THE END
of
THE POINT

THE END

of

THE POINT

A NOVEL

ELIZABETH GRAVER

HARPER

www.harpercollins.com

HarperCollins books may be purchased for educational, business, or sales promotional use. For information, please write: Special Markets Department, HarperCollins Publishers, 10 East 53rd Street, New York, NY 10022.

Grateful acknowledgment is made for permission to reproduce the following:

"As I Walked Out One Evening," copyright © 1940 and renewed 1968 by W. H. Auden, from *Collected Poems of W. H. Auden* by W. H. Auden. Used by permission of Random House, Inc.

"What Have They Done to the Rain" taken from the song by Malvina Reynolds. Words and music by Malvina Reynolds. Copyright © 1962 Schroder Music Co. (ASCAP). Renewed 1992. Reprinted by permission of Schroder Music Co.

"The Idea of Order at Key West" and "Sunday Morning" from *The Collected Poems of Wallace Stevens* by Wallace Stevens, copyright © 1954 by Wallace Stevens and renewed 1982 by Holly Stevens. Used by permission of Alfred A. Knopf, a division of Random House, Inc.

"Dulce et Decorum Est" from *Wilfred Owen: The War Poems*, by Wilfred Owen. Editor John Stallworthy. Copyright © 1994. Used by permission of Chatto & Windus and the Wilfred Owen Literary Trust.

FIRST EDITION

Library of Congress Cataloging-in-Publication Data has been applied for.

ISBN: 978-0-06-218484-9

13 14 15 16 17   OV/RRD   10 9 8 7 6 5 4 3 2 1

for my daughters, Chloe & Sylvie & in memory of my father, Lawrence Stanley Graver, 1931–2010

When I began to tell you children about the different ways in which plants sent their young out into the world, I had no idea that I should take so much time and cover so many pages with the subject. And now I realize that I have not told you one half, or one quarter, of what there is to tell.

You have learned that seeds are scattered abroad by animals that eat the bright cases in which they are packed, and by animals into whose hair or clothing they manage to fasten themselves.

You know that sometimes seeds are blown through the air by means of silky sails to which they are fastened, or else by their little wings.

You discovered that certain plants actually pushed their young from their cozy homes in no gentle fashion, much as a mother bird shoves her timid little ones from the edge of the nest.

And in the last chapter you read that occasionally seeds were floated by water to distant shores.

—Mrs. William Starr Dana, *Plants and Their Children*

CONTENTS

THE END
of
THE POINT

FIFTEEN AXES, FIFTEEN HOES

O N THE STILLEST, emptiest days, you can almost but not quite imagine the place when it was lived on by its earliest people, the trapping
and fishing, tying and smashing, the waves the same, the rocky beaches
too, but no army base, no bisecting road or fighter planes up from Otis
Air Force Base, Code Red. No houses unheated, built for summer, or
mansions with heat, Wi-Fi and central air. No blinking eye on a metal
gate (no gate). Neither headstones nor written alphabet. Later: *Here Lies
John Cornell. Here Lies Tabitha Brown.* Here, a stone fishing weir at the
foot of the creek. Here, a summer *wetu*; inside, a woman labors upright,
giving birth. Did they dunk the baby in the creek, wrap him in a new red
blanket, dress him, as he grew, in a pair of woolen breeches? One year,
they had to find another place to grow him into a man.

    *A deed appointed to be recorded. New Plymouth. November
the 29th 1652.*
    *Know all men by these Presents, that I, Wesamequin, and
Wamsutta, my son, have sold unto Mr. Wm. Bradford, Capt.
John Standish, Thomas Southworth, John Winslow, John Cook
and their associates . . . all the tract or tracts of Land lying
three miles eastward from a river called Cushnett, to a certain*

Harbour called Acoaksett, to a flat Rock on the Westerward
side of said Harbour . . . with all the rivers, creeks, meadows,
necks and islands that lye in or before the same, and from the
sea upward to go so high that the English may not be annoyed
by the hunting of the Indians in any sort of their cattle. And in
consideration hereof . . . We the above-mentioned are to pay to
the said Wasamequin and Wamsutta as followeth: Thirty yards
of cloth, eight moose skins, fifteen axes, fifteen hoes, fifteen pair of
breeches, eight blankets, two kettles, one cloak, £2 in wampum,
eight pair of stockings, eight pair of shoes, one iron pot and ten
shilling in another Commodity.

One iron pot to fill with corn mush, or with a rabbit trapped, skinned, boiled down to bone. John Cooke, signatory, will be the first to farm the rocky, wind-scoured fields of Ashaunt, the Point barely two miles long, half a mile wide, hardly an appendage, more a stub, a neck without a head. A peninsula, as in *paene* (almost), as in *insula* (island). *Ashaunt,* "lobster crawling backward" in Wampanoag. The shoes have brass buckles; each shoe fits either foot. The blankets are woolen, red. An acre for a shoe, two acres for a shilling. Fifteen axes, fifteen hoes. One by one, they bend, they sign. *In the presence of* JOHN WINSLOW *Jonathan Shaw* JOHN COOK *Samuel Eddy* WAMSUTTA. + + *his mark.*

To crane this far back bends hard the mind, fills it with things crude and small, with other things whose necks have been wrung dead. Also with nostalgia (and its kissing cousin, anger). The place breeds it—for this old house, this old couch, this old tribe, one-speed bicycles, driftwood naturally distressed. At one time, a saltworks stood at the foot of the Point. At another, a bootlegging outfit. Table salt hardens here. Books mildew. Diaries flip open. *Private Property: Please Turn Around.* Sometimes arrowheads or bits of pottery and china show up in the churned soil of the few fields still farmed. How fine they would look set in the antique printing box above the bed made up with white Wamsutta sheets, to the left of the nightstand where the clock has stopped again.

On the Point you can still find bones—fox skulls, rabbit femurs, porpoise vertebrae and, on the shore in the crevice between two hard-lodged stones, a milk tooth lost by a child no longer a child. From May through October, swimmers—mostly women—swim, and men dunk, and children jump from the top railing of the dock. One year (and then the next and next) a bloom of jellyfish will come up in August from the Gulf of Mexico on a wave of warmth. To swim among them is to swim inside a living body, a dividing cell.

A deed appointed to be recorded. From a certain Harbour to a flat Rock.

Two kettles, one iron pot.

Bargain, theft or gift.

JANE'S ALL THE WORLD'S FIGHTING SHIPS AND AIRCRAFT

1942

I

THE ARMY HAD paved the road. It was the first thing Bea noticed, coming back with the Porters that summer when most other families stayed away—how the rutted dirt, grassy bumps, heaves and jolts were gone. Instead, a ribbon, gray and smooth. Mrs. Porter complained about it; the two older girls did too. People will speed now, army trucks. A gash on the land, said Helen dramatically. A wound. Bea didn't think so. Bea, sitting in the far back seat with Janie half on her lap and one leg asleep from the long trip, was glad for the change. Where are the soldiers, asked the older girls, craning and peering. Where are the U-boats, the enemy planes? If it wasn't safe, we wouldn't have come, their mother said, but her voice was vague; she was trailing her hand out the window, gulping in the sea air. And even Bea, who silently resisted coming every year—and especially this one—inhaled and felt the salt air rush, moist, into her throat.

Other things had changed too; you could see that right off, although the bigger changes, the ones that might make a life swerve or stay on course, did not show themselves until later on. There was a high wooden spotting tower as you drove onto the Point, where civilian volunteers took turns staring through binoculars at the sky. There was an army truck parked by the path down to the boat dock and, farther down—

shouting distance from the Porters'—a high wooden gate across the road, with wire fencing on either side. On one side of the gate, a soldier, pink-faced, boy-faced. On the other side, another soldier. Sit nice, Bea said to Janie, for the girl was awake now, leaning out the car window. Who are they, asked Janie. She was eight; it was 1942. She knew nothing about war, though something about suffering. No one you should talk to, Beatrice said.

At the house, it was almost like any other year, Stewart hauling Mr. Porter into his wheelchair, and inside, the three girls flying about, skipping, galloping, Janie running after Helen and Dossy, who were up the stairs, down the stairs, shouting like banshees while their mother went into the kitchen with the maids. The trunks had been sent ahead, the maids and Agnes too, along with Blackie, Janie's dog, who was yapping now, pushing his nose into people's palms. Bea went upstairs to her room, which was next to Janie's on the second floor. There, the white nubbed bedspread, the maple bed frame, the watercolor by Mrs. Porter's mother, where the rosehip looked less like a flower than like a startled, open mouth. There, her trunk. She opened it, hung a few dresses in the corner cupboard, propped her photograph of her mother on the bureau, slid her shellflower supplies beneath the bed. Then she closed her window—the curtains were flapping, the room windblown—stopped in the bathroom to relieve herself and splash water on her face, peeked into Agnes's room (not there) and went back down.

Take the rest of the day to settle in, Mrs. Porter had said, but Bea wanted to collect Janie, get some food in her, brush her hair, scrub car grime from her face. All over the house, windows were open for airing. The wicker set was on the porch, the clothesline hung with sheets. In the living room, there was, as always, Mr. Porter wheeling himself to his spot by the picture window. There was the ocean outside, framed by the window so that it looked more like a painting than an actual sea. Bea caught Mr. Porter's eye as she walked by, and he smiled at her. She liked him when he wasn't angry. He cared about things more than the usual man, and unlike his wife, he did not begrudge Bea her attachment to Janie and hand the child off to her at the same time. And like Bea, he lived far from where he had begun—for her, Scotland; for him, a body strong of limb.

"The girls are happy," she admitted to him, their laughter sounding out around the house as if the three of them had split and multiplied, Janie's voice ringing out the highest notes.

He nodded. He was a large man, his torso powerful, his legs like sticks. "Out of time," he said.

She did not know if he meant outside of time or running out of time, and she did not ask. Sometimes, even after all these years, she still felt the language here as foreign, hardly English at all, though the family itself, so full of nicknames, shortenings and codes, had become for her almost a second tongue.

"Tea?" she asked.

"Yes, Bea. Thank you."

"The girls must be hungry. I'll round them up."

They were always wild on Ashaunt. She needed to set a schedule right away, remind them of how things went in Grace Park. Tea at three, supper at six. Janie listened, most of the time. With the other two, Bea had more or less given up, and anyway they were mostly Agnes's, and hardly hers at that.

Outside, in front of the house, then, a tremendous rumble, a dreadful, rolling, grinding noise, and the children's laughter stopped. Bea looked out the window at two lorries going by, soldiers in the back and on the sideboards. For a moment, she felt a great surge—of fear or patriotism, excitement or remorse. Her brother, Callum, his right leg shorter than his left, was an air raid warden in Glasgow. Two of her cousins were in the war. Still, until this moment, it had all seemed, had all been, quite far away.

"What on earth—" said Mr. Porter, but by the time Bea got his wheelchair around, the lorries—trucks—were gone.

~~~~

"IF IT WASN'T SAFE, we wouldn't have come," but it wasn't safe, not safe enough, or else why would most of the other families have left their houses empty, Ashaunt a quarter as full as it usually was, except for the end, which was overstuffed with men, machinery and guns? People disliked the noise, claimed Mrs. P., but the Porters came—Bea was quite sure of it—not because they were sure that it was safe, but because to be here was as close as they could get to Charlie, who was off at Army Air Corps training school in Texas; as soon as he earned his wings, he'd be shipped off. He had grown up in New Jersey except for school and summers, but if you asked him where he was from, he'd say Ashaunt. *Charlie's Beetle Cat is still at the boatyard and needs to be put in; Don't carry off the pieces—that's Charlie's favorite puzzle,* and his room was kept ready and empty, his fishing poles in a corner, his Yale pennant and a photo of his girl, Suky, on the wall. He was their firstborn and only boy, handsome, charming, fast and funny, and he loved this place as nowhere else. Bea was not fond of him, especially—he brought the devil out in the girls and did not pay her much mind except to tease—but even she was startled when she came upon his empty sand shoes in a closet; even she saw, in the faces of the youngest soldiers on the Point, Charlie's face.

Every day, the moment the postman came, Mrs. Porter was at the box. Often, a letter arrived, and once a week or so, a phone call. When Mrs. P. got a letter, she took it off to read it before sharing it with her husband and daughters. One day, she passed Bea and Janie on the stairs— they coming down, she going up. Her hands were empty; the postman had just come and gone. She met Bea's eyes. "Be grateful you don't have any," she murmured. It was a terrible moment, one Bea would never quite forgive her for, though as the years passed, they became in their way dear friends.

Suffer your tongue, Bea wanted to tell her. It was something her grandmother used to say. But she said nothing, Janie said nothing. They were alike that way. It was nearing lunchtime, but Bea took a hunk of bread, two apples and some cheese down the path to the beach and did not scold Janie for soaking her hem as she bent over the tide pools. Up above them, the sky was empty. In the distance, the Elizabeth Islands lay green and low. Skip a stone with me, said Janie. Her brother knew how, her sisters too. Bea's brother had also known how. She, in her memory, had never tried. Together she and Janie found flat stones, bent their wrists in, flicked and watched the stones sail over the water and sink down.

"No matter," said Bea.

"Yes, matter." Janie flung a stone over her shoulder in the wrong direction, where it disappeared among its kind.

"You'll learn," Bea said.

"You've got to teach me."

"Aye."

If not Bea, then who? Janie's sisters ignored her, mostly. Picked her up now and then, whirled her or bossed her, then ran off to places where she was not, under Bea's watch, allowed to go. They disappeared down paths. They went up to the attic, where it was too hot to breathe, and came down dressed like tramps or vamps and laughing too hard, for show.

"You can't." And now there was a hard fury in Janie's eyes. Now there was a blue-black rage she'd never let her parents see. "You can't. You don't know how."

Never enough, never enough, and why should it be, water not blood, wages not a womb. Except that Janie loved Bea, and in no casual way, and Bea knew this—had always known it—to be true. Except that the love she felt for this child was the thickest love, aside from what she'd felt for her own mother, that Bea had ever known.

II

THE OTHER TWO untethered, set free: it was what Helen lived for, and why, as spring in Grace Park showed itself each year crocused and forsythiaed, the changes registered for her not as themselves but as signals of migration toward Ashaunt. She was, by temperament (how often had she heard it?), a high-strung, restless girl, and thus subject to constant chiding—from Agnes and Bea, from her teachers. Don't leave a trail of clothes and shoes and broken-backed books; go to bed before midnight; organize your desk—you are no longer a child! Finish finish finish what you've begun! Live up to your potential (her end-of-year marks were high in some subjects but not in all, and she had not gotten Best in Class). Even her mother, who largely left her children's manners to the nurses, found her daughter's energy an irritant: stop *circling* (Helen walked as she talked, walked as she read. When forced to sit, she jiggled; her right leg had a little motor of its own). Or worse, her mother saying, almost desperately, Could you just stop *talking*, darling, and Helen's eyes would prick with angry tears.

Of all the adults, only her father, locked in his wheelchair, seemed unbothered by her, and only he could stop her in her tracks. A tidbit from the newspaper, she'd offer forth to him, or a Shakespeare sonnet she had memorized, then feel hope rising: Say it, Daddy—*Sharpest knife in the drawer,* or even just *Good girl*—his eyes resting, settling (and so she'd settle too) on her face. Or not. Increasingly, as his body warred against him, as the war warred, his dark moods intensified. If no response came from him, her own seep of darkness, but she did not have to stay with it; she could leave him there, stuck in his corner. She was young, she had legs, she could run.

On Ashaunt it was first to the water with Dos, no matter how cold it was. Most years they stripped naked at the dock, but this year, soldiers, so they swam in their underclothes, then darted to the house, to the tub with its familiar ring of rust, water sputtering out cold, then lukewarm, the two of them peeling off their clothes, stepping in (when had her sister gotten so pretty, with her mop of ringlets and little sorbet mounds of breasts?). With the water finally right, they were jostling for space, and soon again out, into peg-leg trousers and summer tops. "Teal Rock," Helen said, and again they were off, past Janie who called out, to their bikes in the garage, down the road to the path behind the Stricklands', to the rock with its cliff faces, and so—finally—they climbed.

There at the top, they stood first in the wind, then back on the path where huckleberry bushes bloomed white-pink among poison ivy and the air was nearly still. Only then did they stop to catch their breath.

"I hope he doesn't die," Dossy said abruptly.

Helen bent to pick a dried-up lily of the valley and inhale its faint scent. "He's in Texas, Dos. Not in a foxhole somewhere. Gosh. You're as bad as Mummy."

"You don't worry?"

"Not a bit."

Their brother—also their father—thought worry was for sissies. This was, after all, a just and necessary war, and Charlie wanted nothing more than to reach the stage when he could pilot his own plane and get shipped out. She would not rend her garments and keen like a woman in a Greek tragedy because her brother was at Army Air Corps training camp. If anything, she envied him. To learn to fly a plane, perhaps even help change the course of history. To fly! Still, from the moment they'd arrived, she'd felt his absence everywhere, even more than in Grace Park. She missed his fun, that was it—missed how he'd have told them to quit making a scene about his being away. She missed how *happy* he made people; he was lighter than the rest of them, fleet. He was cocky, headstrong and only sporadically interested in school; still, somehow, he was the golden boy and impossible for even her to resent. When she was six and he ten, he had snuck her out on a sailboat to Penikese Island, just the two of them. He was the one who had named her Hellion. He was madly in love, now, with Suky, her best friend, making Helen at once linchpin and third wheel. His letters were filled with jokes, patriotism and cheery complaints about the food. All of them wanted and did not want him to earn his wings.

In front of them, the sea was ruffled by a light wind; a lobster boat passed in the distance. You could look and never even know there was a war.

She turned to Dossy. "Let's go meet the soldiers at the gate."

"Really? Just like that?"

"Sure. They must be lonely and bored, out here for months on their own. It's our duty to cheer them up."

"What will we say?"

"Good day, good soldiers." Helen curtsied in her trousers. "Welcome to Ashaunt!"

"But they're already here. We've only just arrived."

"So? It's ours." She scowled. "Do you think there's one passably handsome or smart fellow in the bunch?"

"You may not fall in love and leave me."

"I never would. They're just ordinary boys from anywhere. Foot soldiers, not like Charlie. You're the one I should worry about."

"Me? I'm fourteen!" When Dossy laughed, curls blowing, dimples creasing, she looked like a cross between Shirley Temple and Rita Hayworth.

"You're too pretty," Helen told her. "And you'd wander off with anyone."

They started down the rock and along the kelp-strewn beach, where sand fleas rose in swarms at every step.

"We could bring Janie too, as an icebreaker," said Helen. "Everyone loves a little girl."

"Janie? Over Bea's dead body."

"Bea too, then. Soldiers love dead bodies."

"*Don't*," said Dossy. "You scare me when you talk like that."

Helen sprinted ahead. At the start of the path she paused to wait, but as soon as Dossy saw her stop, she stopped too, waiting until she started up again, and so Dossy matched her pace—start stop, start stop—the distance between them remaining stubbornly the same. They reached the road, continuing on like this, and might have kept it up the whole way home were it not for the army truck approaching from the end of the Point. Dossy broke into a trot and Helen stopped, so that by the time the truck passed, they were standing together, arms linked, ready with a smile and a wave.

III

IT WAS A week into summer, as Bea returned from swimming with Agnes, that she met Smitty for the first time.

"Good afternoon, young ladies." He took off his cap.

They laughed. Beatrice was thirty-six, Agnes thirty-four.

"Good afternoon, young soldier," Agnes said, bolder, prettier. As a girl, she had won medals for her dancing, the Sword Dance, the High-land Fling.

The soldier was tall and broad, red-faced from the sun, and no boy himself from the look of him. "Oh," he said. "Blimey! Not from these parts?"

"Scotland," said Agnes. "And yourself?"

"Me? Shipped to this hunk of rock from Saint Louis, Missoura." He turned to Bea. "And you, miss?"

Bea wore a towel coat over her bathing suit. Her white rubber swim shoes stuck to the paved road. Her hair—always her best feature, thick and brown—was damp; the swim cap never kept the water out. The rest of her was pink and salty, a slab of fish. Behind them, the maids were coming along; they always swam at the dock at the same hour, and those who could not swim watched. "Me? Scotland as well."

"Better to be here right now," he said. "You watch the little blond girl, don't you? And the older ones? They come to the gate."

She nodded. The maids, all four of them, had caught up now, hovering. Their hour break was almost up.

"Cute kid, the little one—reminds me of my niece," he said. "Bring her by when I'm on gate duty. I'll take you to the P.X. when I get off. She can pick out a candy bar. You ladies too."

Bea shook her head. "I thought . . . the sign says—"

"You're neighbors, I can get clearance in a flash. Anyway, we're all in this together, aren't we?"

He looked at her, then. Later, she would have to wonder why, with the flock of them all there, it was she that he fixed on. She should have said no, the child's parents would never allow it. She should have stayed on her own side of the fence. Instead, her mouth twitched into a small smile.

"Sergeant Raymond Smith." He tipped his cap. "Smitty. And you?"

Her voice was thin. "Beatrice. Bea."

"She's Nurse Beatrice Emily Grubb," Agnes said, and the others rocked with laughter.

"A nurse?" he asked.

Stanching the blood, cleaning the stumps of soldiers. It was the most important work, and in another life she might have done it well, but she was grateful not to have to.

"Children's nurse," she said. "Janie'll be needing me. It's time I get back."

"Jane's all the world's fighting ships and aircraft," said Smitty.

She had no idea what he meant.

IV

SPEED BONNIE BOAT like a bird on the wing, onward the sailors cry, carry the lad that's born to be king, over the sea to Skye. Her grandmother had sung it to her mother, and her mother had sung it to Bea (no matter that none of them had ever been to Skye), and Bea sang it to Janie when the child came to her in the night and slipped into bed and asked for nothing, just turned her back and lay, waiting for a cuddle and a song. The songs rose of their own accord from Bea's half-waking body: *Can you no hush your weeping-o, ah the wee birds are sleeping-o . . .* Once Janie was asleep, Bea would lift her up, take her back to her own room—it was getting harder as the girl grew bigger—and tuck her in. In Grace Park, she had to walk out her bedroom door, into the hall and through Janie's door to return the child, but on the Point their rooms were connected by an inside door, and each also had a door to the hall. They never spoke of these visits in the morning, so that sometimes Bea wondered if Janie even remembered that she'd come.

When Bea was small and woke with a fright, it was her mother she'd gone to, crawling out of bed, squeezing past her brother's trundle into the kitchen where her parents lay heavily sleeping. There, she would lean through the curtain and prod at her mother, who would heave toward the middle to let her in. Her father always smelled of sweat and railway yard, her mother of soap and Colman's Starch, and one night Bea came upon him moaning and atop her—she looked, then looked away—and the next day her mother told her she was old enough to stay on her own all night. And so she did, that night and the next and forever after, until she grew up and her mother grew sick, and then her father moved in beside her brother and Bea slept with her mother in the kitchen bed, which seemed to grow bigger as her mother grew smaller. And then it was pennies on her mother's eyes and rest in peace and ache.

It was not that Janie's mother did not love her. Was it? No, there was love there, but it was of a most peculiar kind. Now and then, Bea would catch Mrs. P. stopping mid-stride to stare at her youngest daughter as the girl sat drawing on the porch or ran across the front lawn. And she read to her, Mrs. P. did, from stories about princesses and India, and books by Mr. Porter's own mother, who wrote about flowers and ferns. This, the reading, took place in the summer during Bea's swimming hour. After lunch, Bea would bring Janie to her parents' bedroom, where Mrs. P. had often drawn the curtains halfway shut and was sitting on the loveseat in the half-light, waiting.

"Hello, Janie." And Mrs. Porter would pat the space beside her.

"Hello, Mummy."

"What shall we read today?"

"You choose."

Have a nice swim, Mrs. P. would say, or Thank you, Bea, or sometimes nothing, turning to Janie and a book. Did they talk or just read, mother and daughter, during this odd, still hour to themselves? Bea didn't know, but she could tell that for Janie, this was the best time of the day, the thing to wait for, though Janie (so thoughtful already, Bea had seen to that, and some children could be so selfish or unkind) knew better than to say it aloud to her nurse.

Bea would leave them, then, together in the bedroom they'd added on off the living room when Mr. P. could no longer take the stairs. She'd walk away, feeling light and free but also wobbly, untethered, a balloon let loose from its string. Then to Agnes and the others, the chatter and water, the sea's cold suck. She liked to swim, especially early in the season, the shock of it around your ankles as you descended the ladder at the dock, the way, as you went in farther, it became the thing you were used to, and it was, of course, the same water as the water on the other side. At Arbroath, where they'd taken the train to her cousins' when she was young, the sea had been colder still, and yet they'd gone in, laughing and squealing (all save her father, who stayed on shore) as the cold hit hard.

From Bea, Janie learned to lace her shoes and plait her hair, to knit and crochet, to sing in tune. She learned bread and butter before bread and butter and jam, and *upsy-daisy hold your nose, swallow hard and down she goes*, and about the Sandman. She learned that a fresh egg sinks to the bottom of a glass of water and a middling egg floats halfway down and a bad egg floats on top. She learned that after breakfast every day, you must go upstairs and do your business, and if your system is sluggish, milk of magnesia will set you right, and if that doesn't work, an enema. She learned to stand up straight and walk beautifully, as if carrying a creel. She learned steadiness and manners and how to remove herself if her father was in a storm, and how not to follow her sisters—sometimes she learned this—into mischief.

Gay things too, she learned—to skip rope, chanting, *"Old Mrs. Mason broke her basin on the way to London Station"*; to play with her doll, Rose—really play, not just plunk the doll in its cot. Bea helped Janie fold a blanket into a swaddle, and they'd fill a baby bottle with water, and by the time Janie was seven she could do basting and running stitch on Rose's clothes, and they'd set up tea parties, invite the teddies and dolls that Helen and Dossy had abandoned right out of the box. Sometimes Bea found herself talking for an hour in the voice of a bear or a doll. She'd rarely done this kind of playing as a girl, and to do it now brought her a furtive happiness: the teacups filled with mint tea, the growly American or high-English voices coming from her mouth, and (mostly) the pleasure it gave Janie to pretend like this, to pretend with her.

From her mother, Janie learned, what? The stories in those books. They were nearly all about orphans, from what the child told Bea. An orphan from India, an orphan from Switzerland. One girl slept in a hayloft; another heard screams coming from a locked-up room. They seemed unlikely stories for a child, but Janie spoke of them matter-of-factly and with great interest, so who was Bea to say? From her grandmother's books, Janie learned the names of plants and flowers: beach peas and heal-all, Plymouth gentian, ladies'-tresses orchid. Janie pointed the plants out to Bea and told her how the apple was a jewel case for the seeds inside and the burrs on her dress were for carrying seeds to a new home, like a tramp stealing a ride from a train. You could make one from your shells, she'd tell Bea when they came across a wildflower, not understanding that Bea didn't aim for her shellflowers to look real, and burrs were for picking off.

From her mother, Janie learned to play Charades and Murder in the Dark, to run three-legged races, to spot hermit thrushes, towhees (Mrs. P. said the towhee's call was "Drink your tea!"; Bea said it was "Brush your teeth!"), and tell the prairie warbler from the Maryland yellowthroat and the great horned from the barred owl by their calls. She learned to think always of one's friends, for Mrs. P. had a great many friends, and when they came (which was not often, that summer), she flitted like a sparrow gathering seeds. From her mother, Janie learned cheerfulness—from Bea too—and never to mention her father's wheelchair or the sister who had died. Over the mantels, both here and in New Jersey, hung oil portraits of that sister, a gold-and-blue girl who had died in her sleep just months after Helen was born. Her name (somehow Bea knew) had been Elinor, but no one ever said her name. From her mother and Bea both, Janie learned about keeping one's word. From her mother, she learned to set aside her old toys for the poor children in Newark and go to the store before Christmas to pick out a doll for a child Santa might forget. From Bea, she learned about Scotland, how beautiful it was. Twenty shades of green, Bea told Janie. Twenty shades of green and little lambs.

From whom did Janie learn more? Well, look at her sisters, who'd had a series of nurses before Agnes and more of both their parents than Janie ever did. It wasn't just good behavior that Helen and Dossy were lacking in. There was ferocity to their actions, an unhealthy desire to be seen. They ran naked across the lawn and no one even noticed. They went camping out of doors one night (they couldn't have been more than seven and nine) and left a note—*we ran away to sleep outside dont worry dont you wish you knew where we where, HMP, DCP*—and their mother said, Oh, they'll come in when they're cold or eaten by bugs. Bea remembered

it; she'd been holding Janie, feeding her a bottle, and she'd raised the
baby for a burp and thought, Not you.

In the early days, during the long summers on Ashaunt, what she
had mostly done with Janie was walk. She'd tie a bonnet on the girl, settle
her in her pram and start down the road, greeting anyone who said hello
to her: the Porters' cousins and second cousins; the stable boy leading
the ponies; the dark-haired French governess one family brought along,
so pretty she turned heads; the local men come to fish; the farmer hauling salt hay for his fields. A child needed daily fresh air, and after Janie
learned to walk, Bea would fasten her to a harness she'd bought at a shop
in Orange and take her out. People thought it strange at first ("Good
Lord, you've put my monkey on a leash!" said Mr. P.), but no one told her
not to do it, and a child could dart before a car or horse, and anyway Janie
liked the contraption, raising her arms for it, crowing "Go!" Sometimes
they'd meet up with another nurse, or Agnes would come with the big
girls on their bicycles, or Charlie would appear suddenly, swoop upon his
sister (Bea had to drop the harness, give her up) and fling her to the sky.
Ashaunt, so narrow across, was nearly two miles long, and Bea and Janie
would often walk the length of it with Blackie at their heels, stopping to
pick blackberries. On sunny mornings, they met up with other nurses
and children at Garrisons—the only sandy spot, the rest a pile of rocks—
and spend an hour there before lunch and nap.

Then Janie turned four, then five, and now (how fast it happened,
even as it felt like several lifetimes ago that Bea had arrived at the family's door) was eight. She was at school nearly all day during the year. She
had a best friend, secrets, a diary with a lock. Moods. She had arithmetic
homework that Bea left to the tutor to sort out. She sometimes grew bored
with long summer days with her nurse, yet she was too young—and for
this Bea was grateful—to keep up with her sisters. "Where is everybody?"
she kept asking that summer, for there were few children about, just the
Andersons, Stricklands and Childs come down for a stretch, and each
with only boys.

Let's sew a pillow for Rose, Bea would suggest. Let's go for a swim. Or walks and baking, checkers, shell crafts; like a suitor, she offered things forth. Sometimes Janie would frown or shake her head, but other times she'd sit by Bea and stitch her rows, or jump her checker piece across the board, or walk (skip, scooter, jump rope, as Bea hurried breathless behind) along the road. Once in a while, Janie would even ask Bea to play Rose and Teddy, or Rose, Annabel and Laura, though not if her sisters were around. Still, it was not like other years when they'd been, well, *in love* was the way Bea had once described it to Agnes, then wished she had not, for something—jealousy? judgment?—had crossed Agnes's face. Agnes was, of the two of them, the more professional, the crisper; if you didn't know her, you might even be afraid. *In love*, but in the easiest, most companionable way.

Lately, Janie's blue eyes had darkened in color, becoming cloudier, almost bruised and who could blame the child, with everything going on and the push and pull of growing up besides? But what to do? And did anyone notice? Janie might have been a half-tamed hedgehog for all her parents seemed to worry about her whereabouts or even Bea's role in looking after her. Set out a bowl of milk; keep an eye out for foxes. But she would grow wild, but she would turn rude and prickly like her sisters. The family would (as was their right; still it felt like thievery) claim her as their own.

When Bea was Janie's age, she had minded her brother each afternoon while their mother finished her shift. She had put the ticket in the window, spread newspaper on the floor for the coal man, taken Callum round to the shops and Green, done everything but iron and cook, as her mother did not let her near the stove. At her grandparents' in the country, she'd fetched water from the well, the buckets attached to a metal hoop that kept the splashing from your legs. In town, she had run messages to her mother's sister in one direction, to her father at the goods yard in the other. She's built like a boy, her father said once in front of Callum, insulting both of them at once. Bea had known how to swim—her mother, who'd lost a sister to drowning, had seen to that—and Janie was a strong swimmer herself, though she was not to go in alone (about this, both Bea and her parents stood firm). At eight, Janie still listened, but there was an out-of-sorts-ness to her that summer, an itchiness, that later Bea would view as partly her own fault—first, for hovering too close, then for letting her attention split in two.

YEARS LATER, BEA, AGNES AND MRS. P. were drinking sherry in Bea's room before lunch—it had become a habit they all looked forward to—and that summer came up, and Bea confessed that she worried she'd not watched Janie closely enough and had let things slip a bit. Jane was twenty-four by then, married to Paul Strickland, a boy she'd met on the Point, expecting her first child.

"There was a war on," said Mrs. P. Just that.

Perhaps it was forgiveness Bea was looking for. Or perhaps a part of her wanted to tell the whole story; even Agnes never knew it all. But it was not her way to hold the past up to the light, any more than it was Agnes's or Mrs. P.'s. "I hope she doesn't name the baby something dreadful," said Mrs. Porter cheerfully, and they went on to talk about nursery colors as Bea knitted a sweater—yellow, with white edging—for Janie's baby. "It will be a boy," said Agnes (a girl, it would be, named Elinor). Together, they drained their glasses, then rose for their separate lunches.

There was a war on—as if that explained everything.

And in a way, perhaps, it did.

V

IT WAS A SUMMER of waiting, eyes fixed on the sky. Grandmother Porter had given Helen a pair of birding binoculars for her sixteenth birthday, and she wore them around her neck, training the lenses on sky, sea or in between. My spyglass, she called the binoculars, and though she'd entered the summer with an interest in bird-watching, it evaporated before the twin pulls of men and war. You could look and look so hard you thought you spotted something ominous, but then the plane behind the clouds would be another cloud, the hump rising in the water a rock made visible by low tide. You could, if situated right (her bedroom window worked; so did the bow window in the attic), aim the binoculars at the soldiers manning the gate—here, one scratching under his arm, there, one cleaning his gun as he chewed gum. "He has a gun?" Dossy would grab the binoculars, try to focus, close one eye and try again. "He's a *soldier*," Helen would say, though her pulse had sped up, as much for the hands on the gun as the gun itself, as much for the face, which had turned in her direction while she watched, rotating toward her as if the soldier (handsome in a blocky, ordinary way) felt the heated pressure of her gaze.

One afternoon, Bea, Janie at her heels, caught Helen and Dossy at the landing window with the binoculars.

"Let me see!" Janie lunged forward.

Bea caught her by the collar, held her back. "Put that away, girls."

"Why?" Dossy asked.

"For one thing, it's extremely rude."

"Not to mention illegal," said Helen.

"Illegal?" Bea's voice went high. She was beautifully easy to shock.

Helen shrugged. "It's all classified information over there. But don't worry—we'll use what we discover for the common good."

Bea reached for the binoculars. Helen ducked away, and Bea turned to call down the hall. "*Agnes!*"

"Call in the troops," Helen muttered.

Agnes appeared from her room. "Well. What's all this about?"

"These two"—Bea jutted her chin toward them—"are spying on the soldiers."

"Give me those glasses," Agnes said.

Dossy, who'd gotten hold of them, dropped them deftly around her neck. "Don't you love bird-watching? I think I saw a scarlet tanager."

"I'll tell your father," said Agnes.

Helen blanched, but she would not let on. "Daddy? That we're aiding the war effort? Just wait—we might spot a submarine. We'll catch a spy. Heinrich Heidelberg. Or Masako Fujiwaka." She liked the sound of German and Japanese, read aloud the words in the newspaper, collected them in her war scrapbook.

"Who?" Janie asked, panicked. "Where?"

"This war," Bea said, her face gone pale, "is not a game."

"Her brother's in it," Agnes explained. "On the other side. Where there's bombings."

"The other *side*?" Janie shrilled. "Your brother's a *German*?"

"The other side of the *sea*, love." Bea's voice shook. "He's an air raid warden in Glasgow. You know, the picture in my room? The little boy? That's Callum, my only brother. It's just the two of us. I've told you about him."

Janie turned to her sisters. "Bea's only brother is in the war!"

"*Your* only brother's in it too," Helen told her. Bea had never liked Charlie; they all knew it. She liked girls better than boys, Dossy better than Helen, Janie better than the Queen of England, which said a lot. "And rising up the ranks. He could get shipped out."

"Enough." Agnes flew into motion, ushering Helen toward her bedroom. "Helen, really—you've got a queer idea of a joke."

Helen sprang away and slipped sideways into her room, where she slammed the door and leaned on it, though no one was trying to get in. A joke? What none of them could see was that she was dead serious—

serious in how she watched the sky and sea, serious in how she wrote to her brother every single day, serious in how she followed the news. The murders in Lidice. The lists of casualties. She had begun reading the newspaper last year in an attempt to impress her father, but it quickly became more than that. If she were old enough, she would sign up to be a lady reporter or join the WAC.

She cracked the door open, expecting them still to be there, but they had disappeared, even Dos. She took off the binoculars, let her skirt drop to the floor and crawled into bed, where, after a run of muffled, cleansing tears, she fell asleep.

SEVERAL HOURS LATER, she woke to a dusk so dense it was hard to make out your own hand and turned on the nightstand lamp to read. She was partway through *A Farewell to Arms*, and while the book's cover—a man and woman naked from the waist up—had announced the romance (which she'd expected, having seen the movie), it was the bits about war that held her rapt. A world limned and burnished. A road. Leaves. Bodies (wounded, dying, longing, healing, dead). Trenches. Big ideas. The book was full of things she could almost but not quite say, nor even quite think, so that reading it was like watching her own mind—a better, smarter, more worldly version of it—cross the sea and come back to report. "All thinking men are atheists," said the young lieutenant, which seemed potentially true to her, though awful, but what then of her prayers, for she'd begun praying some nights before bed, a new thing, a secret she kept even from Dos. Her prayers were childish—she saw that now—at once too specific and too general (*Let Charlie go to active duty AND keep him safe. Let us win the war*), and worse, arrogant, for even if God existed, why should He listen to her, she who knew nothing, who'd been nowhere and made of war an attic game and thought her own brother the only brother in the world (it turned out Bea had one. Nearly everybody did). As for love, she had always felt it to be—as Frederick Henry had too at first—a sort of game, but as she read on, she saw that it was not a game for Frederick and Catherine; it was something else, a religion almost, and so was God love, sweating, tangling, in the bodies of a man and woman together? The thought upset her; she had always thought God, if there was such a thing, would be spread across the sky or, if embodied, be a giant brain of sorts, quivering, brilliant and alone.

I loved to take her hair down, Helen was reading as her mother entered without knocking and went straight for the windows, lowering shades with a flick of her wrist and a snap. Helen slid the book under the bedclothes. While her parents didn't much bother with what she read, to be interrupted now felt like both a risk and an affront.

"I was outside and saw your light," her mother said. "You need to *think*, darling. If you don't pull down the dim-out shades, the soldiers can see you clear as day!"

"How thrilling for them." Helen propped herself up. "The shades are so the *enemy* can't see us. And our ships, which get lit against the coastline if there's light on shore."

She had broken a central rule from "Additional Restrictions If Your House is Visible from the Sea"—and she the one constantly to remind the others. She had pasted the flyer in her war scrapbook, where she kept every little thing—ration cards, newspaper clippings, the stamps from Charlie's letters. *People living in these areas visible from the sea must not only shade those windows and doors visible from the sea, but they must not allow any light to shine upward from any window, skylight, or lightwell, no matter what direction they face. Like everybody else, you must keep shades drawn as low as the bottom of the lowest light in the room.*

Her mother stepped over her skirt. "Get dressed for dinner, please." She peered at Helen, who had slipped back under the sheet. "What is it? Are you ill?"

"I'm fine."

"Then what?"

"I'm just lost in my book. And not hungry."

"Reading is not an excuse to malinger in bed at dinnertime."

Somebody else's mother, or even Helen's mother at another time, might have phrased it differently—*please come down, we'd like your company*—or offered to have Lizzy bring up dinner on a tray. Somebody else's mother might have set herself on the edge of the bed, kicked off her shoes and brought her feet up onto it, sunk into a pillow, asked *what are you reading, what are you thinking about?* or said *it's not easy, is it, to have Charlie away, to have Daddy ill, to be sixteen?* Her mother stood, neither going nor staying, and then, in a motion so fluid that Helen didn't see it coming, flipped the covers back, leaving both Helen and the book exposed.

"Why are you hiding that? It's"—her mother picked up the novel— "Hemingway. *A Farewell to Arms.* Why are you hiding Hemingway?"

"I wasn't."

"I suppose the cover is racy. I didn't like that book—it's my copy, you know. I found it cynical, and the ending too sad, in a hopeless, unredeeming sort of way. Sad for no good reason."

The ending of the movie was oddly dim in Helen's mind. Birds flying, music swelling, Helen Hayes and Gary Cooper in an embrace. "I didn't think it was so sad."

"You've finished it? And you still won't come to dinner?"

"I saw the movie." Charlie had taken her, with a friend he'd brought home from Yale. Helen's elbow had grazed the friend's elbow all the way through, which had been thrilling—to watch two lovers while her skin grazed a college boy's skin—though in daylight the boy was pompous, his skin too pale, his lips too red.

"Does she die in childbirth in the movie?" her mother asked.

"Mummy! You've ruined it!"

"I'm sorry." Her mother held the book against her chest, the front cover turned in. "Now you can read something else."

VI

THERE WERE NO tennis tournaments that year, no clambakes or Beetle Cat races—not enough people and you couldn't sail beyond the Red Nun (one day, the Childs boys did and got escorted back). The bicycles got lots of use—the paved road was great for them if you could avoid the trucks—but the stable stood empty, the ponies and donkey back in New Jersey. The grass on the lawns went longer without mowing, which made the place look neglected to Bea, overgrown. During other summers, the houses had been lit at night; headlights bumped along the road, boats blinked on the sea, company of sorts. Now, on cloudy or moonless nights, it was as dark out as the dim-out shades themselves, except for the army's searchlights on the water and the odd car inching along the road, headlights straining, watery, through curtained slits.

Yet even at night, even in the dark, the place was filled with men and boys, and it felt, well, Bea felt strange thinking it, but it felt most like a party, or just before a party. The soldiers were a cheerful, joking lot and seemed not to have a great deal to do. On the base—you could see from the lawn—the men slept in tents and shaved outside, using mirrors nailed to poles. They washed their pots and pans on benches, drawing water from vats that looked like dustbins (the water itself was piped from the Porters' and stored in Hollow Hill, the army's well too far out and dry). Sometimes Bea would catch a glimpse of a soldier dressed only in an undershirt and trousers, his underarm hair visible, dark clumps. It wasn't anyone's fault, they had nowhere to go, but there was a nakedness to this war she did not like.

Still, on the base, it seemed as if things would not stay like this for long. The army was fast building up and out—officer quarters shingled and edged like summer cottages, the beginning of a radar tower designed to look like a civilian water tower, barracks going up to replace the tents.

More roads kept getting built, cutting through fields and scrub brush and what had been the Wilsons' lawn. Trucks from the concrete company came and went; the lumber mill delivered wood. The noise was terrible. Sometimes, during drills, guns went off, and that was one thing, a kind of necessary, almost holy noise—it made Bea stop and think of her brother, of the war across the sea—but most of the time the sounds were of hammers and trucks, and the gate stayed open almost carelessly to let soldiers and workers through.

"Such a shame," whispered Mrs. Porter one day as she wheeled Mr. Porter near the gate. Bea, Agnes and the girls were all there too, hovering around the sentry box, Helen and Dossy making conversation with the soldiers standing guard, the adults keeping an eye on the girls but also looking in. Sometime over the previous winter, the army had taken over the Wilsons' Point House, and now there were tents pitched right beside it, and a long sheet of black canvas covering one wall, and pipes protruding from the roof. There was the Wilsons' barn, become a rec hall, and the Wilson children's playhouse with its peak and weathervane. The Wilsons had not come—nowhere to stay, and two of their own sons already shipped off.

"It's necessary," Mr. Porter said as his wife turned his chair around and began to wheel him back. "If they needed our house, we'd let them have it."

He would have been out there fighting himself if his legs had worked, even at his age, and Bea admired him for that. On the day in April that Charlie had come back on leave before going to flight camp, Mr. P. had put on his old World War I uniform, which smelled of mothballs, and Stewart (butler and manservant but also friend to Mr. P., almost, it sometimes seemed, a sort of aging son) had propped him in a corner next to Charlie, also in uniform, for a photograph. Bea had not liked it—a boy playing at being a soldier, a cripple playing at being a boy.

"Not that they'd need our permission," said Mrs. P. "And I didn't say it wasn't necessary, just that it's a shame. Anyway, nothing is happening here. It must be so dull for them. Nothing *will* happen."

"You have no idea of that, darling," her husband said. "They're guarding the mouth of Buzzards Bay. This is a crucial location. Anything could happen."

"Like what?" asked Helen, who had caught up.

Bea glanced at Agnes. Janie was behind, still, showing Dossy something cupped inside her hands.

"Things are escalating, is all I'm saying," said Mr. P. "This may be our last summer here for a little while."

Janie caught up and released the moth she had captured—a brown flutter—to the air. "What's 'escalating,' Daddy?"

Her father looked over at her, and his face softened. Mostly he was kind to his children, though now and then he played cruel, childish tricks, like getting Stewart to dress up in a bearskin and leap out at Janie from the dark woods. Janie had not been more than five then; she'd wet herself from fear. Or he would instruct his youngest daughter to spit into the river and run to the other side of the bridge to watch her spit get carried by the current, and Janie would do it—running, looking, increasingly frantic: *Where is it? I can't see it, Daddy! Where?*

"Like an escalator," he said. "Like at Macy's."

"The army's putting in an escalator?"

"And some Christmas windows." Helen laughed. "And a dress department."

Janie looked at Bea, who took her hand, but the girl brushed her away. "Mummy," Janie asked. "What could happen, really?"

In Amagansett on Long Island, not even a month previous, four Germans had come ashore in a collapsible rubber boat. Stewart had read about it in the paper and told the rest of them. Later, Bea saw pictures of the men. They looked like anybody else, but one of them, the most handsome of the lot, had the middle name of Harm. Saboteurs, Stewart had called them. They had buried their gear, put on civilian clothes and taken the train to New York, carrying fishing poles. A few days later, four more Germans came ashore in Florida. By then, the Porters were beginning to pack for Ashaunt. Don't forget the handkerchiefs. Don't forget the tisane. Mrs. P. needs it for her sleep.

"What could happen, Daddy?" Janie tried.

Just then the mail truck drove up, and there was the postman, holding out an envelope. Mrs. P. let go of her husband's wheelchair and ran to retrieve the letter. The rest of them stood there, watched her take it, watched her move swiftly toward the house. In his lap, Mr. Porter's left hand quivered. His coordination had gone before his strength, but if you put a rubber thimble on his finger, he could still flip the pages of a book. When Bea had first come to the family, he had been walking. Now, on a good day, he could move his chair around inside but not on grass, though he still swam nearly every day (in Grace Park, they had built him an indoor pool; they took him to Bermuda every winter), Stewart hauling him in and out. She felt the air grow quiet the way it always did before one of his rages came on and nudged Janie across the lawn.

"Get that letter from your mother, girls," Mr. Porter said. "What always gives her the first right?"

Helen and Dossy froze.

"*Get it*," he told Helen.

She looked once at her father, then ran toward the house. Bea was at the porch by then. She opened the screen door and ushered Janie upstairs. She could hear Helen calling, a door slamming, maybe two, and the sound of Mr. Porter's voice, aimed everywhere and nowhere at the same time—a roar of sorts, a howl.

"Bath time!" she said to Janie, though it was not.

In the vast bathroom with its small claw-foot tub, Bea started up the bath, readied the towel, found the bar of soap. Unprotesting, Janie stripped, climbed in. With the water running, you could not hear anything. Once the bath was full, the water off, the child lay on her stomach and plunged her head, staying under for what felt to Bea like a beat too long. When she came up, Bea handed her the soapy washcloth. It was quiet outside by then, except for the noises from the base. It was quiet downstairs.

"I'm hungry," Janie said.

Bea scrubbed behind her ears. "That's fine. And you'll be shiny clean for lunch."

Jane looked up at her. With her curls wet and forehead bare, her eyes looked bigger than usual, and the sadness in them was a sea all to itself.

Bea readied her robe. "Come, poppet."

As Bea wrapped, Jane leaned, and they stood there rocking, the child's hair spreading dampness across the front of Bea's dress. For a moment Bea found herself grateful for the trouble in the family, grateful, even, for the war. For here was Janie babylike again, letting her full weight cave in. And if it all exploded? If the war arrived, Germans climbing from the sea onto the shore? If it happened, it happened; she had long ago given up trying to steer life's course. She would be a shield to Janie, that above all. She would take her away somewhere, just the two of them if necessary; she knew country life well enough from her grandparents and could get by on almost nothing—a house built into a hillside, greens taken from the beach and fields. Once as a child on tattie holidays, her grandmother with a broken wrist, her grandfather in the fields, she had wrung a chicken's neck.

Janie moved away and shook out her hair, sending spray.

"I need to give it a quick brush," said Bea.

"Not now. I'm too hungry."

"We don't want a rat's nest, do we?"

Janie ducked. "I'll do it myself."

"Good." Bea held out the brush. "Go on, then."

"After lunch."

"Sit *down*." Bea leaned forward, brush in hand, but already Janie was heading for the door, robe flapping. Bea grabbed the child by the hood and pulled her back, her own anger blooming suddenly, and bigger than the moment.

"Before lunch, I will brush your hair and dress you," she said, and when Janie jerked away again, Bea grabbed the brush and rapped her three times on the bottom.

And then the child was weeping—real, loose, gulping tears, not the practiced kind. "You hit me!" she said between gasps. "I'm not a baby, you can't hit me—I'll tell Mummy!"

It was not a hard rap, nor on bare skin, nor was it the first time Bea had done it—perhaps the third or fourth; Janie was a girl who rarely needed spanking. Still, it unsettled Bea, because she had not planned it. Her father had given her the willow rod when she broke a rule (no talking back, no wiggling of her ears in church—it was her special talent, and she often did it without knowing), though Callum had gotten it more. What reason here? Something had snapped; her hand had closed over the brush.

"Sit," she said, her voice more a plea than a command.

Janie folded herself onto the squat white stool, knees pressed together, arms around her knees. She bowed her head. They did not speak. The girl would not tell her mother; both of them knew that. They were in this together—whatever this was, wherever they were. Outside, three shots sounded, and Blackie barked three times as if in answer. In the bathroom, Bea brushed, working slowly at the knots, and after a time, Janie relaxed. Bea would bring lunch up on a tray, with a rosebud tucked inside the napkin. No need for Janie to go downstairs.

Such curls the child had, a gift from God. If you started at the ends and worked your way up, it would not hurt.

VII

AFTER THEIR FIRST meeting, Bea often saw Smitty on the road. He
seemed to do a lot of walking, away from the base, off the Point, or
he'd be in an army truck, heading into town for supplies, or on evening
leave. Hullo, Nurse Beatrice, he'd say if he was on foot. Or Hello, ladies,
when she and Agnes were together, and if Janie was there, he'd kneel
down and let her try on his cap, or toss a stick for the dog, or tell jokes.
*What's the best kind of story to tell a runaway horse? A tale of whoa. What
do you call a pony with a sore throat? A little hoarse.* Since neither Janie
nor Bea tried to answer the riddles, he soon came to deliver both question and answer at once, and both Bea and Janie would break into a grin.
"What does it mean if you find a horseshoe?" (Good luck, no joke, thought
Bea.) *"It means some poor horse"*—Smitty snorted, and Bea laughed too,
before the punch line—*"is walking around in his socks."*

Why were all his jokes all about horses? She always meant to ask; she
never did find out. Janie was shy of him; they both were. He was a large
man, and in uniform, his hair shaved close to his head, and he had a flat,
nasal accent and a cigarette often tucked in the corner of his mouth, and,
if he was on guard duty, a bayonet gun at his side. Later, at home, Janie
would repeat the jokes to her sisters, and if they laughed (fondly, or auto-
matically, or with real pleasure, it didn't matter), she shone.

At the beginning of the summer, Bea had assumed they shouldn't
talk to the soldiers, but as the weeks passed, it became clear that this was
not true. "Our boys," Mrs. Porter called them, even as she complained
about the noise from the base, and Annie made snacks for the sentries,
and Helen and Dossy brought them pitchers of ice water and sometimes
lemonade, and one night Mrs. P. had ten soldiers (had they been chosen,
or volunteered? Smitty was not among them) over for dinner, and Annie
made shepherd's pie and corn on the cob and a sad green salad from the
little victory garden Mrs. P. had put in (the big girls had planted a sign

that read "Victory for the Rabbits," until their father made them take it down), and Stewart used up gas rations to drive to New Bedford for a keg of beer. Bea would not have known that she wanted Smitty to be part of that dinner until he wasn't, and then she felt a little stab of disappointment, followed by a bigger stab of irritation at herself.

Usually she ate supper with Jane upstairs, and the other help ate in the kitchen, but that night everyone sat on the back porch together—on chairs and boat cushions and the steps, with three soldiers sprawled in the hammock, and the older girls wore flowered skirts and sleeveless eyelet tops and ballet slippers with winding ribbons, too pretty for their own good. Mr. P. had his dinner on his card table and talked about the Great War, and Mrs. P. asked the soldiers small questions—Where are you from, Do you have brothers and sisters, How's the food on the base?—and Helen asked them big questions—Do you think people will always wage war, Does religion do more harm or good in the end?—and Dossy crossed and recrossed her legs and said, "Oh, *stop* it, Hellion! Leave them be!" and Mr. P. said, "She's all right, Doss," and then, to the group, "Helen's smart as a whip, top of her class," and Helen wrinkled her nose at her sister. The soldiers talked and talked and drank and drank, and as dusk came and the fireflies blinked (the porch lights out, no lanterns or candles lit, though nearly a full moon), Annie brought out shortbread, then blackberry pie and huckleberry pudding; she must have used up the sugar ration for a week. "Enough to feed an army," she'd say each time she or Lizzie set down another dish, and each time, the soldiers would salute her and applaud.

Bea and Janie sat together to one side. Agnes sat closer in, talking to this one or that one, and as Bea watched her, she had a sudden flash of fear: Agnes would marry one, leave. While they were both from Forfar, they had come over separately, not knowing each other, but over the years, they had grown as close as sisters. "Tweedledee and Tweedledum," the big girls liked to tease, and it was true that Bea and Agnes bickered like a married couple, mostly over the children, for Bea was cozier, less strict, although still stricter than the parents, who couldn't seem to bother much with rules. Once, when Dossy was younger, she had told Bea that it was her bosom that made her cozier than Agnes; Bea's was wide and pillow soft, while Agnes was narrow like a boy. "That's nonsense," Bea had said, blushing, but she'd been secretly pleased, her body mostly a weight for her to haul around, though she did enjoy the feel of a baby on her hip. Dossy was the moodiest of the children—quick clouds came over her, replaced by gusts of joy—and Agnes didn't understand that it was sometimes best to simply let her be, or that Helen, who had an opinion about everything, was more likely to do your bidding if you pretended she was boss. "If you nagged less, they'd mind you more," Bea would say, and Agnes would snap back: "Ach, if I nagged less, they'd burn down the house!" Or they'd switch sides. "You know, Agnes, Janie likes to know what's expected—a little regularity can't hurt with the big girls, too." "What's expected?" Agnes (pin neat, clock regular; she made Bea look slovenly) would answer. "What's expected around here is nothing at all! *You* try to change it"—for Agnes had been there longer and could lord it over Bea. "And wake me when you're done!"

Now Agnes was leaning, talking, her chin cupped in her hand. Years before, in Scotland, she'd had a fellow, but he'd gone to Australia, and Agnes ("Did he really think I'd set up with the thieves?") had come to America instead. Since then, nobody, for either of them. Funny how when you were small, you assumed it—*when I marry, when I have children.* All the girls did, even as all around them, the men were without work or booking passage or lost—body, soul or both—to the war. Then along went your life until you were smack in the middle of it and had stopped expecting, without quite realizing it, and your life was nothing like you'd pictured, but a good life—an entirely good-enough life—nonetheless. Agnes was pretty, and on the clever side, but it was hard to see her married, too full of her own ways, and what man would marry a Scots nurse past her prime and met on an outpost army base?

The soldiers were bored—that's what everyone kept saying. They were away from home, from jobs and girls and wives (more than a few had wedding bands), and most disliked Ashaunt, the beaches rocky, the wind stiff, the air cold in winter, muggy in summer and always damp. Oh, they knew how to laugh and have a good time, but this made Bea suspect them, for it all seemed too much like a holiday, and they were American in a way that seemed, well, *coarse*. She reached for a glass of beer and took a sip. She didn't like it, never had; still, she sipped again. Leaning against the house, she felt the shingles rough beneath her arms. The ocean was flat calm. Every few minutes, the searchlight made its sweep. One soldier kept stuttering, and she had to stop herself from supplying the jammed word. Another fellow played a Jew's harp, the music twangy, grating, without melody. Her father had played the Jew's harp when she was small, and suddenly she missed him—not as he'd been when she'd left home, but as he'd been back then: harp to mouth, head bobbing side to side, the buzzing, tuneless tune. "But *can* we see the path of history while we're inside it?" Helen asked, fixing her gaze on a soldier a good five years older than herself. Would the child ever stop?

As they finished dessert, the soldiers starting singing again—"*Beer, beer for Battery B! Shake up a cocktail, shake one for me!*"—and chanting—"*Hey Abbot! I'm a b-a-a-a-d boy!*"—and that was when Bea told Janie it was past bedtime, and the girl went to her mother and father for a kiss, and then she was being passed around from soldier to soldier, all of them kissing her cheek or tousling her hair, Jane cringing, giggling, and finally back to Bea. Upstairs, as Bea closed the muslin and dim-out curtains, turned on the light, and readied the child for bed, she could hear the soldiers singing on—"*Say goodbye to them all, to the long and the short and the tall!*"—and the Porters singing with them. Unconsciously, Bea began to hum along, until Jane interrupted for her lullaby.

After Janie fell asleep, Bea might have gone back down—Agnes was still there—but somehow she did not want to. Instead, she took out her shellflower box in her room, sorting stamens, gluing on a shell or two, triple-twisting wire stems; the green would have to wait, for she'd run out. She worked even more slowly than usual, drawing out the time.

Ordinary shells were everywhere on the beach, but the rest of her supplies were hard to get in wartime and the hobby itself felt slightly wrong, not useful enough, though she'd been knitting too, muffler after muffler for the soldiers. She might send a shellflower to her brother or father, or to Charlie, or to the aunt in Arbroath who'd taught her how, but they'd likely get damaged in the post. Setting her supplies back in their tin box, she went to do her washing up. Then, closing the window to the noise outside, she said her prayers and went to bed.

"IF I'D BEEN ON THAT LIST, I'd have been there in a flash," Smitty told her later. The soldiers were invited in groups into family homes for dinner; he had gone to a house on Smith Neck Road, where the only drinks were black tea or lemon water and the hostesses were Quaker ladies. Spinsters, he'd reported, his arm loosely around Bea. It was nighttime on the beach. She had shivered against him for a moment, then pulled away. When was this? Later on, of course. It must have been mid-August. Several of the saboteurs had been executed by then. Charlie had been transferred to a base in Oklahoma. No enemies had shown up on the Point. Perfectly nice ladies, Smitty had said, but not you—as if she were something altogether different from what she knew herself to be. As if she were young, not a spinster, a girl in a sleeveless eyelet blouse.

After the dinner where Smitty was not present, something shifted inside Bea. She did not welcome this feeling and did her best not to think about it, nor even to admit it to herself. Still she felt it, in a wordless, almost dumb way, the way you might sense a small animal, mouse or vole, crouched beneath the rafters, looking out. She was waiting. There was, for the first time in years, a man who fancied her. Agnes was sure of it; Bea claimed to be less so, but still she knew. She did not like change, had never courted it. Even leaving home had been a last resort, a decision made largely of grief and not enough money and because Tilly from upstairs was going, and so was the girl to her left at church, and so was the girl to her right.

Now, as she walked down the road, or sat mending on the porch, or ran the girls' bathing suits through the wringer, or picked thyme for Annie on the lawn, or had tea with Agnes and the others, she was waiting, trying to make out the figures in the distance. That one in khaki; was it Smitty? No. That one in dress uniform, his tie stuffed in his shirt? He came closer: a beak nose, curly hair. A group of them, heads tipped in the wind, hanging off the back of a truck. "Top of the day, Beatrice!" one soldier called, trying and failing to sound Scottish, but it was Louis; at dinner, he had pretended to be fascinated by Helen's questions and leaned too close. Still, she waved hello.

We'll meet ere hills meet—one of the sadder songs she knew, though as a girl, she'd thought it perfectly possible for hills to meet. And yet she and Smitty did cross paths again, more than once; he did keep finding her somehow. Of course it wasn't difficult. With the base adjacent to the house and Ashaunt akin to a small village, it was harder to be lost than to be found. Still, it kept surprising her, for shouldn't he have been planning, drilling, protecting, having more "shams," the fake attacks they staged? He was a sergeant, in charge of training new soldiers at the guns, but there he'd be, strolling along the road, so relaxed; it was what she liked about him and what threw her, the jokes coming fast. Sometimes she wondered if he was only out to poke fun at her, or on a dare. "Halt, who goes there? Oh, it's Honeybee," he'd say. Or "Bee-bah-bee, caught you lookin' at me," and she'd blush, and he'd heave in silent laughter.

How old was he? How old did he think she was? Bea's skin, which was her mother's, had a creaminess to it, except when she rashed up from sun or shame. Her face, on the round side, had kept a certain girlishness, though she knew herself to be no beauty. Mrs. P., a few years older and elegant no matter what she wore, had once told Bea she envied her young looks, but now they could be sending out false messages. Or was it Janie that Smitty really liked, because she reminded him of his own niece, or of civilian life outside the base? "Where's your sidekick?" Smitty would ask, and Beatrice did feel better when Janie was with her; it took his eyes off her and gave her something to do with her hands.

"Watch this," Smitty said one morning when he found Bea and Janie on the road, a folded newspaper under his arm. Tearing a piece from the paper, he began to make an airplane, his fingers quick for a fellow on the portly side, as hers were too, her shellflowers better, she thought secretly, than some in the craft magazines. He folded, tucked and creased; soon wings appeared, then a nose and a fin. Next, he took a pen from his pocket and made a mark, the tilted pinwheeled sign the Germans used. Before Bea could stop him, he had handed it to Janie.

"A Heinkel He 111 heavy bomber monoplane." He bowed. "For you, madam."

Janie held the plane by one end, as if it might explode.

"So do I know my airplanes?" he asked.

The girl nodded.

"Do you think I went to airplane college?"

She shrugged. She was not and would never be a flirt like her sisters, though she wanted their attention, especially Helen's, so much it was hard to watch. She liked her solitude, to read and draw and play games filled with characters known only to herself, and sometimes Bea. Her affections were few, fierce, and private. Mostly (Bea told herself), she loved Bea.

"Nope," said Smitty. "*Jane's All the World Fighting Ships and Aircraft* is how I know. It's an army book, big as a St. Louis phone book. *Jane's*. Named after you! Did you know you were all the world?"

"I'm not." Janie shook her head, her voice loud, almost angry, surprising Bea, who touched her shoulder.

"You're all the world to Bea," said Smitty.

And then he looked at Bea, straight into her eyes, his gaze solemn, knowing and exact, and she began (was it then? It must have been) to fall in love with him, but in the most impossible way, for what he said about Janie being all the world to her was true. She met his eyes, then looked away, and as she did, her stomach turned; for a moment, she thought she might be sick.

"Let's see how she flies," Smitty said to Janie, and the girl gave a toss to the plane, which plunged onto the road.

"She needs a tighter nose." Smitty picked up the plane, made adjustments and handed it back. "All right," he said. "Throw her way up this time, and I'll be me, which means manning the 155-millimeter small-calibers here on the Point when—*High alert, men! Resume stations!*—along comes the heavy bomber!"

"Except it won't," interrupted Bea. Just that week, she'd read an advice column in the Women's Features section of the paper: *Do not bring up the war before the children. Do not warn them not to be afraid. Do not mention fear. Do not warn them about death and danger. If the subject comes up, tell them you will take care of them always, all they have to do is to stay by you and do what you say.* With Helen and Dossy, it was too late and they enjoyed drama far too much, forcing it on their sister, filling her head with tales.

"The war," Bea said firmly, "is not coming here."

During the Great War, two zeppelins had passed right over her town. Everyone had thought it was the war come to land; they'd even heard explosions in the distance. In the end, nothing had happened there—except, of course, for the knitting of mufflers, mitts and socks; except for soldiers filling the infirmary, the men going off and not coming back, or coming back quietly (her father) or violently (Tilly's) undone.

"We're only playing," said Smitty. "She knows that, don't you, doll?"

Janie threw the plane straight up, and he stationed himself behind an imaginary gun. "Shoot!" she cried, her little arm taking aim.

And they were blasting bullets, both of them, Janie and Smitty, their eyes narrowed, throaty gun sounds popping from their mouths, and the plane had landed again, a good ten feet from where it started. Smitty laughed and so did Janie, right out loud, and then he picked her up and hoisted her onto his shoulders. She looked so small up there, even at eight. She was wearing blue pedal pushers and a striped blouse, a sailor suit. Her curls had turned white-blond from the sun; her face was lit with joy. She put her hand on the brim of Smitty's cap, and for a moment he was Charlie, they were playing Chicken Fight or Drop the Handkerchief or Cops and Robbers, out of time.

It was then, as Smitty lifted Janie from his shoulders and set her down, that he asked Bea: There was an OSO dance at the base on Saturday, he was on the entertainment committee, would she like to come?

"What about Agnes?" she stumbled. "And . . . the others?"

"The more the merrier, as long as they're female. They're bringing in girls by the busload from New Bedford. We've landed a first-rate bandleader."

"I don't dance."

Bea's voice came out peevish, and she saw Smitty stiffen. In fact, she had taken dancing classes as a girl—nearly everyone had at home—and had not disliked it. Girls danced with girls until the end-of-session dance; then they brought in the boys. The girls from New Bedford would be pretty and young but also common, with painted red lips, and what would she wear, and why not stop things right where they were, there on the road, with Janie at her side? It was nice. It was plenty. It was enough.

Janie muttered something, and Bea bent toward her. "What is it, love? Speak up."

"Can I come?" Janie whispered.

"It's not a dance for children," Bea said aloud. (Break your own rule and the rule stays broken; not whispering in front of others was a rule.) "I'll make a dance for you and Rose at home."

"You'd turn too many heads for a girl your age," said Smitty before he looked again at Bea. "So what do you say?"

"I'll . . . I'll see what the others say."

"What do *you* say?"

Smitty cracked his knuckles as he spoke, and she had an urge, at once tender and angry, to still his movements with her hand. Give the child a morsel, her mother used to tell her father, who after the war held everything—food, words, money, love—tight inside his fist. Just a dance, it was; support your troops. She had a pair of blue brocade shoes, recently passed on to her by a neighbor of Mrs. P.'s. She had, for Porter family events and her own and Agnes's birthdays (when Stewart drove them to the Grand Café in Orange), a blue silk dress, passed on to her by Mrs. P.'s sister with the tags still on. Bea had brought both items to the Point, thinking that this summer she might finally look for a church that suited her (only Annie, who was Catholic, went regularly to church, irritating the rest of them with her need for rides, her endless fingering of beads). The shoes were tucked in tissue, barely worn. The dress would pinch at the waist unless she let it out, and then there was the problem of fabric—she might have to sacrifice the sash.

What was her own? Not her room, either here or in Grace Park, though both were pretty and clean and hers for the duration. Not her time, not most of it, though she loved raising Janie and didn't mind mending or straightening up. Not her money, really; Mr. P., who was still president of Mrs. P.'s father's insurance company, insisted on investing most of it for her ("Someday you'll thank me."), and what pocket money she had left went mostly to gifts, craft supplies and workaday clothes. Give the child a morsel. She could not have said, just now, if she was giving it to Smitty or herself.

"I'll come," she mouthed over Janie's head. Janie's eyes met hers—*Break your own rule*—and Bea spoke the rest aloud. "As long as it's all right with Mrs. P."

VIII

I F THINGS HAD turned out differently, she would have begun the story
here—or no, Smitty would have told it; unlike Bea, he loved an audience, he'd have made it funny, drawn it out. *Drop-dead gorgeous in a blue
dress . . . had never done the jitterbug . . . the whole place stank of feet . . .*

Smitty met Bea and Agnes at the gate and escorted them in, one on
each arm, but not long after they got there, they were separated from him,
ladies to the left, gentlemen to the right. Bea had never heard of a Cinderella dance and didn't know what to think when the bandleader told the
ladies to take off a shoe and let it fly. By the time Agnes had bent gamely
toward her own foot, shoes were sailing through the air—ivory, pink,
black and red—and landing in the middle of the floor. Bea took off her
right shoe but could not bring herself to throw it. Instead, she thrust it at
Agnes and watched her friend run forward to place their two shoes at the
edge of the heap and back off, hands before her face. Across from them,
on the other side of the rec hall, the soldiers were clustered in a group. Bea
could no longer see Smitty. She could not see much of anything. It was
crowded, smoky and noisy, the lights dim, the floor in places already slick
with beer. Everywhere were elbows, and girls in lace blouses and short
satin evening skirts (her own dress fell just below the knee), and darting
glances and craned necks.

When they had first arrived, a lieutenant in loafers (you could have
taken him for Clark Gable) had clicked his heels together and greeted
everybody, and the band had started up on "Night and Day." Even with
the music in full swing, though, almost nobody had danced, the girls
talking among themselves, the soldiers suddenly awkward as young boys.
Smitty had stood next to Bea but seemed tongue-tied, or perhaps he was
listening to the girls behind them, who were babbling in another language. There were Portuguese in New Bedford; there were Greeks and
Jews. The city had seemed, the few times she'd gone, dirty, crowded and

unsafe, a thousand miles from the Point, though in truth it was only twenty minutes by car. New Bedpan, Helen had called it once, and Bea had suppressed a laugh. Now here they were, the girls from New Bedpan, herded like marked sheep into the Wilsons' barn, wearing Fighting Red lipstick and too much scent.

"Show some spirit, Battery B!" the lieutenant had called out. "Come on out, boys! Find yourselves a partner!"

Still, almost no one had come forward, except for the lieutenant, his wife and a few others. Bea had been surprised: When your boss said dance, did you not dance?

"Even once they split us up, I had my eye right on you," Smitty told her later. "And on that blue slipper of yours. But I couldn't be the first one to cross the line—my boys would've never let me live it down."

Her shoe was not hard to find; it might have been the only blue one in the heap. Standing without it, she'd felt lopsided, listing, but then there was Smitty at her side, and his arm on her elbow had felt surprisingly familiar, and somehow she had gotten her shoe back on and then they were dancing the jitterbug, which she knew just a little from watching Helen and Dossy practice in the kitchen, and then the waltz, which she knew well. She was not light on her feet, exactly, but she was sturdy and had always moved easily, winning the girls' division of the running races set up by the church, and now, as she danced, she fell into a rhythm that erased, quite beautifully, her thoughts. His hand on her back was broad and sure, and she felt suddenly as if she were someplace entirely outside the Point, outside the several different lifetimes she had known so far.

Other soldiers asked her to dance as well: Louis Biglarderi, who was often posted as a sentry at the gate; Corporal David Laux; several privates who looked young enough to be her charges. "I'm not much of a dancer," Bea would protest each time, but they were in a merry, even riotous mood; they took her along, twirled her out, and while she must have been a good decade older than most of the girls, the men seemed to either not notice or not care. Agnes danced with Smitty too, her eyes on Bea, and when the bandleader called an all-ladies dance, Agnes took Bea around, leading like a man, and afterward Smitty said they'd been the best pair of the lot.

"By all means go—I mean, if you want to," Mrs. P. had said when Agnes brought it up with her two days earlier, and before they'd left the house that evening, she'd come onto the porch and offered each of them a little rhinestone brooch—Agnes's shaped like a star, Bea's like an anchor. Annie, nearly fifty, had not wanted to come. Lizzy, who had a Scots fellow from another house in Orange, had considered but finally said no. Have fun, said Mrs. P., and then she laughed, and something about that laugh (more of a yelp, it was, involuntary, like when you stepped on Blackie's tail) had made Bea nearly turn around and go back inside. But Agnes had her by the arm, and one of the Childs' maids, an American, was coming toward them from down the road, and two busloads of local girls had already gone by, waving handkerchiefs out the open windows. Dossy and Helen were nowhere to be seen. Janie, through a fail-safe recipe of active play and early supper, was already in bed.

It was not until a good hour into the dance that Bea saw Helen being whisked by in a soldier's arms, and Helen locked eyes with her and smiled in her devilish way. In her embarrassment, Bea ducked her head onto Smitty's shoulder so that it must have looked—must have felt—like she was embracing him, and he leaned full up against her and whispered Darling, and she pulled sharply back.

Too many things, then: wanting to yank Helen away from the soldier; to find her own privacy again; to stay in the moment as it played out, fast and rollicking; to flee its soak of aftershave and beer. Smitty's belt buckle was polished brass; his hands were scrubbed, clean and callused from the guns. Underneath his spearmint gum, beer breath and big laugh, he seemed a large and milk-sweet baby, and underneath that, an animal, at once dumb and powerful—one of the Angus bulls penned in the cattle yard at home. Her father had preferred working Goods, but when they were shorthanded he got put in Livestock, the bulls broad-shouldered, dim-eyed, worth a fortune (buyers came from Argentina). "Dangle down," the yard boys used to call as they passed the pens, clutching their trousers and doing jigs; how Bea had hated running messages down there. *Dance,* she told herself now. Smitty was guiding her again, and once you got on you could not get off, or was it a joke, his courting of her—it would not have surprised her, at the same time that she was (Mrs. P.'s words returned to her) *having fun.*

"I've got to get back," she gasped, breathless, when the music stopped.

"Back?" Smitty had been steadily drinking between dances, leaving his cup on a shelf and taking a gulp each time they went by. His hair was sweaty, his face red and flecked with salty peanut crumbs. He leaned toward her, and she had a brief, untoward urge to draw him closer, followed by an equally strong urge to back away. "Already, Cinderella?" he asked. "Why?"

"Janie." She both meant it and did not.

"Why? Isn't she sleeping?"

"If she wakes."

"You have the night off, Bea. Live a little! What about her mother?"

"It's me she wants. And the older girls snuck in here." (Where Helen was, so too was Dossy, though Bea had not yet spotted her.) "I've got to get them home."

As the music started up again, she wove her way through the bodies, off the dance floor, and Smitty followed her out of the rec hall, past the P.X. and a row of tents, onto the road and through the gate. There was the sentry, slow dancing with his gun; he gave it a loud, smacking kiss as they walked by. Smitty waved him off and lengthened his stride, moving ahead of Bea. He was angry with her, it was clear to see, and suddenly— she felt it in her steps, her quickening blood—she was angry too. Go find Agnes, why don't you, she wanted to blurt out. Agnes will dance with you all night. She was prettier than Bea and knew more about men, and she had her complaints (Mrs. P. was a skinflint, Janie was spoiled, Charlie thought he owned the world), and talked, now and then, about moving back to Scotland, or had, anyway, before the war, though she had promised—they both had, to each other—never to leave Bea. Empty your pockets, Bea thought suddenly; she could not say why. Empty your pockets. No lint or coins, nappy pins or handkerchiefs, just outturned pockets, holding nothing, clean.

She turned to Smitty, then, and stood stock-still. He was a good man (though drunk as a skunk) and they had danced all night; it was a little kindness she could give. He kissed her first in a series of dry pecks, and when she did not move or protest, his tongue muscled its way inside her mouth, his hand rising up to press her cheek. They stood on the side of the road for a good five minutes. First he tasted salty from the peanuts; then he did not. It had been years since anyone had kissed her this way, but after the first shock of it, it did not feel like that long, it felt, well, regular, though she had expected, she realized, something different, more *American*, more *soldierly*. This had a plainness to it, in a good way; she might have been here, or home. Her anger was gone. A calmness, now, though she was aware, as she'd not been inside, of how full of drink she was, her bladder near bursting.

She did not kiss him back at first, but neither did she resist, letting his tongue move about inside her, bump up against her teeth (she was missing a back one, did he notice?). And then, despite herself, the prying open of a door long painted over, swollen shut. The sea breeze had started up by then. The music came fast and loud and jolly from the rec hall. The searchlight made its sweep. Even drunk, Smitty was a gentleman, his hands on her waist but lightly, their two chins shifting, two necks moving in their own kind of dance. Without quite meaning to, she kissed him back, finding there a sweetness, full and male, a foreign but sustaining food. Oh. My. It had never happened before, not like this, and the place where she found herself was watery and shape-shifting, a current tugging her along, and Bea gave in to it, queer feeling though it was; she fell inside.

Not since tending Janie as an infant had she come so close to someone, not since tending her mother on her deathbed, though this was even closer, to be inside his mouth this way and he in hers. He wanted her, that was the difference—he was no baby or old woman; he wanted her because he wanted her, because she was a woman and he a man, because (perhaps?) she was herself. She shut her eyes and raised a hand to touch his cheek, clean-shaven but still rough. She cupped his square-jawed, oddly handsome, oblong face and drew him further inside the kiss. It was he who finally pulled away and bent to look at her. She saw, to her dismay, that he was laughing.

"What?" Her skin grew tight with shame.

"See?" he said.

"What?"

"You liked it. I knew you would, under all that grumbling! I knew it!"

He was triumphant as a victorious child. He drew her toward him, kissed her brow, released her, laughing all the while, and then she was laughing too. She had never known a man to laugh like Smitty did. It took up his whole body.

"Oh," she said, and felt another wave of laughter come on. She gasped and bent over; she had to stop or she would wet her pants. It hurt, this laughter, even as it was a relief. "Stop!" she snorted, finally, straightening up and wiping her eyes.

"Was that your first real kiss, honeybee?" Smitty asked

She shook her head, annoyed. Did he really think she'd never done it before, at her age? She'd kissed a boy from her church, another, named Donald, who worked at the ropeworks with her brother. She had let that boy, or man, really—he'd been twenty, she nineteen—go down her knickers, up her dress. Donald had been fevered when they kissed, shy but friendly when they went on walks and, twice, to dinner and a show. She had rather liked the kissing and felt complimented and worried that he drank too much and was not from Forfar; his family had come for the mills and attended no church. Still, if he'd asked her to marry him, she'd likely have said yes. Then there were layoffs, and her mother took sick, and Donald had no work and moved to Glasgow, sent two letters, disappeared. Bea had minded less than she'd thought she would, glued, as much as she could be, to her mother's side. In America, Stewart came after her a few times in the back hall when he was drunk; he'd tried the same with Agnes (they all thought him a ne'er-do-well in this regard, though a few years later he would marry a nice Scots girl who also worked in Grace Park and be happy enough until Mr. P. died, when he'd fall apart).

Smitty began to whistle, one of the songs they'd danced to. Bea looked back at the sentry, who quite politely, if against all regulations, was facing the sea now, not the road. In the house, the light in the Porters' bedroom blinked off, the windowpane gone black. The dim-out shades were supposed to be down, but Mrs. P. must have forgotten, and this seemed abruptly a sign of something bad. Then a shade lowered, a hand came with it. Was Mrs. P. watching, waiting up? Bea moved toward the partial cover of a stunted tree.

"How old are you, anyway?" Smitty followed her, looping an arm around her waist.

"Me?" She ducked her head. She had been dreading the question. "Not young."

"How much not young?"

"Twenty-nine." Her mouth lied for her, lopping off seven years (and her birthday coming up in September).

If he doubted her, he did not show it. "That's nothing. I'm thirty-five. Are you surprised?"

"No. I mean, yes—" Surprised in which direction? "You—"

In fact, he looked his age, which was nearly her own, a mere year younger, maybe less depending on when his birthday fell. So why isn't he married? she could hear her mother ask. So why is he courting you, or is he just out for a grope and poke? Smitty reached for her again.

"I've got to go," she said faintly.

He lurched toward her.

"Thank you," she said. Now her voice was firm. She sidestepped. Prim, she was. Prim and proper. Desperate. Horrid—to herself and, no doubt, to him. She might have curtsied; she might have dropped, a possum playing dead, into a still, small ball.

"Don't go," he said. "Don't . . . why?"

"I'm sorry. Thank you," she repeated stiffly. "And good night."

And then she was lurching too—down the road, along the lawn, onto the porch, through the front door (still, she did not let the screen door slam). She stopped in the W.C. to release an urgent stream and was off again, up the stairs to the landing, across the landing to the top. She was running, stumbling a few times, and Janie's door was three-quarters open as Janie liked it and Bea had left it, and there was Janie, one arm bent over her head, the sheets twisted around her legs. Bea lowered the child's arm to her side, fixed the covers and sat at the foot of the bed.

Right. All right then.

She did not remember about the big girls being at the dance, not until later, when she was finally in her own bed, nearly asleep, her knickers washed in the sink and hung to dry (or gather damp) inside the closet. She did not picture Smitty going back through the gate, returning or not returning to the dance. She did not dwell in her own body, where she might, if she'd looked, have found her own well-guarded version of desire.

All right, then.

For a long time she sat there, catching her breath, watching Janie sleep.

IX

TWENTY SHADES OF green, or was it twenty shades of gray? In the town where Bea grew up, the buildings went right down to the pavement; it was, like the smell of the jute mills, something you didn't notice until you left. The buildings were stone and so were the sidewalks, with rarely a patch of dirt or grass between, not even on the side streets. Only the drying greens and graveyard interrupted all that rock, and Castle Hill, which you reached from the bottom of her street. You got the key from the chemist's, slid open the iron gate and climbed up the stairs up to the top, where a turret sat without its castle, most of it missing, she'd realize later, though as children they never wondered why. There was a bit of grass at the top of the hill, and you could see the town below you, and beyond it in spring, fields and hills in twenty shades of green, and the train tracks heading out.

As a girl, Bea had liked to climb up, not to think about leaving, for she rarely did, but rather to have a good look around. There, the prison set on a hill. There, the train yard, the steam laundry, the stern brown gables of her school. Often she would take her brother along, and a few of the younger children from the neighborhood. She liked to drop the key into her pocket and feel its weight there, to chide the little ones to stay away from the edge or to organize games for them, King of the Castle, Duck Duck Goose. Later, when they were older, she and Tilly would climb up together after work. Tilly was the one to talk of leaving. *Pah*, she'd spit out from up above the town, dismissing the whole place at once. One day at dusk, Tilly gathered pebbles and began to throw them at the rooftops. Don't, Bea pleaded. You'll break a window or hit someone. You should throw one, Tilly told her. It might cheer you up. Bea had not thought herself uncheerful, though this was early on in her mother's illness, when she was just beginning to understand that things would get harder and harder in ways she did not care to imagine. "If you live in a glass house—" she began, but Tilly just laughed at her, turned toward their own rooftop and lobbed a stone.

Her mother had begun in the sorting room at the laundry, where the smell of dirty linen could kill a pig, but for years, until she took sick, she'd been in ironing, doing fancy work on the hand irons, and when Bea finished up school she'd started there too, but on the gas irons. It was not a bad place. Unlike at the mills, you could hear yourself talk, and there was something about the work itself—stained collars turned clean, tea towels pressed, folded and wrapped in tissue, bachelor bundles made presentable again—that pleased Bea and also her mother, who had grown up doing laundry in an outdoor tub. At Pearl, steam ran almost everything, and if the windows stayed closed, if the air was heavy and the gas irons could give headaches or watery eyes, you learned to live with it, for it was a job and better than most. Once a year, the proprietor had a social at McLaren's Tearoom, and when, after New Year's, months of unclaimed fancy work sat on a shelf, there was a drawing. Bea had gotten two lace collars that way. One went with her mother to her grave; the other, she brought to America. And while her mother had taught her to iron by hand at home, she preferred the machines, to have just her little piece to worry over—two weeks of nothing but collars, then a month of nothing but right cuffs—while behind her, on the other side of the room, her mother spat on flatirons and changed a big iron for a small and sang under her breath, her voice still girlish, pure and pretty, and she seemed to sing for herself alone.

They shared their dinner, she and her mother. They sat together at break, with Tilly and her mother's friend Harriet and a few other ladies from ironing or church. Some girls would not have liked to mix home and work like this, but Bea had always wanted to follow her mother to work, to get a little more of her, and now she could. My shadow, her mother used to tell the neighbors. Never had to worry about this one running off, and Bea looked like her—the same mild gray eyes and broad shoulders, the same capable hands. As long as she had her mother, everything was fine, for her mother got up clear-eyed each morning and made the tea and chatted steadily though rarely complained, and while Bea was not a spectacular student nor a beauty nor anyone of significance, her mother loved her and told her so often. You're my best girl, her mum would say (no matter that Bea was her only living one), and sometimes it felt as if it was just the two of them, something sisterly about it. Underneath it all was the assumption that eventually Bea would end up with a husband, but they were in no hurry; their arrangement suited them. Her mother did not primp or preen her, did not send her out, except to dancing classes, which were, anyway, all girls.

Her mother's sickness began in her privates and spread to the rest of her, taking over two years to do her in. At first she talked right through her pain (though rarely of it) but as she grew sicker, her words grew scarce. Sometimes Bea would come home from work and stand on the stairs for a good five minutes, wanting to hear a sentence pass between her parents or come from her mother, who had always carried on a wandering patter, even when she was alone. Finally, Bea stepped inside with the food she had brought for her mother: strained cheese, pears for compote, chicken livers for blood strength.

For her father and brother, nothing. For herself, nothing. She didn't notice; her appetite was gone, and theirs meant nothing to her at the time. The stairs were dirty; it was her family's week to clean them, and her mother would never have let them get that way. For the first time in her life, Bea had grown irresponsible, so focused on the task at hand—to force life back. Three times that month she scorched goods at Pearl and had her pay docked, and she couldn't be bothered to cook for her father or Callum, whose two lives she would have traded for her mother's one in a flash.

Like farm hands, the men ate porridge for every meal, letting it harden on the counter and cutting a clammy slice to fill them up. Her father did not complain. He seemed in his own daze, doing nothing for her mother for weeks at a time, then coming home having spent a day's wages on flowers, or on sweets that Bea ate when he wasn't looking—so that he would think her mother had eaten them, she told herself. Never did he offer one to her. Callum had met Kate, his wife-to-be, by then and often ate with her family on the other side of town. Without Bea quite noticing, he had become a man, large and meaty, nearly as silent as their father. Where had he gone to? How? Tired though she was from so much tending, Bea would have preferred he'd stayed a little boy for her to tend.

Every day for a time, she found a moment to stop at St. Margaret's and pray, if only for five minutes, though by near the end, when it grew

clear that prayer would not work, she gave up even that (Pray for peace
for her soul, her mother's friend had told her, but Bea prayed singularly
for one thing—and more to her own mother than to God: *Stay*). In the
final months, her mother lost words entirely and developed a noxious
swelling in her belly, though they had already removed parts of it. She
died wordless in hospital while Bea held her hand and Bea's father paced.
After she died, her mouth relaxed, her belly too. The nurse detached Bea
gently but firmly, one finger at a time, but as soon as she was cut loose,
Bea knelt again and took her mother's hand. This time the nurse let her
sit for a moment, and then she said her name—*Beatrice*—commandingly
and with the greatest tenderness, as a mother might. Fueled by a strange
and momentary hope, Bea dropped her mother's hand and stood. By the
time she turned around, a sheet was covering her mother's face.

"Over," said her father as he led her from the building—just that,
"Over," as if he were announcing the name of a town along the railway
line: *Over! Take your parcels! Mind the gap!* Then he stopped and put
a hand on her arm, but it seemed like someone else's hand, just as her
body seemed like someone else's body. What was over? She'd let go of her
mother because the nurse had made her. She'd left the hospital because
her father led her out. What was over? She stepped away from her father.
She was twenty-three years old. She knew how to iron; she knew how to
love her mother. That was all. Poor lass, said her father when, finally, they
were in their kitchen, among the cups and plates, sink and drying rack,
a foreign country now. Poor lass, her father said again; whether he spoke
about her mother or herself or both, she did not know. That was the last he
spoke of it all, except to bring up practicalities around her mother's burial.

Only once did she cry, a few weeks after the funeral, walking and
walking on the roads through town and then out of town, nearly to
Padanaram, feet pounding, tears starting up only when the houses gave
way to fields, her jaw set, fists balled against the sand-soft crumbling wall
of grief. It was December and cold and she wore a hat but no scarf and
the air scoured her lungs, and at some point she turned herself around,

set one foot in front of the other, started back. When she got home, she cleaned out her mother's clothes and sundries and brought them to the poorhouse, saving only a necklace, a shawl and her mother's crochet needle (made from an eagle bone, her mother said) for herself. She cleaned the kitchen, stepping around her aunt, who was living there by then. That night, she cooked for her father, her aunt, Callum and Callum's fiancée: smashed parsnips, beef in dark gravy, stewed apples. Then, without pleasure but with a plodding, almost endless appetite, she sat at her mother's place at the table (her aunt occupied her own) and ate.

At the laundry the next day, she tried to increase her hours, which she'd cut back during her mother's illness, but business was slow and her mother was not there to stand up for her, and they said maybe by spring if things pick up. She offered to watch the three-doors-down neighbor's infant two afternoons a week, and this was her comfort in the months to come: the firm weight of the boy as she rocked him by the stove, the way he woke reaching for her face. The neighbor paid her in sewing notions, which Bea accepted, and hemp bags from the mills, which she had no use for and refused. You need to get out, Tilly would chide her, making her walk to High Street to look in the window of the hat shop, or go to a dance now and then, though everyone knew there was only one man for every five girls and Bea's mouth had no words inside it, and she had gotten, after having grown so thin, quite fat.

Where was her father through all this? Her brother? Only years later, when she watched the Porters try to move through grief, would it occur to her to wonder. At the time, it seemed to her that sorrow was entirely her own territory. Her brother was getting married, after all. That he broke the news a few months before her mother's death, and that it brought her mother some measure of peace, did not escape Bea's notice, but more potent was her sense that both she and her mother were being quickly and practically replaced. Her father did not seem particularly changed after her mother's death, though he must have been. Anyway, they were men, cut from a different cloth. She washed her brother's and her father's clothes and made their food and beds and said hello to them, good-bye, how was your day, have you got a cough, and that was that.

It had not always been like this. When he was little, Callum had been her doughy, funny, white-faced, freckled boy, set apart from the other children by his limp and made Bea's own by the fact that she cared for him after school when her mother was at work, fetching him from the neighbor's until he was old enough to attend school himself. It had been Bea, for a time, that Callum wanted when he called out at night. It had been Bea who defended him from teasing, Bea who bathed him, until they grew older and he bathed himself. As Callum grew, a sullenness set in with him. His hands got rough from the ropeworks; he wore his apron when there was no need to, scissors poking from the pocket, jute clinging to his clothes like body hair. He began, at random moments, to say cruel, coarse things to Bea: about her weight, about what people said about girls who worked the laundry. He began (was it he who started their father in this direction?) to drink. And then he met Kate, the girl he would marry, and a certain pleasantness came back, but not toward Bea, especially, though he did stop being cruel. "This is my . . . sister," he said once as he introduced her to a friend, and anyone might have noticed how he paused before the word, as if he couldn't quite remember who she was.

With her father too, Bea had once had glimpses of a person she could talk to, but that was years ago. One time, when she was six or seven, for some reason she could no longer remember, her father had taken her and Callum to work for the day. "This is where the china is," he'd said, leading them to a side room where a sign read "Fragile Goods." "You need to be banking that with straw, or it'll break." He told them that if someone wanted to send a plover's egg or honeycomb as freight, it was written right into the books that the company was not responsible if the egg broke or the honeycomb got crushed, but it wouldn't break, not if *he* had packed it. He was a proud and quiet man, her father (this was before the Great War, and she was younger than Janie; he had set her on a packing crate, said Do not swing your legs, and she had not).

It was more words than she'd heard him say in years. She would always remember that—how he'd looked at her more than Callum as he talked, and she'd stared at him and listened as hard as she could, though she was, more than anything, confused. Why, anyway, send a plover's egg alone on a train, or honeycomb? Over time, in her mind, the plovers' eggs and honeycomb came to have something to do with her father and the Great War, with her father and the way that, after he came home from France, he scrubbed each night, scrubbed and scrubbed but always stank, for it wasn't mostly glassware and china he was loading at the rail-road; it was coal and ballast and manure, it was filthy sheep marked with chalk, bulls with crimson parts, and first her father was a Good Templar, not a drop of liquor in the house, and then, after her mother took sick, he brought in whisky for her pain, then his; he and Callum drank after work; he stopped washing; he "let himself go" (it was a phrase Mrs. P. used about people, along with "He's lost his marbles" or "She's got a screw loose"). And then her mother died, Callum married, her father's sister Mary moved in, and when Bea brought up the idea of Canada with her father, he barely looked up from his newspaper.

"Tilly's going," Bea said, mostly to fill the space. "Also her brother."

Her first response, when Tilly had brought up the idea, had been panic: first her mother gone, now Tilly. Then, as she was trying to absorb it, only half listening to Tilly talk on, her friend had suggested that she come too. Me? To Canada? It had never occurred to her, not once in her livelong days. Tilly laid out the arguments: how there was no work at home, even the laundry laying off, their own hours just cut by a third. And there are strong, handsome men in Canada, said Tilly. Loads of them, with beards. *Beards?* Bea laughed but felt repulsed. And money, said Tilly, and their own log houses—Scotsmen, loads of them, and the whole lot needing wives. Not long before Bea's mother had lost the ability to speak, she had told Bea to look after herself now. She had not said find a husband. She had not said take care of your father and brother. Just "Look after yourself"—a release of sorts, though all Bea had wanted was to look after her mother, poultice to forehead, spoonfuls of Benger's Pap, Soothing Nourishment for the Very Young & Very Old.

"Mr. Stewart on High Street arranges it," she told her father now. "I'm sure you've seen the adverts"—she pointed—"in the paper."

He turned the page, took a sip of ale.

"You could come too," she said.

"Me?" He snorted, and some ale slopped into his lap. "What would I do in Canada?"

She shrugged. "They've got railroads."

"Ha! To cart my coffin to my grave."

"Don't." Her hatred burned white and sudden.

He shook his head at her. "You'll see when you're old. You'll want to end up where you started. So you're off on an adventure, are you, Beatrice? I didn't think"—he drummed his feet on the floor, a sudden, surly little jig—"you were the type."

She was not the type. She did not want to be. Still, something nudged her on: the sense that she had little left to lose, but also a bit of hope, even excitement. "Would you manage all right, you and Mary, with me gone? Callum would be here."

Her father grunted; what this meant, she could not say. Aunt Mary was childless, timid, not unkind. She had come from Dundee, supposedly to help her brother keep house, but also, Bea knew, because she was recently widowed and could not make the rent. Her father played cards with his sister. They talked at night, in low voices, more than he'd talked to Bea or his wife for years. She did not listen in, though the sound of voices, any voices, was a comfort to her, and seeing her father rise a little from his stupor a relief. Her aunt had not gotten on with her mother for reasons Bea didn't understand or care to investigate, so whatever they talked about was not her mother, and nothing else interested Bea just then. Eventually, her aunt would come climb into the recessed bed, while Bea pretended to be sleeping in the trundle bed below.

"I may just look into it a bit," she said.

She knew almost nothing about Canada, though she remembered her mother teaching her the letters of the alphabet from the white bags: GOLDEN WHEAT CANADA. One time, when a bag was empty, her mother had cut out the letters and made new words from them. Or no—it had been her father. Had it? Had he sat with her at the kitchen table, spreading out the letters, rearranging them: DEN, TEN, WET, GET? Her mother was no reader, but her father used to be. She had been happy sitting there, watching her Da move around the dusty, flour-soft squares. She remembered it; she thought she did: OLD, GOLD, HOLD, TOLD. *Ask me to stay,* she thought to him now. *Or at least say you'll miss me. I asked you to come, now ask me to stay, if only to be polite.*

Years later, in America (not Canada, though Tilly ended up there, and worked on a farm, and married a farmer, and had, at the moment of her last letter to Bea, three boys), she would be reciting "Humpty Dumpty" with Janie and find that there—in the big white egg, the smashed white shell—was her father. As a child, Bea had coaxed splinters from the fingers of the neighbors' children and carried the widows' groceries upstairs. She liked looking after people; it came naturally to her. But her own father? *All the king's horses and all the king's men.* His forehead was too broad, his body too big, his mind too breakable, not like the china cups he prided himself on packing well, but in the way of something cracked beyond repair. He did not try to do kindnesses for other people, hardly ever. He did not try, as far as she could tell, to help himself.

Still, I asked you to come, ask me to stay.

"Suit yourself," her father said.

X

AKING HER WAY through it, toward it, along New Bedford's side-walks, Bea felt at first as if it were a carnival. There were Boy Scouts with banners, women in cross-strap aprons singing rounds, a clown—or no, Uncle Sam, his nose clown-red—on stilts. Along the street, fire trucks and loudspeaker trucks inched along, and just inside the entrance to Acushnet Park were rows of kiosk games where you could throw bean-bags at airplanes or sponges at submarines, and there was a garden plot in a big raised box—*Plant a Seed, Feed a Nation*—and a brass band playing a bright march. Children darted, people laughed, popcorn popped and was passed out in paper cones for free. The scene reminded Bea of nothing so much as the feeing fairs at home, where there'd been rides and music and dancing exhibitions, and once an elephant on a tightrope, though it turned out later to be two circus men in a clever suit. Her parents had met at a feeing fair, her mother in from the country looking for factory work, her father selling Forfar bridies at the pastry stand, and you ate the meat at the center but threw away the pastry, as the men's hands—the women's too—were dirty from work. "It looks like a carnival," her mother had explained to her once, "but it's where you go to find a job."

The week before had been a claustrophobic inside time, the weather rainy, Janie with mumps (where she had gotten them, nobody could fig-ure out), Mrs. P. with a head cold. Bea had spent the week inside nursing Janie and had not seen Smitty, though he'd sent a note in with Helen and Dossy inviting them all to the Civil Defense Exhibitions, with a special p.s. to her: *B. there!* Now, Janie was finally herself again, pleased to be out though tired of Bea, and Bea ready for a bit of air herself. Stewart had driven them to the bus, then gone back to fetch Mr. and Mrs. P. and take them all the way to New Bedford in the car. Now he was pushing Mr. P., and Dossy and Helen were forging on ahead as Agnes struggled to keep up, and Mrs. P., in her wide-brimmed platter of a hat, was turning this way and that: They've really outdone themselves, this is quite a production!

Bea held fast to Janie's hand. It was not often that the family went out all together, but it was the day before Mr. P.'s birthday, and this, he said, was all he wanted as a gift: to go to the exhibitions and take everyone to supper afterward, "my treat" (what was not his treat?). Bea was in her blue silk dress again. At the dance, Smitty had liked it. Would he notice? Would she even find him among the throng? She had put Janie in a white smocked frock and done her hair in ribbons and ringlets, though most of the girls they passed wore simple smocks or sailor suits with britches.

"This way"—Helen looked at her program—"for the demonstrations," and they all followed her; such confidence she had, hatless with her hair in a high bun, her long legs striding, and Dossy behind her, laughing, happy, though later that evening she would complain of a headache and start to weep and say she wished she hadn't gone.

Lined up for inspection were army vehicles, and in front of them signs—"Peep Weapon Carrier with Mounted 30 Caliber," "Cargo Carrier"—and beside the signs, on a stand, a toy-size model of the vehicle. "Oh, Charlie would think this was over the top!" said Mrs. P., as if her son were a little boy still. In his youth, he'd made model after model; they still took up several shelves in his room in Grace Park. At each exhibit, soldiers were posted, clean-shaven, doing their best to stand at attention. Some had sweets for the children in their rucksacks. Others gave out paper flags on toothpicks; Bea slid one into Janie's hair. The men from the base were here somewhere, most of them were, though a few had stayed behind on guard. "If I were a Jap or Hun in Buzzards Bay," Helen had declared too loudly on the bus over, "today's the day I'd make my move, for sure." Smitty was here, though he had neglected to tell them in the note precisely where he'd be or what he'd be doing, and now she wondered if this had been on purpose, for there were pretty girls scattered everywhere like candy, younger than she was, more decked out, laughing louder. Already she was sweating through her dress.

"Hand. Stay close," she kept instructing Janie, and even Mrs. P. had been concerned enough about the crowd to come up with a plan if anyone got separated: Meet at the leaflet table of the air raid warden's demonstration site at four o'clock. "*The war,*" boomed a deep voice over a loudspeaker on a slow-moving truck, "*is being fought on our own door-step as well as abroad. We need more volunteers in many lines.*"

"I thought I might roll some bandages," said Mrs. P. when the voice had moved on. "Just for a few minutes—there's a table down that way. Come with me, Helen and Dossy. We'll catch up."

Before Bea could answer, she was off, Janie straining after her. "No," Bea told her firmly. "You stay with me."

One by one, their group diminished: Mr. P. and Stewart stopping along the way to inspect equipment and talk to soldiers, the big girls following their mother to the Red Cross tent, until it was just Bea, Agnes and Janie, and then Agnes took up Janie's other hand and they went along that way, their own tight chain—past a massive searchlight operated by remote control, past a War Bonds table, past a group of girls tying rags together in a long chain—for tug-of-war, or something more practical? Janie tried to stop, but Bea and Agnes pulled her on. On the map on the back of the printed program, there was a *Storytelling & Crafts Tent for Our Youngest Citizens.* This had become their destination, and while Bea could not make heads or tails of the map, Agnes thought she might know which way to go.

And so it was not at all by intention that they ended up, the three of them, near the gas mask demonstration. It was, it seemed, the crowd that took them there, the swell of it, its buoyant, nervous energy. Each time Agnes tried to move them one way, they got jostled or shuffled or distracted by the next exhibit, until Agnes had turned north to south and then, somehow, dropped the program, so that not only were they separated from the others, but they also had no idea where they were. Later, Bea would wish they had asked directions, gone back to the edge of the green, sat down and had egg sandwiches (she had packed them at home but forgotten to bring them), or found the Youngest Citizens tent and heard a story about ducks.

At first, she was not sure she was really hearing someone call her name: *Bea, Beatrice! Hey there! Over here!*

"It's Smitty!" said Janie, tugging toward him, and then there he was, dressed to the nines, his khaki uniform pressed, his necktie out. He'd gotten a haircut, scrubbed his nails. He was *handsome*; it was the only word for him just then as he stood there smiling at Bea, like a soldier in a musical revue.

"Found you," he said, out of breath. "And just in time. I've been looking out for you—so have some other fellows. Where's Helen? Henry's had his eye out."

"With her mother," Agnes said. "Henry knows to leave her be. The child is barely sixteen."

"Sixteen? That's all? Is that right?" He looked at Bea.

"Barely sixteen," she confirmed.

"Her birthday was in June," said Janie.

"Hmm." Smitty smiled. "The social committee. She does seem older than that."

Agnes had, Bea knew, spoken to the P.'s about Henry after the dance. Helen had not come home that night until three in the morning; Agnes had waited up. Soon thereafter, Mr. P. had gone to the gate when Henry was on guard duty and had a word with him (Bea would have gone straight to Helen, but the girl's parents were afraid of her and thought—perhaps rightly—that if they told her no, she'd act out even more). The P.'s asked Agnes and Bea not to tell, and Bea hadn't told a soul, not even Smitty. She'll only get wilder, Mrs. P. had said, if she knows we're tracking her whereabouts. Apparently Helen had told Henry she was eighteen, heading off to Smith College. "At least that's what Henry told my husband," Mrs. P. had said. "If it's true, she's asking for trouble, and if he made it up"—fat chance, thought Bea—"I trust him even less." Another family might have come right out and told their daughter to stay away from a soldier four years her senior—but the P.'s were not another family. At least, said Agnes, they were giving some attention to the child's behavior.

"So listen, ladies," Smitty said. "Battery B's gotten in on the gas mask demonstration. I wasn't sure till the last minute—they keep us guessing so we're ready for anything—but we hit the jackpot. This one is first-rate."

"What will happen?" Bea asked.

"You'll see." He bent toward Janie. "I'll get you an ice cream after, doll, all right?" He tipped his cap at Bea. "Nice dress."

Her eyes found her feet; by the time she could look up again, he was gone.

DID SHE THINK THE DEMONSTRATION was real? Of course she did not. Did it terrify her, someplace wrapped and wordless in her gut? She had been Janie's age during the Great War. Her mother had kept her safe and kept her safe again, but still she remembered the air raids, the zeppelins passing over, the churches and infirmary filling up with men who were not from there, while all the men from her town—finally even her father—went off to war. Now, as the smoke poured forth, Bea found herself trying to pull Janie and Agnes away from the scene, and then, when the crowd would not part for them, piling her body on top of Janie and pulling Agnes down along with her, until the three of them tumbled— somehow, they did, all wrapped together—into their own rough heap at the feet of the crowd, which briefly gasped and parted to make way, then turned its attention back to the spectacle. On the grass, Beatrice covered them, her best friend and her baby. She could not tell where her body left off and theirs began.

When she finally lifted her head, it was because Janie was crying and Agnes was poking her in the ribs. Somewhere above her, she heard laughter coming through a long tunnel, and she looked up to a goggle-eyed green insect stretching out an arm.

"Need a hand?" said a muffled voice, and then the creature lifted off its mask and was a soldier, a tall, broad-shouldered boy, red-faced, spike-haired, grinning; he looked familiar, but he was not, to her relief, Smitty.

"The demonstration's over," the soldier said, and let out a high-pitched, girlish giggle. Then he lowered his voice. "Sorry if it spooked you, ladies. I guess we did our smoke screen pretty well!"

"No," said Agnes, pushing past Bea and getting up. "No, we're fine. Excellent work, sir," and she had Bea by the arm now, she had Janie too. "You're fine," she said to Bea, brushing her off, but Bea did not feel fine; her dress was dirty, her mind torn up.

"I thought . . . ," she said slowly to Agnes. "It seemed . . ." She looked down. There was Janie, not crying any longer, but rather staring at Bea as if she'd never seen her before.

"You hurt me, pulling me down like that," the child said.

"I was protecting you," Bea said instinctively.

"It was *fake*." Janie plucked at the grass on her dress. "They did it on purpose." She turned to Agnes, tears starting down her face again. "Right?"

"Of course." Agnes pulled out a handkerchief for her. "Bea was just playing along. You're supposed to get down low. It's what you do in a fire drill. Same thing here."

Janie looked around. "Where's Smitty? He said he'd buy me an ice cream."

"I don't know." Bea tried to hide her disappointment. "They're busy today."

"Where's Mummy?" Janie asked with sudden urgency. "And Daddy? Where *is* everyone?"

Bea looked at her watch: 3:30. "Seeing the sights, like us. We'll pay a quick visit to the Youngest Citizens tent and then we'll find them at our meeting point at four o'clock."

As they started to walk away, the men laid down a second smoke screen, but this time Bea was far enough away and prepared enough that she could turn and watch. From a distance the smoke was almost beautiful, curled and blue and rising—and not real, anyway (it smelled of fire but also of something sweet like shaving cream, and had no heat). And there were the men, wandering through it, first with their gas masks in their hands, then putting them on, hat over head, hands on masks, fingers adjusting, pulling levers or pushing buttons. Though it was hard to see through all the smoke, it looked difficult, whatever they were doing, and there must have been forty men, maybe more, all fumbling and arranging at the same time, all disappearing into their masks.

"Battery B! Ashaunt Point! Best of the best!" she heard someone call, and then, in front of her, a soldier was waving—to her, or someone just behind her, or the crowd.

"Wave." Agnes raised her hand, and Janie's too. "It's Smitty. Go on!"

Bea lifted her arm, but by then the soldier was gone, the smoke clearing, the crowd applauding, the loudspeaker voice starting in about searchlights—"*pierce the darkness up to a distance of twelve miles . . . eight hundred thousand candlepower*"— She dropped her hand down; her arm felt heavy, prosthetic. Did a gas mask really help you breathe or just give you a small green tent in which to die? It was at that moment that her heart cracked open for Smitty and—like a sea creature flaring forth, then muscling in—coiled tightly closed.

"What's in the children's tent?" asked Janie.

"Youngest Citizens tent," corrected Agnes. "They have stories there. And crafts."

"Am I a young citizen?"

"Of course you are!" Agnes craned her neck. "Oh—there's Helen and Dossy! *Helen! Girls!*"

The big girls glanced toward them, then ducked into the crowd, but Agnes ran after them, and soon they were all together, the five of them, Bea and Agnes walking side by side, Janie skipping happily between her sisters.

"We saw a gas mask thing," Janie told her sisters. "With Smitty in it."

Dossy began to recite:

"Gas! Gas! Quick, boys!—An ecstasy of fumbling,
Fitting the clumsy helmets just in time;
But someone still was yelling out and stumbling
And floundering like a man in fire or lime."

"What *is* that?" Bea stopped, hands on her belly. The words described precisely what she had just seen.

"Winifred Owen," Dossy said.

"Who?"

"It's Wilfred. A British poet. Has anyone seen Henry?" Helen asked.

XI

IT WAS ON a hot Wednesday in late July that Grandmother Porter swept up in her long black dress and sat herself down with the newspaper on the porch. Nearly all the soldiers had gone off to Fort Rodman for training, leaving the base unusually quiet. Helen was on the porch, writing Charlie a letter. Henry had dropped her quite suddenly after the dance, leaving her stung and newly obsessed with him, then irritated with herself for being obsessed. *Dear Charlie,* she wrote. *I've never been so bored in all my life. I almost wish a submarine would come along to stir things up.* She balled up the paper. *Dear Charlie, I'm curious about whether the soldiers there seem more or less religious than, say, a group of college boys.* For goodness' sake, be cheerful, she could almost hear her mother saying. Light and cheerful, newsy, breezy. *Dearest Brother, I'm out to lose my virginity. Do you have any good-looking friends without diseases?* He might have had a laugh from that one; still, she shredded the paper and dropped the bits into the sewing basket where she kept stationery and pens. Nearby, Dossy was reading *Jane Eyre* for something like the fifth time. Bea was sorting shells and dropping them into jars filled with food coloring, and Janie drawing, busy little bees.

"*Supreme Court Is Called in Unprecedented Session to Hear Plea of Nazi Spies,*" Grandmother P. read from the *New York Times*. "That's astonishing! They want to overturn the law of war! Do we really have to give a jury trial to Nazi saboteurs?"

"It's like the Milligan case in the Civil War," Helen said.

Her grandmother lowered the newsprint to look at her. "What?"

"I already read the story," Helen explained. "That's yesterday's paper."

"The article"—her grandmother's finger traced down the column even as she spoke—"says this situation is *not* like the Milligan case. Kudos to you for reading the paper, Helen—it's more than most girls your age do—but there's nothing worse than acting like you know what you're talking about when you don't."

Grandmother P. had been visiting for several days by then, disappearing down the paths with her notebook to look for flowers, returning peppy and full of reports and questions. Sometimes she took Helen and Dossy on her nature walks. Helen wrote down the names of flora in the calf-bound nature diary her grandmother had given her, then memorized them so that she could recite them back and impress her grandmother (and thus her father). When Grandmother was not talking about flowers, she liked to discuss the status of immigrants, or the pros and cons of women serving on juries (she was pro but sometimes argued the other side just for fun) and of course, the war. Or she'd invite Helen and Dossy to pull chaise longues off the porch and lie under the night sky reciting poetry, and it wouldn't matter how old anyone was, or how late the hour, or how much poetry they remembered. The sky opened, words rose.

"Where's your father hiding?" asked Grandmother P. now, as if he had the ability to hide.

Helen, still too stung and humiliated by her grandmother's critique to speak, pointed toward the living room.

"He needs more fresh air, don't you think? And where's your mother? And Agnes? She took my handkerchiefs to mend, so kind of her."

"I don't know."

Grandmother walked over to where Bea was sitting on a spread-out oilcloth with her shells and jars. "The lost tribe," she said to no one in particular. "My, what have you got there, Betty? Some sort of science experiment?"

"No, just shells."

"She's *Bea*, Grandmother." Jane looked up from her drawing. "Not Betty. Beatrice."

"Beatrice. Of course—I knew that! Pardon me! You make shellflower crafts, don't you? I remember from Bermuda a few years ago."

Bea nodded.

"Your hobby, is it? Everyone should have a hobby. I tell my son that— there are so many things he could do, even from that chair, instead of slaving over insurance papers on holiday. My mother used to make shell- flowers. I've even made a few myself, though they're a poor substitute for nature. But to each his own. Everyone needs a diversion."

Again, Bea nodded. Helen put down her pen to watch. Talking to the Help; it was one of her grandmother's many projects, though she dis- coursed more than listened. "My mother went for natural colors and a more realistic look," she went on. "We have some still, kept under glass— they're quite durable, the way she made them. Have you ever considered not bothering"—she pointed at the jars of dye—"with that extra step?"

Bea, wearing rubber gardening gloves and a kitchen apron over her dress, released a shell into the red jar. "It's no bother."

"Real flowers have colors." Janie got up and put a drawing at Bea's side.

"What's that, darling?" asked her grandmother.

"Real flowers have colors."

"Of course, but not colors like these—I need sunshades!" Grand- mother Porter laughed. "Around here, our flora is much more mixed up, shades of things. Think of Queen Anne's lace or wild clematis—both white but with such subtle variations, or even the goldenrods—we've got a softer, more subtle palette here in New England, don't you think, whether it's in shells or flowers? Also in Scotland, except for your bluebells. Those are just splendid on Skye."

"I like Bea's flowers," Janie said.

"Of course," said Grandmother P.

Bea's creations were in fact garish, Helen thought. She gave them out as gifts in the form of boxes and little frames. Janie's room was full of them. Helen had several gathering dust.

"That's a lovely drawing, Janie," said Bea.

"It's for you."

Grandmother P. stood, smoothed her dress and let out a hoarse laugh. "Compliments all around! Well, then. Shall we go, Helen? Doss? *Dossy?* Hello?"

Dossy looked up dazed from her novel.

"Tea?" said her grandmother. "Remember? My invitation? I asked for sandwiches and petit-fours. I thought we could have tea on Teal Rock. Stewart said he'd bring the hamper down. It's probably there already, drawing flies. Your book will wait. Let's go."

"You can go too, dearie," Helen heard Bea say softly to Janie. "I'll come along if you like."

Janie shook her head. "I wasn't invited."

"Of course you were." In spite of her own near daily exclusions of her sister, Helen felt her protective instinct rise. "You should come."

"Why?" Janie shuddered. "I'm sick to death of Teal Rock."

They all knew Teal Rock was Janie's favorite place on Ashaunt. Its beach had more sea glass than the other beaches. In July, blueberries ripened at the top. You could look down to the other side and see the salt marsh and, often, a pair of mute swans (who were not—Helen knew from Grandmother—actually mute).

"Poor Teal Rock," said Dos. "It's always loved you."

"Shut up, Dossy."

"Tsk," said Bea.

Grandmother Porter, who had been standing silently, spoke. "Janie, I'd have asked you too, but I thought the climbing might worry your parents, and it's a long way in this heat. I keep forgetting how big you've gotten. Teal Rock is nothing to you. Join us! Please do."

It was then, with all of them watching, that Janie dropped to the porch floor and made her legs go crazy, shaking and bumping them in front of her, heels drumming as if she'd been struck down by a fit. Then she sat up. "It *is* too far," she said sweetly. "And in this heat. Over a mile! I can't walk. I've got"—she stared into the sun—"something wrong with my legs."

No one spoke. Janie thumped a leg, a hollow sound. Still, no one spoke. Then Bea was at Jane's side, hauling her up by her armpits, dragging her, though Jane kept her body stiff.

"Get up, child. Now. That's it. Enough theatricals. You're going inside."

Janie bucked away and thudded onto her back again on porch planks, splaying her legs; you could see the white of her underpants. "I can't," she whined. "I can't get up."

"Well." Their grandmother stepped up and towered over Janie, the skin on her patrician nose stretched tight. "Then we'll leave you here, little miss! We'll buy you a chair and strap you in for days and see what kinds of jokes you're making then."

Janie stood, ran down the porch steps and disappeared behind the house.

"What you said"—said Helen to her grandmother before fear or decorum could stop her—"was unkind."

"Me? Unkind? Ha! And what was her performance?"

"Unkind too." In fact, Helen was filled with a new admiration for her sister, though she hoped their father hadn't heard. "But she's just a little girl."

Grandmother turned to Bea. "Is that right, Beatrice? Is that your perspective—that children should be excused for doing terrible things, for mocking their elders and making light of suffering because of their young age, their so-called childlike innocence? Tell me, as a professional child minder, what do you think?"

"Sometimes," Bea said softly, "she feels left out."

"Don't we all?" said Grandmother P.

XII

A FEW DAYS later, Bea came across Mrs. P. on the back porch, staring at her mother-in-law out on the lawn. The lady was turned away from them on the far, seaward slope of parched grass, peering through binoculars; the next day, she was scheduled to visit friends in Newport and then return to Katonah. She was wearing a wide-brimmed straw hat and long brown gown, despite the heat.

"Is she looking for birds?" Bea asked.

Mrs. P. laughed sharply. "One bird. He's having his swim, with Stewart. She's always convinced he'll drown. He's fine in the water. He's *strong*. You've seen her watch him like this, haven't you? She's like an eagle. She can't help herself. She does it every day."

In fact Bea had not noticed, too busy standing watch for Janie, for Smitty, and keeping an eye on the big girls, especially Helen, in case she ran off with that soldier Henry. "A mother will worry," she said.

"*A Mother Will Worry*. Why don't you embroider it on a tea towel for her?" said Mrs. P., and then, "I'm sorry, Bea. That wasn't nice. You're right. And he's her only one. I should be kinder, shouldn't I?"

A streetcar in Mexico had killed Mr. P.'s father, who had been an important government official, when Mr. P. was still a boy, and he'd had a sister who died as a child. Grandmother Porter had lost another husband too, before that—a sea captain by the name of William Starr Dana, who'd died at sea, or was it war? In her first widowhood, she wrote the nature books the family was so proud of—*How to Know the Wildflowers*, *Plants and Their Children*, *According to Season*, by Mrs. William Starr Dana. An Authoress. In her second widowhood, she had focused her vision on her only child. Throughout, she busied herself in her spare time with politics—the Poor, the Rights of Women, now the War Effort, and she liked to drop the names of her famous friends. Bea wanted to find something to like in her—because she had suffered, because she was, like Bea, a woman alone, because her son was Mr. P.— but could not.

She made fun of my shellflowers, she had a sudden urge to tell Mrs. Porter. Bea's shell hobby was not something she advertised, but still the family seized upon it, wanting to know what to get for her birthday, what to compliment her on: Bea and her flowers, Bea and her shells. In Bermuda at Christmas a few years earlier, Mr. P. had bought her a sailor's valentine—a beautiful, expensive trinket with "Timeless Treasure" written on it in shells. Bea had wanted to appreciate the gift. He could be so thoughtful. He had a soft spot for her, and she knew he did. In fact, though, the present had upset her: Mr. P. was not her sailor, nor she his valentine, and the sailor's valentine was better than anything she could make herself. With the money he'd spent, she could have bought enough loose tropical shells to keep her in supply for years.

"She's leaving tomorrow, is she?" she asked Mrs. P.

"Oh yes she is!"

"Mr. P. will miss her."

"That's one way to put it. The girls had some sort of tiff with her, didn't they?"

Bea nodded. What had they told their mother? The three sisters had gone to Teal Rock that day without either their grandmother or herself and come back two hours later without the picnic hamper (We forgot) just as Bea was about to send Stewart out.

"She was quite upset, she said you—" Mrs. P. began, when her mother-in-law raised her arm and waved. "Oh Lord, what do I do now, Bea? I'm absolutely running out of things to say to her. Where's Janie?"

"Reading in her room."

"Have her come down, in something reasonable. A dress."

By then Grandmother Porter was nearly upon them, binoculars dangling from her neck. Mr. P. must have finished with his swim, or his mother would not turn back toward the house. Stewart would have strapped him in (the rocky beach demanded it) and begun the arduous, long work of maneuvering the wheelchair over the rocks, then the easier job of pushing it along the grassy path. Mr. P. would sit on the porch in his towel coat, rosy, dripping salt. "Nothing like the sea," he might say. Or he'd recite the poem he'd made the children—and, by proxy, Bea— memorize two summers before, and which she recited to him now and again. *I must down to the seas again, to the lonely sea and sky / And all I ask is a tall ship and a star to steer her by.* Mrs. P. would sit beside her husband, perhaps place her hand on his hand. This, the after-swimming hour, was their best time. He would be thirsty. He would be happy.

"And would you mind getting some lemonade?" asked Mrs. P. "I have no idea where Annie is." She made her voice bright and pitched it forward. "Hello, Fanny!"

Bea went inside, poured three glasses of lemonade and took them out, then went back in to pour two more glasses, one for Janie, one for herself, though the drink was on the sour side and watery, both sugar and lemons being scarce. If anyone had asked why she carried the two drinks upstairs, sat on the window seat in Janie's room and sipped while the child read and gulped and read, she'd have said she had forgotten about Mrs. P.'s request to bring Janie down. Pushed further, she might have answered that she missed Janie, their quiet time together, and that downstairs Janie was likely to be overlooked, misunderstood or judged.

No one came up to look for Janie. No one even called. The family forgot things; one moment broke over and erased another. If it suited you, you could just sit back and wait. Forget.

But were you angry? the questioner might have asked (except no one ever would).

Angry, no—why?

About your shellflowers, or Teal Rock, or not knowing what Grandmother Porter said to Mrs. Porter about you. Or about being left out or ordered round.

I wasn't ordered. I was asked.

You were asked to bring Janie down. Did you forget?

I brought her lemonade.

Because you were angry?

The child was thirsty.

How did you know?

I knew.

XIII

THERE ARE MOMENTS in every life when something terrible happens to someone you love in a place where you are not, and you don't know what has happened until afterward, and if you had known, you'd have altered the course of things by placing yourself here, not there, a restraining wall, a force of nature: *Stop*. At the time, though, the peacefulness that follows you about is plump and full and generous, as if the day itself were tricking you: *Come, my pretty, look away!*

The Sunday morning that Bea left the house to go for a walk with Smitty, Mr. P. was sitting on the porch with an old college friend—

relaxed and talkative, a martini on the table by his side. Janie was off
playing, for they had, that weekend, right after Grandmother Porter left,
a set of houseguests, the college friend, Mr. Lyall, plus his wife and their
children—a girl a few years older than Janie and a boy her age. With her
mother-in-law gone and friends visiting, Mrs. P. was gayer than Janie had
seen her in months. The day before, she had even forgotten until evening
to check the mail. Stewart had pulled out more porch furniture, set up
the croquet set. It felt almost like before the war.

"Happy walking," Mr. P. called after her and Smitty, and then, to Mr.
Lyall but knowing they could hear, he began to sing: *"A fine romance,
with no kisses, a fine romance, my friend, this is . . ."*

Bea walked faster. Why must he always tease her? He had the velvety,
rich voice of a vigorous man, and sometimes his eyes rested on her in a
solemn, appreciative way that made her freeze for a moment before she
moved away. It being Sunday, the workers on the base had stopped construction, and Mr. P's singing followed Bea and Smitty down the road—
"We should be like a couple of hot tomatoes"—and Smitty took it up from
there—*"but you're as cold as yesterday's mashed potatoes!"* They were
around the bend by then. Bea stopped. She stood very still, a soldier at
attention. She wiggled her ears. It never failed to make him laugh.

"Does the boss know you can do that?" he asked.

For an odd moment, she thought he meant the corporal. "Who?"

"Mr. P. They should pay you extra for it."

"Oh, he doesn't know," she said, although he did. In fact, in the days
when Mr. Porter's muscles still obeyed his brain, he'd been able to do it
himself. The children had tried but never found the proper muscle, and
other than saying that it required a certain amount of concentration, it
was not a thing Bea could explain. "I don't do it for everyone," Bea said.
(Was she learning, at her late age, coyness? Was she learning, taught by
her charges, how to flirt?) "It has to be the right time."

"I'm honored." Smitty touched her earlobe, stroking it between his
thumb and index finger, and the sensation was like nothing she'd ever felt

before, radiating up her scalp to the roots of her hair, and down her neck and into—somehow—the very soles of her feet.

Then he kissed her, tongue thrusting at her lips.

She turned her face away. "Not here."

She'd have liked him to keep on with the earlobe bit, do it for longer. When she was ready, she could touch his earlobe too, return the touch. Like snails, they would proceed, or perhaps not even proceed, just stay right there, taking endless pleasure in this small but exquisite part of each other.

"Where, then, sweetheart?" His hands were at her waist, squeezing a bit too hard.

She straightened up. "I—well, we could . . . we could sit at the dock and talk."

"I might be all talked out. Guess I went on for a while, huh? You must be sick and tired of my voice."

"No. Anyway, we can sit."

They turned and made their way down the steep path to the boat dock, then reached the bottom of the hill and walked out the dock to the wooden floats, where they sat on an overturned dinghy (first he dried it with his sleeve), their knees lightly touching.

The day before, he had, without her asking, told her that he'd been engaged to be married, but his fiancée had died suddenly (Bea had pictured something violent—a house fire, or a milk truck slamming in), that he lived next door to his mother above their hardware store and was a part owner in the shop, which turned a nice profit and had expanded a few years ago to include small kitchen items, steady sellers with the ladies. The speech had felt rehearsed. He'd seemed nervous, which made her nervous too. It's a shotgun apartment, he'd said and then explained that it was one room and another and a third, you could shoot a gun straight through, though of course they never did, and she'd remembered the coldwater tenement where she'd held her first job in America, working for a Jewish family with one small boy and the mother on bed rest, expecting a second child. They had drunk black coffee in that family; they would not mix milk and meat; they had not liked it that she'd throw out tea leaves to make a fresh brew when there was still tea in the pot. The family had been thin and dark, full of strange customs and cheap (as she'd been told, growing up, that Jews were), and she'd thought, So this is it, this is America, and then (lucky for her, for she'd grown attached to Samuel, the little boy, and might not have left him on her own), the new baby was born and the mother climbed out of bed and they did not need her anymore. At the agency, she had requested a house outside the city, one with other Scots help if possible, and she'd landed at the Porters' tall front door.

Smitty had gotten some of this out of her. He liked to ask her questions, bit by bit, here and there, and had a way of making her say more than she meant to. Later she'd forget she'd told him something until he brought it up—"like those Jews you lived with," or "What do you reckon your mother would've thought of me?" or "We could use your ironing on the base."

"I hope I didn't make you worry," he said suddenly, "telling you about Greta."

At the time, she had felt surprise and pity but not worry, exactly, but now, hearing the name again, she had a sharp sense of what might have been: he'd been engaged to a woman named Greta but Greta was dead, as her own mother was dead, and if either woman had lived, she and Smitty would not be sitting here today. As a family man, he might well have been exempted from the war, and if he'd ended up on the Point, he'd be writing home to his wife each day; he wouldn't have stopped to meet her on the road. With her mother alive, Bea would be—where? Why, with her mother, of course. Home in Scotland with her mother. She had, then, a sudden, chill presentiment: Smitty would die in this war. He'd be shipped off (they all would, eventually, as other, greener men came in to take their place), and he would die.

"It's just—" Smitty stood up and turned away so that she had to strain to hear his words. "I thought you'd want to know, and it's not like it matters—I mean, it *did* matter a lot, of course, but I'm a new man now, I don't want you to think—"

"It didn't make me worry."

People did not take her into their confidence often, not even Janie or Agnes, nor she they. She did not court confessions. Everybody had a past, and everybody's past had its share of grief and trouble, some more than others. Friendship helped. Routine. Staying busy. Moving on. Singing. Prayer. Greta, like Gretel in the fairy tale. Was Greta German? Big-boned, like Bea, she must have been. Or thin and blond and American, fast on her feet, brainy and sassy (she pictured Helen), or dreamy and poetic (she pictured Dossy). Greta. It was not the name of anyone she knew. Smitty was too close to the edge of the dock, rocking back and forth, his feet half over the edge of the wooden planks, and without thinking she stood, grabbed his arm and yanked him back.

"Be careful," she said, "or you'll fall in."

He laughed and stepped away, and then, before she could register what he was doing, he'd stripped off his shirt, trousers, shoes, and vaulted from the dock in his skivvies and done a heavy cannonball into the water. The splash was tremendous. When he surfaced, his face was upturned, streaming. "It's like bathwater! Come in!"

"Me? I can't!"

The splash had splattered her dress, wet her face. She tasted salt. If there was one thing she loved, it was water; still, she could not possibly join Smitty, who was—for this, she was grateful—entirely submerged, except for his head, which, soaked, looked smaller now, sweeter, and at the same time, unfamiliar in a way that took her aback.

"Why?" he called up.

"I haven't got my bathing costume."

"Go in your . . . whatchacallit, slip. I won't look. I'll swim to that thing—"

He pointed to the Red Nun buoy, bobbing in the distance, one of the army's efforts to keep civilian boats inside a circle that Helen complained was the size of a bathtub, though to Bea it looked vast. Before she could answer, Smitty was off, doing the crawl, his stroke confident for a man from the middle of the country. When he reached the only moored Beetle Cat, he stopped and wrapped his arms around its hull. Don't climb in, Bea thought (the boat, *Little Brown Jug*, was Charlie's). Then he was off again.

On the dock, she knelt down and struggled to unzip her dress, then took off her dress and sandshoes. She moved calmly but quickly, trying to outdistance both potential onlookers and her own second thoughts. Was she? Would she? Could she? She tucked the dress under an oar. In the ocean, Smitty had reached the Red Nun and was treading water, facing out to sea. There were no real steps at the boat dock, just a vertical wooden ladder slick with algae. In her full slip, Bea descended carefully into the water, feeling the fabric balloon around her legs before it plastered itself, a second skin, along her thighs. What was she doing? What was she thinking? And if someone came by? Good Lord.

But the water was fine. And it was her day off. The Porters often swam in the nude, all of them, from grandparents to children, though whenever Bea took Janie, she made the child wear a suit, and she put on her own in private (once, when Janie was three or four, Bea had caught her peeking in, wanting a look). The water at the dock was unusually cold; she might have been in Arbroath swimming with her cousins as a girl. Smitty had turned now, heading back. She swam toward him, her slip making it awkward at first, then not. When they reached each other, he hovered next to her.

"I didn't think you'd come in!" he said happily. "You're a good swimmer. A regular little duck."

"Quack quack," said Bea.

He dove under, disappearing and coming up on the other side of her, so that she laughed and turned around. She swam too, trying, each time she lifted an arm, to keep the rest of her underwater. The sea was green and murky, and unless you looked hard, you could not see much, though once she saw the white flash of his army-issue skivvies, and once, as he came up near her, he must have seen her own self underwater—cycling legs, cotton-plastered middle, her belly bigger than she'd like it, pale hands cutting through.

He did not touch her during their swim, not once, and they barely spoke, Smitty first at her side, then swimming away, diving under, gone. Bea going under too, though not too deep, quietly aware of how at home she felt in body, sea, with him. When she surfaced, he was several yards away, sun gleaming on his head. She gave a little wave. For a time, they swam parallel, she in breast stroke, he in slow crawl. When she said she was ready to get out, he swam discreetly to the buoy. On the dock, her slip was dripping buckets, but she wrung the hem out and forced her dress on over it, then turned to face the land while he swam in, got out, got dressed.

"Nothing like a swim," he said.

And then he did something that astonished her, coming from a man, coming toward herself. He laid a hand low on her stomach, flat over the front of her wet dress, so lightly that she could barely feel his touch.

"I'd like to have a baby in here someday," he said.

It was noon by then, or a little after, the tide coming in. The few boats in the water clanked against their moorings. The ocean slapped against the dock.

"Me too," said Bea. She had long ago given up the idea of having her own child—not given up, even, just never let the desire quite take shape, until in its shapelessness, it evaporated, slipped away. Now, fresh from the water, met by his words, she felt as if anything could happen: inside, out.

Later he would repeat it to her, stubborn as a child, belligerent, all gentleness bled out of him: *You said me too you said me too you said me too.*

Now he kissed her brow. "Well, then."

She laughed. "Well."

In the distance, she saw a figure coming down the path, onto the dock, and knew from the stride that it was Stewart, in his black trousers and white shirt.

"Mrs. P.'s wanting to have a word with you, Bea," he called as he got nearer, and when she reached for the railing, he added, "She said it's nothing to worry about, so take your time. I've got to get back to the Mister, myself. Good day!"

He turned and started marching back, his duty done, but not before giving the two of them an open look of curiosity and, Bea was quite sure, disdain. How she disliked him—his high-Scots airs, his thinking he was better than the rest of them, knowing all the news—though he did take proper care of Mr. P.

"What's this about?" Smitty asked, hands on her shoulders. "On your day off?"

"I . . . I've no idea. I hope nothing has—oh my Lord. What could it be? Smitty—I must go."

"He said it's nothing to worry about!" Smitty called, but she was already climbing the stairs, then the steep path up the hill, moving as fast as she could.

A summons, a word with you. On her day off. Nothing to worry about. But the Porters treated days off like holy days; it could be nothing good. Smitty was behind her, calling, then at her side on the road, but while she let him take her arm, she did not slow down, and when they reached the house, she left him to make a sharp right turn across the lawn. She was out of breath by then, but only Janie could have stopped her, so great was her fear—formed and grown larger as she walked—that something had happened to the child, who was not making chalk pictures on the road, or skipping on the lawn, or reading in the hall on the way to Mrs. P.'s bedroom door.

Bea knocked.

"Come in." Mrs. P. was at her roll-top desk, writing. How could she write at a time like this (like what?).

She put down the pen and turned to Bea. "My, you came quickly. You're soaking wet! What happened?"

Bea looked down at her dress, which stuck to her in all the wrong spots, and crossed her arms over her chest. "I was . . . I went swimming in my slip. What happened? Stewart came—"

"Everything's all right. Don't you want to change? I don't mind waiting—"

"No, please, tell me now. I won't sit down."

"That's not what I meant." Mrs. P. sounded exasperated. "You're just soaked, you'll catch cold."

"You know I never do," said Bea.

XIV

HELEN MUST, SHE realized later, have been up in the attic in the sodden heat when it happened, trading back and forth the binoculars with Dossy, two stupid, childish girls. They'd thought they'd seen something at sea—a pipe, a sub—and trained the spyglass on it for a good ten minutes, only to have it disappear, and should they report it to the soldiers when it was probably just a piece of driftwood, or nothing at all? But if it wasn't? If it was something? Dossy thought for sure that they should tell.

Summer was almost over, and nothing had happened. Not true. Charlie had proposed to Suky, she'd gone out to Oklahoma, they'd eloped. They were married; Suky was back with her parents in New Jersey, a war bride (Married, Helen's mother kept saying with disbelief but also admiration—seize the day. It helped that she'd been friends with Suky's mother all her life). Helen was happy for them, and disdainful, and jealous of them for getting more of each other while she got less of them, and, mostly, astonished—that life could actually move forward like this into adulthood. A ring, a signature, ta-da! Bea had a fellow. The war was heating up, Charlie still stateside but rising through the ranks. Still, for Helen, nothing had happened. No enemy had come ashore. After the dance, she had not set foot upon the base. Henry had not fallen in love with her; in fact he'd barely spoken to her after the dance, just a nod and hello if he passed by. Was it something she'd said? Something she'd done (she'd told him brashly that she viewed the belief that God was literally in the wine and wafers as akin to voodoo, not to mention unsanitary. She'd been tipsy, even drunk). Had she let him go too far with her? Was she too loose? Too rich? Not pretty enough? Too smart? Not smart enough? Whatever it was, it stung.

Helen had cracked no codes, broken no hearts. She'd kept her nature diary, written letters, read several novels and half a history book on the Civil War, but she was no closer to understanding (much less participating in) the workings of the world. Soon school would start, the grind of homework, the press of proper clothes. The summer had been largely miserable; still, any thought of packing up for New Jersey incited in her the same feeling she always had in August as the parting date grew close: a low-level, constant nausea, laced with dread. The sea was her refuge, and she swam long and hard, entirely purposeless but in the best way, and she'd stay down for as long as her breath held out, eyes open in the murk. Afterward, in the outdoor shower, she'd strip off her suit to find her torso covered with seaweed, brown feathered fronds and bright green blades.

Might she have seen it happen that Sunday morning, if she'd turned the spyglass toward the land? Seen it and actually have done something useful by stopping it, instead of watching flotsam or a product of her restless imagination bobble in the waves? Janie told her mother first, who told her father and then Bea, and it was only by chance that Helen, down from the attic by then, heard her mother's voice coming from the master bedroom, the door shut. She listened from outside for a moment—*need to stay calm, not turn this into*—before pushing open the door to find her mother by the bureau, gripping its edge, and Bea by the windowsill.

Her mother turned. "Helen? What are you doing here?"

"What happened?"

"Nothing. Don't look like that. Goodness. We're just talking. It's nothing that concerns you. You may go."

Helen moved forward. "Why are you all wet, Bea? What happened? Did someone drown?"

Bea shook her head.

"Then what?"

"It's just . . ." Her mother sighed and sat down on her bed. "Janie had a little incident. I'm telling Bea, I only just started. Please, dearie. Go."

"You can't just start to tell me and then make me leave—" Helen couldn't stop moving, from bureau to bed to window to chair. "She's my sister. I won't say a word if you let me stay."

Her mother exhaled. "Fine. Close the door. And sit. And *stay still*."

Helen closed the door and sat on her father's bed, forcing her leg not to jiggle. Her mother stood and cleared her throat. Bea moved away from the window, her skin too pink. Watching them, Helen had the sense that they were rehearsing a play, blocking out scenes, stage left, stage right, "The Mistress and the Maid."

"It's—I don't quite know how to say this . . . it's just that something has happened to Janie, and I, well, we're trying to figure out—"

"Oh, oh—" Bea reached to steady herself on the sill.

"*Shhhh.*" Helen hissed. "Let her talk."

"The main point is that Janie is fine, unhurt—it's nothing terrible." Her mother's voice sounded stiff, almost angry. "All right? So try not to over-react, both of you, for everyone's sake. For Janie's most of all, and mine. You don't even know what happened yet, and I've told you, she's *fine*."

Out playing, her mother went on to say. Out playing Sardines with the two children of the family that was visiting—Katherine and Christian— and some of the soldiers joined in the game, they must have been off-duty, and one soldier, well, he, according to Janie, and we're inclined to believe her because why would she make up such a thing, hid with her in the field, just the two of them, and he—well, apparently he lay on top of her for a moment, and then, thank goodness, Christian came along and found them . . .

Bea let out a moan.

"We must stay *calm*." Mrs. P. glanced toward the door. "That's all that happened. Janie seems fine, though she did know it was worth mentioning to me, and I'm glad for that. It couldn't have been too bad; she waited until she'd had her sandwich and brownie, which she gobbled up."

"So that's all she said?" Bea asked. "That's everything?"

"That's all. If she says anything about it to you, tell her very calmly that she's fine and it will never happen again and she's entirely safe, and then let me know precisely what she said."

"Oh, Lord, I haven't seen her since breakfast." Bea looked at her wristwatch. "I—I took a walk."

"You took a *walk*?" Helen said. "While this was happening? You're supposed to be taking care of her!"

"It's Sunday," said her mother. "Bea's day off. Helen, really—you must let me handle this."

"No, she's right," Bea said. "I should have been watching her. And to think—all this time, we had our eye on the wrong one."

"Excuse me?" said Helen. "What?"

"Not now." Mrs. P. gave Bea a warning look.

"Which one?" said Helen, though she already knew. "*Me?*"

Her mother sighed. "We were a bit concerned about your friendship with the soldier. Henry. Daddy was, especially. You know how he tends to worry."

"Henry? *You* were keeping me from Henry? Without telling me? How dare you?" Her fury mounted, though behind it was a small measure of relief that it wasn't Henry who had jilted her. "Are you spies, all of you?" she asked. "Don't you have anything better to do with yourselves? We just *danced*." She turned to Bea. "Speaking of which, I might have ratted on you and that . . . Smitty, but I didn't—"

"Bea," her mother said, "is a full-grown woman."

"I should have been watching Janie," Bea repeated woodenly.

"No. It's your day off. You should not have been. They were just play-ing in the field, like the children always do."

"Which field?" Helen began to circle the room again.

"Behind the stables."

"Did she say who—"

"It was one of the soldiers who came to dinner. The one with the stut-ter. Do you remember him? He seemed so young to me, pathetic really—I remember thinking that—and with something not quite right. . . . Do you know who he is, you must—" She winced. "The *bastard*," she went on, in an altogether different voice. "They'll take anybody for this war, they're so desperate, whether they're fit or not. And then send the best ones overseas."

Helen knew who her mother meant; the boy was tall and skinny, all legs and spastic arms. The other soldiers teased him for his clumsi-ness. He stuttered when he spoke. They called him Scarecrow behind his back. What was his real name? Drew, she thought, or Dale. At first she had wondered if he was, in fact, not quite right in the head, but he was assigned gate duty like all the others, and he was popular because he had a car on the base and drove the boys to town. He's rich, Henry had said about him once, with something like disdain. Rich but not the brightest bulb. Helen had felt for him pity mixed with revulsion but also amuse-ment, for he'd done tricks for them on the road—ungainly leaps over fences, spidery hobo dances. They'd fed him dinner, sung with him on the porch, laughed both with and at him. He had seemed harmless. She might even have said he seemed the most harmless of the lot.

"I wish—" Bea looked up. "Oh Lord, I wish I'd been with her."

Say *So do I*, Helen thought to her mother. Was there not a blood-borne mother love, a throwing yourself before the approaching train, a clawing at the grizzly bear? Instead, a sort of coldness.

Her mother shook her head. "You didn't know, Bea. This has always been the safest place in the world. Anyway, we can't look back like that. She's fine."

"Where is she?" Helen asked. It seemed, suddenly, of great importance to be able to locate her sister precisely, as if on a map with a thumbtack, the way her father and Stewart charted the progress of the Allied troops on a map.

"Janie?" said her mother. "With Agnes."

"Agnes? Why not with Daddy? Where *is* Daddy?"

"He went to speak to the colonel at the base."

"Oh." So it was serious. Very.

"But where, *exactly*, is Janie, Mrs. P.?" Bea asked.

"I told you, she's with Agnes. And Mr. Lyall and the Lyall children. Please, you two, we can't lock her up, or any of them, for that matter. They're at Garrisons while Clara Lyall packs up—they're leaving today. We need to keep her from the soldiers, that's all. She knows that too, poor thing, so it won't be hard. We all need to watch her more closely. I do, and"—she paused—"we all do."

Helen spun around. "I'm going to Garrisons."

"Good." Her mother nearly pushed her to the door. "Just don't mention anything. Not to Dossy, either. You must let your father and me handle this."

"I'll go too," Bea said.

"Actually, Bea," said her mother, "stay a moment longer."

In the doorway, Helen turned. "Why?"

"I need to check in with her about some household matters."

"Like what?"

"Clothing."

"Clothing?"

"*Go*," her mother said.

"You lead," said Helen, and her rage was an undertow she could neither master nor resist, "such fascinating lives."

XV

W ITH HELEN FINALLY out the door, Mrs. P. smoothed the bedcov-
ers and sighed. "We'll be leaving earlier than usual this year, Bea.
I don't want the girls to know yet—they'll kick up a fuss—but it's only a
few weeks until Labor Day, and Mr. P. and I feel that the whole situation
is just"—from the floor, she picked up a pair of her husband's dress shoes
with their braces still attached and set them side by side—"too much.
With the war. I know you like to plan ahead. With Jane's clothing and
everything." She laughed weakly.

"Oh." Bea stood, then sat, the breath knocked out of her by this second, sudden piece of news. "So will we leave today?"

"Today! How could we possibly be ready? It's not an evacuation!"

"Tomorrow, then?"

"I don't know, I don't think so. In a few days, when we're organized. I
haven't thought it all through yet. Just sooner than we'd—"

Bea started toward the door. "I'll go find Janie. She can help me pack."

"No, please don't. I'd like to spend some time with Janie myself. And
say good-bye to our friends. And it's your day off."

Bea stiffened. "Well, then, pack."

"If you like, but you could start tomorrow."

"No harm in being ready."

Mrs. P. looked hard at her. "Listen, Bea, are you—I hope you don't
mind my asking—but are you unhappy being here?"

Bea shook her head.

"I don't want to pry—don't answer if you'd rather not, it's entirely
your own business—but I'm wondering if something has happened
recently, besides the incident with Janie. Concerning your soldier friend,
maybe? Smitty? A matter of the heart, as they say? I've been concerned."

Bea shook her head.

"Oh, good. And you're not unhappy? I'd like to help, if I could, that's all. As your friend. I do hope you consider me your friend, after all this time. I"—she flushed— "consider you mine."

"I'm—" Bea struggled for words. "I'm very grateful for everything."

Mrs. P. looked perplexed, almost angry. "We wish you every happiness. You're part of our family. You always will be, no matter what happens. We'd be devastated if you left us, I can't even imagine—but for you to want your own . . . that's natural, of course, every woman wants—I just . . . I don't want to pry, but I hope he hasn't hurt you or taken advantage in some way. You seem . . ."

"He's been"—in her own voice, she heard Mrs. P.'s—"a perfect gentleman."

"Of course he has. And you . . . I mean—I hope you don't mind my asking . . . will you be staying with us?"

What was Bea to say? It was not as if she had a choice to make, not in any concrete way, though it did feel—between what had happened to Janie and her own ricocheting heart—like she was being flung, a rag doll, through the air. Staying? She was not *not* staying, except that she was leaving, wasn't she, leaving with the Porters, which meant staying—as in leaving together, as in staying with. She would hardly remain here, the only female for miles, when they left. She would hardly move onto the base, take up residence in a barracks, or live by herself in the Big House, rattling round. So "staying with us," yes. Of course she was. She did her best to nod. Mrs. P. gave a great sigh, came forward and hugged her—a stiff hug, as awkward as it was kind. She was taller than Bea and much thinner; they almost never touched now that there was no baby to pass back and forth.

"Oh, I can't tell you how relieved I am, though of course we'd have supported you whatever you did. But Janie, I don't know how she'd manage without you." She pulled away, laughed and wiped at her eyes. "Or how I would! Dear Bea. What a day this has been! We need to stick together, don't we? The world's"—she looked out the window—"so much more complicated than it used to be."

~~~

BEA PUT THE BLUE SILK dress in the trunk first, folding it flat, wrapping it in tissue, not because she'd ever wear it again but because her father had taught her how to pack a thing of value. Then her shellflower supplies, their box inside the trunk. Next, wrapped inside a pair of stockings, the box she had started making for Smitty; her hands moved faster and faster. A pile of underclothes, a nightdress. Better, wasn't it, to leave no note. Better to leave no shell box; it wasn't finished anyway. *Go if you're going*, her mother used to say when she dawdled. And the children chanting outside the loo in the courtyard: *Shit or get off the pot!* Better to go back to New Jersey and think on it, for in fact, though she'd nodded to Mrs. P., she hadn't decided, had she? She had not. Better to wait, to give it time. She told herself this even as her hands kept folding. Better to get Janie settled, inspect her for signs of damage. Think the whole thing through.

When Agnes came into the room, her trunk was already half full. Bea left her trunk. "Is Janie back?"

"No. Why are you packing?"

"Where is she?"

"At Garrisons. Listen, Bea, what's *happening*?"

"With who?"

"You tell me."

"No, I mean, who's watching *Janie* at Garrisons?"

"Mrs. P. came, and Helen, and the Lyalls. Half the world." She tugged at Bea's sleeve. "Why are you packing? What has *happened*? Are you getting married?"

Bea shook her head.

"What, then? Has someone died? Your brother?"

"Lord, no."

"What, then? You've got to talk to me. Just spit it out! I've never been so confused in all my life."

"Help me pack."

Agnes took a blouse out, unbuttoned it with swift fingers, removed it from its hanger. "Go on now, dearie. Talk."

WAS IT THEN, WHILE THEY filled the trunk together and Bea recounted what had happened to Janie, that Smitty, with a bit of help from Henry, broke all the rules and beat up Dale, who (bruised, battered and having learned his lesson or nothing at all) was sent home with a demerit on mental health leave and dropped forever from the family's sight? Or did it happen while Bea, Agnes and Lizzy swam together, and Annie watched? Or was it later that afternoon, while Bea, weary of hearing how it was her day off, finally got hold of Janie and took her up to her own room to draw, the child quieter than usual, exhausted? At one point Janie put down her crayons, rested her head on Bea's lap and lay dozing while Bea stroked her tangled hair.

"Poppet," Bea said.

It was what her own mother had called her. Little child, little doll. When Janie was fully asleep, Bea undressed her and put her in her nightclothes, then carried her to bed, no matter that her teeth were not brushed nor her hair combed. Bea climbed in next to her and lay there for a good half hour, eyes wide open, far from sleep, before she returned to her own room.

XVI

THE NEXT NIGHT, later than was considered polite, Smitty knocked on the door of the Porters' house for the first and last time. Stewart answered and called Bea, and Smitty asked Bea for a walk, during which he told her, with no small amount of pride and satisfaction, how he'd beaten Dale to a pulp. They were, by then, on the road again, heading in the direction of town.

"I knocked the wind right out of him, gave him two shiners, might've broken his arm, left him for dead in the grass."

Bea knew she was expected to applaud him. Instead, she ducked her head and walked faster. His violence frightened her—its energy and strength—at the same time that she almost envied his ability to get even. Except there *was* no getting even. No scouring clean or turning back the day. Smitty quickened his step. "I did it for you."

"For me? But *I* should have been watching her. I should never have gone off like that!"

"It's Sunday, Bea. She's got parents."

"No matter. I should *not* have gone swimming."

"Well, I'm glad you did."

"Glad?" The breath drained out of her.

"Swimming's got nothing to do with what happened to Janie," said Smitty. "She wasn't on your watch. That bastard—I really let him have it. I don't care what they do to me for it. I got him good, I can at least say that." He stepped ahead and faced her, his voice almost pleading now. "Our swimming's got nothing to do with it. You see?"

In the water with his hair wet, he had looked smaller but stronger too, a muscled seal. The buoy was red; she'd swum toward it, toward him, until she was close enough to see his face lit with surprise. Swimming wasn't the problem, not by itself. The problem was her falling for Smitty in the first place, for she'd fallen badly, hadn't she, and she was falling still. *Keep your eye on the ball*, Charlie used to shout as he tried to teach Janie to play baseball. Bea had been good at it, surprising Charlie, surprising all of them: the thwack as the bat met the ball, the ball sailing out. *Out of left field*. Was that the expression? She had not kept her eye on the ball.

"I heard you're leaving early," he said.

She nodded.

"When?"

"I don't know. It always takes time to pack the summer up."

"The summer?"

"Their things. Everybody's things. And Janie wanting to take home half the beach."

Smitty took her arm and she let herself lean against him for a moment, her forehead against his jacket. She turned her face sideways, laid her cheek on his chest and pressed her ear close. He held her, then. Through the fabric, through skin and muscle and whatever else lay mysteriously inside a man, she could make out the faint but steady beating of his heart.

IT WAS ON THE HEELS of this moment that he asked her to marry him, pulling back, clenching his fists, a longish silence, then the difficult question pushed bravely forth: He hadn't come just to talk about Dale but for this, really for this. The timing wasn't great, not what he'd hoped for (a ring in hand, dinner in New Bedford, flowers, the works), but with her leaving, he figured it was now or never, and so . . .

And then the words. Marry. Will you. Me. Perhaps he said them in order, perhaps not; either way, they reached her oddly warped, so that she wondered if she had misunderstood.

"I—" Bea said. "I . . . I—"

His question did not come entirely as a surprise, not by now, even as she had a peculiar sensation that she was someone else entirely, this not her own life, but one she might read about in one of Agnes's romance novels: *War Bride* or *Lest All Soldiers Fall*.

"What?" he asked.

"Did you just ask me to marry you?"

He laughed. "That I did!"

"I can't, I—"

"Are you . . . gosh, Bea, are you saying no?"

She shook her head. "No. I can't think right now, that's all. I'd like to . . . to marry you, I just need—" She turned away from him, facing the wall. She felt—though she knew it was awful of her—as if she might be sick.

"What? What do you need?"

Two whole lives, a person might have. Three or four or five. If only. Never before had she felt this fanning out of possibilities; one life had seemed plenty, difficult sometimes, other times fine. Either way, her lot. "I don't know. I need . . . some time."

"To think on it?"

She nodded. She half wanted to lay her open palm on his cheek, out of love or sorrow for one thing or another (Janie? Smitty?) left or lost, but something stopped her. They were on a brink; he would take her touch as a yes and kiss her, and the kiss would crack her open, into what?

"So what do you need? A day? Until tomorrow?" Smitty groaned. "This is—come on, Bea, you've got to help me here; I don't ask this question every day. What do you say? We could, if you want, if the war is a problem—we could do it right away. You could board with a family in town—other girls do that. Remember Louis, he met that girl Lydia at the Rations Board, and there's a fellow who brought his wife here from—"

"I need a little time," she interrupted and had a flash of Janie a few days earlier, holding up a sprig of the thyme that grew on the lawn—*Time for thyme!*—the joke itself time-worn, passed from one child to the next, and Helen looking up from her book to say, "Time for a new joke," before declaring (from her book? from her head?): *"To live is so startling it leaves little time for anything else."* Board with a family in town? Which family? Bea pictured dark Portuguese with strange food and customs, or Quakers who slept on wooden planks.

"What?" Smitty was pacing now. "Is there someone else? In Scotland? Or New Jersey?"

"Of course not. For goodness' sake."

"So what? The war? If it's that, we can wait until after. It's not my first choice, but if you want, we can get engaged now . . ."

Again, she shook her head. "I have—it's just, people depend on me. Janie—"

"*Janie.*" Smitty pounced. "You're worried about leaving Janie. That's it, isn't it? It's nuts, but that's it! Good grief."

Bea nodded miserably. "I . . . I love her like my own. It's not like you think. I've raised her. She depends on me."

"Ha! She'll grow up before you know it. Can't you see that? She's half-way grown already, and then what'll you have? They'll let you go tomorrow if they feel like it, out into the streets. Don't you want your own children, your flesh and blood? With me, you could—"

Bea touched her stomach. "I might not be able to."

Through the dark, he stared at her. "Do you mean . . ."

"I'm . . . yes, there may be something wrong—"

It was a half-truth, based on half-knowledge, though her intuition told her it was true. Her monthlies were not monthly but came every six weeks or so, sometimes every two or three months, and when they arrived she either bled like a stuck pig or let out a mere rusty dribble of a stain. Either way, something was wrong, too much or not enough, though the one time (she was in for a rare visit, with a cough that would not go away) the doctor asked her how her monthlies were, she mumbled Fine. And she had hairs—five or six, dark and wiry—that grew out of her chin; daily she looked for them and plucked when they appeared. That was unnatural for a woman. No one but her mother, who'd bought her a private pair of tweezers in a discreet brown case, ever knew. Her mother had borne Bea and Callum, but four or five other babies had died in the womb, and then there were the two who did not make it past the first year, something in the heart for Lucy, the girl before Bea, something in the lungs for the other one, a boy called Collin, born between her and Callum. She remembered that sweet, sad baby; he had looked wrong from the beginning, a tiny old man, and he would not feed from her mother or even from a bottle, but had to be given goat milk dripped from a boiled rag into his mouth. Bea, two and a half, had stood by the pram and tried to help.

Smitty looked at her. "You can't? You never told me . . ."

He would hold on to this, she realized. This was something he would hold on to all his life if she allowed him to.

"I might have trouble," she said. "I have some . . . and I'm not young—"

"Young enough—not even thirty."

So she had lied about that too; she had forgotten. She was not a liar, any more than she was a woman standing on a dark road in America with a soldier from St. Louis asking her to marry him.

"I lied," she admitted. "I just . . . I'm thirty-six." She could see now that his hands were shaking, and she had an overwhelming desire to still them with her own, but she did not.

"Oh? And with a husband in Scotland? And with a kid or two? For Christ's sake, Bea, what else haven't you told me?"

"That's all," she whispered.

"Why should I believe you?"

"I don't know."

"You said, 'Me too,' " he said.

"Sorry?"

"That morning. When I said the thing about the baby. Did you forget? You said, 'Me too.' "

She was crying again now, as mosquitoes buzzed around them and the humid air pressed over them and, in the distance, fireflies blinked. He sat down on the stone wall a few feet away on the edge of the road, with a soldier's manly posture, rigid, staring out.

"What else?" he asked.

Nothing. Nothing else.

"Are you really thirty-six?"

She nodded and went to sit beside him, and when she had trouble getting on the wall, he reached over and helped her up, his thick hands around her thick waist, and she thought this, this was what she wanted, to stop right here, on a stone wall like the walls at home, with a silent offering of help from a good man, the sort she might make a life with, if only . . . what? How many lives could you have in this world, how many times could you pack your bags and step away from the rooms you knew, from the people, or was it that she did not want a walk-up flat, to stand behind a counter—*Good morning, may I help you?*—in a strange city in the middle of a strange country (here or there, it would never be home), measuring out nails and screws for petty change?

"Would you think of moving there, to New Jersey?" she asked. "So I could stay on with her, maybe? With the family? Just for a bit, to get Janie used to the idea?"

He stared at her.

"It's very nice there," she went on. "They . . . they have a beautiful house, a mansion with a pool, in a lovely neighborhood called Grace Park. There's a hardware store in town, maybe you could—"

"You want me to move to *Grace Park*? To be what? The stablehand? Or sweep floors at someone else's store? I have my mother, Bea. A good business. We own the building. We have friends and family. I'm offering you a life."

"I have a life."

"So," he said, "do I."

ALREADY SHE COULD FEEL HIM beginning to move on; he would pluck another shoe from a pile, meet another woman. He would be a jolly, kind father, a fine husband. If he was not shipped off, if he made it through the war. He would be a family man before long with someone else, if she said no. And if she said yes? She moved closer to him and placed her hand over his, and he allowed her to, and so they sat. *Do not die*, she wanted to command him, for if he did (or if she never heard but spent her whole life wondering), her heart would surely break. Better to say nothing, though.

Just sit. After a time, he took his hand back and placed it in his own lap, and then, without looking at her, got up.

He turned to face her. "You're no spring chicken, you know. You won't get another chance."

So he could also be cruel; she was glad to know it. On the base, a siren sounded, blaring, then stopped. Early on these sounds had frightened her; now they ran together with the wind and waves. She held out her arms to the night, then dropped them to her sides. For a moment she had the strangest thought—that if he were a child, she would surely leave Janie and go with him. She could see him as a boy, a bit wide in the hips, chubby in the face, with a child's goodness and a child's sense of wonder; she would clean him head to toe and keep him well and teach him things as U-boats rose and bombs dropped down. There was something about a boy, purer, straighter, less cunning than a girl. Something about a boy, but not a man.

By then his back was turned; he was walking away.

"Smitty," she called. "I'll write. Soon, I promise. I just . . . I need time to think—"

He turned around. "So you haven't decided?"

She shook her head.

"Don't play games with me."

"I . . . I've been making a shell box for you." The words fell like stones. "It's not quite done, but nearly. Shall I get it? I can run and get it now."

He was a good fifteen feet from her. He did not move or speak. Later, when she looked back (as she would—daily at first, then less often and eventually only once or twice a year, for the rest of her life), she would wonder what might have happened if she'd gone to fetch the shell box. She'd wonder too, what might have happened if he'd said, No, forget about the shell box, and walked over and kissed her. She could see it all, Smitty hesitating, then backtracking, how she'd let herself drop into the kiss. Would it have changed the course of things? Or if he'd *insisted* she marry him, called upon his need, her duty, for she was no shirker. Or if he'd said, Yes, I'll move, and you can have us both, even if he wasn't sure he meant it, as a way to help her through? Or this: Pulled her into the long grass, the scrubby pines. Lifted her dress, dropped her drawers. Given her his seed. A child. Over the years, the image would slip between her other thoughts: Smitty forcing himself on her—no choice, an act, and with it a violence but also a pleasure, no less real for being forced.

In truth, he kept his distance, would not look at her.

"I'll send it," she said. "Battery B, Ashaunt Point. Right?"

He answered slowly, as if she were dim-witted. "Fort Rodman. New Bedford."

"Oh. Why not here?"

"Here? Nothing but stones and rich people on vacation. You thought you saw some soldiers? Ha! Look again! Address a letter here, and you'll get yourself turned in."

"Fort Rodman," she said. He was frightening her now, something jumpy, steely, in his tone. "Still Battery B?"

It might have been roll call, then, the way he spoke: *"Battery B Fort Rodman New Bedford Massachusetts Sergeant Raymond Smith."*

As if she did not know—as if she might forget—his Christian name.

THE NEXT DAYS WERE A dream and a daydream—getting Janie up, putting her in the bath, washing her hair, tucking the girl inside her towel, setting out their breakfast—Annie had made scones again, and there was compote from the blackberries they'd picked, and poached eggs, though Bea had little appetite. Downstairs, they passed by Helen, who was still giving Bea the silent treatment. In a few rooms, paintings had been taken down. Couches and tables were draped with sheets. Everyone kept saying, too often, too brightly, that they'd be back next summer or the summer after that (seven years, it would be before they returned). After her bath, Janie surprised Bea by doing something she rarely did anymore, flinging her towel down and asking for baby oil, and so the child stood there, spine bent, blond hair darkened, straight with water, and Bea smoothed the oil on her legs and arms and up her back and shoulders and squeezed some into the child's palm so she could do the rest herself.

Bea would not walk with Janie on the road, or sit on the front porch, or go anywhere at all where she might run into Smitty. Anyway, Janie knew they were not to go among the soldiers. They would have to stay near the house, or at the very most follow the path behind it to the beach. There was, besides, Janie's packing to do.

"You'll soon see your room at home," she told the child as she began to sort and fold her clothes.

Janie flopped onto her bed. "Will there be soldiers?"

"I shouldn't think so. Not like here."

"Will it be just like before?"

Bea nodded.

"With our same rooms?"

"Of course. Why would we change around the rooms?"

Bea's room in Grace Park was bigger, less damp, than her room on Ashaunt, the floor not slanted. Her coverlet there was dotted with sprigs of blue flowers. She had a card table, its dark green leather top outlined in gold, where her shellflower supplies could be laid out. The bathroom she shared with Agnes had a small white porcelain sink. Her room with the first family had been a bed-size closet, with a strung-up curtain for a door. When she'd first arrived at the Porters' and seen that sink—the brass spigots marked *C* and *H*, hot water flowing clear and fast—she'd grown teary at the sight of it, then mocked herself for crying over a sink.

"Are you sad?" asked Janie now. "To be leaving?"

It was a surprising moment. Rarely did the child ask Bea about herself, not even *Are you hungry, are you cold?*

"A bit," she admitted, and felt her eyes well up. She took a breath. "Well. Let's start to pack your toys."

"My collections."

Bea sighed. Every year, it was the same battle. Janie saved horseshoe crabs and rocks, beach rose hips, butterflies and beetles, every manner of broken and chipped shell, bits of driftwood and sea glass, lobster claws, smelly, rattling strands of seaweed. This year had been worse than most, as Janie suddenly fancied herself—at eight!—too old for toys, and had been scavenging, foraging, pocketing all summer with a fervor that Bea found at once irritating and, in its intensity, a little strange.

"A few favorite games, and Rose and her things," Bea said. "And your few best shells. We can't be bringing half the beach."

"*You* take shells home."

Bare as bones, hers were, and not even enough to fill a canning jar. She sorted and sorted, threw away, bleached down. "Only what I need for my projects. I throw away nearly the whole lot and clean the ones I take."

"I'll clean mine. I promised Charlie."

"Charlie? That you'd bring home your collections? Why?"

"To send him things. So he could see Ashaunt."

"I'll help you pick the best," said Bea, knowing that this year, she would let her take it all.

THEN SORTING THROUGH TOYS AND soaking and scrubbing Janie's collections, and as time passed (an hour and then another and another; it felt like days), Bea began to feel more herself again, calm and returned but also full of her story—*he asked me to marry him last night*—but she said nothing to anyone. It was not a bad thing, anyway, to guard a memory or two inside you. She would revisit that night, when he asked her to marry him, for the rest of her life, though less and less frequently as she grew older, first serving as nurse to Helen's children, then, for a time, to Janie's, then nurse to nobody, just a bit of mending and dusting and helping Mrs. P. and bathing a grandchild here and there, and a lot of sitting around twiddling her thumbs, and finally (*But why?* Janie, in her mid-forties when they left, would ask her. *Why now, after so many years? I'm not passing judgment, Bea. I just don't—I don't understand*) moving back to Scotland with Agnes, where they purchased a fine house on a hill in Forfar and opened a crafts supply shop. Once a year Janie and her husband Paul would visit, sometimes with their children, or Helen's daughter, Caroline, would come, or Janie's daughters, and they'd go on outings—to Kirriemuir, where J. M. Barrie wrote *Peter Pan*, to Glamis Castle (and on the way, the gravestones of her grandparents, though Bea never pointed them out). Mrs. P. came twice, before she grew too old, and her funeral was one of two trips Bea made back to America, this time on her own, Agnes too frail by then to come. Once when Janie was visiting, Bea told her a little about that summer and Smitty, and Janie said yes, she knew the story, except her version was this: how Bea had gotten a marriage proposal from a soldier and asked for her, Janie's, permission, and Janie had said no.

"Did I keep you from happiness? I've always worried, Bea; I've never dared ask."

"Don't be silly," Bea told her. "You couldn't have forbidden it. How could you have? I never told you a thing about it."

"Are you sure? Dossy said you'd asked my permission. So did Helen. I've thought so for years. I've always felt—"

"Rascals, those two!"

"They were, weren't they?" Janie smiled. "I don't remember much about that summer—mostly just everyone waiting for letters, and how we didn't go back after that for years. Your soldier friend was nice, though. I remember that. Friendly, wasn't he?"

Bea nodded. "He liked to joke."

"But you just weren't in love with him, I suppose. Is that it?"

"No. No. I don't know. I liked him very much. I was—"

How could she say it? In love with you more? Frightened of change? Of him dying? Of a life spent sorting nuts and bolts in a hardware store? There was no one answer; there were too many. And perhaps she'd made a mistake. People did—big ones and little ones, all along the way—but who was to say, and it was by now long ago, and not worth dwelling on. She'd been, she thought, largely lucky in her life. She could not complain.

"You were what?" asked Janie.

"I'd left a lot of things behind already," she said. "I couldn't see leaving you as well."

"I did. I kept you from your life," said Janie. "How awful."

"Oh my, no," said Bea. "You were such a good girl. I've always been so grateful to your mother for letting me have you. And look at how well you've turned out."

If Janie's face flickered then, Bea did not notice. Janie was silver-haired, elegant, in a smart linen suit that had not wrinkled from her travels; she looked the picture of Mrs. P. Janie's husband Paul had walked to the chemist's to pick up medicine and the newspaper. He loved to walk and would come back from his outings having made friends with half the town, which was not an easy thing in Forfar, where people kept to themselves. In the next room, Agnes lay in bed, half taken by a stroke. On her bedroom wall, as on Bea's, hung photographs of the Porter children and grandchildren. Above the mantel of the gas stove in the living room hung a photo of the Big House and one of Grace Park. Above the blue sofa was a seascape by Dossy, and above that in a shellflower frame a faded picture of Bea's mother, and a picture of Callum's adopted son Ian with his wife Marcy and their children, and a small brown print of Agnes as a girl, with a solemn expression and a fringe. In Bea's room were two photographs in matching silver frames, one of Helen's daughter Caroline on her second birthday, the other of Janie at around the same age, both girls already with watchful, deep-set, slanting eyes. The house was homey; Bea thought so, and Janie remarked on it each time she came. From Agnes's rose garden, you could see both the country and the town, twenty shades of green and gray.

In the kitchen, the teakettle whistled and Bea rose: instant beef broth for Agnes, tea for herself and Janie.

"How old was I that summer?" Janie asked. "Seven? Eight?"

"Eight."

"Eight," Jane repeated. "A thousand years ago."

XVII

TWO WEEKS AFTER she got back to Grace Park, Bea finished the shell box she had started for Smitty (though she would never send it) and began a note. It took her a whole night to write it: *I'm sorry . . . if I could . . . I wish.* She wrote a different note, then: *Yes,* she wrote, to see what it felt like, and tore it up. She was no writer, never had been, but it was more than that: she had no words for this. For hours she did not so much think as sit dumbstruck. She tried to pray. It was Callum's birthday, September 5, but she didn't remember until she wrote the date down, and then it was with shame—for the first time since she'd come to America, she'd forgotten to send a card. Finally, she wrote, *September 5, 1942, Dear Smitty, I am sorry but I cannot. I wish you much happiness and will keep you always in my thoughts and prayers and wish you the very best of every-thing. I am sorry. Sincerely Bea.*

Then she wrote her address at Grace Park on another slip of paper so she could know where he was, *if* he was.

She put the address in the envelope next to the note.

But it was too unkind.

She took it out.

LATER, SHE WOULD THINK BACK to this as the summer before. The summer before her brother lost half of the longer of his two legs as he ducked into the air raid shelter, the warden always the last one in. The summer before Charlie was called to active duty where, on December 28, 1943, he was gunned down over Italy on his twenty-fourth combat mission (though it would be more than a year before an officer arrived at the door at Grace Park with the news). The summer before her life with the Porters became something she had decided upon in a way that felt quite different from the path her life had placed her on up until then: staying at home because her mother was ill and needed nursing; coming to America because her mother had died; staying in America because— why? A tightly wrapped bundle that mewed like a cat. Bea fed the bundle and it grew. The sheets at the Porters' were crisp and clean. The water ran from taps. People were kind to her. Everywhere she went, really, people were kind. She found Scottish shortbread and tropical shells inside her Christmas stocking. She rode on a private railway car and spent her summers by the sea. She made friends that would last a lifetime. All this was true, though none of it quite hers. That summer, finally: a choice.

PLANTS AND THEIR CHILDREN

1947–1961

I

Dearest Mummy and Daddy,

Today I went to see Charlie's grave. I really don't know what
to say except that it was very sad and I'm glad you can't come to
Italy. My new English friend, Sandra, came with me. I brought
purple and white crocuses, and Sandra brought a large white lily.
A rather nice Lieutenant Haley brought us from Mirandola to the
cemetery. It's a large field covered with hundreds of white crosses
arranged in different plots. We found Charlie's quite easily. It
has just his name, his division, etc., and the date of his death on
a tin placard nailed to the cross. No birth date. To call the scene
plain does not quite catch its essence. It's almost nothing, but
nothing multiplied and multiplied until your eyes might cross
from looking. I took a few photographs, which I will send (and to
Suky too). The man told us that the U.S. cemetery at Mirandola
is not a permanent one, and that by 1950, any graves that haven't
been moved to the United States will be taken to the National

Cemetery in Florence for all U.S. soldiers killed in Italy. So if it means a great deal to you and to Suky, we should apply to have Charlie's remains brought home. The only thing against this would be that the government does not want too many brought back, but they are sure to let us. If I liked Italy, I might think all the American soldiers should stay in the country where they were killed as a sort of reminder to the people of that country of what happened, but I really don't like it at all. I find it degenerate, lazy, depressing and both tremendously rich and luxurious and, at the same time, poor and sordid. Of all the countries I've visited, it's the most fascinating for being so full of life and mystery, but I think I will remember it as a bad dream.

The feeling I got when I visited the cemetery was one of misery and absence, but when I think of Charlie himself, I know he was someone who, at twenty-one, had already gotten more out of life than almost anyone I know of any age, and who never lived to see any part of his life disintegrate, as most people do. He had the wild fun of youth, and then the sense of real achievement in the Army Air Corps. He had his perfect happiness with Suky, and the most wonderful family a person ever had. I can't bear to think that because he died with so much to look forward to, it was more of a tragedy. I guess the chances of continuous happiness in life are practically nil. Sometimes when I think of all the dreary people that live on and on, year after year, in the same way, even if it's not a miserable way, I wonder if they've ever really been happy at all. You, Mummy and Daddy, are exceptions, but I guess to most people, life turns out pretty disappointing, though it certainly never turned out that way for Charlie. I've been trying to remember the inscription signed by Roosevelt on your desk, Daddy, something like, "He died in a way that humbles the undertakings of most men." Could you send me the exact quote? The important thing, of course, is to remember him as he was—I did this much less at his grave, when I could only remember

that he was dead, than when the American soldier who took us back
to Bologna in a jeep pointed to a rather famous statue of Garibaldi and
said, very dryly, "I never can figure out who that joker is!" They might
have been words out of Charlie's mouth, don't you think?

I hope you're glad I went to the cemetery and not too disappointed
in me for what I thought of it. I've come to think I'm not cut out for
cemeteries of any kind—the whole concept feels off to me, unable
to hold or even evoke the actual life. I should like, when I die (in
my old, old age!) to be cremated, my ashes flung into the air and
sea, and to leave my mark not with a grave or stone or dreary cross,
but by having contributed something of significance to the world
during my life, as Charlie did.

Love, Your Ever Cheerful daughter, Helen

p.s. I know I am probably wrong about Italy, as I haven't given it a
real try.
p.p.s. Write me soon! I treasure every word!

LAUSANNE, SWITZERLAND
29 October, 1947

Read to the End!

Dearest Mummy and Daddy,

Please don't let anyone else read this letter until you have fully
considered what I am proposing. At first it will sound preposterous
and it will take me ages to fully explain my plan so continue
reading, please. First of all to reassure you, it does not affect my
coming home on Dec. 10.

I have spent most of my time lately in the office of the dean of
the University of Lausanne trying to figure out some way I could
get credit for work done here. At first I thought it entailed simply

staying here to the end of the semester and taking an exam, but upon investigating further, I discovered that I was working in a department called École de Français Moderne, which is part of the Faculté of Lettres but actually a separate school devoted almost entirely to the study of French—French composition, history and literature. This is the only school I can study in, as I am not, of course, entirely fluent in French yet. Also, it is this department that makes the university famous all over the world. The professors I have are the most brilliant lecturers I have ever heard, and I am absolutely fascinated with my work. Unfortunately, the credits I got from one semester's work will be of no use to me in an American university, as everything is directed toward giving students a perfect knowledge of French, and the lectures are held only once a week and the credit system is not the same.

My next discovery in the Office of the Dean was this: I showed my record from Wellesley and Bryn Mawr to the chancellor, and he was evidently impressed—also that I could speak French, as I am apparently the only American here who attempts to do so. He said that if I would inscribe this year for two semesters, he was sure I could get my <u>diploma</u> at the end of the second semester! Now, before you worry, I must explain a difference between American and European universities. At Bryn Mawr or another college like it, obviously one cannot suddenly leave in the middle of a term and return home for two or three months. One has daily work constantly and tests or essays, which count almost as much as the final examination. At a European university, this doesn't exist. You are told at the beginning of the semester the work you will be responsible for in the exam, and you can do it exactly when you want to.

To get my diploma I would have to become fluent in French and read about thirty books, but I am not responsible for any of this until the final exam, and I've been working hard already. I have a focus here I don't have at home, where I get diverted so easily by friends and my own doubts (and laziness!). I know I wasted time at Bryn Mawr and Wellesley by trying too many different things. Here I am singular about learning French, not just the language, both spoken and written, but also the history of the language and its countries—all of which they teach here in the most rigorous way.

Now you may have guessed already what I'd like to do, but don't think I am crazy until I finish. Please continue reading! I spoke to Professor Guillard several times (my particular professor who watches me work and is known as the best professor at the University of Lausanne). I told him that I absolutely must return to America for between two or three months this winter and asked if he thought I could surpass the exam this summer if I did that. He said *bien sûr*, easily, if I read the books and keep speaking French at home and return in the spring. With the diploma, which certifies that I can read and speak French perfectly, I could get a job teaching or go on to graduate study. Even more importantly, we will all know that I have really accomplished something. I don't know why this matters so much to me, but I suppose it has something to do with Charlie and wanting, now, not to waste opportunities. It feels almost like a moral obligation to live life to its fullest.

This is what I propose: I will come home Dec. 10 as planned and stay until Feb. 10 or a little later, at which point I will take a boat to either England or France. This would give me at least two months at home, during which I would see you constantly. I would study about three hours every morning and schedule conversation hours with a French native speaker, which I can find in New York or closer. Of course it must seem to you the most extravagant thing you have ever heard, but I've also figured that out. You have already paid for my ticket home. I would then need, at the very most, $800 for the whole journey here and back again. My return ticket, first

class, Queen Elizabeth this time, is $425 one-way, and the trip back
$390. Next time I would not travel first class, and traveling across
the continent is cheap. In the spring, after I have bought my clothes
and paid the university fees, it should cost me at the most $200 a
month to live here. This time is much more expensive because I
need to buy winter clothes and Christmas presents, and because I
am in the most expensive pensione in Lausanne. So $200 a month
for 4 months = $800. The whole trip then, throwing in $400 for
good measure, which I won't need, will cost from $1,600 to $2,000.
If I can sell the diamond tiara that Grandmother Porter gave me
for $800, which is low, that pays for the voyage already. If you
remember last winter, not only did you have to pay about $1,600
for Bryn Mawr, but I spent well over $300 on skiing weekends, and
since I wasn't counting my money, I spent more on clothes than I
am spending now. I don't think it will cost you more, <u>provided</u> I can
sell my diamond tiara. Also I will use the $500 of clothes allowance
partly for clothes and partly to live here. Also I think I must have a
small income of my own that I would love to get hold of now.

If you think Europe is dangerous now, you have got the
most peculiar idea of it. You keep writing to me about imminent
Revolutions that no one in Europe seems to be aware of. Every
weekend people go to Paris or Rome, but I promise I will go nowhere
unless you approve of the trip beforehand (as with Mirandola). For
instance, I had an invitation to go to Paris this weekend with four
very nice American boys—one from Princeton—and some girls,
but I refused on account of my promise to you, Daddy, about not
flying (they are flying back). Other girls from my pensione went to
Scotland. I'd have liked to go, if only to send a postcard from there
to A. and B., but I said no.

My gosh—this letter is long and I have so much more to tell!
One more thing, which may be a real reason not to come back
here: When is Dossy getting married? I shouldn't think Phillip's

law school would finish until the end of June, and in that case they
would not get married till about 2 or 3 weeks after. I can easily
make it then. In fact, if I am not her Maid of Honor, I'll never
forgive her. I must get dressed now. I'm going to a party with André
Benoit, the Swiss doctor I told you about. The party is for his uncle,
who has just been elected to the Swiss legislature. His uncle is a
Communist—not a Russian Communist but a Swiss Communist,
which is different. It is very rare for one to be elected in Switzerland.
I hope you will write me as soon as you get this letter. I love every
bit of news. Oh, how excited I am to see you again on December
10! I hope you will find me changed for the better, but that you and
Daddy have not changed a bit.

Much love,

Helen

November 3, 1947

Dear Dossier,

Thank you for your letter, and especially the poem. You have a
wedding date!! I miss you terribly and must ask of you a tremendous
favor: Please convince Mummy and Daddy to let me stay here! I
am absolutely happy here—I wish you could see it now. I feel more
at home in Lausanne than in any place in the world, except maybe
Ashaunt. All the leaves are red and orange along the roads, and
the mountains across the lake are completely covered with snow.
There are thousands of students wandering the streets and sitting
in cafés, and in the morning when the cathedral bell rings at eight
o'clock, all of them walk up to the university on the very summit
of the town overlooking the lake. I am listening to lots of courses
besides my own—Psychology in the Medical School, and Russian
History and Philosophy. Professor Guillard, who is head of the
École de Français Moderne of the university and my adviser, was

the tutor of the Tsar's children, a great friend of the Tsarina's, and was in Russia during the Revolution.

Missing my friends and family—you most of all—is the only really hard part; the rest is freedom and flight. I know that getting married is going to be a new freedom for you, especially as you've found your perfect soul mate who loves you precisely as you are. I agree that you should just let Mummy plan what she wants for the wedding, as it interests her and will be lovely and doesn't interest you. I'm doing splendidly in my courses, and I do think that in Europe an intellectual woman is less of an oddity. Here, I could be anyone. I've even given most of my clothes away to a girl I met who loves fashion and has almost nothing.

Last weekend André took me to Italy for the day, driving up over the Saint Bernard Pass where monks train mountain dogs, and you can see the ramparts from the war still, and it's where Napoleon crossed over. As I stood alone in a little empty stone chapel at the top, it was as if I could see Charlie, way, way off in the distance in the Italian part of the sky, flying like Icarus in that Breughel painting. Of course it wasn't really him—it was clouds—but it cracked me open and I wept and have felt lighter ever since. André knew to stay outside and gave me a sprig of alpine flowers when I came out. He knows just when to come close and when to leave me be, in a very European way. I've been reading Flaubert, who writes, "La vie doit être une éducation incessante; il faut tout apprendre, depuis parler jusqu'à mourir." How is your French coming along, ma petite soeur? Traduction: "Life must be a constant education; you've got to learn everything, from speaking to dying."

Please lean on Mummy and Daddy to let me return to Switzerland for the second term, and don't worry—I'll be back in plenty of time to help you get ready for your <u>wedding</u>! I'm scouring Europe for the perfect wedding gift.

All my love, Hellion

15 Mars 1948

Chèrs Mummy and Daddy,

    Only three weeks that I have been back here, and already I am
homesick and also having more adventures. The ski jacket you got
me for Christmas is perfect, and everyone here thinks it's hilarious
that it was made in Switzerland. I must tell you about this weekend,
which was like a fairy story. I think I told you that André and his
friends, Francis and Jean-Claude, and I were going skiing together.
Well, on Saturday we took the train from Lausanne with nothing
but ski clothes, as we had decided to go to the inn at the summit
of the mountains, where everything is very primitive. We went for
an hour by train to Bex, then changed to funicular, which started
slowly to climb into the mountains and the snow. Everyone on
the train was going skiing, and we were all singing and laughing
together. After another hour we arrived in Villars, a perfectly lovely
little village, closed in on every side by high rocky peaks. There are
few automobiles, but the whole town is full of sleighs and bells and
little inns. Mostly everyone got out here, but we changed to another
tiny funicular that climbed for another hour, slowly crawling
around precipices, slipping under snowbound fir trees, until finally
we came out into the open, where there were no trees, no roads or
rocky cliffs, nothing but brilliant sunlight, deep blue skies and white
everything. Finally the funicular stopped at a little inn and we got
out. It was very warm and blindingly clear. We had a delicious lunch
and then discovered our rooms. I had one alone, very clean and
simple and practically free, it was so cheap, and the boys had one
with bunks. André's friends went to ski down the most dangerous
part, but he and I walked and then skied in the high mountains
for about three hours. It was truly a magic land. You went for
ten minutes up what seemed like a tiny hill and suddenly, as you
reached the top, miles and miles of Alps stretched before you, and

it looked as if you could ski forever down. There was a sense of
nothingness—a kind of empty desolation, a universe of snow and
sky together alone. I wonder if you can catch the atmosphere.

We came back around six thirty, just when the mountains had
turned lavender, and found Francis and Jean-Claude in the bar. We
all had something that was supposed to be a martini but was mostly
vermouth, and then a dinner of roast beef, French fried potatoes, and
red wine. I slept like a baby. At about nine the next day, we began
to ski again. Francis and Jean-Claude rode up to Chamossaire, but
André and I did something that was really the best of all—we skied
down the trail to Villars, a long, long way but not too difficult. The
snow is well packed on the trail and winds around the mountains,
first completely open, then under the trees. I was terrified at first, but
André stayed at my pace, and soon I wasn't scared at all, but rather
in a state of calm rapture that felt almost religious. It was again a
brilliantly sunny day, and I thought as we glided over the snow,
looking at mountains, deep ravines, snow and sky, that it was worth
all of life's difficulties to get to do this just once. I believe there must
be a few moments in every life like this, at least I hope so. Oh my,
this has become a very long letter, and I must study now.

Lots of love,
Helen

P.S. You may be worried because I mention André a lot, and I
think perhaps it's best to explain, as the truth may not worry you
as much as if I say nothing. As I've said before, I'm practically sure
I will never marry André, but he is one of the best friends I have
ever had, perhaps the best, and he always will be because he is
<u>such</u> a kind, charming and intelligent person—and European in
all the best ways. He is not going to live in Switzerland because he
feels he can do no good there, but wants to go to Africa or China
or someplace where doctors are really needed. You needn't worry

about my being hurt, because I can handle this perfectly, but I am so afraid I'll end up hurting someone else. It's too late for me not to now, but I know I'm doing what is right, which is all one can do. I have told André that as the choice is either to hurt you (my family) or him, I would have to choose to hurt him. This is a fact that I can't analyze myself, but absolutely true. André, I am afraid, would be a doctor anywhere I wanted, but he has absolutely no money aside from what he earns and he would much rather die than take a cent. In fact, he has a nature ridiculously proud about everything. His father is rather like André but sterner. He used to have a great deal of money that he inherited from his mother, but he gave every bit away when he became a minister, because he believes that money is the greatest evil in the world, especially when it is inherited. The family is full of idealists about everything. You would definitely love André, and it is terribly worrying to me that I am going to have to hurt him soon. I know it is all my fault, but also that I must make up my mind definitively, that there is no way I can escape doing it in the end. For myself, I was right to go home in December, because once you are faced with the realities of a situation, you realize the impossibility of it, which you don't if you are right up close. The fact is, it is impossible for a person to have a household if he is a doctor at the age of thirty and has literally not <u>one cent</u> of money beside his living and won't take one cent. I hope you don't worry, but I think I should write you, especially as it may set your mind at ease. There is only one thing that could make me mad—if you ever say anything against André. You can say anything at all against me.

II

1960

July 28. On to a new diary, as I have filled up the previous one. A rainy day, which I love on Ashaunt as nowhere else. I walked anyway for an hour, and saw a fox. Tonight I read <u>The Highwayman</u> to the children, and "I will arise and go now, and go to Innisfree." Charlie and Will are keeping diaries too. They call them "diarrheas" and hang the keys around their necks. I remember when Grandmother P. first gave me a Nature Diary, instructing me in no uncertain terms to be an "eye," and not an "I." Now Dr. Hoffman has told me to "write whatever comes to mind" on the page until we meet again. How times have changed! Charlie writes in his diary every night. I got Caroline a little book to scrawl in so she wouldn't feel left out. She wrote SAD HAPPY SAD HAPPY for pages, two of the only words she can write. I guess they more or less sum it up.

As for me, I don't know. Last summer I found being away from analysis a relief, but this summer I miss it, a dangerous dependency. In my last session before coming here, I said how first I was the third child, and then, when Elinor died, I was the second child, and then, when Charlie died, the oldest, like a game where you shoot down the toy ducks at the fair, but always a kind of poor replacement—and might this explain how I've always felt a sham or is it a shame? Dr. Hoffman got (for him) quite animated and said, "That's extraordinary!" and I felt elated that I'd cracked his shell and gotten him to praise me but also angry, for he knows how much I hunger for praise and also it's <u>not</u> an extraordinary insight—it's quite obvious. What I strive for is true brilliance and truly being seen and appreciated, and there's nothing I hate more than a fake (though I believe Dr. H to be quite genuine, so it was all the more confusing). If my ideals are unattainable, either because I'm not up to snuff or because no one can ever reach such an idealized state, then I must strive to be happy with a life of mediocrity, which means accepting it in the people around me as well. What of the bright things, though, what Wordsworth called Spots of Time? I live for moments of intense connection with other people, with nature, with my own mind. If I did not strive, I'd give up all hope, and yet in striving, I am often so unhappy. Of course, I'm hardly the only unhappy person in the world.

Tomorrow everyone arrives, and then it will be dinner parties and houseguests and endless charades and cocktail parties and little spats. If no one came in August, I would be lonely, desperate. As it is, I imagine building my garden wall up and up and just sitting there, not answering when they call.

Aug. 1. Everyone is arriving today with cars and help, and it feels like an actual change of season. I had the strange idea as the cars came down the road that the children and I were the native animals, and now the actual humans will arrive and spoil our peace. Weeks ago, on July 4th weekend, Daddy brought me the new book about the Great War and I still haven't read it, nor the Freud biography, and Mummy will want to see what I've done with the garden. What <u>have</u> I done in all this time? But I have been happy (mostly) spending time with the children. All three are darling when they're cheerful. We wander about like I'm their older sister, not a Mère de Famille. I know Belle expects me to act more my part, but tant pis. Last week I let them eat as many cherries as they wanted, and Belle told them it would make blood come out in their Big Jobs and urine, voodoo nonsense, of course, but they believed her. When André arrived, he said, "Oh yes, this is of grave concern, oui oui, wee wee," until finally we got it, and even Belle couldn't help laughing. She doesn't like me—of that I'm quite sure—and while she is capable with the children, I cherish my privacy and look forward to the day when we no longer require live-in help. I taught Charlie and Will about puns, and Charlie promptly came out with "Surely Shirley Temple likes puns!" His cleverness is second nature to him. I hope he never loses his natural ease.

Aug. 7. Dossy and Phillip were barely here a week and already left today. Holly and Lil-Phil (as the boys call him) have moved over to the Big House. Mummy does not seem capable of understanding how someone blessed with so much can be so unhappy. I think she views it as a kind of moral failing, but I understand it; Dossy just goes <u>down</u>. I hate the Portable being empty and for Dos to be gone, but Mummy and Daddy are glad to have the children at the Big House, and it keeps Bea and Agnes happy, scrubbing and scolding and braiding Holly's hair. Will asked Little Phillip, What does your mum do all day in New York? and Phil said, Oh, she sleeps and talks on the phone and sticks her head out the window to sunbathe. Holly is so brave and cheerful, a little mother to them all. Holly and Charlie love each other so. I could see them getting married someday, except for the inconvenience of being first cousins.

August 15. I took the train back from New York because the plane trip down was so terrifying. Lightning, gale winds, fog. The plane went down a hundred feet every few minutes and seemed to be falling rather than advancing. The train trip back along the coast, in contrast, was so peaceful in the late afternoon post-storm, all quiet harbors with rowboats and outboards anchored, and little salt rivers flowing inland with children fishing at the edges. I felt myself going farther and farther away from New York and toward Ashaunt. A man across the aisle was crying openly with a little boy sleeping on his lap. I think the mother must have died. I felt very sorry for them both and glad to be going home. At Columbia, I settled everything at the registrar's office, but my textbooks were not in yet. I felt extremely nervous and excited just to be on the campus. I think a university may be the place where I feel most myself in the world. When I am thinking hard about ideas or talking about them or working on a paper, my mind finds a kind of shape and concentration that feels almost spiritual, monastic even. I lose all track of time, and of myself. It may be the purest feeling I have ever felt, though it's very hard to come by, especially when my insecurities (not to mention my life) interfere. To be a true scholar and professor would fulfill my dreams; I only hope I have what it takes. Dos is already doing better. We had a nice lunch out and a walk in the park. Her doctor told her she is too reliant on her sleeping pills, and that this could account for a large part of her troubles, so she is entering a strict regimen.

Aug. 20. The fuzzy pale pink steeplebush is just beginning to open on the path from the Stricklands' to Teal Rock. Will identified sea lavender in Grandmother P.'s book. It said it grew near marshes, so we hurried to the creek and found a cluster just coming into bloom. André has been here for nearly two weeks and leaves tomorrow. He is bored, though he will not say so, and he is pleasant enough to everyone but keeps his distance, even from me, so that it feels lonelier to have him here than not. I grow impatient with his perpetual outsider status and envy Jane for having married Paul, though at the time it seemed a safe and even tedious choice. We grew up not <u>knowing</u> how to be bored here. We are trying (my idea) to speak more French with the children, which makes me remember Lausanne and how free I felt there, and how romantic it was to be wooed in French. One day I realized I could live in Europe forever and survive. That was when I told André that we had to move back if we were to marry; the realization was just too frightening to me.

You might lead 1,000 different lives for a time, and then it comes down to one. Nature flings herself about, though, profligate. We walked at the end of the Point where the army roads have nearly disappeared.

Caroline stepped in a thicket of poison ivy. Belle took her home and washed her right away, but she is already getting a rash and is panicked about it, so prone to overreacting. The boys found sticks and an old empty rifle shell and played on the gun emplacements, singing "Beer Beer for Battery B" with all their might. With their scabby knees and puffed-out little chests, they made cunning soldiers. I played the enemy and died several times over, which of course they loved. They have no idea what war really means, and I pray they never learn.

August 29. Over a hundred morning glories in the garden. Charlie counted 92 yesterday and 116 today. Mummy, Caroline and I went to the Packet and Mummy bought us mother/daughter dresses on sale, fussing about choices for much too long. Tonight I let Caroline sleep in her dress. This afternoon we sat on the dock and looked at a fishing boat drifting back and forth through the fog and tried to remember it for the winter. Charlie said he was afraid he would not be able to remember it, as it would be such a long time till next summer. Jane said take a picture in your mind, so all the children did, pretending to click. I told them they could draw it or write it down when they got home. Of course, I am the only one who did. People are so inherently lazy, or is it that the memory is better left alone? The Big House is packed with houseguests. Gaga and Grampa have a hotel, Will said. Dossy left yesterday after having barely just returned, and took Holly and Phil away with her. At least she came for a few days. We did our gardens together, rotating days, and swam. The ocean is so warm, it feels heated in spots. I swim and swim.

Sept. 2. I'm reading a fascinating book about King Philip's War, which literally happened right here, an extraordinary thought, the Wampanoag burning Padanaram! If only I could go back in time. As it is, I intend to do a serious search for relics and enlist the boys.

I got a book from the library about how to cordon off an area and do
a little dig. Charlie found two flat, pointed stones he is convinced are
arrowheads. I offered to take them to an archaeologist at Columbia,
and he nearly bit my head off. Either he doesn't want to let his treasures
out of his sight, or he's afraid of finding out the truth. I hope for the
former but suspect the latter. I looked up "Ashaunt" in a booklet of
Indian terms in the Historical Society and discovered it means "lobster
crawling backward" in Wampanoag. No one here appears to have
investigated this before, but Daddy was quite interested, and we looked
at other words too. I remember a friend of Mummy's—a houseguest
here, no less—saying she thought Ashaunt allowed one to retreat from
the real world in dangerous ways. At the time, I was so indignant I
began to argue with her, but she would not budge, and finally Mummy
had to intervene. Only now, watching the children turn savage and
dreamy in a particular, back-turning way, do I understand what she
meant. Shouldn't a boy <u>want</u> to know if his arrowhead is real?

Sept. 3. All the guests at the Big House finally left, and Mummy
asked me for a walk. She told me she is concerned I'll be overtaxed this
fall between my studies and the children (and she doesn't even know
about my analysis!). I assured her that I'd be fine and told her that going
back to school means the world to me, even if to her it might seem like
a strange and unnecessary thing to do. Then she confided in me that
when Daddy first got sick, she'd been making plans to go to college. I
asked why she couldn't have gone anyway, with Stewart, etc. to help
out, and she said it just felt wrong to expand her world as Daddy's grew
smaller—and also he simply needed her more. I said, Well, you could go
to college now, he'd be all for it, and she laughed and said that my going
for my master's is good enough for her. Then she gave me a little silk
bookmark for luck. I don't remember her ever having confided in me
this way before.

Sept. 6. Today a few glorious clumps of wild sunflowers on the road to Barney's Joy. They have a spicy marigold kind of fragrance. The clematis smelling like orange blossom covers the stone at the Big House and the walls around Jane and Paul's. Today felt like the end of summer and the first day of autumn. I went swimming with André, Will and Charlie this morning, and Daddy came down with Stewart to watch— quite a coterie of men! Along the road, even the latest summer flowers are wilting. Later, we took out the Beetle Cat, and I wished I could store the day's golden light. The children are horribly moody, not wanting to leave, especially Charlie, who says his saddest times on Ashaunt are equal to his happiest times in Bernardsville and that he hates school (which is not true). Caroline has gathered half the beach. Labor Day has always brought me an almost physical pain, a little death, but this year, unlike any other in my memory, I am ready to leave, so excited by what awaits me.

Sept. 12. This morning, Hurricane Donna raged through New Jersey, taking down our dear enormous willow tree, and now it has hit Ashaunt! I talked to Mummy, who said the docks were all right—they took the swimming dock out ahead of time and the boat dock was holding on—but now the phones are down and I hate not being able to call. Paul drove there yesterday to help get the boats out and is still there. Jane is frantic that he'll get swept away or crushed by a tree and has called me five or six times, so I finally told her to just come over with the children and spend the night, and they're on their way. On Block Island, there are wind gusts of 130 mph, according to the TV news. Here, it is just raining now, and we did not lose power. I should be glad we are not on Ashaunt, but I hate to miss a hurricane, to feel its power and walk out to the end where the wind might flatten you and the gray waves crest high, then curl and teeter and finally fall. There is almost nothing so beautiful and, at the same time, so frightening, as that curved lip. If the storm is anything like the one in '38, it could do terrible damage, but it does not seem to be that bad.

Sept. 14: The children's first day of school was today, delayed a day because of Donna. Tomorrow I take the train to New York for my first class and start analysis again. Perhaps the hurricane is an omen (but of what?). When I left Caroline at kindergarten, she looked so stiff and pale, but I told her we were both starting new schools and must be brave, and I've hidden a trinket in her lunch. In the car, the boys discussed shoes as if they were torture devices and refused to put them on until the last second, when they limped dramatically into school. They are disconsolate about missing the hurricane on Ashaunt, and generally full of complaints. Thank goodness I have a driver lined up to take them to school after this.

I had a dream last night of buying school supplies for myself and finding that instead I had a sack of sawdust and ashes with a hole in it, everything leaking out. If dreams are always screens for something else, my screen is awfully thin! I will have one course on early American history, another on primary sources, a third I'm not sure of yet and an adviser who won a Pulitzer Prize.

Sept. 15. An exhilarating day of classes! On Tuesday I was too afraid to speak, dizzy with nerves, but I practiced with Charlie at home, which made him feel important, and today I simply forced myself to raise my hand. The professor seemed to think my comment reasonable, and after that I was off and running. At thirty-four I am one of the oldest students and one of only a handful of women in the department's master's program. Every small thing—getting a sandwich from the machine outside the bookstore, hearing people debate ideas in the halls—is thrilling to me. I was exhausted by the time I got to analysis. Dr. H. said I could just drift and nap if I wanted, but I told him I've never slept in public in my life and would not, anyway, waste the money. "Public," he repeated (I could have predicted it), and I said I was aware that he thought it was a mistake for me to take off the whole summer and had a need to make me feel like I'd lost ground. "<u>Ground</u>?" I said then before he could, and I played me and him for a good five minutes, back and forth, and even got his New York Jewish accent (I think he is Jewish, though he won't say). He didn't laugh. I got the sense that I've grown tiresome to him in my absence. I arrived home at seven to find the children fine and glad to see me. Hurricane Donna has killed hundreds of people, according to the newspaper, but no one in Massachusetts.

Sept. 20. An A on my first assignment! It was only an annotated bibliography and account of research methods, but I'm still pleased. I just hope I can keep it up. Belle told me she wants three weeks off in December to go to Haiti. My courses don't end until just before Christmas, but her mother is sick, so what can I say? I will have to find someone to substitute. Meanwhile Dos is back at Four Winds. We've told the children she has hepatitis. The doctors say she has an agitated depression, and they have her all doped up on drugs (after saying that drugs were part of the problem . . .). I have a great deal of reading to do tonight but can't seem to concentrate. I cut back to three times a week for analysis and feel unsteady now, though that might have nothing to do with it. I do hate it when Dos is at Four Winds. There is a woman professor at Columbia who came to speak to our seminar, quite mannish and knowledgeable and an expert on captivity narratives. The professors all seem tremendously busy, even harried, which I don't quite understand, as I'd thought the academic schedule was constructed for the life of the mind. I am starting to be able to tell which students are full of hot air and which have real ideas. There are an equal number of both, along with a terribly shy and agitated girl who reminds me of Caroline. I offered her a mint, but she wouldn't take it. She does not speak, which makes her seem mysterious and brilliant (I should try it).

Sept. 25. I'm in the middle of reading <u>Of Plimouth Plantation</u>—and to think that we're direct descendants of Governor William Bradford! Charlie was interested, so I told him about some of it, and he asked question after question—about the Indians, private property, religion, governance. He has such a first-rate intelligence, coupled with such natural curiosity, and he is already the best little companion at age 9. I commented on how hard it must have been for the English colonists to arrive in the middle of winter to a "hideous and desolate wilderness, full of wild beasts and wild men." Charlie said, "But Mummy, to the wild beasts and men, <u>we</u> must have looked wild," which is of course true and shows a highly developed capacity for empathy. And then to make a life from nothing and built on such faith. I'd have found it terribly exciting if I didn't perish along the way.

Oct. 7. Back for the weekend. We arrived at eleven yesterday evening and carried the children to their beds. The house was all put away, sheets over the sofas, screens off the doors, shades pulled. Some porch furniture got blown off and ruined and some trees got uprooted and boats damaged (not our Beetle Cat, which was out of the water), but it could have been much worse. Last night I wished we had not come, for it was too bleak, but the morning changed everything. Such a wind, and such clearness and colors, I have never seen before, everything scrubbed clean. The yellow and red chrysanthemums are in full bloom now, and the dahlias. The roses have turned to red berries and the huckleberry bushes and bay bushes to purple russet. Though the sun shone brilliantly and the sky was cloudless, the land and sea seemed in the middle of some polar night where the sun has neither risen nor set. The rocks were dark and jagged, the sea black and blue, the land all shades of blue and red.

Now the boys are off wandering, set free, and Caroline is chattering and hopping about like—my nickname for her—a Carolina wren, happier than she has been in weeks. As we came back from a walk, tiny birds with brown wings and white breasts flushed from the ground, but we could not see them well enough to identify them in <u>Peterson's</u>. In the afternoon Jane and Paul took the children to play with Ellie, leaving André and me alone in the house for a time, which turned into a romantic interlude. He took me by surprise today, covering my eyes with his hands while I was reading. Afterward I wept, though I cannot say why.

Being here, I find myself more than ever two people instead of one. One longs to live day by day, for sparking driftwood fires, and closed doors, the wildness of my fall garden, harvesting vegetables to boil on the stove. The children. To keep them young. To keep them from the world and all its pain and disharmony. When I am in that state, I can imagine abandoning all ambition and just living inside all this beauty.

And yet it is never enough, for I also long to study, to create something lasting in words, to achieve things that the world will recognize as unusual and distinguished and escape in complete absorption into something outside myself. To talk with others about things that matter and go for Truth.

The first longing offers a joy that is closer to my physical being, my animal nature, the other perhaps a more permanent, solid satisfaction. This weekend I can forget for hours my intellectual self; sometimes the mere attempt to move toward my comprehensive exams seems absurd and without purpose. The only common motive that I find in these two selves is the desire to be completely absorbed, to be so preoccupied with life that time becomes unimportant, the moment itself everything because so <u>full</u>.

Oct. 15. We are staying home this weekend. I've got so much reading
to do for my courses already and cannot spend hours in the car going
to and from Ashaunt. The children are protesting, but I will not change
my mind. Anyway, no cousins are there, so they would be bored. Jane
is pregnant again! Ellie and the new baby will be little more than a year
apart, like Charlie and Will, which has its advantages and disadvantages.
Jane came over quite upset earlier, seeking my advice. There had been a
drama, because Bea has already offered quite enthusiastically to move
in for a time and be the nurse. Jane feels utterly determined to raise
her children herself and in her own style, and that also Bea is too much
like a mother to her and would stifle her. I told her she must simply say
no, as nicely and firmly as she can (she will change her mind about a
nurse once she sees how different two babies is from one, but regardless,
the nurse should not be Bea). I realize now that leaving Caroline with
Bea when we went to Japan was a mistake, though at the time I had no
choice if I was to preserve my marriage. Janie credits Bea with her happy
childhood (was it really all that happy?), which makes her feel torn up
about saying no. Mummy will simply have to tell Bea that she can't
manage without her, as tending the grandchildren is a full-time job.
How glad I am not to be in the middle of it all!

Oct. 22. I stayed up too late last night reading Grandmother P.'s
memoir, thinking that the parts on Teddy Roosevelt might point me
toward a subject for my thesis, which I'm already panicking about.
I'd skimmed the memoir before but never read all the way through.
It's filled with name-dropping about Kipling and the Roosevelts,
along with bits about her own work with women's suffrage and
the Republican Party and the occasional fascinating, beautiful or
historically important scene, as well as lots of boring ones. There is a
quite amazing letter from Teddy Roosevelt to Daddy, sent to him when
he started at Harvard, all about Daddy's father and what noble work he

did as a private man and public servant before he died. TR says Daddy's
father was literally one of the two or three finest men he had ever met,
because of his extraordinary character, courage and mental capacity.
I can't bear to think of Daddy losing him when he was just a little boy,
but the letter must have been an inspiration. Of Daddy's baby sister
who died, Grandmother includes almost nothing, nor does she say
much about the books she wrote or even her love of nature, a strange
omission. She dedicates the book to me, Dossy and Jane but barely
mentions us in it, and then only in passing. She led such an impressive
life, but the overall tone is not one of happiness exactly, even though I
remember her as full of enthusiasms. I wonder if her personal diaries
said more, but she ordered them burned when she died. Her nature
books are where her brilliance lay, and it is no wonder that unlike
them, this reminiscence was privately printed. Charlie has been reading
<u>Plants and Their Children</u> and going out to look for "seed sailboats"—
asters, milkweed, clematis, goldenrod and the like. To me, the best
thing about that book is not the facts it imparts, though they are
marvelous, but the way it connects each thing to the other and requires
that the children learn to <u>see.</u>

   Nov. 10. I cannot <u>believe</u> what has happened, just as I was finally
getting back to myself. I don't want another one, but if I have it, I'll have
to love it, not just because it's my duty, but because I'll be unable to help
myself, couldn't with the others—they just come in. I don't have the
energy or desire to start over again, not now. I'll swear off sex altogether
after this, or get my tubes tied. I've told no one, not even André, and
have never felt so alone in all my life. I thought we were careful, and we
did use a sponge and foam, but Dr. Elliot says the blood test never lies.
Anyway I'd know from how I feel, a machine forced into production,
despite its every fiber saying no. I called Dr. H., but no one answered
and I don't see him until Tuesday, and as soon as I hung up the phone it

occurred to me that I don't even have to tell him, I could just take care
of it, if I could figure out how. It is no one's business but my own.

Nov. 11. I'm going completely mad with my secret, but if I tell André
he'll think I'm cold-blooded and want me to have it—at least I think so,
as another child is not so big a thing to him, one way or the other. It will
not devour his soul. And Mummy and Daddy would never understand,
nor Jane. Which leaves Doss or Suky, but Suky is so far away with her
Englishman and only one child, having wanted more, and Dos is still so
up and down. The children know something is wrong, and I swear Belle
does too from how she looks at me, as if I'm emitting a new scent. Twice
today I've not been able to breathe, drawn into an acute panic state.
The first time I thought it might be the start of bleeding, which is all I
can wish for now. To think back on when I learned I was pregnant with
Charlie—how full of joy I was, how proud, the start of a great journey.
Now I feel pressed into service, blindsided. I must burn this page.

Nov. 13. I did not sleep last night. Today I dragged myself into the
city and to class, then to Dr. Hoffman, who spoke more in this one
session than in all the rest of them combined. I'm still not entirely sure
what transpired between us, but I believe he is giving me the devil's
choice of either ending my psychoanalysis or ending the baby. First
he asked me to try to imagine coming to see him three to four times a
week when I was pregnant and had a newborn and was still in school
(I told him I won't drop school no matter what). Then, when I said I'd
find a way to manage it, he said that patients are highly discouraged
from making major life changes during a course of analysis and that
pregnancy, in particular, is discouraged, as the rigors of the analysis are
thought to potentially harm the developing baby. This is the stupidest
thing I've ever heard! He claims that he informed me of the No Major

Change rule when I began, and that he has been flexible in many ways (sleeping pills, my master's, blah blah), but I'm sure he never told me about this despotic dictum, as I'd not have agreed to it.

Then he said, in that hideously neutral tone of his, "I'd be interested in hearing you explore why you got pregnant." My blood was boiling, but I kept my voice level, and said I am married and have conjugal relations and the birth control failed. End of story. *Fin.* But then I begged him, really begged him, to give me his honest opinion, knowing me as he does, my past and present and my innermost private thoughts. I said I wanted to do the best thing for myself and the children and André and my career, but I simply couldn't figure it out on my own, nor turn to anyone but him for advice. He said he couldn't tell me one way or another, nor did he think I'd want him to, as that would be him playing God, but that he'd meet with me for a few more sessions to help me come to a sense of what I wanted. "And then what?" I asked, but he wouldn't say. We were nearly out of time by then, and someone else was waiting. Write me a letter and I can go to one of those places, I told him, but he said he couldn't, not in his position as my analyst. Will you continue to see me if I go ahead with the baby? I asked, but he refused to tell me. I was nearly blind with fury and panic by the time I left. I vomited on the stairs—I only wish I'd done it on the couch.

Nov. 14. I told Dossy, I had to. She was remarkably calm and seemed not the least bit shocked, and I am truly the luckiest person in the world to have her for a sister, for she is the best friend in the world. She had the brilliant idea of calling Dr. Wendall. Besides being an old friend of Mummy and Daddy's, he's an esteemed psychiatrist and has seen Dossy before, and he is known to help women in my condition. Dr. Wendall agreed to write a letter in total confidence to a doctor who performs the operation, saying that having a child would pose a grave danger to my health and the health of my entire family, which it would, as I have never before felt such despair. For the first time in days I can breathe again, so relieved to have a plan, if I can only follow through on it. Dr. Wendall gave me the name of a doctor, and I called and made an appointment for next week. I'll of course tell André someday, just not now. He wouldn't understand how this threatens my very core, for though he loves the children, he does not feel charged with shaping them, drawing out their potential and being their mother all the time, even when I'm not physically with them. André got home late, and I avoided having to talk to him except to say good night. If he had so much as kissed me or taken me in his arms, I think I would have broken down and told him, but he did not, and it is partly because of these wide gulfs between us that I cannot think of this as anything but a disaster. Now I'm in my study, exhausted but far from sleep.

Nov 17. I went to do it but could not. I don't understand what happened, only that the city seemed suddenly tiny, my courses, my books, my desires, all so tiny and vain and in vain, and instead, this life inside my every cell, not even a life separate from myself but my own life, was how it felt. I could not stop it, I wanted to but could not, which does not mean I want another child, as I do not. The place was so well appointed and discreet in a funeral-parlor way, drawn curtains and the smell of furniture polish in the anteroom. Tess of the d'Urbervilles was on the bookshelf, which, if intentional, is the sickest joke and made me and Dossy break into a sort of hysterical laughter—thank God we were the only ones there. I was called in and put on a gown and got on a table, but I was shaking horribly from head to toe, and then I vomited violently and left. It all still feels entirely unreal. In the taxi Dos started crying, telling me how relieved she was, that she'd been afraid it would hurt dreadfully, or I'd regret it later, or die in a pool of my own blood. So then we were crying together, and soon enough I was back to calming her down and things felt almost normal. Today

I wanted to go to my classes but was simply too drained. I'll go on Thursday if it kills me, but I will never see Dr. Hoffman again (nor pay my outstanding bill).

III

1961

May 28. We arrived on Thursday evening to find the herbs and the roses in the garden mostly gone. This has been the coldest winter in many years, and the harbor was frozen beyond the breakwater in Padanaram. The roots of the plants froze too long in the ground to live. It has been a warm, quiet, misty day, changing from fog to pale sunlight. I bought lilies, lantana, pink and blue petunias to plant, but I am too fat to bend, so André put them in with "help" from Caroline. The honeysuckle is still in bud, and the pink bushes outside the door are the only ones fully blooming. Charlie saw a ruby-crowned kinglet out of his window. He can name scores and scores of birds now. Ellie has started running, and Jane must chase her everywhere, a comic sight as Jane is huge. Put her on a leash, I told her—the way Bea kept Jane close when she was young. Jane didn't remember and was shocked. She's obsessed with the Dr. Spock book, which is about kissing your baby all day long and letting him roll in mud and never taking a moment for yourself.

To return here is always a reminder of time's passage. This has been a difficult year, with Dossy's troubles and Daddy's fall, and Caroline not saying a word, not one word, in school all year, and of course my situation, which I've come to accept but still cannot welcome, and to lose my analysis. I must remind myself that I have nearly completed a

full year of my master's, which is no small accomplishment, especially
toward the end, as people at Columbia looked at me as if I'd grown
horns. Mummy and André both want me to take the fall semester off
after the baby comes, but I shall not, as the risk of losing momentum is
too—one might leave and never return.

Once all this was before me, the children pure, unformed innocents,
and before that, my own life waiting, or not even waiting, just living
itself. This morning I woke before everyone and walked the paths. The
warblers flit from bush to bush and are easy to find, flashes of blue
and gold and an endless piping of song. Yellow star-grass carpets the
path from the Stricklands' to Teal Rock. I watched the most amazing
tree-swallow courting behavior today, the male swooping and circling
overhead with a large blue jay feather, showing it off to his mate. Then
he would drop it from very high, and as it floated down, she'd collect
it in midair. They did this several times, until finally the feather was
placed in the hole in the tree where they must have their nest. I tried
to see but was dive-bombed. I brought Charlie later, but we could not
find them. Tomorrow we must leave until June. I have two twenty-page
papers to hand in between now and then, but the course meetings are
over so I need not go into the city, which is a good thing, as my ankles
are swollen and my bladder has a mind of its own.

June 9. I turned my papers in and took the children out of school
two weeks early and do not regret it, especially as this is the last year
I can do it. Charlie's schooling is becoming more serious, and Will
has already learned how to charm his teacher without doing a lick of
work, and I'll have comprehensive exams next spring, if I can keep on
schedule. Jane and Elinor are here too, and will stay until Jane needs to
go back to have the baby. It's cozy both being pregnant. I'm as large as
she is, though due a month later. She knit a sweater set. I tried a cap but
have no aptitude, so she undid it and took it over. I know I should want

another girl, so it's two and two and Caroline can have a sister. Either would be fine, but I find myself hoping for a boy.

June 12. I spoke to Professor Sheridan on the telephone today, and he thought my new idea about the French attitude toward FDR's New Deal promising, but he also seems skeptical of me lately, dismissive (because of the baby coming? because I postponed the first set of exams? Or has he read my paper and decided I'm a dolt?). André says it's mostly in my head, but he was not on the phone and tone is everything. He thinks I exaggerate and so doesn't take me seriously when he should, a source of immense frustration to me. Everyone loves André. I love him too and believe he loves me, but does he <u>like</u> me, which is not the same as love? Or understand me? Perhaps it's too much to ask of anyone, as people are almost entirely mysterious to each other. Still, I want to think and talk about things that matter, to have conversations I return from changed. I might have done well as a missionary. I'd have gone somewhere strange and beautiful and talked to people about God, and seen astonishing things every day. Of course there is the problem of belief.

June 14. My birthday. 35. I celebrated it at the Big House with everyone on Sunday, but today, with just us, was happier. The wind swept through the house. André made a fire in the living room and gave me several books I've wanted and a gold bracelet with an inscribed charm for each child and a new blank one for the baby (surely Jane or Mummy picked that out). The children each made me a card. Suky did not call or write, which is a disappointment, as she always has, but she is so far away. We ate lobsters for dinner, and now the fog and the wind have blended together in a strange, unearthly mix. The Swiss chard and lettuce in my garden are two inches high. The radishes are already bulging and ripe. Some beets have pushed above the ground, along with the rows of feathery carrot tops. My vegetable garden is surrounded by wild roses, daisies and the sea. I wonder if there is another garden like it in the world, a neat, cultivated rectangle of soil and vegetables in rows cut out of the wilderness of cedar, pines, blackberries and grass.

I would like to stay just where I am or go backwards. I still cannot seem to embrace or even grasp this new adventure we are headed toward, though the baby will be here so soon. I think of the past with longing, of the future with worry. Only nature can hold me, in its obliviousness to all that consumes me. So I love the Maryland yellowthroat that comes each day to bathe in my garden pool, the birds that whistle in the thickets and flash past me, green and yellow over the grass and sea. I love the rabbits that hop in the garden, and above all, the sea that gives us the illusion, at least, of timelessness. On these things, I must fix my gaze.

June 17. I got more plants for the garden today—asters, alyssum, marigolds, petunias. A lovely evening—watered the garden and filled the birdbath. I want it all to be in bloom for Mummy when she arrives on July 4th. I thought with horror tonight, not of the baby but of all that is coming, especially the nurse—and it seemed to me that the more I thought, the louder the TV grew in Belle's room—and the more I longed for solitude. In September, somehow I must arrange to go off by myself, if only for a few nights. Charlie was so sweet tonight. He is utterly removed from any such thoughts as mine and yet so curious about them. "Don't you ever hear the television at night?" I asked him. "Sure, but I shut the door and think about something else," he said, and when I said I didn't have such fortitude, he said, "But why not, Mummy? You've got the most interesting thoughts in the world!" He is a darling and companionable child, and I think he admires me most for what he has been able to achieve, feeling somehow that I've pushed him to distinguish himself, but also recognizing that he finds attainment and recognition pleasing. I think he feels too that we both recognize the importance of this, and I know he is grateful for my guidance. Someday he may feel the opposite—but he will never, I hope, stop wanting to learn and accomplish unusual things.

July 3. Fog and honeysuckle at the dock. A heavy sweet smell. Caroline and I walked back home after watching Will and Charlie sail off into the fog with Kenneth, the Padanaram boy we've hired to tutor and teach them sailing. We went and admired the roses on Dossy's wall. I just hope she can come before they are gone. Will and Charlie's fairy garden is enchanted. Everything grows quietly, untouched by weeds, blight or rabbits. We don't know why. It is the most exquisite little spot; an opening in the woods lets the sun through the shadows. The earth is quite black, and each separate flower almost glows in the darkness. Charlie told me his friend Rusty peed on it as a supposed joke, but Charlie didn't find it funny. I don't think a best friend should pee on your garden, he said very seriously, and I told him I thoroughly agreed. Tomorrow is Mummy's clambake. After, André will take the children to New Bedford for fireworks. I am tired but more peaceful than before. Jane and Paul leave tomorrow, as their baby will arrive any day.

July 4. I'm terribly upset. I was with Charlie and Daddy and Daddy's friend Bert Adams and his wife on the porch. Charlie was reciting poems he had memorized, and Daddy told me I should be careful about not turning my son into a performing monkey. It was so humiliating, especially in front of other people! To have poems stored in one's brain is a great gift, and who taught me that but Daddy, who used to make us memorize not only poems but <u>bad</u> poems, while Charlie knows Frost and Yeats and some wonderful funny ones by Kipling and Edward Lear?

What's worse is that Charlie disappeared afterward—he must have run off. I looked for a little while but couldn't find him. I've sent Will and Phillip off to try. Perhaps there is a grain of truth in what Daddy says, but it seems entirely unfair coming from him. I work so hard to engage the children and teach them things and cultivate a love of learning. What he did feels like an old humiliation, one I am helpless against.

July 6. Tonight the children and I went swimming after dinner. The tide was a foot over the tide rock. The water was a pale green-gray in the evening fog. To plunge into it felt like immersing oneself in another substance, more buoyant than water, more tingling than winter air. I am so glad everyone else is gone. We plunged many times into the pure, deep surface and drifted below it, and then ran back to the house and the fire, feeling as if we had changed our shapes and were part of the night sea air. In the water, I don't feel pregnant at all. The ocean was so lovely in its gray depth that I was afraid to leave.

July 8. The little playhouse Mummy had built for the boys is finished! It's set in the low woods between the Big and Red Houses, like a rustic birdcage in the green. There is no place where one can really see it. It is almost hidden away in the bushes, and I think the children will love to watch the birds flit in and out of nests where only they can see them. I would like one for myself and am more than a little jealous. Tonight the boys are sleeping there, and I haven't seen them quite so excited for a long time. It began to rain as I was reading <u>Mary Poppins</u> out loud, and Charlie began to whisper to Will, "How snug it will be to watch the rain from our cabin." He is terribly happy today. I think he feels released from his friendship with Rusty, who has gone to Europe for two weeks. Charlie plunged down to the dock ready for his sailing lesson and later came to me, his eyes rolling with anticipation, and suggested that he and Will spend the night in their sleeping bags in the cabin. He accused me of not watching the Maryland yellowthroat long enough from the bathroom window. "It almost seems as if you were getting <u>used</u> to it, Mummy." "Well, aren't you?" I answered. "Of course not," he replied. He is happy and childlike and I wonder if he wouldn't be more at ease with Will and Phillip than with the enervating kind of companionship he seems to have with Rusty—the difference, perhaps, between a "best friend" and blood relations. Mummy only had two beds built in the cabin, so it is a bit unclear if it is meant for just my two or also for Dossy's children, though I do think Holly would be afraid sleeping there, and Charlie and Will are already calling it their own, though I have told them they must share. Charlie said to me that he will live there when he grows up.

July 10. Jane had her baby! A boy, Stephen, nearly eight pounds. They will be here as soon as they can and stay through August. She sounded entirely herself on the phone and so happy. Mummy offered Bea for a few weeks, mostly to chase after Ellie, and Jane accepted. Talking to her, I felt the stirring of something like hope, for how can it not be a miracle, a whole new life? The cousins will be nearly the same age, like twins, which pleases Jane immensely after a life of trying to catch up. I am myself enormous and uncomfortable and I must go home next week, as the hospital in New Bedford is subpar. I've set myself a page count of things to read each day and am so far managing it. If I can take even one course in the fall, I won't be too far off track.

July 12. Charlie ended up at the hospital today after attempting to make gunpowder bombs from old shotgun shells and having one blow up in his face! I was in Newport and did not even know until it was over. He is all right, with only minor burns, but could have been blinded or even killed. I am furious. What a stupid, stupid boy! At ten, he should know better. I was going to leave the children here when the baby comes, but now I must bring Charlie back and leave him in Grace Park, where I'll instruct everyone to be extremely strict with him. I can see him getting ruined before my eyes, ruining himself, and I must stop it before it happens. He's been given too much freedom, and he is lacking in judgment and also hypersensitive, girlish even, and weak, though he tries to hide it with his bullish antics. What was he thinking, building bombs? Janie said, Well, you were wild too, when you were young, but I told her never like that—I did not self-destruct or do violent or dangerous things. He found the shells in the Big House, in a closet in Charlie's room, where he was rummaging around.

I must bear in mind that my own brother might have done such a thing and would, if alive, have forgiven Charlie for doing it, as I must try to do. Charlie's face is covered with bandages, his beautiful eyelashes are gone, his hand is all bandaged up. The truth is that for weeks and maybe longer, he has often seemed sullen and unreachable, and that worries me even more than this particular incident. André brought him to the hospital but is otherwise of little help and sets a weak example, as if, being foreign, he has no idea how American boys should behave. Will was very worried, and I saw in him a kind of pure sweetness that does not show itself often—he spends so much time trying to keep up with Charlie or clowning around. He could tell how upset I was and set out to comfort me by singing little songs and telling jokes, such a dear boy. I am again regretting the baby coming. I'm just so tired and do not welcome the responsibility of another child.

July 15. Waiting for the baby at Grace Park, my due date tomorrow. I'm actually glad to have brought Charlie back with me, as we've found some of our old ways together, and I'm teaching him early colonial history as a way to pass the time and engage his mind. Something has happened to him this summer—a distance or lethargy or restlessness—

that worries me, as he is too young for it. He says he made the bombs—
or "firecrackers"—as a science experiment, and because Rusty had bottle
rockets and he had none, and the boys are all obsessed with astronauts.
This does not excuse what he did, but I think he is sorry and also glad
to have time with me and be able to act himself and not like some
delinquent in a movie. André is being very attentive, and Mummy too,
and except for not being able to swim in the sea, I am happy enough
to be here. The agency sent two baby nurses for me to interview. One
was Scots with glowing references, but she got hired away before I
could make a decision, and I'm not sure I want to start up with a Scots
again—even the accent makes me feel like a child. The other one seemed
humorless but capable and will probably have to do. Belle we will keep
on, though it is not ideal; it's simply too much trouble to find someone
else. It's horribly hot and humid here, and I'm about to burst. Even so, I
have the feeling of wanting to suspend time. Tomorrow, or the next day
or soon after, I will be a mother of four, an incomprehensible fact.

July 30. Back to Ashaunt with the baby, Percy Russell Benoit. But
I knew nothing at all about this baby until he came—that he would
be a new star, a new existence, that I would love already so deeply and
imagine him in the years ahead, see him running around the garden,
loving the birds and flowers, counting morning glories. It is a great
happiness, and I think of what has happened with gratefulness, and of
my state over the past months with disbelief and no small amount of
guilt. Tonight the wind is blowing at sixty miles an hour, and the dock
almost down. Uncle Barney, the new Beetle Cat, blew loose from its
mooring this afternoon and washed ashore. All day, Charlie, Will and
Rusty have been watching the waves, some twenty feet high, from Gaga's
dock. Paul found a lobster pot blown up on the rocks with two live
lobsters in it and put them in a pail and brought them home for him and
Jane to eat. The boys have gone through the wind to their little cabin

to spend the night, and the baby is sleeping by the garden window, and Caroline, when I checked on her, was peacefully asleep, and André is here beside me reading, my little fur family, all I could ever want.

Aug. 7. I found out I have been given permission to go on to the PhD program! This is of course fantastic news, and I will accept and just hope I have the willpower and stamina to see it through. It could mean a great many things in the long run, like going on the job market and having to consider moving (people move to all kinds of godforsaken places for tenure-track jobs). For now, it is a great boost of confidence and means I can go much further with my studies. Also, I must have been wrong about them thinking the baby was a problem. I will paste the letter in here as a memento. I called André at work, and he was sweet about it and even told his secretary, who got on the phone to congratulate me. He is quite lacking in ego and competitiveness, which is mostly a good quality, though it may help explain his lack of ambition. It's not that he's not successful, but he does not seek out recognition, nor does he even seem to want it much. It may have something to do with his not being American and also with his family, as his father was the same way. I'd always thought I'd marry a powerful man, but I suppose the downside of that is I'd have to be a powerful man's wife. Dossy did not answer when I called, which of course leads me to worry. I will bike down to Jane's now to share my news (I'm so glad finally to be back on my bike!).

Aug. 10. Sick with anxiety—it is one o'clock in the morning, and André, who is driving from New York, is not here. I think that something dreadful has happened. I am waiting to nurse Percy, with the wicked old nurse guarding him in the other room. What has happened? It is too terrible. The whole day has been ghastly, and I don't know what to do. I can't sleep, can't wait, and yet I feel I shouldn't wake Mummy and Daddy. I can't even imagine what has happened to André, but I don't think he will come now. At moments like this, my love for him is crushing, and I know I could not survive without him, much less raise the children on my own. Also Charlie is very worrying still and keeps me up nights fretting. I am very far from him. He seems grown up and yet discontented. There seems to be no way to reach him, and he is not really interested in anything. Mummy says he might be jealous of the baby, but I don't think so, for if he softens toward anyone, it's Percy. If André is not here in a half hour, I'm calling the police.

Aug. 20. A happy few days. I went to buy chrysanthemums (coral pink) and put them in the garden in the evening. The baby has eyes as wide awake as stars at night, and when I feed him, he locks eyes with me and I am everything and give him everything he needs. He is so like Charlie as a baby that it is strange. To think that only a few weeks ago I was dreaming of ways to escape him—and now he feels as much a cornerstone of my life as anything else, for truly a baby of that age is part of yourself. It is easier to love him completely than it is to love a child who is a person on his own and who angers and provokes you and is constantly struggling to be free or not to be. A baby is utterly good with no power to hurt anyone. Everything you do for it is good. There is no agonizing choice, no reasoning, and yet with its pathetic powerlessness, it is the beginning of everything. Already I see in the intense blue eyes someone eager to know the world. Already, he follows me with his eyes. It is more intense than any joy I can find in flowers and the sea, or even good conversation or great books. It draws a circle around us that no one can disturb. Caroline is like a little mother, fetching diapers and hats and whispering secrets in the baby's ear. André arrives tomorrow by dinnertime, as long as no one else has a heart attack he has to stay for. I've told him he must call next time he's running so late or risk <u>my</u> having a heart attack from worry. The patient from the other week survived. That André has such power to heal and help dazzles me when I let myself think of it, which I don't often do. It unsettles me terribly to think of life hanging by a thread. I would prefer him to do more research and less private practice, both for my nerves and because I think research is where one can ultimately have a greater effect.

Today I love Ashaunt—my first true love—and it is physical pain to imagine leaving it. The world is so uncertain that perhaps we should just stick to what we have, like Percy sleeping in the moonlight in the next room, or Caroline with her red hairband and long brown hair. I think sometimes that I should stay here forever, stop striving, find meaning close at hand. But is this a cowardly philosophy? I don't know.

TRESPASS

1970

I

SOMETIMES HE WENT to break windows. Sometimes, once summer was in full swing, he went to read, bringing along a book and a Coke or beer he'd taken from one relative or another's fridge. (Stolen? Gifted? Doors were open. Help yourself.) Mostly, stepping over the collapsed barbed wire that had once kept the army in and the summer people out, Charlie went to look for things: in May, prairie warblers and quail nests, windflowers, wood anemones; in midsummer, wood lilies and pearly everlasting; later, bayberries that he dropped into his pocket, hoping to melt them into candles (they ended up in the wash and turned to gray, clotted clumps, leaving a waxy stain on his pants). Sometimes he brought his camera, an old Canon his father had given him after his own camera was stolen. It was slightly broken, so that what you saw was not always what you got—a cluster of leaves transformed into a green clipped corner, a cloud turned into empty sky. Still, he liked how the camera narrowed his field of vision and gave him something to do with his hands, which, like his jaw, still shook if he let them go slack.

Sometimes he went to make out with a girl in the grass, or in the one remaining barrack with its rows of corroded metal beds, or in the open crow's nest of the concrete radar building, the only problem being that there was no girl, just the bright throb of his body, just his own tongue inside his mouth, his own hand down his shorts. Just (it was how things were, then, at the best of times; at the worst, no throb at all) the bright throb of his thoughts. Some of the others—Rusty, Phillip, even Will, if he was to be believed—had taken actual, real girls who were neither their cousins nor sisters to the base and done things that seemed to Charlie like the primitive and miraculous acts of feral monkeys. His own penis looked remarkably like a stinkhorn mushroom—a *Phallus impudicus* or *Mutinus elegans* (its head picked clean by insects, a delicacy in China, edible if you could get past the smell), and while he was not yet the mushroom expert he would later become, he knew a fair amount and noticed mushrooms everywhere, just as he noticed bones half buried under leaves, a fox's bleached white pelvis, the fissured skull of a rabbit or weasel.

It was 1970. The summer before, he had graduated from St. Mark's School in the bottom third of his class and gone to Woodstock, where he took photographs of garbage for an hour and left, fleeing the mud, the crush of bodies, the throngs of people losing themselves in addled celebration while he, watching himself watching, watched. That fall, he went off to a middling (by his mother's standards) college in Ohio. To escape the draft, he supposed. To escape the draft, or something else? His destination proved problematic in a number of ways: (1) Ohio was land-locked; (2) his college was in a city; (3) in order to attend college, you had to bring yourself along. He applied too late to get on-campus housing, and although his parents would have paid for something better, he found a dirt-cheap basement studio on the edge of the ghetto and didn't lock the door, and it was with great detachment and a certain amount of curiosity that he watched a burglar in a ski mask enter the room one early November Friday night and steal his camera and wallet as he lay not-sleeping in his mummy sleeping bag, which smelled of soil, salt and sea.

It was on the Saturday following the burglary that he first did LSD, though his therapist's later attempts to string the two events together into cause and effect would not convince. He was at a dorm party, vaguely trying to get into the spirit of the times and conquer a dim sense of malaise, when he accepted a tab from a guy in his Greek class: Check it out, man, this is the real goods. Even in the moment, part of him knew it was a terrible idea. The tab was small and delicate, a mouse's pocket handkerchief; he set it on his tongue and sent it down. For the first hour or so, it had no effect at all, but then he smoked a joint on top of it and it took him up and tumbled him, filling his lungs, his thoughts, his every cell, then spitting him out, leaving him shipwrecked, shorn. A week later, he did it again, convinced, through a sort of desperate, inverted logic, that the second pill might take him backward and so undo the damage of the first.

Peeling, he thought instead as the drug took hold—or did not think, exactly, he *registered*, witnessed—his brain peeling back and back and back, and at the center, nothing. No me, only an I—a consciousness, an I without a Me, except that there he was (and there he knew himself to be), crouched in terror on the floor of the dorm lounge, bent over his knees, wrapped around himself but also disembodied, a batch of molecules coughed into the air. Johnny, someone said to him at one point, or was it Charlie or Jimmy (each name arrived as unassigned and tinny as the next), and Hey, Cat, you don't look so hot, and he was rocking underneath a chair; they might have been poking him with sticks, the other students in the room; he needed to be gone from them, to cross the wall, the fluorescent lights grown too bright, the ceiling sunk too low, its lines unpeeling, running through him as if his body occupied no space. His self (despite the fact that it, when skinned, parsed and set in wobbly view, did not exist) was shuddering. There was laughter in the room, too loud, and the magnified weave of a girl's wool sweater coming toward him (briefly, it was beautiful—how he could see every color, twined shades of brown, rust, green, blue, how he could *see)*, and then the arm swung away, and he was shuddering and shuddering and gone.

FIVE HOURS, IT WAS SUPPOSED to last, then back to ground control clutching the keys to the kingdom, only it didn't work that way for him, not once, not twice. (You *idiot*, his mother would say to him later, sympathetically, cruelly. Why take a chance like that? Why, for once in your life, did you decide you had to be like everyone else?) After the first trip, he'd woken on a floor, groped his way to his apartment and slept for two days. This second time, someone got him to the college infirmary. He awoke to learn that they'd prescribed him a supposed antidote to the acid that made his entire body break out with a rash like poison ivy. He didn't mind, even, the itchiness on his arms, the sight of the welts rising up, how distracting it was and how familiar, and he could look at the arm and think *arm*, could feel the itch and think *itch*. He was grateful to be in a hard, high bed under a white sheet, tucked in so tightly his legs were pinned.

"*W'll it turnit 'round*?" he asked the nurse bent near his bed, surprising himself with both the slurred quality of his own voice and the phrase itself, old-fashioned, as if out of his grandmother's mouth (and Charlie as a boy, distraught over something—a broken bike, a wounded bird, his mother in a rage because he'd bombed a test or built a bomb—and Gaga, always calm: "Don't worry, Charlie, we'll turn it around").

The nurse looked over the expanse of bed. "What you asking me about?"

Her skin was light brown, her accent lilting, reminding him of Belle, his Haitian nanny for a time (she had married a postman, moved to Queens, sent his family annual Christmas cards of three scrubbed, clear-eyed sons in light blue suits and dark blue ties).

"What they gave me—" He lifted an arm, displayed the rash. "Willit make it go away, whah-I . . ." He shook his head. His tongue was pickled, floating in a jar of brine.

Damn fool thing to do, Belle would have said. Throwing away your future. Wasting your fancy education. She'd been strict with them but also kind. She had believed in both Jesus Christ and voodoo, and in the power of Special Milk to put a child to sleep (it worked).

"Might." The nurse took his chart from the end of the bed, glanced at it and put it back. "Sometimes it helps. Won't nothin' turn it around for sure, save for you and your Maker."

"I don't believe in a Maker."

Charlie was expecting a lecture, wanting one even—to be chastised like a child, set on a path—but instead the nurse turned toward the sink, washed her hands and dried them briskly with a paper towel. He tried to speak, but his jaw was trembling, his hands shaking. It was not over— once again, it did not seem to be—and as it started up again, the mind withdrawing, the body bucking (he kicked off the sheets, drew up his knees, grabbed hold), he had his first real glimpse of how far this day would stretch into his future, even as it looped insistently into the past.

"Easy, child." From some unseen place, the nurse produced a brown paper lunch bag and held it open to his mouth. "Breathe."

Not until then did he notice that there was a person in the bed to the left of him, and another in the bed to the right, both watching him with open interest. He ducked his head away from the bag. Was the nurse trying to suffocate him? He was—would be, intermittently, for the rest of his life—jumpy. Do not touch me without warning. Do not send me to closed spaces. By then her hand was on the nape of his neck, half forcing, half guiding him.

"In and out," she said. "That's it. Slow down. Go nice and slow."

He inhaled into the bag and felt his own breath come at him, dark, papery and sour. He jerked his head away; she brought it back.

"Breathe in," she said. "Breathe out."

LATER, IN A SMALL OFFICE down the hall from the room where he'd woken, a doctor called his parents in New Jersey and handed him the phone. First, his mother's anger, shrill enough that Charlie held the handset away from his ear while the doctor shuffled paperwork on his desk. Really, really stupid, I mean *asinine*, his mother said, and then (how fast her mind moved, skittering from room to room, slamming, opening doors along the way), but we're willing to forget about it, we won't tell anyone, just get yourself out of the infirmary, put this behind you . . . come home for a few days to find your balance . . . don't fester . . . worst thing you could do for yourself . . . bad element . . . think about transferring, I'll make some calls . . . Columbia . . . Astonishing lack of judgment.

At one point Charlie put the receiver down on the doctor's desk, but the doctor, smiling slightly, gave it back.

"If you won't come here, we're coming there," his mother said finally after he refused a plane ticket home.

"Don't," blurted Charlie. "You'd only make things worse."

HE STAYED AT THE COLLEGE infirmary for two nights, hardly the only drug-addled student there, and then there were the ones who'd been tear-gassed by police or had burned their arms in protest, and a few vets, and a clean-cut, anachronistic girl—she might have been his mother or Dossy twenty-five years ago—with a velvet headband and Peter Pan collar and a petite sprained ankle up on ice.

When he left the infirmary, he started going to classes again and felt, toward his piles of books and lecturing professors and—especially— the algorithms in his calculus class, something new, strange and deeply grateful, akin to love. He could, he realized as the weeks wore on, appear almost entirely normal to the outside world, especially since that world hardly noticed him at all. Sometimes, in the middle of class, the floor would fall out from beneath him. Other times, as he walked along the sidewalk, a panic attack would overtake him, his legs losing any but the most formal relationship to his body. Eventually, the attack would pass. He'd feel fine, almost totally fine, except for two things: the constant press of knowledge that another attack lay in waiting, and the fear that he'd forever lost his sense of self and, with it, all ability to feel a part of the outside world. Only one thing he had left—his mind, his thinking power (his mother thought him a genius, and while Charlie had tried for years to escape her definitions, he'd also secretly come to think of himself as, if not a genius, then at least extremely smart). Now the world was a movie that he, bloodless and implacable, was watching. A few times he tried to go to an actual movie. On the screen, a man struck down by gunshot, a car chase, a funeral, a garden in Italy, a couple having sex. Or a baby had died, its mother-actress pretending to be hysterical with grief. Charlie watched himself watching, moved only by his inability to be moved.

His parents never came to Cleveland. The Midwest wasn't on their map, nor was a son in his particular condition. They sent money, called with names of prominent doctors (could any doctor in Ohio really be prominent in their eyes?). His father wrote letters detailing financial and practical arrangements and ending, always, with *I hope you feel better. Love, Dad. We've had five days of rain here when I'd so prefer snow,* his mother wrote in her oddly girlish hand, like a pen pal from a foreign country. And, in the same round handwriting, in the same letter: *Is it over yet? It must be over by now, promise me, you'll never do it again! I won't do it again,* he wrote a few days later, easy enough to say since it was true. Days would pass before he managed to put a stamp on the letter (his mother sent the stamps and envelopes), days again before he found a mailbox and dropped the letter in. For a few seconds he'd stand there, envying the letter's passage, terror-struck at having let it go.

On the phone, sometimes, if his mother caught him at the wrong moment, he was more honest: I can't explain it, Mom, okay? I'm pretty messed up still, but I can't really explain. His siblings still called her Mummy, but he'd stopped once he'd realized how out-of-step it was, how high-WASP. He said tom*ay*to now, and *fridge* instead of icebox. He told people he was from Massachusetts, not New Jersey, but left out the part about the summer house. Now and then, his mother reiterated that they would visit or told him to come home when school got out. "I feel sure you'll soon be yourself!" she'd say. And, "What dreadful times we live in!" And once, with surprising candor and sympathy, "You remind me of myself after I found out my brother died. There was no language for it, not even in my most inward thoughts. For months I didn't even keep my diary. It was the most alone I've ever been."

Briefly, then, he saw how selfish he was, for he'd suffered no untimely loss (though his grandfather's death the year before had felt like one); he'd lost only, through his own stupidity, his Self. He might have said he was sorry then, but for what—the death of his mother's brother years before he was born? For bearing his uncle's name (hardly his own choice) and being, like him, a blue-eyed firstborn son, but lacking his mother's brother's upbeat, charismatic nature, along with—so far, anyway—his tragic fate? For the fact that he'd turned his own mind to cottage cheese while boys his age, boys he could have been but for flukes of birth and circumstance, were coming home in body bags? He *was* sorry, for all of it, but his mother would take any apology wrong, twist it her way: I'm sorry for being a disappointment, for not going to Harvard or not becoming a war hero like your brother, though by now, she, like most everyone else he knew, thought this war—this *conflict*—was a mistake (still, she did enjoy her heroes, until they let her down).

Instead he said nothing. His breath was speeding up, the sweats starting. His mother's brother Charlie had jumped from the plane he was copiloting on his twenty-fourth combat mission. They'd been on their way to bomb some railway lines, having recklessly set off without the normal fighter escort, and were attacked before they hit the target. Charlie— a family myth by now, an Icarus—had done a swan dive from the plane. His parachute had opened. He had unwrapped a hard candy and put it in his mouth before an enemy gunman broke the rules of engagement and shot him down. Everyone else in the family seemed to find the detail of the hard candy reassuring, even whimsical—for how it showed the young man's spirit of adventure, his calm in the face of danger, his *joie de vivre* until the very end. Didn't anyone see how bizarre it was that the Italian priest who came across the body had pried open the dead boy's mouth and rummaged for a peppermint half-sucked? Or that in the priest's flowery letter to Gaga and Grampa, he'd lamented the poverty of his village church, so that his missive was, among other things, a plea for money (duly sent) to a family that he'd deduced, from a corpse's uniform and gold wristwatch, to be of means? And the letter, along with another from the copilot, coming years after the death, and the hard candy like a pill, diminishing in size, enlarging in effect, and the soldier (brother, uncle, son) with Charlie's name, one war joining with another except that back then it was all patriotism, victory gardens, joining up, and now it was all slash and burn and duck and hide and shout and spew.

The psych ward at the university-affiliated hospital was not a bad place to spend the night when the panic attacks came on. People were nice there—the nurses, especially. Especially the pretty ones. No one made you talk. He was not the first in his family to check into such a place. His aunt Dossy had stayed at a more upscale one, Four Winds, for more than a year when Holly was ten, and had gone back for shorter stays since then. Dossy has hepatitis, they used to tell the children, or Dossy is resting, the place both peaceful and disturbing in Charlie's memory (his mother took them to visit a few times), long, green lawns, birds in cages, giant jigsaw puzzles, distant screams, his sweet, drugged aunt turning to him—Charlie!—as if it were was a happy coincidence that she'd chanced upon him on this other planet, far from home.

By day, now, he still sometimes went to classes—because they distracted him, and because it turned out that away from the masters at St. Marks and the trembling eye and ego of his mother, he loved to study and learn. He loved, he discovered, Ancient Greek, and physics, and poetry, especially Wallace Stevens:

> She sang beyond the genius of the sea.
> The water never formed to mind or voice,
> Like a body wholly body, fluttering
> Its empty sleeves; and yet its mimic motion
> Made constant cry, caused constantly a cry,

That was not ours although we understood,
Inhuman, of the veritable ocean. . . .

From the outside, he knew it might seem peculiar that he could attend class, do his homework and spend every third night or so in the loony bin. But these were not normal times. There was a war going on. His friends and cousins had not been drafted, hiding out at their Ivy League schools, but in the current climate they had still learned, faster than seemed possible, to flick a switch: Carry a protest sign, fuck your girlfriend, take your exam, eat your dinner, smoke some grass, watch the splotch and splatter on the evening news (*Hell no, we won't go*). His split was just a little different: Panic attacks and hospital versus beige desks, round clocks and the lucid, gearlike workings of the mind. The psych ward let him come and go, as long as there was an open bed. One night, when he showed up to find the place full, an Irish nurse with a soft spot for him set up a cot in the linen closet, where Charlie slept beautifully, starched and clean.

His family was all on the East Coast. He needed the distance and hated it, missed his mother and hated her. He missed, most of all, Ashaunt. All winter, landlocked in Ohio, he dreamed of it.

In spring the lottery was drawn, and he lucked out, his number 218, though the loony bin might have been enough. Then in May, the shootings at Kent State, just a few miles down the road. At his own college, classes became teach-ins, finals were canceled, grades turned to pass/fail. Charlie carried a few signs, marched in some demonstrations. Everyone was chanting so he chanted too, but in a thin voice from a distant land piled with jammed machinery: *Onetwothreefourwedontwantyourfuckingwar.* He did not decide to drop out of his college, any more than he had decided, in a way involving all his faculties, to attend. One sticky, humid midwestern morning, he hauled his mattress and milk crates to the curb, flushed all his medication except the Valium down the toilet and left the key in an empty Navane bottle (before, he'd had a beautiful sense of humor, and it still struggled, cockeyed, to emerge). Outside, he left a stack of books next to a sleeping homeless man, stuffed a garbage bag of clothes and his grandfather's lamp into his car, felt in his pocket for the Valium. Drove east.

IT WAS MID-MAY WHEN HE got there, Ashaunt empty except for the Ballards, who farmed the land at the foot of it, and the occasional squadron of cleaners, mowers or gardeners, and Joe Olivera, the caretaker (the summer before, he and Charlie had gone fishing, Joe's son and stepson both in Vietnam), who was turning on the water in the houses, painting the gate, launching the Whalers and Beetle Cats. Charlie's parents had wanted him home in Bernardsville, and his cousin Holly had invited him to crash in the living room of her Cambridge apartment, and Dr. Miller had suggested that he stay in Cleveland for their sessions, then said (so kindly, in words that would stay with him for the rest of his life) that these past few months had been the hardest Charlie would ever know and life would only get better from here. He drove barefoot for some twelve hours in his VW, the windows open, his eyes on the horizon. When he got to Padanaram, the Village Market had just opened and he said hello to Rich, stocked up on food and cigarettes and drove on, over the bridge across the harbor, down Gooseneck Road, past Salvador's until the road dead-ended at the two points with their gates and Private signs: Windy Point, with its tightly clustered houses, other people's; Ashaunt Point, his.

If it was not peace he felt as he parked in front of the Red House and got out of the car, if it was not a settling, a solace, then it was the closest thing he'd come to peace since the night the drugs had pithed his mind. It was early afternoon and foggy, and the lawn smelled of wild thyme and his stone wall was just where he'd built it, hauling the rocks up from the beach in a wheelbarrow, and around back, the shadbush was in bloom and the honeysuckle rising in greening, acquisitive humps, and beyond it all, the sea. And as Charlie stood barefoot before it all, among it all, he could finally feel (if it was not a solution, might it be a start?) the ground beneath his feet.

II

I N A WORLD both rattled by and rattling with change, what had changed in Forfar? Not much. If anything, the town seemed quieter, more tucked into the past, than it had been on Bea's last visit eighteen years prior. She took great pleasure in seeing it again: the stone buildings squared with the sidewalks; the Green where laundry still hung, though a self-serve Laundromat had opened on High Street and Pearl Laundry had closed, council housing gone up in its place. Still, look (Bea pointed ahead, but she might have pointed anywhere): the same bridie pastries lined up in the tea shop window, the same sewing notions store where her mum used to take her on her birthday for a cross-stitch kit. A charity shop had taken over the spot where a beauty shop used to be, and there was graffiti on some walls, and several shuttered factories, and a few long-haired hippie boys, but not near as many as in America. Forfar was still civilized; people took pride. Shopkeepers wet and swept their bit of sidewalk. Schoolgirls wore their blue skirts and ironed blouses, toting satchels, and the boys in blue britches, chalky-kneed. And Castle Hill. Shall we go up? Agnes asked, but of course they should—even being there together felt as if it had always been this way, both knowing about the key, both knowing how to get around. At the chemist's, they borrowed the key. On top of the hill, the patch of grass was smaller than before, a chips wrapper caught in a bush. Still, you could see over the rooftops to the edge of town and beyond, the same hills, the sheep and lambs, Bea's favorite time of year, though she had forgotten about the rain, which came often and without warning. Even this she welcomed, raising her face to it, struck, suddenly, by how far they were from the sea, which they'd seen appear and disappear from the plane, Caroline gripping her hand each time they hit an air pocket, *speed bonnie boat like a bird on the wing* (Bea had hummed the girl through the turbulence) *over the sea to Skye.*

Louisa and Caroline were both fifteen, one girl (Jane's) sunny and open, the other (guess whose?) edgier and sensitive, quite unlike the placid baby she'd been when Bea had cared for her in Grace Park while Helen, having birthed her, abandoned her for Japan. Mrs. P. liked to take her grandchildren places, show them the world, especially the girls, especially now that Mr. P. was gone and she was "free" (but why keep *saying* it?). Janie had agreed to Louisa's coming on the trip right away. Helen, forever jealous of Bea's bond with Caroline, had hemmed and hawed but said yes in the end. Bea and Agnes had been presented with the trip by Mrs. P: Ladies, how would you like to go to Scotland in June, after Louisa and Caroline get out of school? It wouldn't have occurred to them to say no, any more than it would have occurred to them—though they had, by now, sufficient funds and leisure time—to plan such a trip themselves. They would all stay in Glasgow for five nights, said Mrs. P., then split up, with Bea and Agnes taking the train to Forfar and Mrs. P. and the girls going to the Isle of Skye to stay with Suky, Charlie's wartime widow, who had married and divorced an Englishman but remained living in London, with a holiday cottage in Skye.

Whether Bea and Agnes were intended to be chaperones, guests or guides was not entirely clear. Tell me the name of a hotel in Forfar so Stewart can make a reservation, Mrs. P. had said, and Agnes had said, Well, there's the Royal Hotel, but it's a bit on the steep— One room or two? asked Mrs. P. One, Agnes said. I used to iron their linens, Bea said. Me and my mum. Mrs. P. looked at her a little queerly, then. Did you, Bea? Would you rather stay somewhere else? Bea had paused, considering. The linens had been delivered by carriage from Pearl Laundry to the Royal, so she had rarely been there; still she could picture the whole thing—red lobby, pale blue bedrooms, white tea room with gold trim. And the boxes in the goods yard marked ROYAL FRAGILE ROYAL, and her father recounting the famous people who'd come through—the La-Dee-Das, he'd called them, or the Hoity-Toits—business tycoons and Brazilian horse traders and Parliament men. We could stay there, she said finally. Agnes had guffawed: Oh, could we, Missy? Oh yes we could! Won't we be coming back in style?

In Glasgow, they went to the People's Palace, wandered through the university, had dinner in an Indian restaurant where the waiters all wore kilts, walked until their feet swelled, Mrs. P. consulting the guidebook, Caroline stopping to pet every dog she saw, Louisa to look in shops and at her own reflection in shop windows. Bea had a hard time concentrating amid the crowds and traffic, worried that the girls would get lost or wander off—that was part of it—but also she was already on the train, heading into the green, except that when they went to purchase tickets they learned the train had been canceled, or not just canceled, there *was* no train, not anymore, not to Forfar. No trains? Line shut down, said the man behind the ticket window. Permanent closure. How can that be? Bea asked illogically over Mrs. P.'s shoulder. The man looked up from his ledger and caught her eye; he seemed oddly familiar, like someone who might have worked in Goods with her father years ago. Town's gone, Missus, he said dryly. Canna have a town without a train. Then he winked and slid them the schedule for the coach.

Bea had been back only once before, in 1952, for her father's funeral— a grim and narrow-visioned little trip, as quick as she could make it, then on to Glasgow where Callum was still living then, with his wife, Kate, and their boy, Ian, an orphan they'd adopted after the war. As her father was lowered into the ground, she had steadied herself on her mother's gravestone and tried to divert toward her father's coffin a bit of the raw grief she still felt for her mother, long lying underneath. She'd stayed with her childhood friend Tilly's sister Laura, who had four children and tended, in a little home nursery, a brood more. Her father's service had been small, his coffin smaller, as if it held a boy or a dwarf. Afterward Bea had ordered a new, shared headstone for him and her mother, black polished granite of the highest quality, but it was only on this second trip, Agnes at her side, that she actually saw the stone and found, on top of it, a bouquet of faded plastic flowers, which she replaced the next day with a dozen fresh roses, and then, the day before they left, with six more fresh roses and a new, bright clutch of plastic flowers, so well made as to appear quite lifelike and guaranteed on the label not to fade.

As opposed to in Glasgow, she and Agnes did very little in Forfar—walked around a bit but mostly sat in tea shops, visited with people—Laura, Agnes's sister Beth, Joe the Chemist, who must have been ninety but was still often behind the counter and greeted her—Hullo, Bea—as if no time had passed. She spent time with Callum, who, a pensioner now, had moved back to escape the Glasgow rents and crowds. On the street, several people recognized her, and one woman even recognized Agnes, being from the same nearby village. A comment might follow—*America suit you? Done well for yourselves, have you? I've got a son gone off to Philadelphia*—or just a nod of hello and the feel of eyes on their backs as they walked on. Have we aged much? In the hotel room, Agnes wondered it aloud. Not to be vain, she said, but compared to Laura (big as a house), compared to Beth (gone hunchbacked), they'd fared well. It was not having children that preserved the body, Agnes said, that and the kind of life they'd led. They seemed to be shifting into something else here—belonging and yet novel. Polished up. Improved. America felt very far away, and Bea could not quite remember her part.

On their next to last day, Agnes's sister's son drove them all out to Eassie, where Agnes was from, knob-kneed lambies everywhere, and the ruined churchyard with its skull and crossbones, and across from it, the tidy cemetery with Agnes's parents' graves, and down the lane, there, the house where Agnes had grown up, trikes now in its front yard and a mean dog on a chain. On the way they'd passed through Padanaram, which had the same name as the village where Ashaunt was, and Agnes's sister took a photograph of Bea and Agnes, arms linked, beneath the sign. Bea liked the look of Agnes's childhood house—it reminded her of Glamis and her grandparents—but Agnes was quiet and later told Bea she'd rather not have gone. *It gave me a peculiar feeling,* she said. *To think we've never been to Skye—now that would have been a holiday!*

Agnes fell asleep quickly that night, while Bea lay awake in the Royal with its fine-pressed linens, nibbling on shortbread from the tartan tin between the beds, feeling oddly young, as if she and Agnes were two girls from another walk of life, the sort who regularly slept in a place like this. Agnes was snoring lightly, holding her pillow in her arms. *We're home,* Bea thought, trying it out, but it wasn't quite right. The flat she'd grown up in was a world away; her parents were dead. Home was Agnes and the Porters, Grace Park, Janie, Ashaunt. Still. A plate put before her. Callum raising a glass to her coming "home." He was good and kind, pale and wide in the face, just as he'd been as a boy. He managed well with one leg and had a pension from the office job he'd landed after the war. He was not a drunk or sullen—he'd come round—and she felt it was in some small part because she'd helped raise him. No one inquired as to why she or Agnes had not married nor how much money they had, which was a lot by Forfar standards; they'd saved a good bit, and Mr. P. had spun it into more. *You've got a new accent,* Laura remarked, *and you've become a bit of a looker!* Bea could see herself that what had been plainness in her youth had become a quiet prettiness, not beauty (she could do to lose some pounds), but her skin was unusually clear and smooth for her age, her hair still mostly chestnut brown, and her weight had settled into something less than plump. Each evening, they came back to made beds, more shortbread in the tin, laundered and pressed clothes. They had brought gifts—perfume and soaps for the women, fine-cut Virginia tobacco for the men, newly minted 1970 silver dollars for Agnes's grandniece and nephews and Laura's grandchildren.

Their last night in Forfar, Bea went for supper at Callum and Kate's, along with her nephew Ian and his wife Marcy, who were expecting their first child. Halfway through the meal, Bea—for the first time in her life, she thought—found herself moved to make a toast: "To my new grand-niece or -nephew!" And then, to her own surprise again, "I'm starting up a little education fund for the baby."

They stopped eating to stare. She swallowed hard. "Unless you'd rather—"

"No," said Marcy, who was a grammar school teacher, though she would give up working after her second child was born a few years later. "That's lovely, Bea. Spectacular. Thank you!"

"I'm making it a wee cot," said Callum. "If I don't chop off my finger in the process."

"Spoiled brat already, isn't he?" Ian said. "I'm making him a set of working papers."

"Could we let the baby be born first?" said Kate. "No use tempting fate."

"Oh, he's kicking," said Marcy. "He hears you!"

"Or she," Bea said.

"Have you become one of them feminists?" Callum asked her.

"Certainly not! It's just, we don't know what it is. It might just as easily"—she could not help hoping—"be a girl."

Kate got up to place her hand on the slope of her daughter-in-law's dress, and then Marcy said, "Bea, would you like to—" and Bea placed her hand there too (again a first for her, to touch a woman with child) just for a second, surprised by how hard and firm the mound felt, and then there it was, a sort of tap, a finger-flick against her palm.

"Oh Lord," she said softly.

After dinner, she rose to clear the plates, but Kate stopped her: Dinner in your honor, your last night, sit. Then, with Kate and Marcy in the kitchen and Ian on a side bench, head in the newspaper, it was just she and Callum left at the round table that had been their parents'. "Short trip, eh," Callum said. "Aye," said Bea. "Too short." Agnes was with her sister that evening. She and Bea had agreed to meet at the hotel by nine to pack and be ready for the morning coach to Glasgow, but now the clock struck quarter past and Bea, never tardy, could not get herself to move.

"I've half a mind to come to America with you," said Callum. "To see that house and ride those horses, if they'd let a lame duck like me on."

"What horses?"

"You know, in the picture you sent."

"No. What picture?"

"Of you, planted on a horse."

"Me—on a horse? I never—"

"Hold on." Callum clomped off and came back a few minutes later with a photograph of Bea in britches on one horse and (Helen's) Charlie on another. Dolly—that was Charlie's horse; suddenly the name returned to her. How the boy had loved that animal, his hands in the photo wrapped in her mane, his eyes joyful (he'd been, early on, a merry, open child, and his hair was nicely cropped so you could see his eyes). On the other, taller horse, Bea sat upright, laughing at something. A shadow was cast across the bottom part of the picture, and she could tell from the angle of the image and the shadow's shape that it was Mr. P. who had taken the photograph from his chair.

"It seemed unlike you," Callum said.

"I had a few adventures. What do you call a pony with a sore throat?"

"A little hoarse," said Callum.

"You know it?" It was the only joke she could remember, and it always got a laugh. "From where?"

"You. Your memory's gone a bit soggy, has it? You put it in a letter once."

Outside, the church clock sounded. Bea turned toward the solemn sound, listening through to the tenth and final strike. "I should go. Agnes will worry."

"Funny to go all the way to America," Callum said, "to find yourself a Scots wife."

"Oh, let her be, Callum!" Kate called from the kitchen. "Forever the pesky little brother!"

Then, ignoring Bea's protests, they all got ready—Ian, Kate, Marcy with her big belly, Callum with his peg leg—to walk her through the night to the hotel.

III

HIS PLAN MIGHT have worked, Charlie would later think. It might have functioned as a sort of self-prescribed rest cure, hibernation, meditation, were it not for several fucked-up forces bigger than himself. If he could only have had, as he did for a time, the place to himself, with a friend or two visiting occasionally and his cousins doing their own thing but essentially leaving him alone, even his parents coming now and then, long enough to say hello good-bye. Mostly, though, the days in their solitude, camera in hand, a diet of pasta and brown rice, beach peas, lamb's-quarters and sorrel, and now and then a sea bass he caught or was given by one of the men who came to fish off Gaga's dock, or tuna from Giffords Market, and when he needed it, a Valium, though he hoarded his stash, taking a nibble at a time. He read when he could concentrate and when the print did not morph before his eyes. He took cold outdoor showers behind the Big House (the house more or less empty until August, when Gaga would arrive with entourage), every morning at six. He ran. From the end of the Point to the gate was almost two miles, then two miles back, and he took paths too, and sometimes Little River Road across the marshes, where a snowy egret often stood in the shallows, and if the bird stayed frozen, good luck, and if it took off, bad. Five miles or more every morning, barefoot and bare-chested, no matter the weather. Running and running until his blood filled his temples, bathed his brain. Then blood, just blood and bone.

He slept in the cabin in the low woods between the Big House and the Red House, constructed as a playhouse for him and Will when they were younger, with two built-in beds and paned windows, and he bought a double-burner hot plate at Mars and a dorm fridge at a church sale and did not trim the path that ran down to the cabin, but kept it overgrown and tangled. Involuted. *Hallucinogen Persisting Perception Disorder/ Depersonalization Disorder/Involuted Depression??* he'd seen on his hospital chart, and later had looked up the word involuted: 1. complicated or intricate 2. having petals or leaves that roll inward at the edges 3. used to describe a shell whose axis is hidden by tight whorls.

"I have a vaginal depression," he'd told Rusty one night on the phone, and Rusty had snorted with laughter and said, "Yeah, you and the *Bearded Clam*" (the motorboat they shared with Will, christened by Rusty. Charlie—so young and virginal for nineteen, so old and wracked— wouldn't learn for a few more years that the boat's name meant *twat*).

How was it, he would later wonder, that during all those weeks spent wandering the end of the Point, he didn't notice the surveyor tags? For days on end he must have walked right by them in a kind of necessary blindness, seeing stones and plants and sky and bones, but never this. And so to find out about the land being for sale over drinks in the Red House living room on Memorial Day weekend, as his mother perched on one couch, and his father made gin and tonics, and his relatives wandered in and out, Jane's baby a round, staring lump except when Charlie bent down and handed her a cracker and then she howled and his mother said, If you'd just cut your hair, Charlie—you're terrifying—you have no idea! And Jane said, No, she's just exhausted, she skipped her nap.

Charlie started to leave then, back to the cabin, away from them all, the din and shrill, but his father put a hand on his arm and said, Stay a leetle, and so he did, lifting a Triscuit to his mouth, mock-boxing, even, with Percy, though his brain was in a shudder, *You have no idea.* He had, off and on, been looking forward to his family coming, but now that they were here he wished them gone. They all looked so familiar, so thoroughly themselves, and at the same time so much like someone else's family: cheerful, winter-pale, abuzz with energy and talk, except for Caroline, who at fifteen, was hunched in the corner with a book. They discussed the Cambodian invasion one minute, the dock the next, and how a tree limb had fallen on the roof of the maids' wing at the Big House—has anyone told Gaga yet?—and how the renters coming in July had no teen-agers, thank god, things were out of control (this, predictably, from his mother)—in the country, the world, the government, the social fabric, everything (her glasses slipping down her nose) falling apart.

"Like this couch. This couch is shot," Will said.

It was worn, soft corduroy, faded red. They'd had it for years; they would keep it for years.

"I love that couch," said his mother.

And for once, Charlie agreed. "I love it too," he said.

IT WAS IN THE MIDDLE of such chatter that someone brought up Dick Wilson and the land. Charlie wasn't paying close attention. He was pic-turing them all as skeletons; he was remembering his pee that morning after his run, how it had come out the color of Coca-Cola, a dark red-brown—should he tell his father or just let it go, for it had seemed, as he'd watched it arc into the bushes, a sort of purging, a purification, *appropri-ate*, even as he'd had a jolt of fear. By the time he tuned in, they were in full swing: three house lots, maybe more, a new road being cut, planning board meetings, and was one of the developers really from Japan, and was it true that the elder Wilsons were getting divorced, and if they didn't want the land, why wouldn't they just pass it on to their children? The land and house had been, before the army took it, in the Wilson family since 1882, but the first time the army shot all its guns at once, every win-dow in the Point House had shattered, and then the radar caved the floors in and the army bulldozed the house, and when the Wilsons returned after the war, they settled on another parcel of their land midway down the Point, where they built a new house next to their old playhouse, which was put on a flatbed truck and moved, like a parade float, down the road.

"Three modest houses might be better than one monstrous one," his mother said.

"What are you *talking* about!" Charlie cried out, and for a moment, everyone was silent, remembering, he and they both, what they all knew—the drugs, the hospital no one would mention out of tact or fear or both. Remembering too how Charlie was, had always been, the wildest of his generation of summer children, burrs in his hair, chokecherry juice on his limbs, and how the end of the Point had been his favorite part because the most untamed, and also rightfully (if you believed in the ownership of land; he both did and did not) half theirs. Throughout his childhood, as new houses went up along the road, as suburbia built and trimmed and mowed (here, in New Jersey, everywhere), the base lived in an opposite cycle—its buildings decaying, bushes and trees growing up from cracks in the road.

Just six years earlier, Gaga and Grampa, together with their old friends the Wilsons, had bought the land back from the army, with the fourteen acres adjacent to the Big House, Red House and Portable going to the Porters, and the twelve acres of the choicest part, the tip, to the Wilsons, since it had been theirs before the war. A hotel outfit from New Bedford had shown up at the public auction; so had—everyone was sure of it—a Mafia man looking for a hideout, who gave up $5,000 before the Porter-Wilson limit. At the time, the purchase, $125,000 for the twenty-six acres, had seemed a cooperative and rightful reclamation: the Porters would hold on to their piece for future generations, and the Wilsons would rebuild on the site of their old house. One house, only, they would build, something in scale, modeled after the not un-grand but quite proportionate and lovely gabled house the army had blown up. Because it was the Wilsons, they would welcome other Point families onto their land, which had become, in the years since the army left, a rough playground filled with weeds and wind and souvenirs of war, occupied almost entirely by the kids. Or perhaps (Charlie had hoped for this) the Wilson clan, busy procreating or divorcing or making money in the city or relaxing in their perfectly fine house down the road, would put it off and put it off until the land reclaimed what was left of the base, and the Wilsons let it go, they let it be.

"Dick Wilson," Jane's husband, Paul, said slowly. "He—you didn't hear about this, Charlie? I thought they'd been showing the property. Dick decided he wasn't going to rebuild there. They had an engineer come in, and it turns out they can't get rid of the army casemate—it's eighteen feet high and ten feet thick, too big to blow up or knock down, so they'd be stuck trying to build on top of it." He shook his head. "They'd never get back that chestnut of a house. I guess Dick needs—"

"*Paul.*" Helen hissed his name. "That's enough. He's not—"

And then she was beside Charlie, hand gripping his shoulder, and he had an infantile desire to sink down and wrap his arms around her waist, even as he wanted to shrug off her hand and hear the rest.

"Dick needs what?" he asked.

Dick Wilson was president of a company that put more breakfast cereals on America's tables than all the other cereal companies combined. Snap, Crackle, and Pop, the boys liked to call the Wilson grandsons, though there were, inconveniently, more than three. Originally, in the 1800s, the Wilsons had bought up the whole Point from the Cooks, a farm family grown tired of battling its rocky soil and exposed fields. Slowly, the Wilsons' friends from New York and New Jersey followed them: the Porters, the Stricklands, the Platts—just five summer houses, for a time, and even now, as the generations multiplied and barns and barracks were converted to cottages and smaller houses went up behind the old ones, not more than twelve. Dick's eldest grandson, Little Dick, was Percy's age and one of his best friends.

"Dick needs the money," said Paul. Big Dick Wilson was his uncle, his mother's half brother. "Listen, we tried. Jane—" He looked at his wife, but she shook her head.

"Nobody's happy about this, Charlie," said his mother. She had sat back down on the red couch and was jiggling her leg. She was no longer—mysteriously, mercurially—on his side. She picked up an old copy of the *New Yorker* and began to leaf through. "You're not the only one."

"Why doesn't Gaga buy it?" asked Caroline, looking up from her book, and Charlie felt a momentary rise of hope.

"The taxes alone would be too much," their mother said almost savagely. "You children have no idea! One of these days, this place will do us in. You'll see."

And Gaga a widow now. And the future unpredictable. And times are changing, and we should be grateful for what we have. Who spoke? Some of them? All? *The times they are a . . .* One of the cousins started to whistle it, and another joined in. Charlie sat down on the edge of the coffee table; he was sinking, flying, all of them against him, carefree, heedless, except for Caroline, who was stony-faced, reading or pretending to read. Jane's baby, Maddie, began crying again, and as her voice rose above the talk, suddenly Charlie saw, in a flash of memory he hadn't known he had, the location of several surveyor tags: one on a stake to the left of Hollow Hill, another tied around a cedar tree near the shore, a third to the right of the army gate.

WHEN HE LEFT THE HOUSE, no one called after him, nor did anyone ask or require him to stay. Outside, the mosquitoes found him quickly, but he hardly noticed. On the base, he came upon the first surveyor tag, ripped it off and stuffed it in his pocket, found the second tag, the third, then more. He circled the place, untying, pocketing. Somebody's idea of progress, was it? Big Dick Wilson's? Like most of the husbands who came to the Point on weekends and for part of August, Dick Wilson looked jovial, casual, a man who liked to sail and amble, wore shorts the color of tomato bisque and napped on his porch with the *Wall Street Journal* spread over his face. But follow these men to work and who were they? They were law school deans, research physicians, CEOs, top attorneys. They were members of Harvard's Porcellian Club, men whom the communal Hog Farmers at Woodstock would, with one red-rimmed, appraising glance, have marked Establishment Capitalist Pigs. On the Point, Dick Wilson (who had not yet retired at seventy-nine) grew heirloom tomatoes and pale yellow raspberries, which he presented with a flourish to the ladies and the little girls. He told slightly off-color jokes. He often swam, as did Gaga, in the nude. At the luncheon after Grampa's funeral last February, he stood up to speak, then sank back down, broad shoulders heaving in his dark blue suit, his bald head catching the light.

The surveyor tags were everywhere, proprietary, like dog piss aimed, sprayed and laying claim. Some were half hidden by the brush, others in full view. Charlie had seen them around before, but not knowing their purpose, hadn't paid them much attention; now, he saw only tags. After he had found them all, he picked up two stones the size of his fists and went to the barracks. Others—his cousins and friends, and the local kids off-season—had come here over the years to smash windows, leaving only a few panes intact. Charlie had gone along with it a couple of times, tossed a stone or two, but until this summer he'd never been a smasher or breaker (*having petals or leaves that roll inward at the edges*); a gentler soul, he, his eyes the bruised blue of overripe blueberries, the lashes so long he'd been told they'd been wasted on a boy. Now, inside the barracks, he threw the first rock high up and watched it sail cleanly through the top pane of a window, above a row of urinals. The glass shattered outward; still his hand flew to protect his eyes. Then the next throw, in the bunkroom, at an already-cracked window. He found another rock and threw it at a solid wall, which lobbed it back. He ducked.

For a few moments, he felt it then: the razor edge of anger, the relieving point of contact: rock to window, rock to wall. And then a pinging sound as he hurled a chunk of broken brick at a metal bed frame and picked it up and threw again, until he saw a human being in the bed, the body of a soldier sleeping, dead or dying or rising, coming at him, out to kill.

And that was when the anger left, replaced by a panic attack the likes of which he'd not had since he'd left Cleveland. He dropped the rocks, knelt on the floor, his fingers scrabbling in his pocket for the Valium. He downed a pill, found his pulse on his wrist and began to count it (it went above 180 during these attacks). By now the sweats had started, his breath was ragged, the number line he used to keep himself on track was jumbling, buckling, no mathematics here, no scaffolding of any kind, just a pile of stones and limbs.

WHEN IT WAS OVER, HE vomited on the floor of the barracks and went outside and peed, a red stream again, though lighter than before. Then he stumbled down the path to the shore, where he pulled off his shorts and walked naked into the water. It was low tide, and the rocks scraped his shins; still he half crawled until the sea was deep enough to swim, and so he swam. The sun, a swollen ball, was setting over Barney's Joy. He shut his eyes, dove down, came up, felt a little better. From the Red House he could hear laughter, chatter, the party going on. He went underwater for as long as his breath would allow, then surfaced, eyes still closed. And down again, a beat longer, experimenting, but his lungs were strict masters, bellows. Thirsting for air, he came up to float on his back, eyes stinging from the salt.

The sky above him was the sky; it had been that way forever. The water too. The beach, no matter where you came upon it or who owned frontage, was open to Point residents, if not to members of the outside world. *Stop! Please Turn Around Here! Private Road, Ashaunt Point Association, Special Police Patrol*, read the sign by the gate at the foot of the Point, though a few years ago Charlie, Will and Rusty had nailed a replacement sign over it: "Stop! Please Take Clothes Off Here! Private Parts, Ashaunt

Point Nudist Colony, Naked Police Patrol." They'd gotten Percy and two of Jane's younger sons to jump out of the bushes and moon the cars and bikes.

Now Charlie made his way along the beach back to the cabin, shorts and boxers in hand, walking up the narrow path, climbing the rickety cabin stairs, sitting—finally—in his bed, where he took up a calculus problem he'd left undone the day before. Soon his hand grew steadier, and he solved one problem, then another. At the end of the bed his toes looked far away, but if he told them to wiggle they would wiggle, so he told them to wiggle and they did. His parents would not come look for him there, though after he got in his sleeping bag, Holly, arrived after dinner from Cambridge, would enter quietly and stand over him, wondering if she should wake him (through one slitted eye, he watched her watch), but deciding, finally, to let him be.

The next day was Memorial Day. On the road, which bisected the Point like flypaper and pulled him into conversation, someone would mention the other Charlie, who'd been only twenty-one when he died.

"He had more life in him than the rest of us put together," Dossy would say. "And endless reservoirs of charm."

"Like me?" Charlie would ask darkly, and they'd all laugh (ha ha), and then his mother and aunts would go down to the beach to remember their brother or say a prayer and come back tousled, seeming younger, secretive, their arms linked. Later that day, everyone would pile into cars and go, leaving Charlie with fifty dollars cash, enough leftovers for a week, a few Valium he'd swiped from his mother, and the place (which he could, with great, blindfolded effort, pretend was his own) until July.

IV

DAYS WITHOUT SPEAKING to a living soul. How do you do it? his mother kept asking. She called almost daily now that he was here (she hadn't called Cleveland more than once every few weeks). He answered every three days or so if he was in the Red House when the call came, but only if picking up the phone felt more tolerable than listening to it ring, or if his guilt or loneliness won out. "How do you go so long without conversation; it would make me positively frantic!" As was her way, she always turned things around to her: *her* psychoanalyst (Was she back in it again? He couldn't keep track) thought the one in Cleveland he recommended was among the best in the nation; *she'd* had panic attacks and yes they were god-awful; *she* believed ("But what do I know?" she'd add—and then go on) the way through was quite simple: top-notch medical care, intellectual stimulation and—more than anything else—structure.

Daddy could get you a lab assistant job, she'd say. Or you could garden for Gaga. Or she'd suggest he take up teaching. She taught high school and college sporadically, part-time, and often complained about how her students lacked curiosity and rigor, except for the rare ones she identified as prodigies; these she took home, offered books, complimented and talked to late into the night. Teaching, she told him, forces you outside yourself and makes you focus on ideas and other people. You could work with black children in Newark, or at that camp where you were a counselor. Oh, and by the way, the housing form for college arrived—Daddy forwarded it to you.

Obladi, oblada. Charlie twisted the curly black phone cord around his leg, up his arm, looping it into a noose around his neck and letting his eyes roll back, his jaw drop into a silent gag. Dead, they would find him. He'd picture his skeleton, the stripped-down, could-be-anybody shape of it, as beautiful as it was frightening:

Death is the mother of beauty, mystical
within whose burning bosom we devise
our earthly mothers waiting, sleeplessly.

What, his own yammering mother liked to ask, do you *do* out there all day, as if the place had not been, for years, her native habitat, and theirs together. When he was five, six, seven years old, she used to take him and Will out of school a month early and return them a few weeks late each fall. They'd stay the whole extended summer, days filling, emptying, filling, time meaningless because there was so much of it. Bedtimes slipped. Mealtimes. Baths. Nearly everything Charlie did back then was clever and amusing to his mother, but she also left him alone much of the time, let him be, and he had Will, Rusty, Holly, Little Dick, a few other kids; from house to house they moved, from path to path, or he'd go swimming with Grampa, both of them naked in the water, Charlie thrashing toward his grandfather—*Head up, kick kick, attaboy!* He had his fairy houses made from the wooden crates the plants came in and furnished with sticks, moss, shells, scraps of fishing net. Holly, Will, Rusty and he each had a fairy house, and for a long time he managed to escape knowing that in the outside world this would be viewed as a deep humiliation for a boy. Together, he and his mother counted the morning glories, put messages in bottles and set them out to sea. It was and would always be (Don't assume, said Dr. Miller. You're still very young) the happiest time of his life.

Obladi, oblada, life goes on. The phone cord could reach out the kitchen door onto the back stoop if you stretched, a dog on a leash, *just cut the cord.* And his mother in her study in New Jersey surrounded by her papers, by research projects she'd start with great gusto but rarely finish, or in the kitchen with a glass of Coke, and when she hung up, she'd call Dossy or Jane or Gaga or a friend; she talked on the phone to many people daily; she played tennis, read the newspaper, maybe gardened, squabbled with Caroline, wrote Percy and Will letters at camp, then complained that she wasn't getting enough work done and stayed up in her study (doing *what?*) until dawn.

What do you *do* out there all day? In fact he had all sorts of things to occupy his time. He'd finally told his father, a research cardiologist, about the blood in his urine, so there were drives to the New Bedford Hospital, where he peed into cups and had (in a moment of pain so excruciating it almost made him forget himself) a catheter inserted into his penis—and peed into more cups (they'd found some albumen, whatever that meant), and was forced to explain that his tremor was preexisting, drug-related and, as far as he knew, unrelated to the wine-dark color of his pee.

There were his showers and runs, the making of food, washing of dishes. He prepared all his meals in the cabin, bringing water down in jugs, heating it for dishwater. There was the digging of holes in the woods for his shit, and the shitting itself (at first, the water in the houses was off, and even after it was turned on, he rarely used a toilet). The beating off. The reading, first more Wallace Stevens, then *Anna Karenina*, then *The Andromeda Strain*; a renter had left it in the Red House the summer before, along with *On Death and Dying*, which he could live without. Sometimes he'd take a copy of his great-grandmother's *How to Know the Wildflowers* or *Plants and Their Children* out to the base with him. She'd died when he was two so he'd never known her, but he liked her books, as much for their stores of information as for their bits of poetry (*a battalion of milky-tufted seeds from the cracked pod of the milkweed float downward and take lazy possession of the soil*). On the base, he'd find flowers described in the book and press them into the pages, some of which already contained papery, sapped versions of what he found.

One morning he dropped to his hands and knees in the brush by the boat dock with the express desire to find a woodcock in the bush. He had arrived on Ashaunt just in time to catch the end of the birds' mating season—the male woodcocks' spiraling evening flights and fast, whistling descents. Now it was nesting time, and there—he'd not yet crawled ten feet—was a startled female woodcock, flying up so fast that she whacked her head on a branch and dropped like a glove to earth before gathering her wits and rising again. He backed away and later returned to part the branches and find a cunning little nest on the ground. His mother had been a passionate birder before her dissertation, before her turn away from this place, which had started as a gradual distancing but seemed, lately, like a full-out war. If he'd told her about the woodcock, would she have shared his pleasure—a bird in the bush, his own sixth sense, the universe briefly, startlingly, in sync? Or volleyed it back on him: *It's not exactly a miracle, Charlie; you've been seeing woodcocks twenty times a week.*

As for hearing other human voices, well, he did. Nearly every night he turned on the twelve-inch TV he'd brought to the cabin from the Red House, fiddled with the rabbit-ears antenna and watched a snowy, staticky rendition of the evening news. Spilled sacks of grain, thatched lean-tos, fire rising up from sandy ground. Soldiers bellying through the mud, a convoy of jeeps in a forest stripped of undergrowth and leaves. Helicopters everywhere, buzzing in, and the president with his bulldog face and oddly high-pitched voice, and occasionally a Vietnamese girl around his age, slight, scared and lovely with a slender jaw, or an old Vietnamese man, or a waving, half-dressed child. Charlie sat on his sleeping bag, hands trembling on his lap or pressed between his legs, and watched. What was happening over there was at once sickening and improbable; still, he *could* watch it, he could sit himself down—as a duty, yes, but also as a way to hear a human voice or two—and think (didn't Cronkite get sick of saying it?): *And that's the way it is.*

It was the home-front footage he had more trouble watching, for who were those college boys with their long hair, suntanned arms, signs and chanting, who were those swingy, angry, passionate college girls, if not the boy he might have been, if not the girls he might have loved, lifting their arms to reveal their downy armpits, nipples showing through their peasant blouses on national TV? In the shots of demonstrations, he saw himself as he should have been, as he was before. Before and after were the only working categories now. Before the hand brought tab to tongue. Before the throat swallowed, peristalsis, and the body began its steady breakdown work. Before the blood received, the body a dumb innocent.

After the brain cried no (too late).

"Don't you think your division is a little stark?" Dr. Miller had asked a few months earlier, as they'd sat in his office in the university hospital psych ward, where old Miss Flower, whose family had endowed the ward, was a patient too, her footsteps audible as she did the Thorazine shuffle in the hall. "From what you've told me, you were not an unconfused young man before the drugs. You were not without a complex family, a complex past—like most of us."

Charlie had laughed. He laughed too often during the sessions, to fill space, or because everything seemed absurd, or because he was trying to be amiable, normal, in *conversation*, and the doctor's double negatives— "not unconfused," "not without"—tripped him up.

"I was—" he tried to explain. "I wasn't like now, it's . . . I—" He raised his knees to his chest.

"What?" asked Dr. Miller gently into the long silence that followed. "What were you, Charlie?"

Myself, Charlie meant to say, but his laughter had turned to gasps by then. To turn yourself inside out and find (if you were lucky) a scrap of plastic fluttering at the center? A box of tissues came toward him, though he was far from tears. *Okay, son, it's okay,* and then the doctor's hand was on his shoulder, and usually Charlie hated to be touched by people he didn't know, but for once he didn't mind. And his gasps slowed and the hand lifted, retracted, awkwardness intruding, each to his own, two men in a room in chairs.

At the session's end, he stepped into the hallway to find old Miss Flower standing over a slow-spreading puddle of her own pee. She had on red lipstick, a silk kimono, fuzzy slippers shaped like lambs. Her hair was white at the part; the rest was dyed jet black. Once she'd been a little rich girl; then, apparently, a student at Radcliffe. Now she lived here, in a private suite on a ward that bore her family's name.

"Looks like it rained!" she said brightly, peering down between her feet.

Charlie laughed. Until that moment, he'd thought she was entirely out to lunch. She took a step, right into her own pee. For a moment she teetered. Instinctively, Charlie offered his arm, and she steadied herself. She reminded him of something, Miss Flower, of *Miss Happiness and Miss Flower*, that was it—a book about dolls, a girls' book, but he'd read it anyway.

Somewhere, Miss Flower had a first name. Charlie sidestepped away from the puddle, Miss Flower still gripping his arm. *You are not without a complex past.* How had he gotten here? How had any of them? How had they not landed here before? Miss Flower smelled of perfume mixed with pee. Abruptly repulsed, he removed her hand from his arm finger by finger, and she clenched her hand as he returned it to her and studied her own knobby little fist. And then a nurse was coming down the hall, followed by a janitor with a bucket and mop.

BY THE END OF JUNE, Charlie had stopped watching the news. He gave up cigarettes, cut the supply off in one day, though he'd been smoking off and on for years, his first cigarettes filched from his mother when he was nine or ten. He added on to his stone wall, repairing it, extending it a few feet more. One afternoon he came home to find the old army gate entirely removed, along with the wire fencing on either side. Just beyond where the gate had been, a white Pontiac was parked on the overgrown army road, and beyond it, a blue pickup truck. Charlie went down to the shoreline by way of the paths, kept himself low, heard male voices near the radar tower: *Trying to get it scheduled . . . one helluva job . . . stop by next week for paperwork . . . all right . . . Lemme know. . . .*

As he hunched in the brush, he was tempted to strip, paint himself with mud and berry juice, and spring out at them, hooting Indian calls. It would freak them out; it would crack him up. *Mine*, he'd call in faux Wampanoag. The whole area had been the Indians' before Wamsutta sold it to Governor Bradford and his cohorts for thirty yards of cloth, eight moose skins, fifteen axes, fifteen hoes, fifteen pairs of breeches, eight blankets, two kettles, one clock, two English pounds in wampum, eight pair of shoes, one iron pot, ten shillings (as part of his self-imposed study regimen, Charlie had memorized the list). A few years earlier, he'd have played Indian, then sat back to watch the story travel around Ashaunt. But things were different now. The men might have been told that a kid was living out here on his own, a rich screwup shut-in dropout. They'd call the cops, or at the very least tell Joe Olivera, the caretaker, that Charlie had "exposed himself," and Joe would be obliged to tell the Point Association, who'd tell his parents, who'd take him back to Bernardsville and make him get a job or go to summer school or see his mother's shrink.

After the men drove away, he returned to the base, where he found more surveyor tags, along with orange spray paint on some trees and rocks. This time he went out after dark with a flashlight and Swiss Army knife, slashing and removing tags, feeling at once righteous and ridiculous, and wishing—mostly—that he was a boy again, playing with the others: Capture the Flag, Freeze Tag, Sardines, Hide and Seek, along with invented games so absorbing they went on well into the night, until the mothers or nurses (sometimes both at once, a chorus of voices, then bodies appearing) forced the children in. They'd played a game they called Casemate, which involved going deep into the bunker and coming back with evidence—a twist of wire or discharged rifle shell. They'd played Sea Serpents' Lair, Pirate Hide-Out, and Underground Railroad (slave catchers vs. slaves, blue-eyed towheads all; his mother had tried to lecture them—*It's offensive, imagine how a black child would feel*—but they'd ignored her, though the memory made Charlie cringe). Tonight's game would be to remove the surveyor tags as fast as you could, bring them to home base and tie them around the wrist or waist of a cousin of the opposite sex. (When they were ten or eleven, he and Holly had tied each other up. Houdini, they called it. She would gasp and giggle, fight him off, pin him—though tiny, she was wiry and strong—in a wrestler's grip.)

Now no game or cousins, just Charlie undone and undoing, removing markings in the night. He knew it would lead to nothing, but he did it anyway, stowing the tags behind the drawer under one of the cabin's built-in beds. Over a quarter century later, cleaning out that drawer to make space for his girlfriend Rachel's weekend clothes, he would come across the tags and be surprised that he had saved them, the sight of them slightly painful even after so much time. Rachel was on the other bed; it was Memorial Day weekend (round and round it came, and always here). He'd built a fire in the woodstove, made them milky Earl Grey tea. "What?" Rachel asked, but vaguely; she was bent over her laptop, working on a paper, her bangs covering her eyes. Charlie held up the tangle of plastic; it was, among other things, a chance to sneak a look at her (they were still so new). "What's that?" Rachel asked. He might have told her then, the whole story, or the pieces that came back to him, but the memory was shameful—all gesture, no action—and from a period in his life he rarely talked about. "Surveyor tags," he'd said simply, and when she didn't press, he threw the tags away.

V

THE FIRST TIME Charlie gave Jerry Silva a ride was not the first time he had passed him on Gooseneck Road, but it was raining that morning and there, on the side of the road, was a guy he'd seen before on his way to town, only today he was soaked and hauling a large canvas bag. Every few days that summer, Charlie was in the habit of driving or biking to town for food, where he bought only enough for a couple of days so he'd need to go back to the Village Market, take money from his pocket, hand it over, receive the change. Speak. He didn't generally pick up hitchhikers (once, earlier in the summer, he'd pulled over at the foot of Windy Point for three teenage girls who'd taken one look at him, giggled and run off), and Jerry's thumb was not even out. Still, uncharacteristically, Charlie pulled over and rolled down the window. "Need a ride?" he asked, and this wet and wordless guy, still nameless to Charlie at that point, got in.

Even once the car started up again, they did not speak—not about the rain, which was sheeting down over the harbor as they crossed the drawbridge, not about their respective destinations. No chitchat, no introductions or how-do-you-dos or it-sure-is-coming-down-hards. The guy was olive-skinned and brown-eyed and looked Portuguese or even Indian (the black ponytail helped), and this pleased Charlie, who liked how dark his own skin got in the summer, some glitch or untold story in his WASP and Swiss-French genes. When they reached the market, he stopped the car and his passenger got out and rounded the corner out of sight. They might have been two animals, foxes or coyotes, pairing up for a time as they traveled across mutual territory, then splitting off without a glance.

A few days later, driving back from town, Charlie saw him again. This time it was a steaming, sunny day and Jerry was barefoot, dressed in frayed cutoffs and a flannel shirt, and holding, again, the canvas bag. As Charlie slowed and pulled over, Jerry turned and lifted a hand in a half salute.

"That bag looks heavy," Charlie said out the car window.

"He's not heavy, he's my brother."

Charlie smiled. "Does your brother need a ride?"

"Lemme see." Jerry put his ear to the bag.

As he leaned down, Charlie saw that what had looked at first like a strip of cloth tied around his head was a dried snakeskin, black and orange, the skin pulled taut.

Jerry nodded. "Lazy son-of-a-gun. He says yeah, he'll take a ride."
Charlie leaned to open the car door.

WHY, OF ALL THE PEOPLE in the world, did you have to take up with a
nutcase, his mother would ask later. Not only his mother. Jane. His father.
Dr. Miller, though his mother's phrasing was the most direct. Why, of
all the people? Was Charlie lonelier than he wanted to admit? Did he
hope to find in Jerry—this from Dr. Miller—a more attenuated, or more
authentic, version of himself, or to find himself normal in comparison?
In fact, Jerry had seemed normal at first—quirky, yes, but in a good way.
And even later, Charlie liked him, admired what he stood for, was trying
to stand for. Felt his pain. Mostly, though, this: Could no one see that no
matter how it played out, there was something worthy, something *valuable*, about the reaching out toward another human being during a time
when nearly everything he did was aimed at the relentless discipline, pro-
tection, preservation of his so-called Self?

During the second car ride they exchanged names, and somehow
Jerry already knew that Charlie was from Ashaunt, and when he said, So
you've got one of the summer houses, Charlie said he lived in a one-room
cabin, then added that he foraged and fished for a lot of his food (which
was true) and would spend the fall out there (which hadn't been true until
he said it, when it became a plan). He had something to prove, or something to deny. Did it matter? For the first time in months, he felt eager to
engage. Jerry said he fished too, and snared small game to eat. Charlie
asked about the snakeskin, and Jerry said he'd found a water snake and
stretched and dried the skin.

"Did you eat the meat?" Charlie asked.

"No. It was too skinny, and DOA. I had some on a snake farm once,
though—blood, heart, eyeballs. They kill it right in front of you. Nothing
goes to waste."

"Where was that?"

"No place you'd know."

"I cooked a snake once," Charlie said. "It tasted okay, but there wasn't much of it. A few years ago I had this idea of hunting and gathering everything I ate. It was harder than I expected. I only lasted a few days."

Jerry nodded. "My cat'll only eat Nine Lives, won't even eat a mouse if I kill it for her—that's the main problem for me with living wild. That and booze. But at least she stays out of my traps."

"You have traps? What do you catch?"

"Chipmunks, rabbits, whatever takes the bait. I set up a squirrel snare a few days ago, but it hasn't gotten anything yet."

"Where'd you learn how to trap?"

"My father, the Mighty Wampanoag."

"You're kidding."

Jerry laughed sharply. "Yup. I read some books."

Could you show me how to build a snare, Charlie nearly asked, but something held him back. Jerry might have been a little older than he was, or even in his late twenties, good-looking but in an already slightly worn-out way. His hair was a glossy, blue-tinged black, his braid secured by twine. Burrs clung to his shirt. He might have been a vet, back from the war, but he could just as well have been a CO or student, or flat-footed, walleyed or a homo, or a hippie getting back to the land. Or he could even have been a guy more or less like Charlie, sponging, squatting at his family's summer place. His coloring was off for that, but things were getting more mixed up these days; on Ashaunt there were a few half-Korean kids among the blonds, and Rusty's older sister was engaged to a (Princeton-educated, lawyer) Jew.

Mostly in Jerry, at first, Charlie saw, what?—a Green Man, a dweller of the forest. *Cultivate poverty like a garden herb, like sage. Sell your clothes and keep your thoughts.* Later, he would learn that Jerry's bag was filled with library books, and, on return trips, a new batch of books, along with liquor, cat food, peanut butter, beans. And what did Jerry see? Eventually Charlie would have to wonder this as well. Somebody curious? Somebody with two ears? A rich boy playing poor? A ride? Or this: a lonely person looking for a friend.

"Here," said Jerry suddenly as they drove along. "Stop."

Charlie veered onto the shoulder. A few minutes earlier, Jerry had told him to take a right onto Rock O'Dundee Road. Now there was no sign of a driveway or house, though they'd recently passed a rotting barn and silo, and after that, a construction site with bulldozers and mounds of dirt. Now, on each side of the road, just woods: the trees grew so well here, with such height and confidence, that you'd never suspect the ocean was a few miles away. Charlie looked for a path or other traces of human habitation and saw nothing, aside from a few No Trespassing signs nailed to trees. Over the years he had explored these woods, crossing over stone walls where farm fields used to be, bushwhacking down to a brook where the water ran copper from tannic acid, coming, once, upon a meadow full of spent daffodils that seemed to have multiplied profusely on their own.

"Here?" he asked.

Jerry nodded and got out with his bag. He looked down the road in both directions but did not move. In the distance, a motor started up, a towhee made its call—*Drink your tea* (Gaga's translation), or (Bea's) *Brush your teeth.*

"I can drop you at home," Charlie said, as much out of curiosity as generosity. "Where do you live?"

"Close to the bone," Jerry said.

He squatted by the door and met Charlie's gaze across the front seat, and what passed between them was strong enough to feel almost erotic— a current stretching, a plea, but some kind of promise too, traveling in both directions: Follow, do not follow, follow me. *I live close to the bone.* It was from Thoreau. Charlie had been reading him just that week; they both had, though neither of them knew it of the other yet.

Charlie was the first to look away. "I live pretty close to the bone myself."

VI

ON'T KNOW, BEA said, for perhaps the fourth time. Maybe, Mrs.
P. said, it should be something of his grandfather's. A pocketknife,
she thought aloud. Or a book they both cared about, but which one? Bea
exchanged a look with Agnes as they sat on the faded couch in the Big
House living room. What did you give a boy who had everything and
thought he had nothing? Who dressed like a tramp and left his own and
other people's bicycles and tools in the rain, and had been living here
on his own, no job, no course of study, no plan, as far as she knew, of
any kind. They had arrived the night before, for Fourth of July weekend.
Mrs. P. had told Charlie in a letter that she'd be bringing his late birthday
present. She took her gift-giving seriously, but Mr. P. had often done the
choosing for the boys.

"I'm flummoxed," she went on. "I should have gotten something
when I was in New York last week. The girls are easier."

"How about a bit of money?" Agnes tried. "He'll pick out something
he wants."

As in drugs, thought Bea.

"I will—I always do, but I need a present too." Mrs. P. sighed, then
perked up. "I know. What about a compass? One of his grandfather's.
Charlie may already have one, but I think he might like the idea. We've
got a gold one in Grace Park, but I'm pretty sure there's a camping one
here—I can picture it."

"Good idea," Agnes said.

"But where might it be? Do either of you know?"

"No," Agnes said. "But I can take a look around."

Bea knew precisely where the compass sat—in the middle drawer
of the child-sized maple secretary in the front hall, tucked in a ring
box behind the fishing lure, twine and flashlights (the top drawer held
Band-Aids, tweezers, batteries; the bottom drawer was swollen shut). In

his last years, Mr. P. used to ask her to get it for him sometimes, to hold it in her palm or set it in his. He'd taught her how to turn the outside dial until it matched up with true north and then move the base plate until it pointed toward Gaga's dock (which she'd not had put back in the water this season), or Scotland, or New York. Where, he would ask, would you like to go today? He had loved geography and maps, to watch the needle wobble in his hand. That she'd half fallen in love with him over the long course of years was a plain fact to her, as her name was a fact, as her body (which she cleaned and fed and otherwise generally ignored) was.

Mrs. P. had not let her husband's death stop her from living, not in the slightest. She made—it was her mantra, and Bea admired her for it—the best of things, but she also seemed almost giddy sometimes since Mr. P. had died, free, and younger and, well, not properly mournful. Not three months after his death in February of last year, she'd offered all his clothing, save his army uniform and the suit he'd married her in, to Stewart and the grandsons, and given the discards to the Salvation Army. When Bea was boxing up the clothes, she took a necktie dotted with red sailboats from the pile, and a monogrammed handkerchief. That summer, Mrs. P. traveled with friends to Italy and France, and all the following fall and winter she went off each week to the opera and art shows in New York, where she'd taken an apartment at the Lowell Hotel. She oversaw her father's small foundation, which supported the Newark schools and museums, and set up several scholarships in her late husband's name. She lunched with her friends, her grandchildren and her grandchildren's college roommates. She visited friends in the hospital, got her hair done in New York. In the Big House, she moved her bedroom upstairs for a better view and because the old room was too sad. She read the *New York Times* and *Herald Tribune* every day and stayed abreast.

Two days before Mr. P. died, he had thanked Bea, said I'll see you someplace, Bea, I'm not a religious man but I do think it more likely than not, don't you, and she'd nodded, utterly unable to speak. He had asked her to put his hand over hers, so she'd lifted it—feather-light, still broad—and placed it on her own. Mrs. P. had been in the room but had politely ignored them. When he fell asleep, Bea returned his hand and tucked him in. She had not been present at the moment of his passing, the door closed—just Mrs. P. and the doctor in there for much too long, and finally the doctor came downstairs with the news and it was just Mrs. P. left with him, and the sound of muffled sobs, and eventually she came down holding a spoon, which she looked at as if she couldn't recall its use.

By the next week, the wheelchairs, braces, bed lifts were disassembled and donated, and not longer after, they began getting organized for Ashaunt. In September, at Mrs. P.'s urging, Bea started volunteering at the hospital in Orange, holding the babies, putting on a pink-striped smock and going up and down the halls with a cart stocked with playing cards, Saltines and orange juice—but she didn't much like it, the smell of the place, babies passing through like cupcakes on a line, and after a few weeks of it, she gave it up. Then, last month, Scotland, a trip designed in part, she knew, to cheer her up.

"I worry about Charlie," Mrs. P. was saying now to Agnes. "They all go through their phases, but this has been going on too long, don't you think?"

"He needs to get a job or be in school," Agnes said.

"Helen"—Mrs. P. paused—"expects a lot of him. And she should—he has so much potential, but there are ways . . ." She frowned. "I'd like to find a way to lift his spirits a little."

"I might know where the compass is." Bea let the words escape before she could change her mind.

Mrs. P. turned. "Do you, Bea? Wonderful! Why didn't you say so?"

"It just now came to me."

She went into the hall, retrieved the compass, shut the drawer and stood with it, closing her fingers over the small brass circle and trembling needle. Then she crossed into the room and held it out. "It's a bit tarnished. I can polish it up."

Mrs. P. took it. "Charlie will love it, if it still works." She put on her reading glasses, turned toward the doorway and held the compass in her palm. "Oh, yes—you see! True north."

VII

G AGA HAD INVITED Charlie to come over, and he'd wanted to, but as he sat there in the living room, an armchair where Grampa's wheelchair used to sit, he could feel her studying him. ("She pays more attention to her grandchildren than she ever did to us," his mother had remarked recently, without apparent bitterness.)

"It must be so peaceful here with none of us around," Gaga said. "I'd love it."

He gave her a look. They both knew she'd be bored to death.

"I hope it's helping a little bit," she said.

Charlie allowed something between a nod and a shrug.

"Your mother's concerned, you know. About your health. The . . . well, the blood issue, for one thing. I don't tend to get alarmed, but it does bear investigating, and by the right people. We know a first-rate urologist in New York. You could come stay at the Lowell for a night. With this sort of thing, there's no reason not to go straight to the top."

"My doc in New Bedford," Charlie said, "won the Nobel Prize for Piss."

Gaga smiled. "Is college interesting for you, Charlie?"

"Sometimes."

"I'm jealous, you know. To think I never even went to college. All those courses to choose from! What's your favorite so far?"

He shrugged. "It's hard to say."

"I can see how with everything that's going on, college might feel"—she flung her hand out—"irrelevant."

She meant because of the war, for him merely a rattling in the distance, especially since he'd stopped watching the news.

"Anyway," she said, "it's nice to have you back. I didn't like your being so far away, though I admire your independence. You're like your mother in that way. Listen, dearie, I have your birthday present. Sorry it's late." She pulled a small box from behind her on the couch and handed it to him. He lifted the lid. Inside sat a little compass, and under it, providing padding, some folded twenty-dollar bills; he wanted to count how many but did not.

"Oh," he said. "Thanks, Gaga. I don't have one."

"It was Grampa's. Bea dug it out from somewhere."

"Wow. Thanks."

"No need to mention it to the others. It's not valuable or anything—it's just a camping compass—but I think he'd want you to be the one to have it. He was a great hiker and woodsman when I first met him, you know. Like you are. Nonstop."

"Thanks," he quacked again, a bird with only one call.

"It gets harder to find you things as you get older."

"I *like* it."

With a sudden violence, he missed his grandfather: the polished shoes in their braces, the kind smile, the sense Grampa always gave off of having come through a storm and emerged bent but not broken. It was Grampa who'd taught him to memorize poetry, to read maps, to tell one fighter plane from another—the P-51 Mustang, the P-61 Black Widow, the F-86 Sabre; Charlie built the models while his grandfather's voice walked him, with slow precision, through the steps. His uncle Charlie's plane, the one he'd copiloted, had been a B-24 Liberator, with compartments for nine men. He was nuts about that plane, Grampa had said, but he never produced a kit of the B-24. It was Grampa who'd taught Charlie that if you sailed from the tip of Ashaunt straight across the ocean, you'd land in Spain. Supposedly he'd had a terrible temper when he'd first gotten sick, but Charlie had never seen it, and he wouldn't put it past his mother and Dossy (whose childhoods were oversized, antic, in their tales) to have exaggerated.

"Enjoy it," Gaga said. "Have new adventures with it. Explore. He'd want you to."

Charlie put the compass in its box and closed the lid. Implicit in her comment, her gift, in nearly everything she said, was a critique aimed at him, he who was not enjoying life, who saw only holes and absences. And she was right, which made it worse. When he was small, being here—in the Big House living room with her and Grampa—had brought him to his home place. There was the grown-ups' black coffee after Sunday lunch, and for the children, a sugar cube—just one—to plunge into the demitasse cup, then set bittersweet and grainy, melting, on your tongue. He could sit at their feet or wander like a cat, come and go, return again, no judgment anywhere, just a sense of *this is where we live*. Now, even here, he felt out of place, dropped down in this room with its painted gray floors, pale blue walls and ocean view, with its dignified, aging woman, bewildered and slightly repulsed (though she did her best to hide it) by his troubles. Like his mother, Gaga wanted him to get a grip.

"So much has happened since I last saw you," she said. "We were afraid for you when we heard about Kent State. Did you take part in the protests in Cleveland?"

"A little. Not much."

"It's frightening, isn't it? But also important. I sometimes wish I were young so I could be part of it in some way. Writing letters to politicians doesn't accomplish very much. Your generation hates people like me, though. We're everything they detest."

"Not everyone's a radical in 'my generation,' Gaga. And you don't just write letters—you've done all that stuff for the Newark schools."

She nodded slowly. "I believed—I still do, I think—that education is the key to giving everyone a fair chance, but I may be wrong. Anyway, it's a slow way to proceed, and it's not enough for them."

"Who's *them*?"

She waved toward the window. "The hippies. The antiestablishment radicals. They'd like to take over Ashaunt like the army did, except turn it into a commune, with sex, drugs and rock and roll. They'd paint the houses neon and cut my flowers to make chains for their hair. Imagine that! Eliminate private property. Would you jump on board, Charlie?"

"Me?" He laughed dryly. "Probably not."

"Why not?"

"I'm not a jumper-on-boarder. And I don't like neon."

"You do have beliefs, though. Values. Don't forget that. You have a moral sense—you always have. Everyone does, but some are more fine-tuned."

"I'd turn Ashaunt into a nature preserve if I could."

"And not live here?"

"Not if it could be a nature preserve."

"What else would you do?"

"Stop the war! Get rid of big business! End racism, sexism! End ism-ism!" He pressed the heels of his hands against his eyes and the headache under them. When he lowered his hands, the air was full of blue spots.

Gaga pursed her lips. "You're much too young to be so cynical. You used to be *engaged*, you know. When you'd come back from that camp and talk about the inner city kids you worked with, you lit up, Charlie. I can picture the look in your eyes. And you do still care. I know you do. What about the environmental movement—doesn't that interest you?"

He shrugged. "I carried a sign on Earth Day."

"What did it say?"

"'Life Is a Gas, Keep It Clean.'" He had shown up and grabbed a sign, hadn't even stayed with the group all the way to the Cuyahoga River, which, while no longer burning, was still a cesspool.

"You're so clever! See? A sense of humor is a terrific weapon—and lacking these days. The country could benefit from a little change. Why not get involved in a political campaign? It could be helpful for you, a way to meet people, if nothing else. Girls, even. You could report back to me. Holly has been telling me how Cambridge has been turned upside down. If you don't want to be in the middle of things, you could write about it; you've always been a good writer and photographer. You could *observe*."

"I don't know," he said.

GAGA STOOD, RELEASING, DISMISSING HIM. He stepped into the dark hallway, then out to the porch, where Bea sat on a bench sipping tea.

"Charlie," she said. "Cuppa tea?"

"No, thanks."

"Are you sure? It's Brodies Famous Edinburgh, from our trip home."

She might have been a statue, a figurine, so installed she looked, so comfortable, once his eyes adjusted to the brightness enough to take her in.

"Nice. But no thanks." He had given up, among other things, caffeine. That morning he'd brewed homemade tea from boiled arborvitae leaves and gulped it down, minty and medicinal, so hot it burned his tongue.

"Oh—" Bea tipped her chin toward the box. "Good! She'd been wanting to give you that. Did you open it?"

He nodded.

"Lovely, isn't it? A compass. I've always wanted one."

Bea with a compass, forging through the wilderness in her flowered dress, carried along by her pale, stout legs. Had she ever, even for a moment, wanted a compass, or was she just trying to be nice? Charlie knew her hardly at all, despite her having babysat him sometimes when he was small. One cloudy day last August, he had happened upon her sitting alone on a flat rock on the beach, facing the sea. He'd stood at the end of the path and watched from behind. He could not see her face, just her back, broad, the shoulders rounded, and her gray hair in its bun. Beside her a cardigan lay folded. It began to rain, a few drops at first, then more, dimpling the sea, staining the rocks. Still, she sat. She might have been peaceful, sitting there; she might have been not. Finally she looked at the sky and reached for her sweater, began to rise. Charlie had left before she saw him, first backing away on the path, and then, when he rounded the corner, turning and breaking into a run.

"It was your grandfather's," Bea said now. "He'd be glad for you to have it. Be careful not to lose it, though."

"It's a camping compass," Charlie said.

She gave him a look filled with judgment, or was it pity, or scorn? She did not much like boys; neither she nor Agnes ever had. (Decades later, when she died, she would leave $10,000 to each of the female grandchildren, and nothing to the males.) She did not like ungratefulness, bad manners or going against the grain. Once Grampa had brought up the subject of Scotland perhaps going for its independence, and Bea had tucked in her chin and said, "What, and not worship the Queen?"

He left, feeling her watch him, her eyes on his back, following him as he went across the lawn and down the path until she could no longer see him. He was in the woods; she and Agnes did not have, though they used to claim they did, eyes in the back of their heads. Probably they thought he should have enlisted, and disapproved not only of his long hair but also of his rummage-sale shirt and half-grown beard, and the way his unhappiness was written plainly on his face.

In the cabin, he counted the money from Gaga—a hundred dollars— set the compass on the windowsill and crawled into bed, exhausted in the way that only social life could exhaust him. He needed a Valium, his sleeping bag, to count the knots on the rafters until he was relaxed enough to shut his eyes. He would sleep, then, for hours, as lunch was served at the Big House, as Gaga and his aunts and mother gathered for a swim, and the truck from Giffords Fish Market drove up with the fixings for the clambake scheduled for that night at the Yacht Club with

Gaga hosting—*Come One, Come All*—handwritten flyers taped on the "Go Slow Children" signs nailed to sawhorses up and down the road.

Like a baby, Charlie slept, waking to the dimming light and his father peering over him—*Are you awake, Chahrlee?*—his accent still strong after all this time, his face worried and watchful. First he filled Charlie in—Holly had arrived with her roommate from Wellesley, the clambake was starting, Mummy had gone swimming with the others—he told this and then more, until finally he worked his way around to what he'd come for. So. He thought he maybe had a diagnosis. He'd been looking into it, gone to the medical library at the hospital. Would you like to know?

Charlie sat up, gripped by fear. Not that he liked his present life, not that he wouldn't trade it in a second for his previous one, but to hear his fate spelled out (*dia*, across; *gnosis*, knowledge).

"I don't know, Dad," he said.

"Oh, don't worry, it eez nothing terrible. I think you have march hemoglobinuria." His father was unable to keep a note of pride from his voice. "You like to run, yes?"

Charlie nodded.

"And when you run, what do you put on?"

"Huh?"

"What do you wear when you go to run?"

"Shorts, I guess. Nothing special. Why?"

"And on your feet?"

"I . . . I—" He felt suddenly forced into a corner, as if his mother had somehow rigged this all, down to the blood in his pee. "Usually I run barefoot."

His father clapped his hands. "I knew it! This is what I told Mummy! You've always hated shoes. After you run, you pee, and this pee has the blood in it! Correct?"

"I guess. Yeah."

"This," his father went on, "is 'soldier's marching disease,' or 'march hemoglobinuria.' Soldiers get it from long forced marches. It is very rare, with only a few reported cases. The red blood cells get crushed as they pass through the pounding feet. You must be running far, and on the road, yes?"

The wine-dark stream, his breath still heaving; even when he needed to urinate in the middle of the run, he didn't let himself, holding it in, the blood that pooled, the pee that pressed; only his sweat escaped, leaving him slick and salty. He loved the deep pressure of running barefoot, loved, even, stepping on a pebble or shell and not reacting. Every day he pushed himself faster, returning, always, to the end of his stone wall, where he stretched, then walked behind the Red House. There, facing the sea, he peed.

His father sat on the edge of the bed.

"So is it, like, fatal?" Charlie asked.

"Don't be silly. Nothing like that."

"Do I have to stop running?"

"For now. The blood will go away and soon you'll be like new. I think so anyway. I'll give you money for sneakers, but you'll take a break from running, and once your urine is normal, you can try running in shoes. Your kidneys are no problem; I checked with the doctor in New Bedford. And he will look into the diagnosis to make sure, and so will the chief of urology at Columbia. You'll need to keep giving samples. Now"—his father made a clucking noise—"get up for the clambake. And put on some shoes. I promised Mummy."

Charlie burrowed down. "Is Rusty there?"

"Of course."

"Who else?"

"Everyone."

Charlie groaned. "That's too much."

His father sat on the edge of the bed and reached toward him as he lay inside the sleeping bag, then withdrew his hand. He looked tired; he looked old.

"Everybody has to eat," his father said.

~~~

MAKING THEIR WAY DOWN THE sandy driveway, they could hear voices at the Yacht Club before they could see people. Charlie followed his father down the hill, past the bicycle rack and peeling changing rooms, onto the deck, which had gotten damaged in a winter storm and was still missing a few slats of wood. There were no yachts at the Yacht Club and never had been; there were no boats at all, the name so familiar that no one gave it any thought, except when a newcomer asked. Every year Gaga hosted the Fourth of July clambake, and each year more and more people came: renters; new girlfriends and boyfriends, new babies; the Pratts, who'd bought land from the Stricklands; plus the regulars. Rusty's mother was there but not his father; the divorce had been finalized the summer before, but it still felt wrong to Charlie to extract Warren (who'd brought them contraband fireworks, who'd been president of the Point Association for five years) from the Childs clan. Next year I think I'll limit it to family, Gaga said each year, but she never did.

Charlie went down to the beach for some steamers and a beer, at which point he told Rusty about soldier's marching disease, thinking that it would make a good story, though Rusty didn't seem to find the diagnosis particularly funny.

"That's good you're okay," he said instead.

It was five o'clock but the air was warm still and stirred by an even warmer wind. Holly went swimming in a crocheted bikini with her friend from college, who wore a bathing suit out of another time—a pair of navy blue boyish trunks and blue-and-white-striped top. As Charlie watched, the two girls climbed out of the water and started back down the long dock. The roommate was taller than Holly and had cropped blond hair, a long torso and loping gait, and as she came down the dock she stopped and turned to face the sea. Then she raised her arms to shoulder height and extended them straight out, and as she did, a band of pale skin appeared between her bathing trunks and top. Holly, ahead of her friend, turned and said something, breaking the moment (*Don't*, Charlie thought), and the girl dropped her arms and turned toward shore.

Rusty drew in his breath, then exhaled. "Howdy Doody, check her out. A siren from the sea."

"So go for her," Charlie said. The summer before, Rusty and Holly had slept together once when they were drunk. Though they weren't technically related, it had seemed to Charlie like incest (which he'd told them) and made him wild with jealousy (which he'd not). This girl was a stranger on whom he had no claim, nor any capacity to lure.

"Right." Rusty shook his head. "She's like a foot taller than me."

"So? You make up in charm what you lack in height."

Rusty cuffed him on the side of his head. "And you make up in height what you lack in charm, Bozo. Has it ever occurred to you that I've never been with a girl even an inch taller? Not"—he threw a stone, watched it skip—"once. You go for her," he added generously. "It could be just what the doctor ordered."

In his nineteen years, Charlie had made out with exactly three girls—two in high school and one in college—but he'd emerged from the Summer of Love still a virgin and remained, several years later, skittish about the whole thing, though he'd suffered staggering, painful crushes for years and performed inventive sex acts in his mind with a wide range of girls and women, including several of his friends' mothers, a few of his cousins, and most of his sister's friends. Still, his deepest love, he liked to maintain, had been for Dolly, a pony Gaga and Grampa got when he was six and who had died a few years later of a perforated ulcer. His love for Dolly was a joke and not a joke; he still remembered draping himself along the solid length of the pony's back, lowering his face into her coarse mane, cupping her chin to inhale her heated, grassy breath. Everyone had teased him, but Charlie hadn't cared. When they stood face to face, Dolly's eyes would look at him with an alert, liquid patience, filled with waiting and (he knew it then and still believed it now) a pointed, particularized love. And because Dolly was a pony, not a *Homo sapiens*, he did not have to look away.

"They're *coming*," he said now between gritted teeth, and there they were, Holly in a sweatshirt over her bathing suit, her friend in a flannel shirt, the two of them crouching down—*This is my friend Melanie from college*—and the girl was looking at him closely: Exhibit B, Holly's Loony Bin Cousin, to go with Exhibit A, Holly's Loony Bin Mother, who almost never came to Ashaunt anymore but spent her summers traveling in Europe with her husband and, when they could be dragged along, Holly and Phil (who mostly stayed here, with a maid or grandparents or, more and more, alone). And Exhibit C, Rusty, who was not an exhibit at all, just a nice guy asking questions, conversing, honing in; so much for being too short, so much for just what the doctor ordered.

Charlie started down the beach, then pivoted, walking to the Yacht Club porch; somehow he found himself there, next to Gaga, between Gaga and his mother, who were sipping martinis and balancing plates on their knees.

"Charlie." Gaga smiled. "I'm glad you came. Get some food, why don't you?"

"I already did."

"Get some more. I always order too much. I depend on you boys to help me get rid of it." She looked at his mother. "You're right—he's awfully thin. Are you eating enough, Charlie?"

He nodded. They were all thin, his family: his father, his mother, his siblings, straw people (*I'll huff and I'll puff and I'll blow your house in*). "I eat plenty."

His mother leaned toward him. "Holly's friend seems nice. And interesting. She told me she's studying art history. Why don't you go talk to her? You don't have to waste your time with us."

He gave her a baleful look. "I'm not wasting my time."

"That's nice of you to say so." His mother frowned.

"All she means," said Gaga, "is that we wouldn't be insulted if you'd rather spend your time with a pretty college girl."

Charlie reached to take a littleneck from his mother's plate.

"You're not wearing shoes!" she cried. "Didn't Daddy talk to you? I sent him—"

"Shhh," Charlie interrupted. "He did. He talked to me. Okay?" The truth was, he'd forgotten to wear shoes, and his father hadn't noticed. They were alike that way—they didn't mean to, exactly; they just forgot. "My shoes give me blisters," he said. In fact, he had no real shoes at the moment, just flip-flops. In Cleveland he'd worn ratty sandals through most of the winter, switching to sneakers only when it was bitingly cold.

"*Blisters?*" said his mother loudly. "For god's sakes, Charlie. You have bloody urine! You could damage your kidneys!"

Several people turned, and Charlie went hot with shame.

"Helen," Gaga said. "Not now, dearie. Discuss it later, why don't you?"

"Later, Mummy? He has blood in his urine from going barefoot, and here he is, barefoot! Of all the asinine things! André was supposed to get him to wear shoes. Where is he? For god's sake. I am truly *furious*. André!"

She strode off the dock, drink in hand. In the distance, his father was walking with Percy along the curve of shore that led to Windy Point, getting smaller and smaller.

"Go put on shoes, Charlie," his grandmother told him. "Before she comes back. For the sake of my party. For my sake. Be a good boy."

"It can't do any harm unless I'm running. And I'm *nineteen*," he muttered. "Not a boy."

She nodded thoughtfully. "You are, aren't you? I was married at your age. I wish I'd gone to college; I envy you that. Still, I don't regret one moment of my life."

"You just said you regretted it. What's wrong with regretting?"

Gaga stood, her eyes glittering, her color high. She scanned the group. "Why, it's a colossal waste of time!"

It was her clambake. She would have fun. Everyone would have fun. Charlie had a rare moment of sympathy for his mother, who was a storehouse of conflicting regrets, always considering the path not taken: to have been a historian with a university appointment, to have moved abroad, to have lived in the city or spent all year on Ashaunt. To

have sold the Red House (which—minor sticking point—Gaga owned)
and bought a house in a summer place where she knew nobody and
could reinvent herself. To have had another child (though they all
knew she'd had an abortion after Percy). To have been a world traveler,
or (her family's teasing masked the sting they felt) a nun. "I wish I'd
never set foot in Switzerland!" she'd once screamed at his father during
one of their more toxic fights. And another time, when she was feeling crowded by her parents, "Why didn't we just stay in Lausanne?"
(She had, apparently, refused to.) Her outbursts were followed by either
periods of long silence or by compensatory chatter about how lucky she
was, how lucky they all were: family was everything, the problem was
having too *many* choices, too *much* money, everyone should have such
problems, and this would eventually feed her back into another fantasy:
of a plain and modest life, stripped bare, like the Amish who had no
buttons or zippers, no TV, not even faces on their dolls. She'd visited a
community once; the women made quilts, the men made maple syrup,
the children seemed happy and were exquisitely well-behaved, but in
the most natural way.

His parents were walking back down the beach together. They had
almost split up several times over the past decade. There may have
been affairs. Their fights—on the occasions that she pushed him past
his breaking point—were monumental, loud and fierce, sometimes in
French, and had no clear root that Charlie could see except that they
seemed largely to be about her *happiness*, her *bonheur*, and his inability to create it for her, or to be what she wanted him to be, a Man of
Importance (he was highly respected at work; he'd won more than one
award for his research; he published papers; he was nearly always kind,
if sometimes distant. *Mais qu'est-ce que tu veux, Helen? Je n'en peux
plus!*).

Still, something kept his parents together, just as something made
his mother continue to live half an hour from her parents and five minutes from Jane in Bernardsville and return, each and every summer, to

Ashaunt. Was it habit, or obligation, or something else—a tugging, chafing, necessary love? His parents had met at the swimming pool in Lausanne when she was a student, he a young doctor. She had challenged him to a race; she had won. It was not hard to imagine—the spark in her eyes; the surprise, and then the spark ignited, in his. The kick-off, the parallel swim, Helen pulling ahead. Did he let her win? She was an excellent swimmer, but he was stronger, bigger. The meeting up again, wet and breathless, at the far end of the pool. Her nearly fluent French. Now, as they came nearer, Charlie could see his mother speak close to his father's ear. Then she looked up and caught Charlie's eye.

"*La-voilà, Monsieur Contraire!*" she called, but she was laughing, dropping his father's arm, heading for the drinks. Charlie turned to watch her go. In her summer skirt she looked suddenly radiant, the late afternoon sun striping her skin, her legs lean and agile on the rocks. She was full of fire; she always had been. As girls, she and Dossy had kidnapped a neighbor's baby and held her hostage in the attic until Bea thought she heard a cat and found the child. At Parents Day at Brearley, she'd stuffed stockings and shoes with newspaper and set them up in the toilet stalls to make each stall look occupied. She was, for all her faults, rarely boring, never bored. For an instant, it occurred to Charlie that one day—how impossible—she would die.

"You." His father poked him. "Get with zee program, Cat. Go find your shoes."

His parents were, Charlie realized, tipsy, maybe even blitzed. "Cat?" He snorted.

"Go," said his father. "Or she may toss me to the sharks!"

CHARLIE LEFT THE CLAMBAKE, WANDERED up to the road, found some mildewed huaraches in a closet in the Red House. He stayed away for a while, but wherever he was, he could hear the voices on the shore, and eventually he returned to the beach, sat down again, barefoot, shoes at the base of the rock. By then the sun had set. Someone had started a bonfire. The adults had left with the littlest kids. A keg had appeared, and a guitar. He got another beer, returned to his rock. The beer was cold and malty, and the edges of things, soaked in dusk and alcohol, had turned pleasantly soft. He hadn't had a drink all summer, and while some piece of him wondered if the alcohol might make him crack again or even return him to himself, he managed, with surprisingly little trouble, to set the thoughts aside. Percy and the younger cousins were gathering driftwood and hauling it back to the fire, along with buoys, lobster traps and washed-up plastic bottles, which they arranged busily, with no apparent logic, on the beach.

Holly made her way over to him. "Why'd you take off like that, Charlie? It was rude. Melanie wanted to meet you, and in the middle of my introducing you, you just bolt!"

"Bolt? I had to get shoes. Who's Melanie?" For a moment, he truly didn't know; the name sounded unfamiliar, the wrong name for the figure in his thoughts.

"*Melanie*," Holly repeated. "My roommate. The one you can't stop checking out. I've told her all about you. I was trying to help you two connect—you know—boy/girl?" She twined her middle finger over her index finger. "Didn't you realize that?"

"No."

"Wow. You're pretty out to lunch." She squatted and peered at him. "Are you okay?"

"Rusty thinks she's hot," Charlie offered. "He was talking to her when I left."

Holly stood. "She wanted to meet *you*."

"Why? What did you tell her about me?"

Holly, who knew him better than anybody—by instinct, or because their mothers had been inseparable as girls, or because she'd spent the better part of her childhood with him—just shrugged and walked away. She was his favorite cousin, at once intuitive and cheerful despite her mother's instability (yet how accepting Dossy was, compared to his own mother, how much less critical, swept by the current, it seemed, instead of fighting it). By this time, he was more than a little drunk. As he watched Holly navigate the rocks back to the group, it occurred to him that he might actually be, for that moment, precisely what he looked like: a college student at a beach party, a barefoot boy in the prime of his life, hands slick with butter and smelling of shellfish, desire rising for a pretty girl.

He followed Holly over to the group, moving easily over the rocks. It was dark by now and the fire had died down, but the moon cast a watery light. He made himself sit next to Holly, who sat next to her roommate. Then, so fluidly it seemed a trick of nature, Holly disappeared.

"Hi," said the roommate. Melanie.

He formed the word back. "Hi."

"I'm Holly's roommate, Melanie. We started to meet, before—"

"Yeah. I know. Sorry. I—I had to get something."

"That's all right." She leaned toward him, chin in hands. "I think I've answered the hall phone when you've called. Holly talks about you a lot."

"Uh-oh," he said.

He should not have had the beers, could feel his mind go loose, the world grow dim, and the girl's voice was talking on unperturbed, something about Wellesley, then about his family, how cool it was, and Ashaunt, how lucky they were, I mean her family rented in Maine but it wasn't the same, not a place like this where everyone could be together and so tight, and he said yeah (vise tight, tight enough to blow a fuse), and then she stopped, gazed at him, head tilted, hands tucked inside her cuffs; it hurt him to look, she was so pretty. He shifted and sat on his own hands, looked down.

Oh to have instinct do the work. He'd watched spotted turtles mate in the sand at the pond near the gate, watched dragonflies do it, a blur of wings, their tails connecting in a circle, and afterward, locked stillness. He'd watched dogs fuck, had even caught Will with his high school girlfriend behind the barn in Bernardsville, bare-assed to the wind. Melanie seemed finally to have registered the fact that he was not fully inside the conversation. She sat back, rocked on her heels, and took another tack: Do you maybe want to swim?

And so shirts off—her flannel, his T—and down the dock and stairs and into the cold smack of the ocean, where he could barely see her, just her wet hair and the outline of her face and rising arms (she started with a strong crawl, slowed to breaststroke). In his family, it was mostly the women who were swimmers; Charlie was usually in and out, and now he struggled slightly to keep up. Across his mind ran, willy-nilly, a stream of standard-issue questions: How do you like college? How long have you known Holly? Where are you from? Instead he asked nothing, nor did she speak, though she slowed down and swam alongside him. On the beach someone played the guitar, the group singing off-key—a song he didn't recognize. Then they had reached the raft and he was on it, and as she tried to get on, his hand reached out to pull her up. There. Very good. She sat dripping beside him. In the dark he could see only the half-outlines of her body. It was windy out of the water; they would soon grow cold. From shore, the song reached them piecemeal: "*Just a little rain . . . falling all around . . . what have they done . . .*"

"I love that song," said Melanie.

"What is it?"

"Joan Baez." She began to sing along: "*And the grass is gone, the boy disappears, and rain keeps falling like helpless tears, and what have they done to the rain?*"

She stopped. He wanted to ask her to go on. The song was sad and lovely; her voice, pure and clear and a little quavering on the high notes, was too—but on the beach they'd started in on something more raucous.

"It's pretty," he said.

Melanie nodded. "The bizarre thing is, it's about the fallout from aboveground nuclear testing. On the record, she says it's the gentlest protest song she knows. I live for Joan Baez. Do you know her stuff?"

"A little. I should listen to more."

"She'll blow you away. She's really political, but she has a voice from heaven. Holly told me you're living out here by yourself all summer, in a cabin with no running water."

"Yeah." Had Holly failed to mention that the Red House and the Big House, with their showers, sinks and toilets, were each not even a hundred yards away?

"Cool. You don't get lonely when no one's around?"

"No," he said, then lied (or was it true?). "Sometimes. A little."

"I crewed on a schooner for June," she said. "It was ridiculously crowded. They bring camp groups for overnights and the crew all gets stuck in one cabin. But I got lonely anyway, maybe because there was no space, if that makes sense. There were, like, ten of us. We slept"—she held up her hands, a few inches apart—"like this."

"I've never done that." He may as well have declared it: *I'm still a virgin.*

"It was a drag in some ways," she said, "but great in others, especially at night when everyone except the night crew was asleep. I'd climb up to the crow's nest and sit there in the dark and wind, just clinging on. It was . . . I don't know, impossible to describe."

"It sounds amazing," he said.

"It was. It was one of those extreme experiences you can't put words to. Existential, even. Does that sound ridiculous? I don't talk about it much. I tried to tell my mom about it, but she freaked out at the idea of me up there. She thinks I take too many risks."

"You held on," he said.

"For my life."

Even in the cold, he was getting a hard-on, and he could feel the attention of everyone on the beach, the silent urging: *Go for it, make a move.* But then he didn't have to. She scooted closer.

"You can"—she leaned until their shoulders bumped— "kiss me if you want. Or if you're not into that, I mean, that's cool too. . . ."

He put his hand on the wet nylon of her bathing suit, felt the small of her back as her lips came toward him, pursed and cold at first, then open—bone teeth, muscled tongue—and for a moment he leaned in, his whole body wanting her, for he was only human, could it really be this easy, to swim through dark water into this? They necked, heads turning, chins knocking, finding new angles. He felt the knob of her hipbone, found her ear and, without thinking, spoke close to it. "I wish I'd been there on that boat with you."

"Really?" She moved back, her smile broad. "Wow, thanks. Me too."

They kissed again, her hand tracing the waistband of his shorts, pulling on fabric, grazing the zipper, and he let out a little moan.

Melanie pulled back. "So, um, everyone can see us. They're going to starting cheering soon. Could we maybe go somewhere, like to your cabin?"

Yes, he should have said immediately, but no words came. He had condoms in the drawer under the bed, bought in a foolish moment of hopefulness a few years back. He had candles, and orange butterfly weed and turk's-cap lilies in a jar. He had a record player. (And prescription pill bottles on the table, and a book called *Understanding Your Panic Disorder*, and a paper bag to breathe into, and a notebook where he recorded, daily, how many miles he'd run, which birds and flowers he'd seen, along with the circumstances that preceded his panic attacks, as if with a pattern might come comprehension, but there was no pattern, at least not yet. He had his mummy sleeping bag—cradle, straitjacket, sized for one.)

Once more, he willed himself to kiss her, but it was already too late; his mind had yanked him back into the long, cold view. It was as if he could see them kissing, two specks—she warm-blooded, open-minded, *normal*, he a body full of urges but with its feelings sealed off, his mind a capsule lodged inside his body. He could peer out, observe, but through a slick-walled, bloodless barrier of glass. If things went forward, even a little, he would feel it more, he knew: how alone he was, how lost inside himself, the isolation easier to tolerate when he was, in fact, alone.

And then, as if on cue, his hands were trembling, his teeth knocking together; she'd pulled back, was looking at him—You're shivering, babe, are you all right?—and he said, Listen, I'm really sorry, I've got to get back, I'm not feeling well (*and the grass is gone, the boy disappears*), and before she could answer he was in the water, turning once to see her swimming after him, and though he forced himself to stay only a few strokes ahead, he did not speak, and when they got to shore, to the group stifling laughter (someone flashed a victory—or was it a peace sign?), he smelled pot, grabbed his shirt (forgot the shoes) and ran.

A FEW DAYS LATER, HE tried to explain to Dr. Miller what he could not explain to Holly, or to Melanie, who'd left early the next morning before he'd had a chance to apologize or say good-bye. How for the body to want and the mind to detach was an impossible equation, and he'd give up beer, he'd give up parties, girls, sex, all thoughts of sex, if only he could just be left alone.

"It sounds as if she liked you," said Dr. Miller, who charged these phone sessions to his parents but asked Charlie to pay a token two dollars a session himself.

"She didn't know me."

"Was attracted to you, then. And maybe to what she'd heard about you. The swimming and conversation sound nice. So does the intimacy. There was a connection, no?"

"A normal person would have felt one, but I didn't."

"What if you'd let it go further? Explored a little more. Physically, I mean. Without thinking about it too much. What would you have risked?"

"You can't do that if—" Now Charlie was stuttering. "You c-c-c—can't—"

A minute passed, then another. The July renters had canceled at the last minute. The Red House kitchen floor was filthy. Over the weekend, his mother had decided to pay him to clean the house and clear brush after they left, but so far he'd done no cleaning and only a little clipping, and he wouldn't cut down so much as a twig from behind the house, where she wanted a better sea view and he wanted a thicket where the cabin could hide.

"You felt desire," said the doctor finally. "Do you see how that could be a good, even a hopeful, thing? Not that you need to act on it. There's no rush. You're young and you've been through a lot. But to feel a connection—"

"Once," Charlie said, "I caught a fish and cut off its head. Ten minutes later, the head almost bit my finger off. I had to get stitches."

"That's a funny story, but you're not dead, Charlie."

"I didn't say I was dead. I said a dead fish bit me."

"And the significance of this is—?"

"You're the shrink."

"But what do you think?"

"Um . . . don't bite the hand that kills you?"

Dr. Miller laughed. "Did you know Freud dissected fish before he turned to people? Eels, to be specific. Of course, others would say a fish is just a fish. I'm afraid we're out of time."

"I need more Valium. Can you phone it in? And maybe something else. Is there anything else? That might get to, you know, the core?"

"We've tried a number of medications already," said Dr. Miller. "You're sensitive to side effects, and none of them have been very helpful. You're making progress, Charlie. Can you see that?"

Thank you, Charlie wanted to say. For having faith in me. For not thinking I'm a lazy, selfish shit. For being, above all, kind. Once he had followed Dr. Miller after spotting him on the street, had lurked half a block behind as the good doctor moved—alone and somehow tentative in the suit and bow tie he always wore—out of the university district, finally disappearing into a low brick office building whose sign announced a Ladies' Depilatory Service and an insurance agency.

"Then Valium," Charlie said.

"How many do you have left?"

He took the jar from his pocket. Three pills, barely enough to make a rattle. "One," he lied.

"I'll phone it in," the doctor said.

VIII

FOR THREE DAYS after that, Charlie spoke to no one and drove to town only once, to pick up the prescription and buy a pair of canvas tennis sneakers at Mars and, even more reluctantly, a pack of tube socks. He did not shop for food that day; he was living off leftovers, first those he'd been given, and then, after he'd made the round of houses, stuff he took from cupboards and fridges before the cleaners came. In the Big House, he found chocolate and orange juice, a carton of milk, stale shortbread, lemons, a few apples. At the Childs', an untouched roast chicken that he smelled, deemed fresh enough, and ate at their kitchen table, tossing the bones into the bushes when he left. At the Stricklands', almost nothing (half his relatives, like Jane, despised waste; the other half, like his mother, let food rot and turn to mold). The Red House was rented now, so he couldn't go there; voices came from the house—children shouting, a mother calling, new people he didn't know.

If the door of a house was locked, he used a back window. If he found food to bring to the cabin, he put it in his rucksack, and the feeling he had was not of trespassing, exactly; it was both dreamier than that and more permissive, each house so familiar, the halls and kitchens of his childhood, when you did not come home for meals, except sometimes for dinner. Hungry ruffians, Bea and Agnes used to call the gang, for they'd charge into the Big House kitchen starving and expectant and depart again two minutes later, leaving crumbs and apple cores behind.

Now, alone, he lingered longer, went into bedrooms, even: Jane's and Paul's one day, not sure what he was looking for. He found a pacifier and books on the nightstand and then, when he opened the drawer, a bottle of talc and a small pink case, and, inside, a rubber diaphragm. He started to touch its rim, then pulled back; it had been inside his aunt (everyone knew Jane had meant to stop at five children, Maddie a surprise, having come just as she'd started teaching reading again). When he was back outside on the paths, the image of the diaphragm stayed with him, its round smoothness, but also how it spoke of a life smack in the middle of itself, and of sex, which he imagined between Jane and Paul as tender, steady, unfrightening, nothing like it would have been for him if he'd gone further with Melanie (enflamed, engorged, obliterating, or— worse—surgical and cold).

He felt, then, something like yearning. Jane seemed to go through her days with a kind of steady, pointed focus—first you do this, then that—and because she had married Paul Strickland, they lived in the old- est house on the Point, the original farmhouse, its central fireplace big enough to park a car in, its rooms a crooked labyrinth. Jane and Paul's children had been born, both sides, into Ashaunt. Their father was not a foreigner. Their mother was not torn, unpredictable and full of judg- ments, nor forever struggling to write a dissertation. Jane and Paul seemed *happy* together, in a steady way (how rare this was, he realized, in the couples he knew). If they had moments of real unhappiness, together or alone—and surely they did—you almost never saw them, nor did you see them battle with their kids, except in the usual ways. Of course, Jane kept things to herself, which irked his mother, who thought herself an open book. Still, it seemed, all told, from where he stood, a smoother, less divided life.

Charlie would have liked to live in Jane and Paul's house. Was that it? He would have liked to be the baby in the crib, lifted, when he cried, by capable hands. But of course there was no choice. You moved forward—everyone did—from your own tangled origins, belonged to your own particular set of parents, whether you wanted to or not. He was cutting a new path that meandered from the cabin to the beach, and as he clipped and sawed, the familiar motions calmed him, and it was not until he got back to the road that he saw the bulldozer, neck swinging down, shovel extending, smashing the far end of the wall he had built, stone by stone, over the course of several summers, from the Red House mailbox to the old army gate.

He ran toward the machine, loppers in one hand, the saw in the other. "Stop!" he yelled. And then "Hello?" and "Stop," again, louder, until finally the man at the wheel shut off the machine, its neck raised halfway up.

From high above, the man frowned. "Can't hear a damn thing. Even when it's off. My ears are shot. What's the trouble here?"

"I, this . . . It's just—" Charlie shielded his eyes from the sun. "This is private property. I live here. . . . My grandparents, my grandmother, owns this land. Margery Porter. Charles and Margery Porter? I built it, this wall. You can't just knock it down."

The man shrugged. "They're widening and paving the road, pushing it out to the end. They tell me where to dig, I dig."

"Who is 'they'?"

"Mr. Wilson."

"Dick Wilson? Why?"

"I reckon so the deal can go through with Cording."

"Who's Cording?"

"Cording and Sons, from New Bedford, you know? Bill Cording, the developer? They cleared it with the planning board. It took long enough to get the go-ahead—it was even in the papers. Kind of a shame, if you ask me. I fish out here from time to time—Mr. Wilson knows. But what's done is done. They'll put up some nice houses with amenities, and *heat*. Imagine that. It might give you folks ideas."

"This isn't Dick's land, not this piece, this is ours—" Charlie's voice was high now, girlish, begging. Did the shoulder of the road belong to the Point Association, or to his family? Might it be protected by some ancient right-of-way law like the one that still allowed the descendants of the Cooks and Cornells, the families that used to farm Ashaunt, to gather kelp to fertilize their inland fields? "I'll call my grandmother," he said. "There must be some mistake. Could you please wait?"

The man wiped his brow. "I've got to get the dozer on to another site."

As he spoke, he looked down at the wall, and Charlie saw it through his eyes: the stones of varying shapes and size, no mortar, just beach rocks tucked and wedged. Building a stone wall had turned out to be harder than he'd expected, the project starting as a whim, a rock in each hand on the beach. How he had labored, day after day, the summer he was seventeen. No one had made him, just as no one, except maybe Percy and Holly, had been at all impressed when he was done. His parents were fighting a lot that summer, on the weekends when his father was around. His mother was considering abandoning her dissertation, but in the most tortured, voluble way. There was the adviser, a renowned historian at Columbia whom she both worshiped and detested; there was the bag of books she carted about, complaining of the weight. She was a caged bird bashing, fluttering, though to Charlie the door had seemed more or less open, if she'd nudged. His wall had grown up topsy-turvy; you couldn't sit or climb on it or it would fall. Still, it had been tolerated, allowed to sprawl across the Red House lawn, unremarked upon, mostly, or the subject of an occasional joke.

He moved around the other side of the machine so that he wasn't staring into the sun. "I can call right now, sir. I'll talk to Dick—Mr. Wilson. He's an old family friend, I've known him all my life. We own half of the end of the Point with him. I'll be quick. Anyway"—he looked up, met the man's eyes—"it's my land you're bulldozing, not his."

"Your grandmother's land. That's what you said, kid. Don't go changing it around on me."

"It's complicated," said Charlie cagily. "If you can wait just a minute, I'd appreciate it—"

The man peered down at him. "What's your name?"

"Me? Charlie."

"Porter?"

"Benoit."

"Benwah? What kind of a name is that?"

"Swiss. French-Swiss. My mother's a Porter. Helen?"

The man nodded. "I knew her brother. Nice guy, knew how to have a good time. We shipped off the same year, but I came home. You named after him?"

Charlie nodded.

"I'll give you five minutes, Charlie Jr., four more than you asked for. Go."

GAGA WASN'T HOME WHEN CHARLIE called Grace Park from the phone in the Big House kitchen, nor was she at the Lowell Hotel when he tried there. He phoned his parents, got no answer, then Holly, no answer, then Jane, who said she thought Gaga was in Newark, and no, she hadn't heard about the road being widened. She wasn't surprised, but still, it was a shame.

"Can't we make him stop?" Charlie asked. "My wall is on our land. He's trespassing."

"I'm sure he's acting on orders from the town planning board. Hold on . . ." The shrieking of children in the background grew louder. "Go to Rosa, doll. Okay, I know it's upsetting, Charlie, but whether your wall stays up or not, the land is changing hands. You can rebuild the wall a little closer to the house. My boys will help. *I'll* help. That fellow must be digging on the public right-of-way, or he wouldn't be there."

"He can't take down my wall without permission."

"The sides are public, sort of—for electricity or . . . gas lines—I don't know. Dick wouldn't have someone go in if it were illegal. He has a law degree, remember, and I'm sure he has a lawyer handling this. He's scrupulous about this kind of thing."

"Scrupulous! Why is he doing this? He doesn't need the money."

"We don't know that. He must have his reasons."

"Will you try to find Gaga? Please?"

"Charlie, try to put it in perspective. Can't you? It's a *wall*."

Charlie slammed his hand on the counter. "Why didn't anyone tell me about this? I would've gone to the town meetings. I'd have *done* something."

"You were in Ohio. And no one wanted to upset you."

"You all just give in," he said. "It's not the wall, it's the whole thing. You all just roll over and let it happen. It's pathetic, actually, more than anything."

"The Wilsons let it happen," Jane said, "for reasons of their own. None of us are happy about it, but it's not the first time things have changed— remember, there was no Red House or Portable when I was little. This isn't the wilderness, Charlie. It never has been, or not for a very long time. It's easy to romanticize the past here. My mother always said so. For a long time I didn't understand what she meant."

"I'm talking about the present—three new houses, and it will go downhill from there. This isn't nostalgia. It's about what's happening now."

Jane hesitated. "Listen, Charlie, keep this between us—Paul and I tried to buy it. We got outbid. Mummy was going to help. A few people know, but not many. We wanted to put a conservation easement on it. Paul came up for all the meetings. He didn't miss a single one. He was as upset as you are. So was I."

"Really, you bid? That's great. But why didn't Gaga just bid to win? She can afford it."

"She's old, Charlie. And there've been financial setbacks with the company, and this all happened right after Grampa died. You know how he always warned us about becoming land poor. After he went, we were all just . . . in such shock, we—"

"Grampa would have bought it."

"No," Jane said. "I don't think so. In fact, I know he wouldn't. He was too cautious. He wanted Mummy—all of us—to have enough after he was gone. Gaga didn't even have her dock put in this year, the expense was too much—"

"This family is *rich*."

"Not like you think. Not anymore."

"I'd spend my own money," he said, though it was not enough—some $50,000 that Gaga and Grampa had gifted him over the years—and he couldn't get his hands on it until he was twenty-five. It was tied up, tucked away, managed by people he'd never met, who sent occasional reports in creamy envelopes. Later he would learn it was in a "spendthrift trust," the name right out of a WASP joke.

"Charlie," Jane said. "I have to go, dearie. It's too late. It's under agreement. The sale will be final by next month."

"Then they can leave my wall up for now. I don't care if it seems petty—I'm calling Wilson."

"Please don't. It will only upset you more, and it won't change anything. You need to get your balance."

"Calling Wilson will *get* me my balance." His mind was, in fact, feeling better than it had in days—focused, steady, needle sharp.

"Write to him," Jane said. "Writing always works better. Gaga taught me that. The 'more in sorrow than in anger' letter. Hold on . . . . Here. Richard Wilson, 125 East End Ave., 02456. Have you got a pen? 125 East End—"

"I'm *calling*." He scrawled the address on the phone list taped to the wall. "The bulldozer's outside."

EVEN BEFORE HE HUNG UP, his resolve had weakened. He picked up the phone, put it down. It was a Tuesday; he was likely to get Wilson's second wife, a bleached-out, jittery woman dwarfed by her husband and dried out from too much sun and booze. He left the Big House, walked back to the Red House. The bulldozer was parked, the driver not there. Charlie left a note on the dozer—*Please wait!* <u>*Thanks!*</u>—and weighed it down with a rock. Back at the Big House, where his grandmother kept a typewriter in her bedroom, he found a sheet of her onionskin paper wither her initials at the top. As he slid the paper in, turned the crank and watched the shaft turn from black to white, something shifted in his thinking, as if the typewriter were itself a sort of brain. It wasn't the wall that mattered, was it? What was a wall but a man-made barricade, and if they knocked it down, he'd return the rocks to the beach, where they would, with time and tide, resettle among their kind. It wasn't the wall, but the land.

> *Dear Sir . . . . As old family friends and neighbors . . . preserving even some small piece of the land for wildlife and future generations . . . hoping it's not too late . . . anything I can do . . . know you care . . . help raise funds, contribute all I have, Yours Respectfully . . .*

On a separate page, he typed: *fuckyoubigdickfuckyoufuccccck kkkkkyyyou.*

He went out again to find the bulldozer still parked across the road from the Red House, its shovel in midair. Charlie rolled up the second letter, tucked it into a crack in the wall and rode his bike toward town. The road was potholed; the Point Association kept it that way to slow down cars. The developers would repave the road, take away the bumps. He bicycled past the low-slung ash tree, past the foxhole and blackberry thicket, along the curve where a few weeks earlier he'd seen a mother skunk followed so closely by her kits that they'd formed one undulating line of black and white.

At the Packet, he mailed letter number one to Dick Wilson, then headed home, stopping for ice cream on the way. As he sat on the picnic bench at Salvie's licking a maple walnut ice cream cone, he pictured the war landing on Ashaunt—land mines and napalm killing off the people,

Agent Orange stripping down the land. He would hide in the old radar tower, or lift up the lid of the manhole at the top of Hollow Hill and climb in. What would be left? And who was the enemy, and who the natives, and what were they fighting for? Freedom? The landed gentry's right to keep its holdings? The birds, the bees, the sycamore trees? A wall?

For close to an hour he sat there, eating the ice cream, nibbling down the sugar cone, a boy in a nineteen-year-old's body, playing war. Around him, people came and went. He filled the radar tower, fired off shots. He led the charge, herded the wild animals into the underground casemate where they waited, trembling and restless, until he could return for them. The grass grew back out of the moonscape. The trees grew up. The Point House rose again, but smaller now, dollhouse-size, and around it, bay-berry bushes, cedar trees, his paths. His mother's brother Charlie came back, just showed up one day—a clerical error, a mistake in processing. The first Baby Elinor came back, the age of Jane's youngest daughter, wheeled in on Grampa's living lap. Charlie's former self returned and set about its days. He set the animals free. *One two three four, we don't want your fucking war.* His mother was young, she held his hand, they named the flowers. I'm glad it's over now, she said.

When he got back on his bike, the air was cooling down. Along Gooseneck Road, a few families had set out tables where, on an honor system, you could buy garden vegetables and zinnias in mayonnaise jars. To the left, beyond Round Hill, the sea was choppy, a sunlit, ever-changing plane of gray and green.

Charlie felt something like happiness as he rode, something like luck. He'd sent the letter; tonight he'd talk to his grandmother. He'd done, as Jane had said, what he could do. Ashaunt, after his blasted vision of it, looked unusually lovely and like itself, the honeysuckle blooming yellow-white along the road. From his moving bike, he reached to grab some blossoms and sucked the juice.

When he got back to the Red House, his wall was gone.

IX

July 21, 1970

Dear Kate and Callum,

Thank you for the letter. Arbroath sounds lovely! We will go
to Ashaunt Point for August as always. Thank you for the housing
estate clippings even though I did not ask for them! Agnes thought
it comical that you sent them and says to tell you she needs a garden
with full sun. It is fun to dream but the truth is we are settled here
and not well versed in caring for a place, much less owning it. I am
hoping you will come to America for a visit if you could manage
getting about. I can buy the plane tickets and would take you to
a Broadway show and the Statue of Liberty, both are sights to see.
Also New York is much friendlier than they say. If you come across
any of the old letters I sent you I'd be glad to see them. Maybe you
could lend them to me or have them photocopied? I know I did
not write often enough, which I now regret. I really would like to
have those letters. I hope this one finds you in good cheer and good
health. I am in both.

Your Loving Sister,
Beatrice Emily Grubb

X

*A*GE QUOD AGIS: *Do Your Best by Doing Your Best,* or *Force through Force,* or *Excellence Because of Excellence,* or *Success through Striving,* or *Attend to Your Business,* or *Do and Be Your Best.* In Charlie's four years at St. Mark's School, no one, not even the Latin instructor, provided a precise translation of the school motto, which seemed, in its impenetrability, designed to foster a dual sense of privilege and panic in the student body. The boys at St. Mark's were Forbeses, Rockefellers, Pulitzers, Fairchilds, Roosevelts, and Cabots, plus one black boy—a prince, apparently—from Ethiopia. The school's graduates went on to become senators and congressmen, lawyers and businessmen, and the occasional (insane) poet like Robert Lowell. When the St. Mark's alumni spawned, they sent back their sons. What of the sons? A few died in car crashes or OD'd or died or cracked up at war, but most *Did Their Best by Doing Their Best* or at least *Attended to Their Business.* They worked hard in the classroom and even harder on the playing fields and would turn into versions—often paler, less effectual (inbreeding? regression toward the mean?)—of their fathers.

Charlie's mother (his father had gone to the village school in St. Aubin and knew nothing of this world) chose the school because her brother and father had gone there, and because she thought a rigorous education might turn Charlie into a Serious Person and draw out his Potential and allow him to Contribute, which was what Brearley had supposedly done for her. His two brothers were sent to lesser boarding schools when the time came; his sister attended a private day school from home. Charlie hated St. Mark's more than any place he'd ever been. He hated the dark Tudor building under whose one broad roof you ate and studied, slept, worshipped, went to class. He hated the daily sessions in the chapel, and the classes, dull and tiny, lectures aimed at nobody. He hated the teachers— Masters—who were either wholly of the place, in love with the sound of

their English or fake-English accents, or mysteriously, miserably trapped
there, spinsters, oddballs and would-be writers, unhappiness turned to
contempt for the students, who sucked the blood out of their days. He
hated the steady climb toward the Ivy League, not even a climb, really—a
sweep of bodies; it was hard *not* to get in if you came from St. Mark's. He
watched the dull and diligent get in, he watched the more or less dumb.

> *Charles is clearly a bright young man but is deeply lacking
> in motivation. . . . Charles wrote a highly sarcastic essay off-
> topic. . . . Charles pulled himself together at the end of the term
> and performed admirably on his chemistry exam, but his lack
> of effort during the long course is of continued concern to the
> faculty here in terms of both his intellectual and character
> development. . . . Charles' test scores show him to be exceedingly
> bright, but his work does not measure up to his potential.*

Still, as bidden, he wore his suit and tie. He did his lessons, sort of. He
shoveled food into his mouth in the dining hall, where his uncle's name
was engraved in a list of dead war heroes on the wall. He neither taunted
the weak boys nor got taunted himself; to be a good target you had to
radiate a desire to belong. He read a lot of books not on the syllabi and
ran cross-country instead of playing soccer and football, and sometimes
he left the course and plunged into the woods. He found a small pond to
swim in, a rocky outcrop with a cave underneath, where he smoked cigarettes and, later, pot in a small clay pipe. Any thoughts of the future were
ones of avoidance. He would not go to Harvard or Yale. He would not go
to college at all, though he had no better plan and wasn't paying much
attention (no TV at St. Mark's, no radio in your room until fourth form)
to what had become a full-scale war.

Years later, he would remember reading in the paper that Martin
Luther King had been shot and being shocked at how little it seemed to
mean to the St. Mark's community. Bobby Kennedy was shot on the last

day of fifth form; this cast a general pall over the day. He would remember when W. H. Auden, formerly a St. Mark's teacher, came to give a reading, the great poet's nicotine-stained fingers, his warm, gruff voice. Watching from afar, Charlie had known that Mr. Auden would be interesting to talk to (and might even listen), were he not sealed off by the sodden formality that was St. Mark's.

O plunge your hands in water,
Plunge them in up to the wrist;
Stare, stare in the basin
And wonder what you've missed.

During Charlie's time at boarding school, he was threatened with expulsion for sitting on the altar inside the chapel (someone took a photo, which ended up in the yearbook), and threatened again for "setting a fire" (a campfire it was, ringed with stones, inside a pit they'd dug on the outskirts of the grounds) with Sean, one of the few friends he'd made, a sardonic scholarship boy from Worcester who was as much at odds with the place as Charlie, though he made sure to get top grades. Once Charlie brought up transferring to his mother (to where, he had no idea), and she told him he had two choices: stay at St. Mark's, or move home where we can keep an eye on you.

As for when it had begun—their tug-of-war, his endless, exhausting swimming against her current—he could pinpoint the moment. He had just turned ten, at the end of fourth grade. It was prize day at his school; the annual awards were being given out. Charlie was sitting on the risers with his class, wearing a suit jacket, his hair cropped close (in the class photo, he was the only boy with belt and tie askew). Beside him was Jeffrey Deacon, the second-smartest student in fourth grade. Every year since kindergarten, Charlie had gotten the grade's award for highest scholarship. This year Jeffrey had worked tirelessly, bringing in extra long division problems and a battery he'd made from lemons and wire, memorizing extra stanzas of a Longfellow poem, sucking up to the teachers, all in an effort to win the fourth-grade prize.

Charlie had looked at his mother as she sat in the first row and seen that her hands were twisted together, her eyes shut as if in prayer. Beside him, Jeffrey sat ramrod straight. Charlie's name, when it was announced by the headmaster, sounded like someone else's—*Charles Porter Benoit*. He stood and wove his way to the podium, where he accepted his prize—a book and plaque—then watched as his mother rose, visibly pregnant, to stand and clap, alone among all the seated parents, her face alight not with joy or even pride, but with almost abject relief. Then his father joined her, awkwardly (was it his wife's odd whim to stand or a custom of the country?), and Gaga, and soon the whole audience rose—because they had to, because she had. Jeffrey's parents clapped and stood. Everybody did. Only his grandfather stayed seated in his wheelchair, flapping his large hand on his shrunken knee.

Done, Charlie decided at that moment, shutting his eyes against the noise. Done. He had, at ten, neither the language nor the distance to call his mother's investment in him obliterating, nor could he articulate the sadness buried under it (he loved her, he had loved her so, child at her side, her firstborn son. They had discovered a bog, once, near the boat dock; they'd sunk deep in mud, found an Indian bridge, made bullfrog sounds in their throats). He wanted to hand the prize off to Jeffrey Deacon, who was frozen in his seat. He wanted to block out the voice of the headmaster, who'd told his mother before the ceremony that Charlie was bound to earn a PhD in nuclear physics by the time he was twenty-four. The fifth-grade highest scholarship prize was given out; then the sixth, seventh, eighth. Each time, everyone had to stand and clap, having stood and clapped for him. It was too hot out. Grandmothers pleated their programs into fans. Babies cried. Will, having won nothing as was expected of him, sat happily with his third-grade classmates, beating a drumbeat on the back of a folding chair.

Smaller and smaller, Charlie grew after that; it was how he pictured it later, his body and brain pressed to one side, sidestepping, until some moment—well into his twenties, closer to his thirties—when he felt his mother's gaze diminish, her hopes slacken—and began, cautiously, to venture forth again. Was he a weak son, too subject to her will? Was she a bad mother? She could have been much worse. Did she love him? Of course. Too much, he thought. She did not pressure his brothers, not like that, and though she pressured Caroline, it was in a different way—to be her soulmate, to write poetry and pour her thoughts out, except that midway through, his mother would grow distracted or turn on his sister, rageful or diminishing, or—worse—just walk away.

It was during the summer following fourth grade that he tried to build firecrackers from the gunpowder he emptied out of twelve-gauge shotgun blanks he found tucked in the back of a cupboard in his mother's brother Charlie's room in the Big House—for fun, and because he was bored. He meant no harm; he wanted something to play with (Rusty had firecrackers, he had none). In the field behind the house, he emptied the gunpowder from a few blanks and wrapped it in paper, then twisted the end to make a fuse. He lit it and sprang back to witness the small explosion. With the sweet, acrid smell in his nostrils, he made another bigger one, and when it didn't light, tore a hole and touched the match directly to the gunpowder. Then *boom*! A blinding heat upon his face.

The burns were scary—on his face, his neck, one hand, his eyelashes gone—but his mother's fury frightened him more, made him grow still as she stood above him with her hugely pregnant belly after he and his father came home from the emergency room. How could you be so irresponsible? Selfish! Stupid! And to his father: I just knew he'd blow himself up, and now he did!

Charlie sat on the edge of the couch in the Red House, knees pressed together, silent tears running over the bandages and into his mouth. His father pulled him up roughly by the shoulder. In the doorway, his brother and sister stood fascinated.

"Sit down, *chérie*," his father told his mother. "You need to take care of yourself." He turned to Charlie, his face white with rage, though in the hospital he had been quite kind. "She will go into premature labor, and it will be all your fault! Go to your room. You are hopeless! *Va t'en!*"

His mother was sobbing by then, loosely, loudly, bent over her belly. For all her moods, Charlie couldn't remember ever having seen her cry, and the sight shocked him into a glassy calm. In his room, he stood before the bureau mirror and examined his face, covered with bandages. His eyes without their lashes looked bulbous and amphibious. He wadded up torn Kleenex and stuffed it in his ears, and when that didn't block the sound of his mother's sobs, got into bed. His face hurt too much to touch the sheet, so he hunched knees to chest, supporting his forehead with one hand. Crouched there, he pictured the baby inside his mother, shaking as she shook, and for the first time, he began to have a sense of the substantial power of his own actions. Please, he prayed to a god whose existence already seemed improbable to him, please let the baby be okay. And if he himself had died from the gunpowder? Indulgently, he let himself imagine it. They'd have mourned him; they'd have had to, even his mother. A good boy. Highest scholarship in grade five years running. Shame he blew himself up.

THEN TO NEW JERSEY. WILL and Caroline got to stay on Ashaunt with Belle, but Charlie's mother packed him up when, not trusting the New Bedford Hospital, she went home to give birth and deposited him with Gaga and Grampa in Grace Park. For a time, then, things were better. There was a baby, Percy. He was tiny, strange and charismatic. Everybody loved him, Charlie too, who viewed him with particular gratitude because he'd been born healthy, a week late, a pet monkey who would stare into your eyes, and if he screamed or messed his diaper, there was the baby nurse descending and you could hand him off. You're so good with him, his mother told Charlie. You know just how to hold his head up; where did you learn a thing like that? She crooned to the baby, grew dream-

ier, mellower. When Percy was just a few weeks old, they went back to
Ashaunt, and with the baby there, everyone seemed to forget that Charlie
had been grounded for the summer. His burns had turned to scabs and
would soon disappear, except for one little scar above his right cheek-
bone. His eyelashes were growing back. "I've never been this happy," his
mother announced one night as they all sat on the back porch eating ice
cream, Percy kicking in his pram. "All that matters is right here."

For Charlie, there were the paths again, there was Teal Rock, boats to
be sailed, tide pools to explore, collections—wishing stones, discharged
bullet shells—to build, birds' nests to find. One day the army showed
up with trucks and men to stage a training battle, with guns, uniforms
and drill commands; the boys installed themselves by the gate. At four
o'clock, the troops left and padlocked the gate, as if that kept anyone out.
The next day, the whole thing felt like a dream except for a new round
of spent shells. There were crabs to be caught: they'd tie a fish head to a
length of string, sit on the bridge over the salt creek and wait for the rock
crab or blue claw to take the bait. There were trips to Salvador's for ice
cream, hours spent at Grampa's side, visits from family friends. Charlie
resolved to stay out of trouble, and amazingly, for the rest of the summer,
he did—or else managed not to get caught.

IT MIGHT HAVE SHIFTED THINGS permanently to have this new person,
who changed the shape of the family, but if it softened his mother briefly,
it returned her to herself more fiercely in the fall. Her work was start-
and-stop now. Bound to the nest she was (by her own choice, he told
himself, told various shrinks over the years), and though the baby could
do no wrong, she snapped at the others and fought with Charlie's father
more and more. At prize day in fifth grade, Charlie won nothing. He
began smoking cigarettes that year, filching them from his mother. The
summer he was eleven, she hired a tutor and signed him up for camp
on Windy Point, where he knew nobody and chafed at the nonstop

schedule—sailing, knot-making, baseball, archery, crafts involving Pop-sicle sticks. On Windy Point the houses were clustered close. A field had been cropped and fertilized into a mini golf course, and the boys were clannish, and Charlie was, anyway, determined not to make friends.

By then, the line was drawn between him and his mother, the two of them against each other, vigilant—and through it all, unsettling moments of détente, when she would relax, make a joke or offhand remark that showed she understood him as no one else could. Or they'd go sailing in the Beetle Cat and she'd give herself in to it, and Charlie too, the wind at their backs, the sail full, and they knew, still, how to sail together well—tacking, trimming, coming about as if one well-tuned human machine. Or his parents would grow warm and playful, flirty, fight again, kiss, fight, kiss. And Dossy in and out of the hospital, which made Charlie's mother, as she put it, lose her mind, and Grampa ever frailer, and throughout it all, Gaga entertaining, volunteering, steering her precarious, huge ship.

When Charlie was twelve he was sent to a sleepaway camp in Maine where you had to salute the flag each morning and make your bed well enough to bounce a penny on. For the next few summers, he convinced his mother to let him go with Rusty, whose mother was a Quaker, to Quaker Wilderness Camp, and that was better: canoeing, fire-building, rock-climbing, even the silent meetings, and finally he was too old for camp. After his second and third years at St. Mark's, he worked as a coun-selor at Brantwood, a New Hampshire summer camp that the school ran for inner-city boys. Charlie liked this job—to show the boys stuff, to watch them start to trust the natural world, to goof around with them—and his one real disappointment was that he was not invited back as a senior counselor after he graduated (a privilege reserved for the boys with the most leadership potential). Every summer, no matter what he was doing, how far away he was, whether he had to come by bus or bike or hitch a ride, he saved the last two weeks of August and as many weekends as he could manage for Ashaunt.

We've become a world without values, his mother was starting to say by then, first a supporter of the "conflict" in Vietnam, then eventually against the war. Each summer, her time by the sea grew shorter; she loaded the car with books and brought them into the Red House, then complained that she couldn't get anything done, too many people in and out (and she over at Jane's or at the Big House, or in her garden, or going with her sisters for long swims). The cabin was unofficially Charlie's by then, and he was allowed to stay there even when his mother was in New Jersey. He kept the path overgrown, used the outdoor shower at the Big House, not the Red House. He found, in his cabin's location (smack in the middle of Gaga's fifteen acres, built as if she'd known, when he was just a boy, that he might need it there), an island in a sea of leafy green.

XI

A FEW DAYS after the bulldozer razed his wall, Charlie picked up Jerry on the road again, and Jerry got in the car, agitated, head bobbing, and when Charlie asked How's it going, Jerry said they're clear-cutting now, and Charlie asked who and Jerry said the Golf-of-Coursers.

"The what?"

"The military-industrial golfplex."

"A golf course? Is that what they're building?" Charlie asked. "Where I dropped you off last time? I assumed it was houses."

"Nope. A golf course for the rich and infamous. They won't let me cut through to get home. They think"—Jerry laughed mirthlessly—"they own the place."

"Who does own it?"

"My family owns forty acres and we're not selling, but the developers keep crossing over the property line. I'm trying to monitor it, but every time they see me, they tell me to leave. They think I'll scare off the golfers." He bared his teeth.

"But there are no golfers yet."

"Some guy stepped in one of my snare traps. You'd think I'd set a bomb. Do you play golf?"

"God, no."

Jerry looked pleased. "Did you know Castro got rid of every golf course in Cuba? The playgrounds of the bourgeoisie. Did you ever notice how green a golf course is? The grass always greener on the other side. Day-Glo green. Rainbow green."

Charlie nodded. "They use all kinds of chemical crap to get it to look like that."

"You know where it's at, man. Do you believe in private property?"

Charlie hesitated. "I believe . . . I believe we don't own any of it, really. That we should be, you know, stewards. In an ideal world. There's this book, *A Sand County Almanac*—"

"I read it."

"What'd you think?"

"I thought, way to go, Aldo, and then I get shipped out, and they're like, 'Only you can prevent forests!' I shit you not—'Only you can prevent forests,' courtesy of Operation Ranch Hand. They give us gloves, like dishwashing gloves, red, white or blue to hold the poison hoses. Somebody in some office is having a good laugh."

"Jesus. Are you, you know, okay?"

"I made it out alive, I came back here, I got *out*, so I was flying high, I was, like, waiting for my girl and my trees and my . . . my *de-formation*, but it turns out she's sayonara and my trees are waiting for the ax." He looked up, his eyes pained. "You know how Agent Orange works?"

"It kills the foliage?"

"It makes the plants grow themselves to death, like cancer. *Grow, grow grow, my pretties*, then"—he clapped—"*Tạm biệt*. It's happening right here."

"I doubt they're using Agent Orange to build a golf course."

"It's the same chemicals, same family. Cording does his song and dance about open space and recreation, but he left out the part about Die-dioxin."

"Cording? Bill Cording? From New Bedford?"

"According to Cording."

"He's developing Ashaunt too, building houses."

Jerry nodded. "He'll eat the coast and shit it out."

WHEREAS FOR THE FIRST FEW trips to town, Jerry had been silent or spoken in spurts, now he could not stop talking, with a mix of logic, knowledge, passion and hyperbole that both drew Charlie in and set him on edge. Jerry had been to the town hall and library, he said. He'd found deeds and records, maps. His mother didn't know anything about the property boundaries; it had been his father who'd bought the land; the developers thought they could screw over foreigners, but Jerry was born here, a draft-card-carrying American, and he had a plan. He was going to put up a fence at the entrance of the construction site to block the trucks from getting in and slow the whole thing down, and then he'd make the developers stay on their own property and off his, and he'd spread the word about the chemicals—did they really want to spawn kids with no eyes, no eye sockets, did they really want babies with two heads, there was a reason it was called *die*-oxin, and it wouldn't stop at golf courses, the chemicals would leach into the drinking water, into the fish, everywhere. He'd gone to Earth Day in Providence and heard Barry Commoner speak. The chemicals were in our fat and bones. We've got, he said, to bring the knowledge to the people.

By now they had crossed the bridge and were idling in front of the bait shop.

"Could you"—Jerry pointed at the ignition—"keep driving?"

"I was going to pick up some food."

"After, okay? We can't—listen, there's something I want to ask you, but it's got to be—"

Jerry put his finger to his lips as Charlie, half knowing he should not, turned the car on and headed down Bridge Street, then onto Dartmouth Street toward New Bedford, past filling stations, the Salvation Army, the A&P.

"Over there," Jerry said as a large brick church came into view.

Charlie turned into the parking lot and turned off the car.

"Okay, so are you in?" Jerry rolled up his window. "Do you want to help?"

"With what?"

"Stopping the development. Keeping them off my land."

"Of course I'd want that, I just—"

"So you're in?"

"Listen, I can't get involved with anything violent—I'm not into that."

"I'm a pacifist, brother." Jerry looked hurt. "Nothing violent—we just got to act now, like tonight. They're at it with the chainsaw and dozers, the trees are coming down. They're defoliating. *Today* was too late."

"So what are you thinking?"

"First fencing. Then the legal part. They're on my land, and I've got to live there—it's the only place for me. They think I'm a goddamn nobody freak, but they'd maybe listen to you with your Harvard education."

"I don't go to Harvard."

"Yale? Princeton?"

"I was in college in Cleveland, but I'm taking a break. Or dropping out."

"I hear you." Jerry handed him a catalogue across the stick shift. "Take a look."

The catalogue showed chain link and chicken wire, split rail, cedar, aluminum, locust wood. Some fences had been circled. Some circles had been crossed out, drawn again. "Free Delivery!" announced the sticker on the cover below the address: Brobart Fence, 12 Cove St., New

Bedford. Civil Disobedience. Uncivil Disobedience. Nearly a decade earlier, when the gunpowder exploded in Charlie's face, he had experienced a moment of pure wonder before the pain hit—that he could do such a thing, that he contained such power. Dick Wilson hadn't answered his more-in-sorrow letter, which must have arrived too late and was, anyway, less a call to action than a mannered whine. In a few days, the workers would widen the road, lay and bury pipes and wires. His grandmother had called to explain but not apologize: I won't sell our portion, Charlie, but I couldn't afford to buy the rest. On Ashaunt, surveyors continued to mark house lots and foundation sites. Earlier in the week, a worker had begun to cut down the scrubby cedar trees on the end of the Point.

"All right, we can put up some fencing," he said to Jerry. "It's not going to change a lot, but it might help draw attention to what's going on. We might even get some newspaper coverage."

"Do you have a little cash for supplies?" Jerry asked. "I've only got five bucks."

"I've got a little more than that." Adrenaline coursed through Charlie. Hadn't Gaga urged him to get involved, to care about things? He could use his birthday money, spread the wealth. "We can make signs. There's plywood at the dump on Ashaunt. I can put it on top of my car. And we'll need paint."

"*Shhh.*" Jerry looked around.

"No one's listening," said Charlie. "Anyway, we're not doing anything particularly illegal. Just civil disobedience. You're with me on that, right? Nothing shady. I can't afford to get in trouble, and I don't want anyone to get hurt."

"Nothing shady, except protecting the shade."

WHAT HAPPENED HAPPENED QUICKLY, the two of them gathering supplies that afternoon, stowing them at dusk in the woods near the construction site, then meeting after dark to put up fencing to block the access road where the vehicles came in, as well as along what Jerry said was part of his family's property line. It was only deer fencing, the stakes pounded six inches into the ground, but while Jerry had wanted barbed wire, and Charlie had hoped for chain link, this was the cheapest and fastest to install. Charlie had stowed two flashlights, kerosene lamps and black paint in his car, and when they were done with the fencing, they dragged the plywood out and turned to making signs: "Road Closed— Land Returning to Nature; Die Dioxin; Golfers Have Little White Balls." They worked quietly and mostly in silence, and though Charlie knew— because he'd drunk one—that Jerry had brought beer to the site, it wasn't until they were quite far along that he realized that Jerry had been drink-ing steadily, and it wasn't until Jerry upset a can of black paint across a nearly finished sign that Charlie began to get a sense of things having already taken a distinctly wrong turn.

"You're spilling," he told Jerry.

Jerry plunged his hands into the paint can, then raised them to his face and smeared. He opened his eyes wide, rolled them. "Camouflage!"

"Stop—you'll get it in your eyes," Charlie said, but Jerry took his shirt off, picked the paint can up and tipped it down his body, turning his torso black.

"Holy shit, Jerry! What the fuck are you doing?"

Jerry turned on him and bared his teeth, which showed white in the moonlight. "Black Power! Power to the People!" He thrust the can at Charlie. "Cover up, man. Camouflage!"

"We don't need to. No one's here." He took a few steps back. "We should go now—we've done what we came for. Come on."

"There's no way out—they're coming, man! We've got to pull it off!"

A car passed on the road, then. Through the trees, Charlie could see the dusty yellow of its headlights sweeping the edges of the woods and hear the noise of its engine and rock music pulsing, fading.

"That was just kids." Charlie tried to slow his breath. "Please. Let's get out of here."

But Jerry had taken the can and was running toward the bulldozer and flinging paint at it. Even in the dark, Charlie could see the splotches land on the yellow flank of the machine and begin to spread.

"Let's go," he tried one more time. "You've had too much to drink. You should sleep it off. I'll take you home."

Jerry dropped the paint can. "Home?"

"To your place. Where you live. I'll—I'll walk you there."

"Have you heard of the indigo macaw? From Brazil?" Jerry's voice was almost calm now, and full of wonder. "It's supposed to be extinct, except in captivity, but I spotted it on my land. You should see it—all different shades of blue, and when it flies, phosphorescent! That bird is *rare*."

"Maybe someone's parrot escaped," Charlie said, but even as he spoke, he caught a glimpse of something else—wild and impossible, crossing continents and time, a flash of blue, of green.

"Slash the tires!" Jerry began pounding the massive bulldozer tires with his fists. "Burn and slash pyrotechnically speaking 'cause there's gooks in the barnyard, they've been coming over in the wheel holes, little buggers but they'll get you when you turn your back, filling up the hoses, and the government is out for us but I know how to blow shit up using your basic trail dust mechanism—"

"Calm down, Jerry."

"I'll cut your ears off!" Jerry cried. "I'll slice your trophy tongue!"

And then Charlie was running barefoot through the dark, down the access road, cutting through the brush, emerging, finally, at the clear, dark, empty road where he'd parked his car at a safe distance, and he was in the car, and in bed in the cabin.

Home.

As he got into bed, he experienced the by-now familiar separating of mind from body, but also something more: a separating from Jerry, a peeling apart, though he hadn't realized until then how much he had twinned them, intertwined them, in his head. *Not me, not I, not me, not I, not me.* He knew how a mind could buckle; he'd seen it in the patients in the hospital in Cleveland, seen it in Dossy, the way reality could bend and stretch, accommodate almost anything—and then his aunt would go away for a while and return, talkative and funny, painting her paintings, writing her poems, all the while carrying this *thing* around with her, this dark possibility veined with gold. He knew firsthand how the ceiling could sink down, your sightline travel through an object, halos appear, the self disappear, becoming approximate, proximate, turned away from itself in parallel play. He'd seen this madness, tracked it in its various forms. He would come to think that it was primarily this, the tracking, the ability to track, that separated him from someone like Jerry (also war, he'd tell Rusty some years later when Jerry was found dead—basically he drank himself to death, Rich at the Village Market said—in the woods behind the Little River Golf and Tennis Club. Jerry went, we stayed).

He took a whole Valium, removed a thorn from his foot, zipped himself inside his mummy sleeping bag. Slept.

And if, some hours later, he heard the distant sound of sirens, it was through the gauze of sleep, and if, in the morning, he woke to find himself stained by black paint, it was nothing that couldn't be fixed by an outdoor shower and a hard scrub, and later, at low tide, by dry kelp that he used (roughly and with nothing like kindness) to scour the last traces of paint from his skin.

THAT NIGHT, AFTER CHARLIE LEFT, Jerry poured sand and water into the gas tanks of the bulldozer and backhoe and plugged their exhaust pipes with potatoes. He cut the valve stems off the backhoe's tires. He piled brush around the bulldozer and set the pile on fire, and a policeman out patrolling for drunk drivers spotted the smoke, knocked over the deer fence and found him ranting and shit-faced, shirtless, painted black with his hair singed off (so went the story, round and round the town). When the cop walked up to him, Jerry apparently stripped naked, waved his penis at the cop and started chanting "Go home, Hogjaw!" into the night.

Charlie learned about it the next day from Rich at the Village Market, the details unfolding at the meat counter—two other patrons listening, contradicting, chiming in: *A whiskey bottle in one hand, a bomb in the other. . . . I heard it was a machete. . . . He might've been a tunnel rat over there, the skinny ones get that. . . . Should've been living with his mother, not right, a kid alone in the woods. . . . Destroying valuable equipment . . . Bad element, maybe a Weatherman . . . Radical signage. It'll be all over the papers, just what we need. . . . Shell shock, thinks he's still over there . . . waste of time and money . . . full-blown mental case. . . . He could have killed himself or someone else. . . .*

"Jerry Silva? He's an empty suitcase," said Rich a few days later, when Charlie gathered the courage to return to the market and ask (as casually as he could manage) about Jerry, who was, he learned, in jail in New Bedford awaiting trial for arson and malicious destruction of property. "Ever since he got back from Vietnam. He was in the hospital for a while, but not long enough. I'm not surprised he got himself into this mess, but hell, it's a damn shame."

"How long has he been back?" Charlie asked.

"Jerry? Long enough to grow that rat tail."

"Hasn't anybody—"

"Excuse me, Rich," said a young, pregnant mother, whose toddler son had squirmed down and was banging his fists against the glass deli case. "But if I could, he's getting—come here, Kenny, stop it—"

"Shoot, Wendy," said Rich. "Don't mind us, we're just gossiping like two old biddies. What can I do for you today?"

She wiped the hair from her forehead. "A pound and a half of hamburger." She sighed. "Please."

Rich weighed and wrapped the meat and handed it to the woman, along with a lollipop for the boy. She paid and grabbed her child by the hand, but not before giving Charlie a hard look.

"Does he have somewhere to live?" Charlie asked after the door chimed shut. "What does he do in the winter?"

Rich gave him his block of cheddar. "Jerry? He's been staying out in the woods, mostly—his family's got property out there, and some kind of shack. His mother lets him run up credit here and pays at the end of the month. 'Course he goes straight for the booze. I can't tell him what to buy, and she can't keep track of him every second. Every day she goes to mass to pray for him."

"He should be—" Seeing a shrink, on medication, Charlie almost said. "Has anybody tried to help him, in, you know, practical ways?"

Rich, who had been stooped over the case, stood. "Help him, buddy? How about this? You leave a roast chicken out for him, he drops it in the neighbor's well—thinks you're trying to poison him. You try again, down the well. Ask my wife. You put the kibosh on selling him booze, he finds it farther down the road. You get him a mass offering card, he calls you the devil. No one dares go out to his place anymore, not even his own mother. He's—" He twirled a finger near his head. "But not dumb. He was always a smart kid, maybe even some kind of genius. He's got a brother who's retarded. Dumb and sunny, the opposite of Jerry. George, their father, was a friend of mine. I'm glad he ain't alive to see this. It would've done him in."

"What happened to him?"

"Dropped dead of a heart attack, some, oh, ten years ago by now. He wanted to have a farm out on that land—you could get it for next to nothing back then. After he died, the wife opened a beauty parlor in New Bedford with her sister. She does all right." He wiped his hands on his apron. "Listen to me, rambling on. Why are you so interested in Jerry, Charlie?"

Charlie reddened. "I gave him rides sometimes." They'd never, he realized, come into the store together; Jerry always peeled off quickly, quietly. "We read some of the same books. He's a good person. I'd like"—he spoke too fast—"to try to help him, if I could. I could, I don't know, try to find a doctor who could help him."

"Were you mixed up in this, Charlie?"

"No." The lie came quickly, smoothly.

Rich nodded. "Good. Stay out of it. It'll get you nowhere, and his mother's not likely to appreciate it. Maybe a little time in the slammer will open his eyes—I've seen it happen before. When does your grandmother get here? She hasn't placed her meat order yet."

"The beginning of August."

"And your mother?"

"Around then too."

Rich flipped up a page of the calendar on the wall. "Six days. Tell them to call their meat orders in. And Charlie?"

He nodded.

"Stay out of trouble until then."

THE VISITING HOURS AT THE Ash Street jail were five to seven on weekdays, noon to two on weekends. Charlie needed to go there even more than he needed to stay away, driven by a toxic mixture of both guilt and fear. The jail was large and brick, oddly situated in a residential neighborhood between triple-deckers, some with the windows boarded up. When he entered, he was stopped by a short, burly guard, who asked to see his license and had him fill out a form: name, address, relationship to inmate (Charlie hesitated and then put "acquaintance"), date and place of birth, history of felonies or incarcerations.

"No food." The guard took the chocolate bars he had brought for Jerry. Charlie had never been in a jail; the feeling was a strange one, like being stuck on the set of a TV crime show, bleak and unreal at the same time. The walls were pale green, the few windows barred, their panes lined with mesh wire. The place was dirty, paint peeling on the walls, and the air held a foul, unidentifiable smell only partly masked by ammonia. The guard led him into a small room divided by an inner wall, its bottom half wood, its upper screened. A woman stood close to the screen talking to a man, both of them whispering in Portuguese.

"Who's he here for?" asked another guard, sitting in a ratty armchair near the door.

The first guard handed over Charlie's paperwork. "To see the Bug."

"Jerry," Charlie said. "Silva. You can tell him it's Charlie. He doesn't have to see me. Only if he wants to. I brought him—" He held out a copy of *Walden*. "I can just leave it—"

The guard in the chair took the book. "Jerry O, star of the show. He should've gone straight to Bridgewater. The doc had to load him up on Thorazine. Eddie, see if our man's awake."

It took Charlie a moment to recognize the person who appeared. They had shaved Jerry's head, making him look exposed and childlike— his eyes bigger, his ears sticking out. They had shaved his beard; his chin was pale, and he seemed smaller, in a green V-necked shirt, too big, that resembled medical scrubs. His arms were wrapped in bandages, his face still stained with the remnants of black paint.

"Jerry." Charlie gave a feeble wave and stepped toward the divider. "Hey. Hi, it's Charlie. I thought you might want—I brought you *Walden*. I know you've already read it, but I thought—"

Jerry stared blankly through the screen.

"Listen, Jerry, I'm—" Get it over with, Charlie told himself. Apologize (for what, though? Joining in? Abandoning? Misjudging? All of the above?). He wanted, also, to make sure that Jerry hadn't ratted him out for his own role in what had happened, but there was no good way to find out. He'd hardly slept since he'd talked to Rich two days earlier. He'd been jumpy—afraid of being hauled off, found out, even as he'd been having fantasies of being back in the loony bin in Cleveland, clean, bound and gagged, *not guilty by reason of insanity* (though he'd never been exactly insane, which complicated the matter and made his own role worse).

"It's Charlie," he repeated to Jerry. As he heard his own name again, he could feel the warning signs of a panic attack, his breath growing shallow, the tightening of his forehead, a rubber band looped around his brain. "I'm . . ." He shut his eyes, then opened them. "This isn't the right place for you, you don't belong here—"

Jerry nodded, his features blurred by the grid of screen. "It's a case of mistaken identity or, like, alias. I wasn't in uniform, see, I couldn't find it in the dark but what I was doing was legit, totally, I didn't hurt anyone, I just—" He shuddered. "Someone was there. Golden? Was it him? Do you remember? Listen, I could use another beer, could you get me a six-pack or maybe a shot of—"

"You can't have alcohol in here. You're in jail. In New Bedford. That's where you are right now. Just temporarily. I'm really sorry about—that you ended up here. Really sorry." Charlie's eyes stung with childish tears. "I'd like to try to help you."

"They said it was R&R, but they'll tell you anything, I wasn't ghosting or anything. Golden was there, but I lost track—"

An empty suitcase. An empty suitcase that read Thoreau. Charlie remembered a patient at the hospital in Cleveland who went in and out of thinking he was a fireman rescuing sexy extraterrestrials or watching them burn, and how the nurse had played along with it: You got her, Mr. Gerstein; ease her down the ladder, nice and slow. Ten minutes later, the guy would be normal. An insurance adjuster. Two kids. Wife ran off on him. He'd round up the patients, including Charlie, to play bridge.

"Golden's okay," he told Jerry.

"For real?"

"For real. Nobody got hurt."

"*Golden's* okay?" Now Jerry sounded skeptical. "How do you know? I'm"—he tensed, then released every muscle in his face—"not supposed to be here." He looked out, his gaze dense and fully present through the screen.

"Listen, Jerry." Charlie stepped closer. "What can I do? Please tell me. What can I do to help?"

"The cat."

"What?"

"She'll starve out there. I've got twenty bucks under the mattress."

"No problem—I'll feed her."

"Naw, I'll feed her tomorrow. She can wait." Jerry laughed shrilly. "Fat cat!"

"You might not be able to get there. When do you leave? What's your bail?"

Jerry spread a hand across his face and squeezed.

Charlie turned to the guard. "Do you know when he'll get out of here? His trial date, or what his bail is?"

"Nope."

Charlie turned toward the screen. "I'll feed the cat, Jerry. Okay? Until you come home. What does it—she—eat?"

"Nine Lives," Jerry said. "But watch for dented cans—botulism, and the chemicals, it's all part of the same— And you've got to bring water in."

"I'll go tonight."

"Not at night! You can't find her at night!" Jerry started bobbing again. "I've got a thing going, Operation Die Marker, an anti-infestation-infiltration barrier—it's got infrared, watchtowers, sensors. Bad idea to go at night, very bad, and if you go in tomorrow, don't walk straight, you have to weave cloverleaf and don't go taking a dump there 'cause I've got this other device that senses shit, a Shit Detector—"

"Okay, okay." Charlie looked frantically at the guard. "He needs help—he should be at a veterans hospital where they know—"

The guard spoke into a crackling walkie-talkie. Almost instantly, the younger man who had led Charlie in appeared on the other side of the screen, where he turned Jerry's face toward him and, in an almost tender manner, held it still, his hand clamping Jerry's chin. "*Shut up*, Silva. I didn't finish my tour to listen to this crap."

"You heard of punji stakes?" Jerry asked him with the enthusiasm of a collector. "I once knew this guy who—"

"*Pare-o!*" The guard let go of his face and stepped back. "*Está mental-mente doente! Pare conversa sobre la guerra! Pare-o!*"

Jerry answered back in a rapid stream of Portuguese. Another whole language, he had; it shouldn't have surprised Charlie, but it did. *Casa*, he heard (was it *house*, as in Spanish?), but other than that, he couldn't pick out a thing.

"What did he say?" Charlie asked the younger guard when Jerry finally stopped. "Did he say 'house'?"

"He's just ranting."

"Jerry, listen. I'll feed your cat"—Charlie stepped close to the screen and Jerry's face—"and keep the indigo macaw safe. Okay?"

Jerry met his eyes and nodded, and what passed between them was a slower, more labored version of the look they'd exchanged on the side of the road in June—*Help me, follow, help*—but something else now too: not knowledge of each other, exactly, but knowledge's bent cousin, shadowy and wordless, an animal low to the ground. Jerry's eyes were bloodshot but also liquid brown and full of pained intelligence. Charlie, holding steady, held his gaze.

Why, of all the people in the world, did you have to take up with a nutcase?

It was the rarest kind of seeing, being seen.

JERRY'S PLACE WAS NOT A rustic one-room cabin in the woods. It had no stump for a table, no roll-up bed. The clearing where it stood was sur-rounded on all sides by brambles, just about as hidden as any place in southeast Massachusetts in 1970 could be. There was a small vegetable garden, but everything in it, save for a few tomatoes overripe on the vine, was dead. All around, for a good half mile in every direction, Jerry had posted a series of misleading markers, painted arrows nailed to trees, signs reading This Way, even Welcome, each one sending the intruder (it might have been a prank out of Lewis Carroll) the wrong way, or no way at all.

All that, though, was farther in. As he first entered the woods, Charlie saw just the familiar sight of trees, undergrowth, and to his left the bulldozer site with its piles of dirt and downed trees, now ringed by yellow Keep Out tape. He'd waited until the late afternoon when the workers had gone home, filled his backpack with cat food, a can opener, a thermos of water, an apple. He'd walked to the spot where he always dropped Jerry off, looked both ways down the road—no one—and darted into the woods. Now, as he followed a rough farm road until an arrow painted on a piece of plywood directed him to take a right, a calm settled over him. Passing through a small clearing, he came upon a rusty old car near what looked like the concrete top of an old well, and beyond it, a brook with skunk cabbage rising, prehistoric, from its marshy banks. There, the mosquitoes and deerflies found him. Swatting, he followed the first arrow to the second, which circled back to the first.

"Here," Charlie said aloud every few minutes as he walked. "Here kitty, here kittykittykittycat!" Jerry hadn't told him the cat's name, and now he wished he'd thought to ask. He must have circled for nearly half an hour before he finally stumbled upon an old fence, the cheap roll-up kind, mud-red slats held together by wire and peeling with age. It was partially hidden by a camouflage screen made from cut boughs. Gingerly, he followed it for some fifty feet until it ended, simply ended, barricading nothing, keeping nothing in and nothing out.

And there, a clearing, the grass uncut and scratchy, up to his knees. To the right stood a ramshackle building—a broken-down stable, maybe, long and low. To the left, a crater of a stone foundation, filled with grass now, and a lone white pine sapling. He walked over to the building, opened a rough wooden door. The place seemed deserted, old hay still on the floor of the open stalls. A bird flew from out the rafters and exited in a clean shot through a hole in the roof. He walked along the row of stalls, kicked a can out of his path, found a rusty horseshoe and put it in his backpack. "Kitty," he called again. "Cat. Kitty-cat. Here kitty kitty, here?"

Jerry's house—home? hovel?—turned out to be well beyond the

other end of the clearing, after the terrain became wooded again. Charlie might have missed it were it not for a tin smokestack poking up, weak sunlight glancing off the silver tube. To get there, he had to lie on his stomach and crawl, pushing through what was not much more than a rabbit trail, a passageway all green, brown and yellow, all scratch and push; his stomach itched, his backpack slowed him down. Around this corner, what, around this corner, who? Finally, the tunnel ended and he looked up to see another plywood sign—"Jerry Silva, Lord of 10,000 Acres"—and behind that a smaller clearing, and in it, finally, the place where Jerry lived.

It was an old metal milk truck with the wheels removed, painted army fatigue green so that it blended into the bush, but you could still see some letters through the paint—an *S*, a *V*. Next to the truck was a small round fireplace rimmed with stones, and behind it a heap of cans, mostly Buds—and empty whiskey bottles. Behind the milk truck, on the other side, a foul smell, and there (he gagged) a bucket full of shit, a cloud of flies. On the third side of the truck, two wide, neatly sawed off, upright log stools (finally, something he had imagined), set up near each other as if ready to host a conversation, and a woodpile, wedge and ax. Charlie came back around the truck toward the door and was stopped by another sign—"Do Not Enter, Signed J.S., Guardian of 10,000 Acres Master of None."

"Cat?" His voice returned, tentative. "Are you inside? I'm—what the hell—I'm coming in."

He ducked into the truck, his eyes adjusting. It was tiny in there, and strange. One small window, high on the wall, let in a slice of dusty light, but the front and side windows were covered with green garbage bags. He pushed the door farther open to let in more light and dilute the rank smell. Jerry's bed was an old cot mattress on the floor. On it lay a sleeping bag, faded green and lined with red flannel covered with deer and hunters—the kind of bag a boy would take to camp. Instead of a pillow, a pile of clothes. Instead of a table, an overturned oil drum—and on it, a food-encrusted plate and spoon. There was a flashlight; he turned it on. There was a woodstove, the stovepipe rising through a hole cut in the roof. In one corner, fishing net hung, creating a hammock for more clothes. And other things, details he would remember years later, mostly for how they didn't add up. A diagram, drawn on the wall in black Magic Marker—lines labeled "a," "b," "c," leading to a jarlike shape. Below it, a piece of delicate embroidered linen was affixed with masking tape. On the floor next to the bed, a pink girdle, lacy and muddy, and a potholder appliquéd with yellow balloons. Two bowls, one empty, one half full of murky water.

Had Jerry done this all alone? Had somebody helped him, or had he come upon the place unoccupied but furnished (such as it was), or had it been his father's—a hideaway or hunting shack? There had clearly been a farm here once, and here, maybe, its milk truck, left to rot. Reclaimed. On the floor, Charlie found a bag, and in it a bar of soap, a pair of new work gloves, a prayer card of Saint Francis flocked by birds: *O Lord, Make Me an Instrument of Thy Peace.*

Then the books, housed in crates. A few were library books: *Silent Spring*, Emerson, a how-to book on electrical wiring, another on trapping. These, dutifully, Charlie put in his backpack to return. There were dog-eared thrillers, a book on foraging for native plants, a mushroom guide, a few tattered copies of *Playboy* (he opened one, felt a stirring, put down the magazine). A *Time* magazine with Barry Commoner on the cover. But it was the last book in the second crate that stopped him short. The *Social Register*, black and red, dated Summer 1968. His parents received one in the mail every year, his grandparents too. His own family was listed in it, he had always assumed, though he didn't actually know how it worked. Did you have to be from a Mayflower family? To make or have inherited a certain amount of money? The *Register* was, to him, like an outdated encyclopedia set—part of the furniture; he'd seen the book but never looked inside. But to find it here, to see it here. Had Jerry taken it from a house in Ashaunt? *Look at Dilatory Domiciles Always to Ensure*

Accuracy, read the small print on the cover. Was the milk truck (Red House, Big House, Portable) a dilatory domicile?

He had just sat down on the mattress and begun to look up his family in the *Register* when something rushed through the door and brushed against his leg. By his feet, a plump gray-and-white cat opened its mouth to show its tongue. As Charlie put down the book, the cat sprang toward the door. He stepped outside to see its tail disappear into the brush. From his backpack, he took out a handful of kibble and scattered it on the ground, then filled a bowl with water and sat back to wait. And there, again, was the cat, trotting toward the food. She ate the kibble. He ate his apple. He opened a can of 9Lives; she ate, cocked her head, meowed. "Meow," he answered and put out more kibble. The cat ate that too, then lapped the water in the bowl.

She was mottled gray and white, missing part of one ear, with a broad, suspicious face, but when she'd finished eating she came up and rubbed against his leg. She circled his calves, weaving, flicking her tail, stopping to look at him through slitted yellow eyes. Finally, he bent and picked her up. Through her bulk, her heart beat fast against his hand. She scrabbled up his chest, climbed her front legs over his shoulder and lay draped over him, a living stole, until a noise—a squirrel in the branches? a cop?—put both of them on high alert. Then, digging her claws through his shirt into his skin, the cat tried to spring away—he yelped in pain—but he tightened his grip and held her fast and took her home.

XII

WHAT BEA HAD not known before her trip to Forfar was that
homesickness was like a virus lying dormant; it could be housed
inside you for years, attached—or so you might think—to a single person, a mother in this case, hers (why go back if she was gone?), only to be
woken by a place itself. Bea had thought herself more or less indifferent to
location; it was people she cared about, children, friends, good-natured
men who could make her laugh. She had never been particularly moved
by either landscape or mortar, but now she couldn't stop thinking about
the shape of the Angus hills, the shades of green, the streets of Forfar,
which she had started walking in her mind.

Also houses, the insides especially. She and Agnes had always enjoyed
leafing through the home-decorating magazines—she for the crafts and
colors, Agnes because she liked picturing herself or the characters in her
romance novels living in this house or that. But now, as they sat in one of
their rooms or on the Big House porch in the August heat, it was adverts
they read. *Seaside cottage for sale. Condo. retirees, all amen, free pkng,
pool.* In Dartmouth and Fall River, Westport, even Rhode Island, the ads
on leaflets left in the mailbox with grocery store flyers or printed in the
classifieds. They learned to read the codes— *2b/1b/hwf/gh*—and translate
the descriptions: *Handyman's project* (piece of rubbish). *Up and coming
neighborhood* (unsafe for ladies on their own). And the ones that truly
played on your emotions: *Victorian cottage, Pfct for 2. Gardener's Delight.
Empty Nesters' Dream. Lil Piece of Paradise.*

It was a game, a sort of amusement, though they both knew without
saying to fold the pages over if anyone came by. The prices were shock-
ing at first, then a little less so, but it was a pipe dream anyway, so didn't
matter. Why would they want to buy here, where the winters were raw
and everyone they knew was far away? Better in New Jersey or even Scotland. In their more sober moments, they agreed that it might not be the

worst idea to consider someday having a place of their own, for what was money for, if not to spend wisely (so said Agnes), and real estate seemed the most, well, *real* investment, a house being something you could enjoy in a daily way, as well as a roof over your head. Money, even her own, still remained a bit abstract to Bea. After a childhood of her parents fretting about it, she was glad it was not a worry for her, but beyond that, she paid it little mind. It was Agnes who read and filed the investment account reports that first Mr. P. and now Paul gave them each month. Bea just signed where she was told to on the tax forms, though she kept her savings and checking account ledgers herself, using the money for gifts, clothing and incidentals, with a bit left over each month.

What she and Agnes felt but could not say, nor even entirely see, was that the air was full of change that year, fomenting, restless. Jump aboard, make a break, take a chance! But in their own way, retracting, stretching out, retracting, snails in their shells, or perhaps hermit crabs (had they, after all these years, outgrown their space?). I'd go for blue for my room, said Bea. Floral curtains with small sprigs. Like your room in Grace Park, said Agnes. Yes, but lighter, and maybe with a scalloped edge. For me, small roses, said Agnes. In the garden and on the curtains. Peach-colored for the fabric—pink roses is too much like a box of tissues, don't you think? Bea nodded. She'd read the same article in *Better Homes and Gardens* but didn't mention it. Peach has a calming effect, she said.

"How would Mrs. P. manage if we left?" she asked one morning, as she and Agnes sat by the window in her room.

"We'd be nearby."

"What if a toilet broke?"

"Mrs. P. fixes the toilets?"

"No, really. What would we do?"

"We'd call the plumber."

"Expensive. Very, I think. Isn't it?"

"We'd ask around for the best rate. We could start by renting. A little flat in Orange, maybe. Then the landlord pays the plumber."

"But why rent when we can live for free?"

"For our independence. To be not so *reliant*, and so the rellies could visit us at our own place."

"I think," Bea said under her voice, "Mrs. P. would be shocked and . . . and hurt—maybe even worried for us."

"Stewart's lived on his own nearly the whole time."

"That's Stewart," Bea said. "He's got a family, and he's a man."

"Women live on their own now." Agnes's eyes gleamed. "Women's liberation! The girls are burning—" She waggled her fingers at Bea's chest. "Don't you keep up?"

Bea pictured her double-D brassieres going up in flames and laughed. "I'd start a forest fire!"

The next week, a forwarded letter from Callum and, folded inside it, a few letters—not copies, the originals—that Bea had written during the war. Reading Smitty's name (*My friend Smitty took me to a picture show*), she tried to imagine the sequence of letters that might have followed: *I'm getting married. I'm moving to St. Louis.* She could have chosen for herself a different fate and written it in a letter—and her brother would have accepted it, found it unremarkable, perhaps because one's own life was remarkable only from the inside (and she did not, anyway, she told herself, regret her choice). Callum also included some housing estate adverts, for small houses, not flats. The codes and abbreviations were different from the American ads, the prices in pounds. Bea put them away in her smaller valise, and it was not until they were unpacking in Grace Park that she even told Agnes that they'd come.

Still, it would be Bea who would suggest the next visit to Scotland the following spring, her niece Marcy newly pregnant with her second by then (who would be Amanda) and pleased to put her feet up while Bea and Agnes took little Jack to the park. It was Bea who suggested to Agnes that they pop into the housing estate office on High Street, where a pleasant fellow young enough to be their grandson pulled out a binder of photographs and called them Madam and took them round. Agnes was the one to break the news to Mrs. P. back in America, in the yellow sitting room in Grace Park, as Bea stood a few feet behind her, short of breath.

"My word. I can't believe . . ." Mrs. P. drew her arms around herself. "Do you mean this? Are you sure? I don't understand—" She turned, first to Agnes, then to Bea.

Agnes prodded Bea.

"My father told me," Bea said (they had rehearsed upstairs), "that I'd want to end up where I started. Before I left for America." She felt both sick and driven, as if she were inflicting a necessary punishment on a child. Also afraid of losing the particular house they'd set their sights on, a new bungalow with a sunny garden on one of the better streets in town, on a hill with a view of the fields. She wanted it badly—for its newness, its address, the garden for Agnes, the light-filled corner bedroom that would be her own. "It seems," she finished lamely, "like it might be a good idea."

"But after all these years?" asked Mrs. P. "And with your parents passed on?"

"We both still have family there," Agnes said.

"Of course." Mrs. P. nodded. "And of course you miss it. It's lovely there, isn't it? You know I think so."

"It's lovely," Agnes agreed.

"But—do you mind my asking, have you been, you know, homesick all these years?"

"No," they said together.

"It's not that. It's just," Agnes said, "with the children grown and us getting on, and my sister and Bea's brother—"

"Of course."

"And, well, we've found a house we quite fancy," said Agnes.

"A house already! Have you told Jane yet? And the others?"

"We wanted to tell you first," Bea said. "I—I was hoping you might break the news to Janie. And then I'd talk to her."

"No, Bea. I can't, I couldn't. Certainly not. That's your job."

Bea stiffened.

"She'd want to hear it from you," Mrs. P. added more gently.

"Do you think," asked Bea, "she'll be all right?"

Mrs. P. laughed, the sound stinging. "Jane? Of course! She has a wonderful life, six children, a career. Paul. Me. She'll be fine. It's just that"— she drew in her breath—"you've been all the world to her."

"And she to me." Bea was crying freely now.

"And you to us," Agnes added, though it did not make sense, not in any precise way.

"And you"—Mrs. P. was laughing now, even as she wiped away her own tears— "to me, dear A. and B. You'll come back often, won't you? Promise me. It's so easy these days, with all the flights. It may as well be part of the same country."

"Of course," they said (they would come back once for a visit, and Bea would return again for Mrs. Porter's funeral, eight years hence).

XIII

T HE SECOND WEEK of August, the wrecking ball came to knock down the concrete radar tower. Ashaunt was operating at full throttle—swimming, conversations on the road, grudges and hurt feelings, houseguests, bicycles, Beetle Cat races, stoned teenagers, roaming groups of barefoot kids. In some ways, the presences made the absences more palpable to Charlie; freshly, he found himself missing his grandfather and noticing how alien he felt among what used to be his tribe. In other ways, though, it soothed him to hear voices in the distance, to be able to show up for dinner uninvited in any number of houses, even to watch the conflicts play out, mostly trivial, mostly among the women:

who wasn't invited swimming; who had overstayed her welcome; who couldn't admit that her son was a bully; whose nanny had quit without notice, leaving her, a working woman, high and dry. In August the husbands came too, for a week or fortnight, and while most of them sailed, fished, swam, played tennis, Charlie's father set himself the lone task of building a shed to house the Red House garbage cans and could often be found leaning over a drawing of his design or squinting at the ball floating in his yellow leveler, as he likely was the day the wrecker came.

If André was not there to watch, nearly everyone else was: Charlie's two aunts and his mother. Rusty, Will, Caroline, Percy, Bea, Agnes and Stewart. A cousin—Marie-Laure, around Caroline's age—was visiting from Switzerland. All of Jane and Paul's kids were there; so were Holly and John, along with two widows, friends of Gaga's from New Jersey, in dresses and straw hats. Gaga, wearing a faded wraparound skirt, stood shielding her eyes from the sun. Big Dick Wilson was there. He'd clapped Charlie on the back the first time they'd seen each other. Did you get my letter? Charlie had asked, and Dick had said, Sure did, and I agree with you, Charlie, every word—thanks for getting in touch! Then he'd fled. He was getting divorced again and had come without his wife. He'd been drinking (or so went the story) heavily and been sent off by his children to a "spa" out west. His grandson, Little Dick, was there, in a purple Williams College T-shirt. Average Dick, Big's son, was not around. An assortment of dogs romped on the edges of the crowd. A child had first sounded the call—*The radar tower's going down!*—and as word spread, people had emerged from houses and paths, from porches and lawns, gardens and boats.

Charlie had been one of the last to arrive, both reluctant and compelled, camera in hand. As a child, he'd played in the tower often with the other boys. They'd pretended to be soldiers spotting U-boats; on the tower's top story (there were four, including the little top one), you could sit in what had been the old control room and see for miles on a clear day. The tower had been stripped of much of its machinery, but they had used a rusty cookie sheet as their radar screen, scratched circles on it, made up lingo and borrowed it from military (pirate, mystery, whaling) books and movies: *Double nine coming in to rest on the haft end! Nose of a sub out there! Ready the shackles! There she blows! A Hun!* Now, as he watched, he felt Jerry—absent, literally barred—at his side, asking him to witness (How many times could one *not* look? How many times could one turn and run away?). He raised his camera, took a photo, then another. The crowd, obeying some collective instinct, turned south, just as the steel wrecker ball began, quite languidly, to swing.

"*Bam!*" shouted Jane's youngest son, but there was no bam; the ball knocked almost gracefully, swung back, approached again.

"Stay back, people!" a man in a hard hat called as the group edged forward. "That ball weighs fifteen hundred pounds!"

"I can't see," Percy complained.

Charlie readjusted his camera to hang at his side and hoisted Percy onto his shoulders, surprised at how long his little brother's legs were. Taking hold of Percy's bare feet, he clapped them together. "Clap for the losers," he said.

"Who?"

"Them." He pointed at the men and machines. "And us."

"Me?" asked Percy.

"No, not you. Me, though. I can't believe we have to watch this happen."

"We don't have to," Percy said. "It's just cool."

Charlie couldn't help feeling a little awed by the ball's elegant, destructive power, even as each blow was a punch to his gut. On his shoulders, his brother's legs tensed when the ball swung forward, released when it swung back.

"I know it's an eyesore," Bea said behind them. "But I'm fond of it. I almost wish it didn't have to go."

"It scared me as a girl," said Jane. "I thought its light was an evil eye. My sisters terrorized me with stories about it."

"Did they, dearie? You never told me," said Bea. "I'd have set them straight."

"We'll have a better view when it's gone," Jane said. "At least for a little while."

"Ladies, I don't think it's going anywhere," said Paul.

It was true: not a chip had come off so far—at least it looked that way from where they stood. Not a dent had been made. Suddenly the whole thing struck Charlie as comical, beautiful. The truck backed up to get more leverage. The group retreated more than a few steps. Even the dogs—some held back by their owners now—were watching, uncertain, keeping their distance as the ball swung harder, faster. Still, nothing gave. And again. Eventually, Charlie's shoulders started to ache. He set his brother down, took another picture. The sun grew hotter. People drifted off, the crowd halving and then again, until there were just four of them left, an odd, ragtag group: Dick Wilson, Charlie, Percy, Bea.

And then the machine itself had stopped, the driver and workers taking a break, pulling out lunch boxes, popping open Cokes. The foreman was speaking into a CB radio in the cab of his pickup truck. All the while, Dick Wilson stood with his back to them. In his untucked light blue Oxford shirt, khaki shorts and faded hat, he looked, from behind, more like a teenager than an old man, except for how his legs bowed in. Off by himself, he'd been, the whole time. Was it true that no one had talked to him? Gaga had not; his grandchildren had not.

"I'm starving," Percy said.

Taking in Wilson's figure, Charlie tried to turn him into a villain, but the man in the flesh looked too human, almost frail. Bleakness overtook him, the pull of a dark mood.

Percy poked him in the side. "I said I'm starving."

"So get some lunch, Perc. Or find Mummy or Anna. I'm not your maid."

"Come, Percy." Bea held out her hand. "We'll have lunch at the Big House, just the two of us. There's a lovely leftover ham."

"I'm sorry, I didn't mean—" Charlie stumbled. "I can make him lunch."

Bea pulled Percy to her side. "No," she said. "We have a date."

In the end, it would take days to get the whole tower down, the great ball swinging and bashing, the structure resisting, then giving in, piece by piece, an elephant slow-buckling to its knees. The bulldozers would lift up the concrete chunks and move them to the shore, converting them to riprap to slow the erosion at the tip of the Point. From far enough away, the pieces of the tower looked like rocks.

In stages, Charlie photographed the tower's demise. In college, his photography teacher had once told the students to take a photo of something ugly, something they hated, and create an image that made it beautiful. Now, he tried to find beauty in the shapes of crane and ball, slab and sea. In one photo, he caught a gull right in the middle. In another, a workman with his hands raised to the sky, as if attempting to grab the wrecker ball—and above it, barely visible, an early moon. He used black-and-white film. Earlier in the summer, he'd gotten his pictures developed at a photo shop in New Bedford, but now he found himself wishing for a darkroom where he could watch the images emerge and control their density and contrast, or even a class where he might share his pictures and view other people's and learn a thing or two.

XIV

JERRY'S CAT DID not like to stay inside the cabin. It either escaped as Charlie was coming or going or complained so persistently that he let it out. Jerry had said the cat was a homebody, but Charlie watched it get into spats with dogs, and it would nose open the screen door at the Red House and peed, once, on the sisal rug (This cat, said Charlie's father, eez not a girl). Charlie had told his family he was taking care of the cat for a friend from St. Mark's who was on a sailing trip. Back in a week, he said, and then, when a week passed, back soon. The cat slept by—and sometimes on—his head, and while at first this bothered him, he soon grew used to it, even to like it. Its using his mother's flower garden as a litter box was more of a problem, and his mother, who claimed to dislike all cats (they'd only ever had dogs), hated this one more. *Keep it in the cabin*, she'd say. *Get it out of here before the weekend, or it's going to the pound* (an empty threat; death made her squeamish, and her meanness—if not her anger— went only so deep). "What's its name, anyway?' she asked once. Charlie did not know but felt an almost ethical obligation not to call it something different from what Jerry had, and, if Jerry had left it unnamed, to leave it unnamed too. "Cat," he told his mother. "I was afraid you'd say that," she said.

One day, after a particularly loud rant from his mother, he looked up "Silva" in the phone book, thinking to call Jerry's mother and drop the animal off, but if his fear hadn't stopped him (Are you the boy who put our boy in jail?), the sheer number of Silvas in the phone book would have. A few days after his first visit to the Ash Street Jail, he had gone back, but Jerry was gone by then, moved to Bridgewater State Hospital for the Criminally Insane, a good hour north. He'd thought of writing a letter telling Jerry that he was caring for the cat, but he never did, too afraid of tying his own name to Jerry's, which would make it harder to deny the whole story if it ever came out.

As for himself, he was doing a little better now. He started running again, with shoes. He still took his pills. His jaw, when he let it go slack, still went on overdrive, his teeth chattering, his face with a life of its own. He still avoided people in general and his mother in particular, and lived in fear (hope?) that Holly would bring back Melanie, but with Holly or Rusty, with Jane or Gaga or on a sailboat or underwater, he was, some days, quite okay. There were blackberries on the paths; he ate until his legs were scratched, his tongue purple and belly full. Underwater, he dove and blindly dug until his fingers closed around littleneck clams, or put on his mask and watched the murky weavings of the water world. There were sorrel leaves to pick; there were lamb's-quarters, oyster mushrooms, black chanterelles, boletes. He gathered and wandered, writing down lists of birds and flowers in his notebook, recording the weather. This was, perhaps, the greatest blessing of Ashaunt (a mixed blessing, his mother would insist, or even a curse): How it could fill you, without effort, with itself.

One day, when he put out food and called the cat, she did not appear. He tried again later, and again at bedtime, then gave up. Animals wandered; she'd return, but the next day, she still wasn't there. Charlie looked a little harder and asked around as he rode his bike, but the cat didn't come back that day or the next, which was when he and Rusty took the Beetle Cat to Cuttyhunk Island and slept in the harbor in the wide cockpit, the boat rocking, the sky full of stars, and in the morning they ate breakfast at Bosworth House and explored the island, with its carless lanes, one-room schoolhouse and paths, on foot. They might have been back in time, a century or more, except for the explosions they saw from afar, Otis Air Force Base testing bombs at No Man's Land (even the fighter planes, in formation, seemed archaic, small, black and formal, like the model WWII ones he used to make). They dug, smashed open and ate an unhealthy number of raw clams. They talked, for the first time all summer, about how they both were doing—not in any major way, just a little here and there, and Charlie told Rusty about Jerry and what had happened, trusting him to never tell a soul.

When, upon their return, Charlie tried to enter the Red House to use the toilet (he felt a diarrhea attack coming on), he found, as in no other time in his memory, the front door locked. Rusty had gone home. Charlie's mother's car was not parked on the lawn. He jiggled the handle— did a key even exist?—and when it didn't budge, hurried around to the kitchen door to find it also locked. So too the door on the porch. Finally he gave up, pulled off his shorts, and squatted in the bushes, wiping himself with leaves.

He should, he realized later, have given more thought to where the cars were and why the doors were locked. But he was sunburned, depleted, his gut in a cramp. People did things all the time that made no sense to him. He was dozing naked in the cabin when his mother burst in. He sat up and pulled his sleeping bag up around his waist.

"Where the hell have you been?" she asked.

Charlie blinked. "Sailing with Rusty. To Cuttyhunk."

She covered her face with her hands.

"What?" he asked. "Is everything all right?"

She lowered her hands and looked at him, and it was then that he saw her bug-eyed rage. "No. No, Charlie, it's not. Absolutely not. I was at the police station."

"Jesus. Why? What happened?"

"What did you do with that wretched cat?"

"The *cat*? I don't know. It's around, I think. Why? What happened, Mom?"

"Call me *Mummy*, like everyone else does," his mother said through gritted teeth. "Some crazy man, some *friend* of yours, came looking for that cat. A criminal, it turned out. He marched right into the house like he owned it. I was napping. Do you have any idea what it's like to be a woman alone in the house and have a crazed criminal walk into your bedroom and loom over your bed? Do you have even the foggiest idea?"

"No. God, I'm really sorry."

"At first I couldn't understand a word he said, but then he said you were taking care of his cat while he was in jail. How charitable of you, Charlie. How very open-minded. This is your old friend from St. Mark's, off for a sail, or did you mean jail? He was going on about . . . I don't even know—private property and Marx and the meek shall inherit. He knew my *name!* Is this what you've been doing here, hanging around with lunatics? I should have known. He wouldn't leave, I had to talk him into leaving—"

"How?" he asked, impressed.

"What?"

"How did you talk him into leaving?"

His mother began to circle the tiny space that was the inside of the cabin. "I told him I'd seen the cat on Little River Road, but that wasn't enough, so I told him he looked like he could use a good meal, and then I offered him ten dollars if he'd vacate the premises and not come back, and off he went." She couldn't keep the pride from her voice. "Money well spent."

Charlie laughed.

"Don't laugh! He could have raped or murdered me! As soon as he left, I called the police and they arrested him. It turns out they knew about him and his prior history with the law. Then I had to go to the station to identify him, which I could have done by his stench alone."

"Arrested him for what?"

"Let's see . . . Breaking and entering? Trespassing? Threatening? Attempted rape or murder? Being a member of a terrorist group? I didn't get the whole list. He's got charges pending for trying to blow up a bull-dozer."

Charlie blanched. "He didn't break and enter—the door's never locked. And Jerry wouldn't rape or murder." He felt the briefest flash of doubt. "He's sick—he was in Vietnam."

"Is he a Weatherman? Does he sell you drugs, or vice versa? Or are you a homosexual, Charlie? Is that what this is about?"

"No." Her barrage of questions, delivered too fast for him to answer them, brought him to the brink of laughter, but he knew better than to show it.

"No to which?"

"All of the above."

"You owe me an explanation." She sat down again in his bentwood rocking chair, which tipped back, causing her to gasp. Then she found her balance, planted her feet. "Go on," she swatted in his direction. "Explain."

"I don't know where to start."

"Start at the beginning," his mother said.

AND SO IT WAS THAT he told her almost everything—not, as he might have expected, as if she were pulling teeth, but in a long stream of detail—first, answering her questions (no, he was not in trouble with the police, nor did Jerry, as far as he knew, belong to a larger group). Then he told her about giving Jerry rides, the books they both read, how it was unclear, at first, where Jerry lived, how he wanted to protect his family's farm from encroachment by a new golf course and keep it free of herbicides, how he'd sprayed—at least Charlie thought so—Agent Orange in Vietnam. How yes, Jerry was crazy, pretty badly messed up, psychotic, maybe schizophrenic—and no, Charlie hadn't realized just how messed up until it was too late—but still, Dossy was crazy sometimes, so were lots of people, was it a reason to dismiss them? Dossy, his mother said, is wonderful, and she didn't break the law. Okay, said Charlie, but Jerry only broke the law because he cared.

As he went on, she asked questions, almost none of which Charlie could answer and some of which he'd never even thought to ask: What do you know about his family? Why did he have the *Social Register* in his house? How long was he at war? How did he walk into the house knowing her name? For a while the story, or maybe Jerry himself, got the better of them both. At one point, it struck Charlie: they were talking. Not about his own troubles or how he had messed up. Not about his mother and her discontents. Was Jerry unstable before Vietnam, his mother asked, or did the war drive him crazy? Did he ever apply to college? What do you think he saw in you? Then they reached the part about the fencing. Charlie was talking loosely by then, his defenses down.

"You were part of this! I knew it!" She stood up, sounding triumphant. "I told Daddy something like this was going on." She flung out one
thin, tanned arm, and for a moment he was afraid she would grab the
sleeping bag, leaving him exposed. "Keep going."

"There's not much to say. I helped him buy some fencing. That's all."

"You've always been a terrible liar. Look at me. Meet my eyes."

He could not.

"What else did you do? Tell the truth."

"I don't have to tell you anything."

"I'll call the police," she said fiercely. "I'll tell them you were an
accomplice to a crime—or a full partner. You'd better tell me *precisely*
what happened that night."

"You're blackmailing me?"

"Oh, you have a lot of nerve! I'm requiring you to tell the truth."

"We put up some fencing and made signs," he said. "I bought supplies
with my birthday money from Gaga. He went crazy on me then, okay? He
just—he'd been drinking and he went nuts—it was like he was still at war.
I tried to stop him, but I couldn't. I—" Tears pricked his eyes. "I screwed
up, I wanted to help him, Mummy. He's a good person and, like, really
sensitive—he's just been horribly unlucky."

"Like you?"

"I didn't say that."

"Good. Because he's not like you. You've been given everything, and
you've squandered it. You made your own bed. You did drugs, dropped
out, whatever they call it—" She shuddered. "Checked out."

"Okay, so I screwed up! Do you want me to shout it? *I screwed*—"

"Stop it," she hissed. "Who knows about this?"

"No one. Just Rusty, but he'd never tell."

"And Jerry, who's a verbal diarrhea machine. Remember, I saw him in
action. This could ruin your future, you know."

"*And he was such a shining star,*" Charlie muttered, but he was trembling, his shame its own motor, his anger at his mother too, and all the

more troubling because he couldn't get a handle on where, in her stream of words, she was right or wrong.

"Don't mock me!" Now she was screaming. "You *do* nothing! You waste your life and other people's money, you nearly got me killed, you sit around sullen and cynical, wasting your talents, taking part in violence, and now mocking me! I can tell you this, Charlie: your father and I are done bankrolling you, and so is Gaga. You'll get a job and earn back that money from Gaga and donate it to a reputable and *moderate* good cause. And you'll find some other meaningful way to make up for what you've done. Really, you should pay for the damage you caused. I should probably report you. Don't expect us to bail you out if you get arrested. You're"—she struggled for words—"expelled from this family. Kicked out. Do you understand?"

He nodded.

Good-bye, he wanted to say. Fuck you. Good-bye.

Also: I'm sorry.

Also: for how long? (Fuck you, good-bye.)

IT TURNED OUT THAT IT was hard to get expelled from his family. His mother didn't talk to him for a week or so, but his father tried to: You make a big effort, Charlie, and she will be okay with it; just say you're sorry, to fix things up. Charlie was, in fact, sorry, but in no simple way, and he couldn't say so to his mother. She consulted a lawyer, who said he could spin the story into one of double mental illness and poor judgment to protect Charlie if the law came calling (upon hearing this, he felt both sickened and relieved). On Labor Day, as with every Labor Day, Gaga had a photographer come to take the Grandchildren Photo, and when Charlie didn't show at the scheduled time, she sent Will to look for him, and when Charlie said he couldn't come, he'd been expelled from the family, Gaga walked down to the beach and told him not to be ridiculous, to come to the porch for the photo: It's an historical record; I have one from every year!

There were twelve grandchildren in the picture—his mother's four children, Dossy's two, Jane's six. It was the second year without Grampa. Gaga stood at the center in a flowered dress. The younger children had been spruced up a little, hair combed, dresses put on some of the girls. Holly wore a bikini top and cutoffs. Charlie stood next to her, off to one side, in paint-spattered cut-offs. As the photographer arranged them, Maddie started toddling away. From the lawn, Jane said, "Escapee! Catch her!" and it was Charlie who seized his cousin's plump arm, so that in the final picture (the one Gaga displayed beside the other Grandchildren Photos in the Big House front hall), Maddie was in Charlie's grip, mad and squirming, and Charlie was looking down at her, amused, long hair covering his eyes.

Not only did he not get kicked out of the family, but his parents even let him stay in the cabin through the fall. He'd been cleaning the Red House and clearing the land to make a better view, not as much as his mother wanted, but more than he did. When it became evident that she was no longer paying him for his work, he drove into town and asked around for jobs: at the Village Market (not hiring); at the boat dock (ditto); finally at the library, where he was hired part-time at low wages, but he didn't mind—he liked the work, ordering and stacking, dusty shafts of sunlight coming down. When his parents asked about college, he said maybe in January, and when they suggested he come home to Bernardsville, it was clearly a halfhearted request. Everyone except Percy would be going off to school that year, though his sister would last only a month at boarding school. Finally, an almost empty nest, his mother free to spread her wings. She seemed to forget about her plan to make him donate money to a cause, though he did save up the fifty dollars eventually and, without telling her, make an anonymous donation to the Sierra Club. Her voice on the phone was distant and distracted. She would not go to great lengths to get him back.

One early morning as he started on his bike ride, he heard a loud explosion coming from the base. Frightened, he got off his bike, changed direction and took a path toward the end of the Point, walking Indian style, his hands close to his sides. There was a silence there when he arrived, and a chemical, smoky smell. Then a voice: *Back up, fellows! We'll give it one more try!*

It was the casemate they were trying to explode with dynamite, so they wouldn't have to build on top of it. Charlie stood watching from the brush, knowing with a certainty rare for him these days that, unlike the radar tower, this structure would not give in. He'd been in there too many times as a boy, pried open the cold metal door in the hill to enter the long, dark, dripping tunnels, the branching, endless rooms. He'd felt the massive circuit boards, wires cut and splayed, traced his hand over a long pillar of what felt like a column of marble but turned out to be (his fingers had read one letter, then the next) A S B E S T O S. He had lain on the racks that might have been for weapons storage or might have been for bunks, holding his breath as a flashlight scanned the corners of the room. The casemate had been there his whole life, and for once he felt a rock-hard faith that unlike the land it sat on and the ever-changing string of owners, the battlement would hold its ground.

The second blast of dynamite went off, so loud his hands flew to his ears. Then a stillness. Three men appeared in hard hats, moving toward the casemate.

"No go," one man said. "I told him, but he didn't believe it. It was built to withstand the Nazis' bombs, for Christ's sake. Ten-foot walls of reinforced concrete."

THE WILD CLEMATIS BLOOMED. The monarchs gathered on the Japanese black pines to migrate, and the asters blossomed purple and white, and the sea turned grayer, and a chill came in, followed, some days, by waves of heat. When Charlie mentioned the asters to his mother on the phone, she said Oh it's always been my favorite time, are you watching the tree swallows gather, and he almost said Yes, you should come see. But then

she started in: When are you going back to college? You need a plan. I
know, he said, but he did not know, would not ask the questions. Each
day presented itself plainly, as it was, a day, and he began to find, that
fall, what he had come for in the summer, which was the slow, unwieldy
process that was healing, or beginning to heal, or learning to live with a
brain that would never be—as his would never be—the same.

Still, small improvements. He could read for longer now. His daily
exercise had made him lean and strong, and sometimes he actually felt
his age. Sometimes, taking off his shirt, stretching his limbs or climbing naked on the rocks, he felt at home in his body. He would lie on the
whale-shaped dark gray boulder after swimming and become part of the
rock as the air raised goose bumps on his skin. He'd drop himself back
in time: just after the Ice Age, or in the 1700s when the Cookes farmed
the land, or earlier, when the Indians fished the shores. He still had
moments—every day, at least a few—when his self seemed a mechanical
object, metal or plastic, bland and smooth, with no openings or face.
Once a week he talked to Dr. Miller on the phone, but the sessions felt
stalled, Charlie as reluctant to say he felt better as to describe how he
was not. Columbus Day weekend, some people came back, but not his
parents—his mother was busy, teaching a course—and not Gaga, who
had sprained her wrist. Holly came, alone this time, and Rusty, and
some friends of Rusty's, and they made a dinner at the Red House, a
feast—turkey, roasted corn, pumpkin soup—and then the pot appeared,
but Charlie did not freak out. He simply went down to the cabin to bed.

The cleaners came after Columbus Day and did the closings, stripping the beds, covering the couches with sheets, dropping mouse poison, bright blue pellets, all around. The water was turned off, antifreeze
poured into the Red House toilets. Still, he stayed on, as three founda-
tions were poured on top of the casemate and to the east and west, as
new power lines went in, trucks coming and going, the noise a constant.
He hated it, but there were only so many times you could let loose a
flare of anger only to watch it sputter and fall. Now and then, at night

and on weekends, he went to the house sites and scavenged shingles and scrap wood for kindling. He found a shiny silver hammer and took it for himself. He had a slight urge, but only slight, to drop sand into the gas tanks of the bulldozers, carve obscenities in wet concrete, but he knew it would be a repeat performance, and self-defeating, and by someone who had not earned the right.

Mostly he was trying—more or less unconsciously—to fold the changes into his sense of things: here this house, there another. The homes being built were big but not enormous. They would have heat, brand-new appliances, interior walls made of drywall, not of the textured particle-board in the Red House and Portable (built on the cheap to house the multiplying generations), or the plaster and horsehair of the Big House (built to last). New people would move in, nobody's relatives. He was inclined to either dislike the newcomers or ignore them, but might there be a pretty, lonely girl?

Largely, now, it was not anger he felt, but rather a kind of bone-scraping, quiet, ever-present sorrow. To come to the place that was supposed to stay the same, to come and find it changed. Dr. Miller had warned him against what he called the "geographic cure." You can't fix yourself by going somewhere else, he'd said. You'll always take yourself along. But Ashaunt's not somewhere else, Charlie had said.

At the library, Linda, the reference librarian, told him how she'd helped Jerry get books on homesteading and trapping through interli-brary loan, how she'd encouraged him to apply to college and he'd started the paperwork for a few state schools but must never have sent it in. He talked to the unhappy, acned high school girl who shelved books after school. Jimi Hendrix overdosed; Janis Joplin overdosed. Both times, the girl had crying jags all afternoon. The second time, Charlie bought her M&M's, and she flung herself, damp, into his arms.

He stopped taking Valium, though he still carried it in his pocket. He left Ashaunt more often, riding his bike to Little River or taking the row-boat to fish for bass or bluefish. One afternoon he went to Windy Point.

It was deserted, the porch furniture put inside, the houses seeming lower, battened down against the fall wind. Another day, he walked to work with a backpack full of books, thinking of Jerry, who, according to Rich (Charlie had finally gathered the courage to ask), had been held overnight in jail for trespassing on the Point. The judge gave him a break, Rich said, and put him on probation with restitution to pay for the damage he had done at the construction site. Now he was living with his mother.

In the folk song, the cat came back the very next day, *thought it was a goner but the cat came back for it couldn't stay away.* Jerry's cat did not come back. Jerry didn't come back, though Charlie watched for him in the library, on the streets. All that fall, he walked around with the figure of Jerry (hair grown back, skin brown, as he'd been when Charlie met him) on the outskirts of his consciousness, unsure what he'd do if he, in fact, ran into him. Run? Apologize? Accuse? Offer more money—here, take twenty dollars, thirty dollars—to get your feet back on the ground, pay the restitution, the chaser after the shot.

When, in November, there were no more fish to catch and the true cold came, Charlie thought he was ready for it. He'd gathered wood, chopped logs, made a woodpile underneath the raised pilings of the cabin. He'd brought wool blankets from the Red House and was keeping supplied with water by filling his jugs in the men's room at the library. The fires he built in the woodstove kept the place toasty. He made tea. Sat by the fire. Talked to Grampa sometimes in his head. He'd doze there, in the bentwood rocking chair. An old man, he was; for now, he didn't mind. A few nights later, he forgot to bring the water jugs inside the cabin and they grew a skin of ice. He woke one morning to the fire gone out. The library, cutting back its hours, let him go. He began to eat his food down and not replenish. He drank the water down. The day he left, he shut the cabin door and put up a sign, thinking mostly of Jerry: "Come in if you like, but close door <u>tightly</u> when you leave to keep raccoons out," and signed it "a spirit storming in blank walls," from the Wallace Stevens poem.

He piled some books in the car, grabbed a handful of clothes, his medicine, his address book, a fox skull, a Joan Baez record he'd bought, a few branches of bittersweet. He put his sleeping bag in the car, his tent. Where would he go? Not to Cleveland, not yet, if ever. Not to his parents. To Holly, maybe, at Wellesley, though he couldn't stay there in her dorm. She might know someone in Cambridge looking for a roommate, maybe in the sublet she'd had over the summer. He might see Melanie, try not to dodge. He might—for a moment he allowed himself to think of it—become her boyfriend, get a job in a bookstore, or he could follow Gaga's advice and work for a newspaper or volunteer for a political or environmental campaign, though he knew so little (and every day, a little less) and had so much to learn.

He passed Salvador's, closed for the winter, drove through the village, then onto Route 6, where he stopped for gas. In the convenience store, he bought an orange juice and, impulsively, a pack of cigarettes, which, just as impulsively, he dropped in the trash bin outside. On Route 24, he switched on the radio. American troop levels had dropped to 336,400. The soldiers would be having canned cranberry sauce, mashed potatoes, and in some cases even turkey, thanks to the tremendous efforts of the Red Cross. Thanksgiving; he'd nearly forgotten, lost track of days, though in their last phone call, a week or so ago, his mother had asked him to come home. Holly would be not in Wellesley but in New Jersey; everyone would be, for the annual meal at Gaga's. He had never, in his nineteen years, not gone, except for the year they lived in Japan. If he went, it would be a triumph for his mother, but Gaga would like it. Holly would like it. His father too. If he didn't go, it would be . . . what? He imagined bringing Thanksgiving dinner to Jerry in the woods, how they'd eat silently and say nothing of the Pilgrims, nothing of Indians or corn or God, just eat because it was time to eat and they were, both of them (of this one thing, he was sure) grateful to the land that gave them food, and Charlie would have dug oysters and clams and foraged wintercress and ground nuts, and Jerry would have snared a rabbit in his trap.

But Jerry was with his mother, and if he hadn't been, he would think the food was poisoned, tell Charlie he was trespassing, Lord of 10,000 Acres, where's my cat? You drew me in, led me on, Jerry might say, or speak extravagantly in five different voices. A bird might fly through the scrub oaks, a flash of blue, of green, extinct in the wild, and the Portuguese settlers farming the land, fishing the seas. A place could turn out so many ways— could it? A place could turn out only one way: divide and conquer. Divide. At the end of Route 24, Charlie got on Route 128 heading toward Boston, though there were still times when he could exit and enter, split to go north or south. He flicked the radio off, his thoughts roaming. Several times he almost turned around, back toward Ashaunt, but the car was warm and the cabin would be cold, the land carved up, though as he drove away from it, he could already feel it returning in his mind to what it once had been.

He was five or six, on the base, deep under a black pine, sitting on dry needles. In the distance he could hear his mother calling: "Charlie? Charlie, where are you? Answer me!" And for the first time in his life, it had occurred to him that he did not have to respond—that he could sit there breathing, hearing his own breath, not answering when she called. For a long time he sat listening to his mother repeat his name, hearing the panic in her voice, the worry, the irritation: "For god's sake, Charlie, is this your idea of a joke?" Eventually, she stopped calling, just stopped. Had she left? Gone for help? Given up?

After a few minutes, he crawled out and stood, his legs cramped. His mother was sitting on the steps of the old foundation, reading a book. He coughed and she glanced up at him and, her face registering nothing, returned to her book. Squinting in the sunlight, Charlie began to cry. Slowly, his mother put down the book and stood. She hugged him tightly to her, his head not much above her waist. She was wearing blue, he remembered, a light summer skirt. Together, without speaking, they'd walked home.

MIGRATE

1999

I

EACH DAY THEY change the garden around, the trucks rolling in on a convoy, flatbeds loaded with perennials in full bloom. Steadily—they've been at it for four days now—the gardeners play with colors as if on a movie set: blue hydrangeas in the back, followed by black-eyed Susans, coneflowers, finally lavender, and the next day, the pattern altered, blue at the bottom, Susans in the middle, new blooms—today it's pink tulips, and salvia, and tufts of stiff, tropical-looking grass, everything still in pots. The garden is sloped, the casemate hiding underneath, but the gardeners have doctored the hump to make it look intentional. Along the outermost rim behind the house—Land's End—they've planted a row of saplings supported by wire, the doomed trunks bandaged white. Below, they've shored up the cliffs with riprap and wire netting. None of it, trees, blooms (even house, in the grand scheme), will last for long out here, felled by erosion, salt spray, wind, but for now, the colors dazzle. Helen, who comes each day to watch, supported by André and her cane, cannot get enough.

Not native, her grandmother would have said of the flowers. *Too uniform*, of the bleached white shells on the path. Such a waste, said Jane the other morning as two trucks from the swimming pool company rumbled past the Big House, tanks filled with water for the plants. The Uh-Ohs are having a party in a few weeks, hence the beehive feel, the furniture delivered; hence the bands of merry Merry Maids, the Sylvan Landscape trucks, the push to get the garden done. *The windows alone cost a million dollars . . . It's just the three of them* (the owner, Owen O'Reilly—they called him O.O. until it morphed into Uh-Oh, plus wife number two or three and a baby younger than his grandchildren). *It makes me feel soiled just to see it* (this, over drinks the other night, from Holly). And Percy: *There's a bathroom with his initials on the wallpaper and a urinal shaped like a conch.* And Will, whose apartment in Dubai has recently been featured in the *Times* Style section: *Give the guy a break, people—at least he made his own money. He grew up in Southie.* And Charlie: *He's not exactly Horatio Alger; he went to Harvard. So did his father. Anyway, he's a nice guy—the house just depresses me. Can't we talk about something else?*

Helen (sharpest knife in the drawer, a critic's critic; she's been called many things in her seventy-three years) contributes little to such conversations. Her focus has narrowed, she knows what she wants; in this case, it's the flowers—to look and look. At night, and in the afternoons when the pain clamps her hard inside its jaws, the garden follows her, a dreamscape unspooling, brighter than the wildflowers and the white-pink roses grown spindly on her own trellises; brighter too than her own walled garden, bee balm blooming now, asters on the verge, the lupine (over) with its fuzzy, blackened rattle pods that could be cracked for seeds to nick, soak, plant.

Once, she used to fertilize, divide, deadhead, mix in annuals for color. Then for a while she hired a gardener, but eventually, she let her garden go. This summer, she has rediscovered it, sitting inside its low stone walls on the green plastic chair (the cedar bench finally collapsed) or watching it through her bedroom window. No matter that it's untended; the blooms impress her with their persistence, and the interlopers—Queen Anne's lace, chicory, goldenrod, thistle—are unruly gifts. Night or day, she does not draw the shades in her room, but even bare, her windows are not big enough for the profusion they try to frame, nor for her pleasure, saturated, magnified (is it the morphine? not just). She'd knock the wall down if she could, let the roof go, lie beneath the sky and spread herself wide. She'd screw the whole world if she could—as in screw its petty cares and intractable truths. As in, make love to it.

She's let it all go, at the same time that she is holding tighter, coming into meaning, into understanding. It's better and cheaper than psycho-analysis, this *thing* she's undergoing, she told Dossy on the phone this morning. It's *fun* (a word she once tried to ban from her children's vocabulary). A few things she has learned: (1) This is her home; (2) She is, when it comes right down to it, an animal; (3) Knowledge is overrated. This last means No to prognoses and timelines, No to Percy's wife telling her that the Uh-Ohs' tulips are fake since out of season, brought in for planning purp— (Helen cuts her off.) No to statistics about the oil spill—this many dead birds, that many contaminated shellfish beds. No to the pain charts with their bloated cartoon faces and scale of 1 to 10. No to the world she has designated the Sassy Sickos or SS: pink ribbons, Susan Love, support groups, self-help, the use of *journaling* and *collaging* as verbs.

Yes to a different kind of order: the Uh-Ohs' garden changing stripes and colors, her own garden wilding itself. The phases of the moon— waning now, with a new moon due in a few days, on September 9. (But they'll be gone, packed up; she has chemo in New York two days before.) Yes to the tides. All summer she has tracked them on the tide chart left by Anchor Real Estate in the mailbox. She swims each day at high tide unless thunder, lightning or (rarely) insurmountable pain keeps her inside. Even the low point of each day, late afternoons, she observes with a certain detached interest—not that she likes them, they're the pits—but they come at the same time every day, though worse right after chemo, and it's oddly liberating to lie in her room with only André or Jane granted access and just *give in*, she who has always been a thrasher, striver, fighter, as in the first time she got sick, when they lopped off her breasts and she put on falsies and got back to the archive a few weeks after surgery and was (twelve years passed, good ones, good enough) fine.

Now it's in her bones. When she found out, a little over a year ago, she disbelieved, then raged, but only briefly; in her bones, she knew it to be fact. André found the best specialists, set up consultations, hauled medical books past her to his room (some years ago, they had tacitly agreed to sleep—or, in her case, not sleep—apart). At appointments in the city, Helen laid herself out, gave herself up to scans and dyes, prods and probes, but she was clear from the beginning: I DO NOT WANT TO KNOW. "Denial Is a River in Egypt," she read once on a bumper sticker. She has not turned her back on treatment—she is no martyr and has no wish to die—but she approaches it like a necessary chore. How have you been feeling? asks her doctor at Sloan-Kettering. Very well, thank you, Dr. Upadhyaya. Good, good, the doctor says. How is your research going? she asks him then, or, Would you ever want to go back to India and be a doctor there? He has an attractive accent and clean, pink fingernails. He grew up in the foothills of the Himalayas, where his parents own a store called Perfection House. He has three young daughters named Mira, Mina and Maya, an engineer wife. Each appointment she learns a little more.

Very well. The truth is more complicated, worse and better. Increasingly, she needs more pain meds; André makes them appear. Always thin, she is even thinner now and has to keep a sheepskin under her hips in bed. She must, she thinks, be a scientific curiosity to be able to take this much pain medication and still not fall asleep. In January, she fell on the ice and broke her arm; it healed but hangs slightly off and aches a little all the time. In her chest they have installed a port for chemo. Her wig is made from real hair; Jane and Dossy took her to get fitted for it as if for a wedding gown, at Joseph Paris Naturally, which might have been a lark—Joseph, the Toupée Titan, was stylist to Frank Sinatra and Burt Reynolds—had Helen not been a customer/client/patient/cancer ghoul. At the hospital, they inject her, hook her up, slide her into tunnels, which whir and bang. Once, she might have been curious to see her body mapped. Now she's driftwood, a jellyfish, single pulse, all egg white slosh and take me where you will.

A pill, another; she downs them without looking. The dosing, the side effects, she leaves to André, who has risen to this role with a kind of devotion that might be slavish were it not so dignified and, she realizes, necessary (she refuses to hire a nurse, cherishing her privacy). He mixes fiber into her orange juice for her constipation and clears a path before her, removing sand spades, tennis balls, beach towels, anything that might trip her up. He brings her water, Coke, coffee, tea, more water (she has never been so thirsty). He runs interference. Over and over, people ask her: What can we do, what do you want?

What does she want? She's done with Freud, done with poking in the bushes of the past or worrying about the future, done, even, worrying about her children—all married save for Caroline, and all employed, though none spectacularly. There's a young man, Bernie, from the New Jersey Historical Commission, whom she still talks to on the phone every few days; he's passionate and smart, fat and scared, half black. He adores her. She is mentoring him and helped him get a grant for his project on Florence Spearing Randolph and the Colored Women's Clubs. She finished one entry for *The Encyclopedia of New Jersey* this summer and has committed to two more, but she hasn't worked on them since April. This bothers her only insofar as she is aware that it doesn't bother her at all.

André, who turned eighty last year, takes her swimming every day. Occasionally he goes in himself; mostly he hovers on the dock. Sometimes the other women come swimming with her—Jane, Holly, Caroline on the Fourth of July. The men and boys jump in, get out; it's always been that way. Only her father used to stay in for any length of time, and only now does Helen truly understand why: antigravity, your limbs return to you, the pain recedes. Horizons flatten, glassy green. And to be touched all over, to be touched without it hurting. She sees her father in the water sometimes, not as a vision nor even a memory, simply *there* as a tern or duck or gull is there, some distance away and apparently indifferent to her presence.

What do you want? For months after her diagnosis, she couldn't say. It was a slog of a fall and winter, but she didn't complain, which caused people to exclaim over how brave she was. In truth, it wasn't bravery at all, but rather the strictest kind of necessity; she had—for the first time in her life, it seemed—no choice. Her body hurt. The house in Bernardsville was at once too big and too small, overstuffed with her parents' and grandparents' gold-rimmed china and dark furniture, the papers in her study endlessly disorganized. She couldn't seem to read for long, a great frustration. Never a television watcher, she nonetheless gave the History Channel a try, only to find that it devoted entire seasons to military blunders, UFOs and the (not even sexy) history of sex.

In February an antidepressant was added to her cocktail of pills, but it was only as spring greened in New Jersey that desire landed in Helen's lap, and it changed everything. She can pinpoint when it happened—stepping out of the car, steadying herself on the hood, looking over the lawn at the frothy yellow wall of forsythia in bloom and feeling a kind of shock, a pulse-quickening surprise. A moment before, she'd had no plans, not an idea in her bald, wigged, wiggy head. Now, she knew what she wanted: to spend the whole summer, an extended one, as summers were when she was small, on Ashaunt.

They arrived in May and have stayed through, with only a few trips back for chemo. To be here has brought her the deepest kind of happiness, of the sort she'd not known for . . . how long? Ages and ages (since Charlie was a newborn? since before her brother died?). How *lucky* she is. She thinks it all the time now. Lucky to have the sky and sea before her at any time of day or night. To have her grandchildren and children for weekends and, in July and August, entire weeks at a time—except for Caroline, who has come once. To have André, become more handsome, even though his own bout with cancer some twenty-five years ago left his face half paralyzed. To see Charlie married, this past December—married!—to a historian like Helen, lively and bright and not contrary like Charlie, the type who could have been a Brearley girl, though when Helen told her this, she laughed and said, Oh my god no, I went to public school!

To have hummingbirds visit. Charlie set up a feeder outside her bedroom window. Never a poet like Dossy, Helen feels a new urge toward verse. *Flit and perch, hovercraft, I follow you . . .* She writes it in the margin of a newspaper; it flutters in the wind of the fan, drops to the floor. Who cares? Writing takes work, and for what? Sleep might be the thing, but still elusive no matter how overmedicated she is. A few times a day, Dossy calls. They talk, hang up. One of them thinks of something she forgot to say and calls again. "They'll write on my gravestone, 'She Talked on the Phone,' " she tells Dossy, and they decide to have an active phone line running between their graves, this despite the fact that Helen cannot, in even the most approximate way, begin to imagine what it will be like to be dead, the project so hemmed in by its own design problems (how to think of a time when you cannot think?) that one may as well bash one's head against a concrete wall. Jane fills the bedroom with flowers in vases, and while Helen doesn't really want them, not indoors, wilting, fouling their water, she thanks her sister and waits until she can blunder out again into the light.

Today after lunch—it's Sunday of Labor Day weekend—Percy's son Charles, age eight, will wander into the Red House living room and tell her fretfully that at Y2K, computers and electricity and banks and the national defense system will all stop working, and time will stop. His parents worry about him; he reverses letters and has odd rituals. Time stopping could be interesting, she'll say. He'll shake his head: We're gonna die. Oh, I highly doubt it, dearie, Helen will say and pat the couch, and he'll settle at her side. If the computer uses four numbers instead of two, he'll say, it might be okay. Like, um, 1999, not '99, which could be 1899 or 1999 or even 2099. Did you figure that out yourself, she'll ask, and he'll say yes, and they'll talk about numbers for a while, what infinity is, what a google is, how a negative number isn't quite a number but more like a number's shadow (his words). He is named after his maternal grandfather, not Helen's brother or her son. His hair, by summer's end, is bleached to nearly white, corn silk; his blue eyes have Gaga's almost Asian slant. The only thing wrong with this child is that he's brilliant, Helen will think, then catch herself. Another thing she has learned, Number Four on her list (it will go in her diary, which she still manages to keep): she has wasted a great deal of energy expecting too much from herself and everybody else.

I'M HAVING THE BEST SUMMER of my life. In the water later that after-noon, she says it to Jane, who dives under without answering and comes up with her head tipped back, her face streaming beneath her white swim cap, and moves into breaststroke again, Helen following her, their favor-ite stroke. The ocean is flat calm and warm with spots of cold, a few red jellies floating—global warming, Holly claims—and there are smaller moon jellies that slip between her fingers, soft, membraned packages. They swim to the raft, stop to rest, swim to the dock, then to the raft again, avoiding the big red jellies (André calls out warnings from the dock), though Helen almost wants to get stung, the pain a zigzag, visible and numbing, the tentacles' lashed trail. Come to dinner tonight, she asks her sister for the second time, but Jane has a houseful, everyone has a houseful. Maybe Holly can come, she tells her sister (Percy has taken the Whaler to Cuttyhunk; Will left on Friday for Dubai), but Jane says keep it small, it will be nicer, you can really talk to them.

Halfway in, Helen floats on her back, eyes shut, arms wide, palms turned toward the sky. She could do this forever except Jane is waiting, André is waiting, Charlie and Rachel are coming to dinner, and then Jane's voice, at once muffled and amplified, reaches her, and she turns her head to let one ear out: Helen! Please! *Come in!* She flaps an arm to show she heard, then tortures her little sister by lying there some twenty seconds longer. *Get out,* André and Jane call in unison, and she rights herself and treads water as she pees, feeling her own warmth spread and dissipate. She swims to the stairs and slowly climbs, then, Jane spotting her from behind, André from above, until she reaches his outstretched arms, her open towel coat, which is when one leg gives out, and she buckles, stumbles, and they catch her, surround her in a humiliating embrace, and who are those people (blurs without her glasses) watching her lose her balance on the dock?

She grabs the railing and her cane, walks toward the people. André slips her glasses over her nose, and her vision clears.

"How was the water?" asks a coiffed blond woman she has never seen before.

"Heavenly," says Helen.

"Warm?"

"Oh yes. Warm as pee!"

With André's help, she gets into the golf cart, then waves a royal good-bye to Jane, who hurries her bike up to the road.

"I suppose that was rude, and childish," she tells André as they rumble up the slope. "I don't know what comes over me. I just didn't like the look of her."

"You're like a beach, marking your territory with pee."

"What?"

"A beach. You know, a female dog."

When she laughs too hard, her chest hurts. "You mean a bitch, dearie," she says. "Like 'itch.' *Bitch*, it's pronounced. Bitch."

"A beach on the beach."

"*Je t'adore*," she says abruptly.

"We do all right, old girl," he says.

ON THE MILKWEED, THE MONARCHS are collecting. Rabbits graze on the Yacht Club's driveway. They come in cycles, and this year they are everywhere. *Having the best summer.* Hyperbolist though she is, cliché though it is, she needs, for reasons she can't quite get a handle on, to have its meaning heard, received. She'll repeat it to André as they return to the house in the golf cart, steering around dogs and relatives, teenagers, trikes, potholes, the Point plunged into Labor Day mode, the air tense, on high alert, toddlers tantruming on the road, people starting to mourn—one more day, school starting, too fast, almost over, but joyful too, legs fast-pedaling, faces to the sun.

On telephone wires, trees and roof peaks, hundreds of tree swallows are gathering to organize their migration. Helen spots a few young females—browner, drabber than the rest—among the metallic blues and clear whites. A group of swallows, she remembers, is called a flight, and she says it to André—"Look at the flight of tree swallows"—and he stops the cart, lifts the field glasses to watch for a moment, then offers her the glasses and returns to driving slowly down the road. The birds swoop and gather, separate and merge, trading places and liquid twitters in a constant, intricate exchange.

And so it is that Helen, bird-watching, does not register the parked oil-spill cleanup truck, or the triple-stranded pinwheeled power lines the Uh-Ohs have put in, or even the septic pile construction they drive past, another cottage torn down to make way for another oversized house. She has seen them before, certainly (the power lines especially took her aback when they first appeared), but she has developed an automatic filter of the sort she never had when she was young. Hers is not a willed oblivion, at least not consciously; her mind is fully, deeply occupied. In the air the birds are clever, acrobatic, but when they land on the road they turn to lumps of coal, then lift together when a person or vehicle draws near. She watches the flight eddies, the trading of partners, the way the patterns form, dissolve and reconfigure like one machine in motion—yet each bird with its own small, muscled heart. When Percy, passing on his bike, calls out to her, she doesn't even hear, in a state of observation so pure it's almost infantile, at the same time that she carries a knowledge that she's been seeing these birds year after year (and always here) and that the medium they pass through is not just space but also time.

II

THE OVULATION PREDICTOR kit turned yesterday, so they had sex last night and are doing it again this afternoon in the cabin, Rachel on top, Charlie traveling the (familiar, startling, plain, dazzling) country of her hips, waist, rib cage, and then she's lowering down, his mouth finding first one nipple, then the other, salty from her swim; he shuts his eyes and sucks. Moaning, he maneuvers them both until he's inside her, then deeper, farther, pelvis to pelvis, and he presses his fingers to her tailbone, urging her closer, into a rhythm, opening his eyes to catch a still (forever) shy glimpse of her most private self—hair swinging, face concentrated—their breathing ragged, matched, and then his eyes are closed again, his thoughts gone or almost gone and they are fucking, nearly slamming bone to bone. I can't help it, I'm coming, he says, so deftly they flip, still locked, and then it's three deep thrusts and over—he's collapsed on top of her, emptied out but still inside. Rachel shifts but doesn't roll him off. Sorry, he says, but it's too late now (no spit allowed, and his hands alone won't do it), and the Clomid exaggerates her every sensation in a way that leaves her jangly, off. On the floor, Major Deegan whimpers softly in his sleep. Charlie raises himself to his elbows. Okay? he asks, and waits for Rachel to say Wait a sec (she does), then waits for her to say Okay (she does), and then rolls off.

At first he'd worried that the mechanics of it all might get in the way, but in fact their sex life, sometimes skittish, has improved over these past eight months, oiled and lubricated by its scheduled appointments and the unsheathed slide of it, the urge toward alchemy: she wants a baby. So does he. For a moment, they lie there in the sunbath coming through the skylight, hands interlaced; then she hoists her legs high against the wall until she's nearly upside down, courting gravity. Impulsively, he joins her, though his legs are too long, the wall too short. Rachel extends a foot to waggle at his and he waggles back, and for a moment, he can almost see it—a rush of dim-witted, driven minnows ramming their heads against the great, round, hard-shelled sphere that is the egg, and he feels for his sperm an almost fatherly affection for how they will strive and batter, head-butt, drop aside.

He lowers back down, gets up, pulls on his shorts. "I'm going to dig the porpoise up," he says.

While the idea has only now just come to him, it feels suddenly urgent on this, the fastest-cycling, quickest-draining weekend of the year.

"Huh?" Rachel cranes her head to look at him. "What? Why now?"

"I'd like to assemble the skeleton with wire and glue and hang it from the rafters, like at the Whaling Museum. If you wait too long, the bones can decompose."

He had meant to do it earlier, last summer, or earlier this summer. What happened? He'd gotten busy. Gotten married. Now and then, he had remembered the porpoise he had buried but always at inopportune times—when he was on the train going to work, or in the middle of a thunderstorm in the cabin, or once last winter when he'd come across a box in his parents' attic (unable to sleep at Christmas, he paced and rummaged), and in the box, among letters, photographs and travel guides, a pamphlet titled "St Ninian's Isle Treasures" that told the story of how, in 1958, a Scottish schoolboy found a hoard of silver objects and part of a porpoise jaw under a cross-marked slab in a church, and how the bowls and bones were believed to date to AD 800. As he'd flipped through the pamphlet, a postcard had fallen out, from his mother to him, dated July 1976: *After Agnes's funeral, we went to the Shetland and to this island, where a little boy discovered treasures that are over a thousand years old! It put things a bit in scale for me, as I'd been very blue. He found them in '58 so must be around your age. Write Bea a sympathy card! Love, Mummy.* In the pamphlet, a photograph of the porpoise's jawbone—slender and long, gray and captivating. That a postcard addressed to him was among his mother's possessions did not surprise him at first (as he plundered, so did she), but then he noticed that it had no stamps. So she'd never sent it, which meant he'd never known that she'd thought of him on an island in Scotland where a boy, now man, around his age, had dug to find an ancient bone.

"Were you thinking about this while we were having sex?" Rachel asks.

"No."

"You were."

"I wasn't," he says truthfully. "But now that you mention it"—he sighs—"I was in love with her. Before I met you. She had a perfect little blowhole, and the way she leaped in the water—"

"Sweetheart, she was dead."

"I didn't mind."

Rachel hoists herself higher on the wall and pulls a sheet across her torso. "Necroporphia. Poor thing. And now you're still tormenting her. How long have I been lying here?"

"At least five minutes." He bends to kiss her. "Plenty long. You should get up."

He reaches to the floor for her clothes, but when he hands them to her, she gives him a dark look and lets them drop to the floor. "I *hate* this," she says, and he sees her mood turn. This, the heading into waiting, is the part she hates—and he, by proxy, hates her hating, for how it makes her frantic, anxious, discontent. "How is it that I can write a book but I can't make a baby?" she asked the last time she got her period. Charlie is more of a fatalist, which almost translates into being an optimist: It will happen when it happens, and if it doesn't, they can always adopt. He adopted Deegan, after all, as a stray found by Rusty's girlfriend on the Major Deegan Expressway, and he loves the dog in a way beyond words.

They've been trying to have a baby for ten months. In July, Rachel turned thirty-five, an age that, though it seems young to Charlie, is considered by the experts to be the gateway to Advanced Maternal Age. That same month, she made an appointment for them to go in for testing. He: plenty of sperm, moderate motility, she: decent numbers, a few uterine fibroids. The doctor filled her with blue dye, and they watched her tubes appear, ghostly and thin, like violin strings, on a screen. Louise Bourgeois, the seventeenth-century French midwife Rachel wrote her dissertation-turned-book on, would advise them to be sanguine, without anger, or offer to purge Rachel of bad blood or improve her womb with a pessary. Instead, a prescription for Clomid, to "give your ovaries a boost."

"Come help me. It'll distract you," he says. "And maybe we'll find an arrowhead or old coin."

She gets up, pulls on her shorts and tank top, then sits on the edge of the bed. "What if someone comes while we're digging up a corpse?"

"They can help. Anyway, who would come?"

"Kids, or your mother."

"My mother hasn't been down here in twenty years."

Does she not understand by now that his parents never visit the cabin uninvited? Almost no one does, except in winter, and then it's raccoons or local kids who swipe the CD player and leave crushed beer cans on the porch. He lets the cabin path stay tangled and unclipped, enjoying the feeling of ducking into a tunnel to his secret world. Over the years, his mother has threatened more than once to raze the cabin. She has called it a hazard, fretted that renters' children will find it, fall off the porch or through its rotten planks and sue. She has talked about wanting to open up the land between the Red and Big Houses, fell the trees, clear the brush, a clean sweep. Once she even hired a bulldozer, though fortunately Holly persuaded her to send it back. For all that, she has let his cabin be, and Charlie can count the number of times she's been inside it since he moved in and made it his own. Even after he expanded it, put in the skylight, and—a little house-proud—gave a few tours, his mother did not come (his father ventured down to admire the post-and-beam construction and smoke his pipe on the porch).

A few months after he'd brought Rachel to Ashaunt for the first time, she'd told him it was the cabin that made her fall in love with him, its tree-house shape, its built-in bed, rocking chair, books and bones; the way he, hardly domestic at home—what she calls home—sweeps and cooks here, catches fish, heats the soapstone bed warmers on chilly nights. It was April that first time he came with her, his daffodils blooming along the path to the cabin. His stucco bungalow, now theirs, in Concord, was still filled with his roommate Andy's stuff: blue leather couch, big screen TV, a poster of Nastassja Kinski winding naked around a snake. Socks and sneakers lay on the floor; dishes were stacked in the sink, awaiting the cleaning lady who came every other week. Though Charlie had bought the place when he was twenty-eight with the money he inherited from Gaga, it had never really felt like home. Here, a different story. Never before, Rachel told him, had she witnessed the way a place could become a person, a person a place, but as she'd walked the labyrinth of paths he'd made, she'd felt as if she were walking the folds of his beautiful (damaged—his teeth still chatter, his ears still ring; he's told her the basics, spared her the details) brain.

"Did you know that there's a disease called seal finger?" she says as they go onto the porch. "It causes numbing if you touch the seal. Sometimes people have to get their fingers amputated."

"Cool, but this is a porpoise, not a seal."

"Oh. What is a porpoise, anyway? I should know that. Is it a kind of dolphin?"

He nods. "Like dolphins but smaller, and with shorter noses."

She stops above him on the steep stairs. "So maybe dolphin means 'big nose.' *Le Dauphin*. I wonder if that's why the French chose it for the title of the firstborn male prince."

Her mood is lifting; he can tell. Her legs are long from this angle, and she isn't wearing underwear; he can see up her cutoffs to the dark thatch of hair. "Come, dauphin." He reaches toward her. Pet names do not come easily to him. Cohabitation, marriage, do not come easily. Rachel is, for one thing, considerably more complicated than he'd first thought. She is Zolofted and Klonopinned, or was until she started trying to get pregnant. She holds her breath past cemeteries, knocks on wood. Now she rubs her belly over her shirt, like a pregnant woman in a movie. The miscarriage in May was an early one—a chemical pregnancy, the doctors called it. Rachel told her parents, sister, closest friends—first that she was pregnant, then that she was not. Charlie told no one.

At the bottom of the stairs, she stops and holds her hands up. "I'll need gloves," she says.

THE PORPOISE IS BURIED IN the clearing next to the cabin. Scrub grass grows over it. A beige rock marks the spot. He'd found the creature several years ago washed up on the beach, tied a rope around its tail and hauled it up the path with the help of his nephews. Lardy and heavy, it had been, out of its element, not pulling its own weight. "Heave-ho!" he'd sung with the boys, and together they'd made pirate eye patches out of leaves and kelp. They had buried the beast, his nephews' eyes alight with the adventure, and Charlie the uncle who'd do anything. (He'd taken them winter camping at Teal Rock, built driftwood rafts, hunted with them under milkweed leaves for monarch caterpillars to hatch into butterflies, the jade-green, gold-seamed chrysalis an astonishment each time.) He'd meant to wait a year for the porpoise's flesh to leave its bones, two at the most (the naturalist he'd asked at the Audubon Center had said that would be plenty), but somehow time had passed, until today.

He ducks into the crawl space underneath the cabin and rummages until he finds two spades, and a pair of men's work gloves stiff with mud and age. He gives Rachel the gloves and a yellow-handled spade, keeping the other shovel, bigger and more pointed, for himself. The grass in the clearing is parched, its roots enmeshed. As he digs, he swats at bugs occasionally but mostly concentrates, enjoying the digging down, but also the smells, the sun on his back, the way, even now, before he finds what he's looking for, he feels closer to imagining it, the bones a vessel for a life once lived. He has loved bones for as long as he can remember—for their delicacy, their architecture, for how they carry traces of the animals they once served as containers for—a brain, a set of eyes, all senses flaring in the underbrush or underwater. At first, as they dig, Deegan sniffs around their hands, but when Charlie tells him to lie down, he settles a few feet away. "Slow down, you losers!" someone shouts from the road as the noise of a truck expands, recedes. Even on Labor Day weekend, the gardeners are busy at the Uh-Ohs'. On the west-side beaches, the oil-spill cleanup crew works overtime, scrubbing and spraying in their plastic suits as they move from stone to stone.

Rachel drops the spade. "This feels like bad luck."

Charlie keeps digging. "It's good luck. The Wampanoag used to chew on porpoise bones for increased fertility."

"*Don't.*" She rocks back and drops the shovel. "Why are we doing this? Do you even know?"

"Sure. For fun."

"No, but why now? Why today?"

"I told you—I've been meaning to dig it up for ages."

"I don't buy it. Listen, sweetie, I can't get pregnant and your mother has bone cancer, and we haven't even seen her yet. We're kind of sneaking around, and we barely finish having sex, and suddenly you're vaulting out of bed, compelled to dig for *bones*—"

"It's not bone cancer."

"What?" For a moment she looks hopeful.

"It's breast metastasized to bone."

She swipes at her face, leaving a smudge of dirt. "What? Did you ever tell me that? How could I not have known that?"

"I don't know. It doesn't really matter." He begins to dig again. His family does not talk about his mother's health.

"So it doesn't change anything—in the diagnosis or treatment," she asks softly, "that it's metastasized?"

"Not that I know of."

Though the thought is oddly inconceivable to him, his mother is in fact dying. In the next year or two in fact, sometime in the undistant future (though knowing her, she'll beat the odds, out of sheer stubbornness), she will do it: go and die.

Rachel takes the gloves off, drops them to the ground. "I wish you'd told me. I have a perpetual feeling of never quite knowing what's going on with you."

He shrugs. "Me too."

"With who?"

"With myself. You." He digs. "With humanity."

"Are you sure you want a baby?" she asks abruptly.

Charlie nods.

"With me?"

"No, with the porpoise."

"I *knew* you'd say that. Please just answer me."

Why must she push him to put words to everything, when they could be here, inside the moment? Here. His previous long-term girlfriend (she had wanted to marry him; it had not—mostly his fault—worked out) used to complain that he was already married, to Ashaunt. Is he wider now, at least a little? Can he come and go more easily? He was, for a long time, opposed to traveling, convinced that if he looked hard enough, he could—like Dorothy in Kansas—find all that was important in his own backyard. Slowly, things changed. He's been to Bolivia. He's been to Patagonia, Tanzania, Baffin Island, Russia, Bhutan. He and Rachel hiked, last June, in Iceland, where the earth spilled steam and horses ran through a night where the sun never set. The prisoners he represents sometimes give him little handmade gifts: an origami dinosaur made from a newspaper, a bracelet woven from hair, something from almost nothing. Last year, he and Rachel had Thanksgiving with her parents, Christmas with his parents. They had a small December wedding, decorating the carriage house they rented with bittersweet and pine boughs, wooden skis, cyclamen in pots, a chuppah made from her grandmother's tablecloth. They put a bandanna on Major Deegan. Charlie wore a flannel shirt and red suspenders, his eyes leaking tears, Rachel a brown velvet dress.

Her head is down; she's turned her back; she might begin to cry. He feels no sympathy, only irritation. Doesn't she know by now that he wants a child, and with her? Before he met her, he'd been exploring having a baby with his friend Bess, a lesbian. For a while, a decade earlier, he was a Big Brother to Marco, a boy from the projects in West Cambridge; they'd rotated video arcade outings with fishing trips until Marco's family moved south and the boy dropped out of sight. For years, he has romped and adventured with his nephews. He loves the on-the-groundness of spending time with children, their branching curiosity, to amuse them with his own still childish high jinks. Being a father himself would be different, harder, but might he not (if generations have told themselves the lie, then so can he) do it just a little better than his parents, pass on his best self, discard the rest, or at the very least, do his best by doing his best?

Rachel turns to meet his gaze. Her skin is flushed from heat, anger or unhappiness. The sunlight finds the copper in her hair.

Say it.

"I want to have a baby with you," he says.

TOGETHER THEY DIG, THEN, the sun on their backs, Ashaunt quiet except for the sound of the breeze in the trees and a few birds calling, and it is in the middle of this motion that they look up and lock eyes, and for a long moment they might be glimpsing, as if through a double-ended kaleidoscope, their future, still unconceived child, who will inherit his blue eyes, the darkness of her lashes and improbable length of his, something of his soulful gaze and the quick intensity of hers. Both of their long faces. I see Gaga in her, Jane will remark of their daughter. She looks just like Rachel did, Rachel's mother will say. She's *herself*, both Charlie and Rachel will protest, even as they'll know it's not entirely true—not of any of them, so much chaining backward and forward, flip and coil, glitch and gift of DNA, no matter how far from the source you might land.

Their second daughter, born a few years later, will have Frida Kahlo eyebrows that come from nobody they know and the broad face of a Russian nesting doll. She will be left-handed like her mother and sister, blue-eyed like her father and sister, a lover of plants and flowers, a worrier with perfect pitch.

That their daughters are dark-haired will give Rachel pleasure, especially at the great-grandchildren photos when, despite a handful of half Jewish or half Chinese or Guatemalan cousins, the palette will remain distinctly blond. A newspaper article on the disappearing blond gene will cite a study predicting that the last natural blond is likely to be born in Finland in 2202. That's sad, Charlie will say, partly to provoke her but partly because he means it (the ivory-billed woodpecker is extinct. The passenger pigeon, the great auk, the wooly mammoth, the heath hen, last seen on Martha's Vineyard in 1932. Jerry Silva is dead, though his signs still mark his woods where Charlie goes to walk, entering the long way to avoid the golf course). What of Rapunzel, let down your golden hair? What of the photographs of his mother and her sisters as little girls with sausage ringlets—flaxen beauties; you can tell, even in black and white. In truth, he will never stop finding his daughters' coloring—dark blue eyes and chestnut hair—beautiful. The blond gene study will turn out to be a hoax.

They go at it from opposite sides, using muscle, digging down. The ground is clumpy at first, then softer, sandy, then clayey. Several times their spades touch and the metal clinks. Rachel finds a disc from the creature's back, the size of a quarter but thicker, and hands it to him. He brushes it off. It is light and hollow, gray and ridged with a complex circular pattern that reminds him of a thumbprint; is each one unique? She takes it back, sets it aside. Deegan sniffs at it, too eager, and Charlie gets a bucket for the bones. They find more discs, and small bones that she says look like the pelvises of miniature women (they are vertebrae). He sets one on his palm and slides a pebble through it. She smiles and pockets the pebble, digs some more. First there are a few bones, then handfuls, pirate's booty. They reach in, come out full.

Charlie finds a bit of plastic from a discharged shotgun shell. Rachel locates something hard, the size of a baseball, which turns out to be a rock. Together they sweat, dig, not speaking until Rachel breaks the silence with nonsense words: *Ashimalongi tallanamanka camunikinga blachh.* Charlie answers: *Tallamoo.* They do this sometimes, speak a nonlanguage language, get into arguments, question, coo, curse. *Kalakali,* she says now and Charlie echoes back *kalakali,* and so they go on, periodically, as they sift and dig. They find more bones—long ones, short ones, thin and fatter, ribs and vertebrae. A few are broken; others are crumbled and decayed. He has waited too long. He won't be able to piece them back together. Still, he is not disappointed, or not very. Finally—they seem to be nearing the end—she surprises him by lifting a bone to her mouth and licking it. For increased fertility, she says. He licks one too. It tastes like soil, and after that like nothing much, the spoon that stirs the soup.

Then, digging farther toward the ocean (he buried the porpoise facing the sea), he hits the jackpot, the skull. Together they dig around it, under it. He lifts it out, brushes it off. How long its snout is, the bone split down the middle. The skull is not broken, or only a little, here. He doesn't actually know it's a female, but he wants it to be. Female and a mother, old, died of natural causes. And somewhere in the sea, her young, no longer young. Their young.

He gets a pillowcase from the cabin, wraps the skull in it and sets it by the bucket of bones, all that is left of a taut bright skin, a muscular blue life. Later he'll soak the bones in bleach, clean and scrub them, bring them inside the cabin, where they'll join other relics—fox and snapping turtle skulls, dried fish, snakeskins—that he's found over the years. Rachel will take one disc for herself. He will hang the skull under the eaves of the cabin, where each year a bird, a chickadee or wren, will enter through the dark, round hole of the spinal column socket to build a nest. The rest of the bones, too disintegrated to assemble, will sit for years muddled in the bucket under the cabin, first dry, then soaked in rainwater, then stewing in rancid sitting water (rusty ice in winter), until one day, Charlie, needing the bucket to go crab-catching with the girls, will dump the remnants out.

III

T HEY REMEMBER THE words, most of them do, though they cannot remember—Callum sometimes cannot—how to button a button or even, for the ones furthest gone, lift spoon to mouth. Still, *"Happy birthday to you."* Nearly everyone is singing it; even ancient, toothless Mrs. McLaren mouths a word or two. Bea almost missed the singing—the bus was late, and when she looked in her purse for her entitlement card, it wasn't there, but the driver knows her and let her ride for free, and now she's here to celebrate her baby brother turning eighty-eight. She makes her way to Callum's table, hangs her purse over the chair, sets her cane beside it, her hat on her lap. Sings.

"Happy birthday, Callum," she says when the singing is through, and he turns, eyes milky, and smiles, then folds over his own big belly, going for the cake.

"No, dearie," she says, reaching with mind but not her hands. There is, lately, a delay between her thoughts and limbs, along with the tremor in her right hand. Mostly she can keep it still, but when she's tired, it shivers in a way that has, more than once, caused hot tea to spill onto her lap. The server gives Callum his cake. "Fork," Bea reminds her brother, and he picks it up. They've laid fresh linens on all the tables and set out a vase of yellow roses on his. They've made a sheet cake, precut into slices, with Callum's name in blue above an "88." They've tied a blue balloon to his chair. You get what you pay for, and Bea believes that even

for the ones whose minds are gone, the details make a difference. At the
ex-servicemen's care home where he was before, it was all men and flags,
grimy lino tables, amputees (which he is too, but she doesn't think of him
that way). Here, it's mostly ladies, which makes for a better atmosphere.
They show old film reels and have a memory board of photographs in
each resident's bedroom, and volunteers bring dogs and cats to visit. Callum enjoys it, especially the animals and desserts. He remembers Bea's
name, still. Some days he seems entirely normal, if a bit more childlike
than before, though he does address his wife Kate (dead eight years) a
good deal and confuses Bea for her in ways that would make her blush if
she were not among people, both staff and residents, who blush at little
and admire her for her independence, and how she went to America and
returned a woman of means and started her own craft shop, which for a
time did rather well.

You're our model, Miss Grubb, the nurses have told her, exclaiming
over her age and good health; she will turn ninety-four in a few weeks.
What do you eat? What's your secret? I'm in God's hands, she says, for
she has found religion in her dotage, returned to her old church, St. Margaret's, first for the people, a place to go, especially after Agnes died, but
then for something else—a blossoming, steadying faith. She prays to God
but talks to Jesus and finds in both good company. Until a few years ago,
she helped in the Children's Crèche, and she still participates in Flower
Club, which has yet to run out of the ribbon, Styrofoam and wreath forms
that she donated when she sold the shop. The church sends a van round
for her on Sundays, and the church ladies have her on their rota twice a
week. She is—for all this and because she can afford to be—generous with
her Freewill offerings and a member of Friends of the Church.

"Hot out?" asks a girl in a nursing smock she doesn't recognize.

"Yes," Bea says. "Even for August."

"It's September." The girl laughs flutily. "Can't keep track of it myself!"

Bea flushes. Of course—it's Callum's birthday. September fifth.

She is given a slice of cake and has a few bites before she slides the plate away. Her appetite has shrunk, though her size, somehow, has not. She has her oatmeal and egg in the morning, then usually nothing but tea and biscuits until suppertime, when her great-niece might drop something off after she picks her baby up from the child-minder down the street, or the Meals on Wheels comes, or the church ladies, or Bea heats herself a dinner in the microwave and eats in front of the telly with the cats. She falls asleep early now, wakes in the night for several hours, naps in the afternoon, though she makes a point of getting dressed and going out most days to visit with a neighbor or walk to the top of the street, often feeling pressed at the end as if she must return to Callum, though it's been over a year since he moved out, first to ex-servicemen's, then to Benholm Care (I can pay, she kept telling Callum's son, finally resorting to ringing Jane's and asking Paul to talk to him, Paul having sway from knowing about money and being a man).

The day Callum moved out was the first time in her life she'd lived alone, except for the brief stretch between when Agnes died and Kate and Callum moved in. Come live here too, said the lady director at Benholm, and Bea did consider it, to be with her brother, to not be on her own, but it turned out that there was something quite pleasant about having a house to yourself. The walking from the shower to the bedroom in nothing but your knickers, for one. The talking—to the cats, Agnes, Janie, herself, Mr. P. To God. The moving about of the shell frames and buying, now and then, a porcelain box or lace runner to put on a table. She has a basket of blocks for when her great-niece stops by with the baby. She has her phone card to call America, Old English Lemon Oil for polishing (her sense of smell has dimmed, but the tangy scent cuts through). She loves her house with a tenderness that makes it feel almost human and has hired a girl to housekeep once a week, though she tidies up before to allow for deep cleaning and not give the impression of a place let go.

"You'll be having a birthday supper tonight with Ian and them," she tells Callum. "I'll come if I'm not too tired."

"Ian's had a baby," he states. "With his girl."

"Two. His babies are grown now. You've got great-grandbabies, remember?"

"Cake," says Callum.

"He'll be needing a shower and nap," Bea tells the aide. "So he can go out with his son. And his nails could use a clipping, or else he digs at the eczema on his feet."

The girl looks startled. "I'm on dining and recreation."

"Oh, he enjoys a good nail clip!" Bea retorts, meaning it as a joke, but the girl just stares at her. They do their jobs, the young people, but nothing more.

"I didn't get overtime for that weekend shift," Callum announces bitterly, "which is a bloody shame."

"A shame," echoes Bea. She yawns. Two outings in one day—church and Callum—is more than she is used to. She'd like to lie down on the window seat and take a nap. She won't go to the birthday supper tonight. The stairs to Ian and Marcy's flat are uneven, and if she stumbles, they'll pounce; they want her at Benholm "for your safety," though she is plenty safe, the council having installed a peephole in the door and given her a Message in a Bottle—a plastic jar in the fridge with her details tucked inside it and a green cross on the outside, and on the front door, a sticker with a green cross, and on the fridge door, the same sticker in case she falls or has a heart attack or dies, but she is afraid of none of these things; she is in God's hands (she pictures them like Mr. P's). If only she could make her world a little smaller—bring Janie and Caroline across the sea, bring Agnes back, bring her mother—if only she could gather them all inside her house and Callum too, she would have indeed found happiness, but as it is, she is all right. Lucky, even, if a bit lonely, if a bit unsure, some days, as to precisely why she is still here. In less than two weeks, she will turn ninety-four, and unless He sees fit to take her in the next four months, she will see the century, the millennium turn, and she would rather like to live to be one hundred so she can receive a personal letter from the Queen.

"I've got to be off now, Callum," she tells her brother, but he ignores her, in a babbling conversation with the lady across the table, the two of them going on about nothing. The room has nearly emptied while Bea was not paying attention, and now someone lifts the cloths from the tables; someone else plugs a Hoover in, the cord stretching, a menace, across the room. Bea gathers her purse, her cane, her hat, kisses her brother on the forehead, and he pulls her face down to him, aims for her lips, but she dodges and presents her cheek. She steps slowly over the cord and sets off for home, where, after changing into slippers and a housedress (its sash is Mr. P.'s red sailboat tie), she feeds the cats some liver treats, lies down on the sofa with the afghan Agnes made and sleeps for hours, waking only to answer the phone and tell Marcy that no, she won't be coming tonight, and yes, she's fine, just tired from a day out on the town.

As she hangs up, she remembers that she forgot to stop on Callum's floor on the way out and ask someone to clip his nails, and she sees, as if in a dream, her brother's child-plump hand laid flat across her own knee, the manicure scissors, the satisfaction of a job well done, and then she pictures the nails grown long and curved, yellowed as old cockleshells, for the nurses forget things at Benholm, which rankles her, and then she remembers that fingernails keep growing even after death, and she prays for such morbid thoughts to stop. The couch does not feel like the right place to be, but the bed is far. Betwixt and between, she is; she could do with someone pulling the afghan up around her shoulders in a gesture at once unthinking and full of love, singing to her, and there's a bitter taste at the back of her throat, just the faintest trace of it, an aftertaste. Swallow hard (she swallows hard) and it will go. And then Pudding the cat has arrived, slit-eyed and calculating, to measure the distance between floor and couch—and jumped up and settled by her side. Bea pulls the old boy close until he's curved against her ample belly, the motor of his purring running strong, and breathes with his breath until she sleeps.

IV

HELEN WAKES ANGRY to voices down the hall, gets up without help, gets dressed—a wraparound skirt, tennis shirt and cardigan, her white sneakers, Velcro-strapped and big as boats—an abomination, orthotically prescribed. She puts on her glasses, her wig. The shades in her room have all been lowered, and she releases them with a snap. André, she vaguely remembers, came in earlier to take her blood pressure and give her pills. Now it's dusk, bats swooping and rising along the lawn, against the sea. Would that she could join them—flap wings, fly blind, beat back her foul mood. Instead, toward social life, her son, his wife.

In early August, when Charlie and Rachel last came over for dinner, it went well, she must remember, but then Jane and Paul were there to grease the wheels. They'd played Dictionary. Helen had given Rachel a copy of her monograph on the New Jersey slave trade (it came out over a decade ago and is closer to a pamphlet than a book, though it received a bit of notice at the time). André had brought up the *Massachusetts Lawyers Weekly* article Rachel sent them about Charlie winning an award for Best Public Interest Lawyer of the Year, and Charlie said, "You *sent* that to them?" and Rachel said, "Sorry, sweetie—someone has to toot your horn," and Helen said, "We're so proud of you, Charlie!" (in fact, because he hadn't told them himself or invited them to the ceremony, she was more hurt than proud). After dinner, they watched shooting stars from the porch, and Charlie brought up how she used to take him stargazing in the Beetle Cat, and Helen, listening, was close to passing out from tiredness but sat there watching and tremendously happy and part of everything—made of stardust—underneath the stars. "My god, she's sleeping," she heard Jane say at one point, and Charlie said, "I've never seen her asleep in my whole life," and Helen—rising from a half-dream state—popped her eyes open and said "Boo!" and they all roared.

The evening had been a great success, Jane assured her the next day. Still, a month had passed, and they hadn't been back for a meal until now.

In the bathroom, she splashes water on her face. Her legs ache, her head too. She remembers something from a dream she had. A bloody diaper. Whose? She finds a tube of lipstick, applies a coral slash and smiles in the mirror, a mistake. Chin up (she hears her mother). Off you go, then (Bea). Sharpest knife in the drawer (her father, who has grown, in her mind, almost monumental, but did he hurt all the time? Did he hurt like this?). She pees and takes three Motrin. She will ask Rachel, again, if she can read her book, which is coming out later this year. She will ask Charlie about his case to limit solitary confinement. She has a present for Rachel, a book of drawings of seventeenth-century French peasants, if she can remember where she put it. In her skirt pocket, she has an article for Charlie about a judge who improved living conditions for prisoners, clipped from yesterday's *Times*. No one can say she doesn't try.

Tip-tapping, she walks down the hall with her cane. There they are, in the living room, talking, and as she stands in the doorway, she has the sense of peering in at a tableau of someone else's life. André is sitting on the window seat, Rachel beside him in shorts and a flannel shirt, her knees tucked under her, her curly hair pulled back. Charlie is perched on the edge of the fireplace hearth, suntanned and handsome, his hand buried in his dog's fur. Holly is there too, on the couch. Everyone is talking. She can be part of it; she just has to step inside. She enters the room, noisy with her cane; all heads turn in her direction. Hi, says Rachel, too brightly. Hi Mom, Charlie says. Helen sits down, and Holly, ever a little mother, leans over to fasten the Velcro on her sneakers.

"Not too tight," Helen says.

"You slept a long time." André brings an extra pillow for her back.

"Too long. I wish you'd woken me. Naps are the pits—they should be outlawed for anyone over three."

"Oh, I love a good nap." Holly stretches and yawns.

"So do I," says Rachel.

"I'm with you, Mom," Charlie says. "I almost never nap. When I do, I wake up feeling like I have to claw my way out of a black hole."

"That's exactly it," Helen says. "I had a dream about a bloody diaper."

As soon as the words leave her mouth, she regrets having blurted out this strange, intimate detail, but it's too late.

"That's terrible!" says Rachel.

"It wasn't as bad as it sounds. It was just there. You know how dreams are. What were you all talking about?"

"The oil spill," says Holly, and immediately Helen wishes she'd not released them into it, but it's too late; they're off, as if into the slick itself. It turns out it's even more than sixty thousand gallons, says Holly. The spill has killed hundreds, maybe thousands, of birds and damaged ninety miles of shoreline, and no one even knows yet what the long-term damage will be. The workers should be wearing respirators, Rachel says. They're cleaning up toxic waste. They'd give them respirators if they needed them; the worst chemicals come at the beginning, says André (the spill was in late April, just before they arrived). There will be criminal proceedings against the skipper and the company . . . the damages to the seabed can last for years. . . .

Helen looks out the window and wills the subject to swiftly run its course. Not long ago, she would have known how to jump in and turn things in a new direction, but she seems to have lost the gift. She slept through the roadrunners' race, slept through the great-grandchildren photo. Her head throbs; their voices are magnified. Wine, she mutters to André, and he says something about her medication and gets her a thimbleful of wine and a cracker with cheese, and she downs the wine in one gulp (lets the cracker slide to the floor, where the dog inhales it) and asks for more, and he gets her water and sits down between her and Holly, putting his hand on her knee. She wants to ask about Rachel's seventeenth-century midwife, to charm and impress her daughter-in-law, to tell Charlie about the tree swallows she saw earlier today. Not to talk about pollution, not, especially, the damn oil spill, which happened months ago and has, along with the Uh-Ohs' mansion, monopolized dinner-party conversation ever since. Still they go on, about the cleanup workers, come all the way from Texas, some of them ex-cons, and how they're taking care to scrub every rock, and how the dead bird count keeps mounting, and how many shellfish beds and nesting grounds are damaged (apparently a new report has just come out).

All summer, the cleanup crew has been fanning out across Ashaunt, parking trucks with giant vacuum tubes and hoses in Jane and Paul's field, dressed in plastic yellow jumpsuits, hauling equipment, wandering like zombies, dropping cigarette butts on the road, and for what? Helen has seen the beaches at the Yacht Club; they are fine. She has seen the cormorants on the rocks, the pair of swans, arrived, as always, to spend the summer in the marsh. The tree swallows, butterflies, gulls. All fine.

"Don't you think," she says, "that it's bit of a charade?"

They all look at her.

"What do you mean?" asks Holly.

"This endless 'cleanup' effort. Think of what those workers could be doing to help some truly endangered species—or in New Bedford, cleaning up the neighborhoods or making parks. Instead, they're scrubbing our stones with toothbrushes. Actual toothbrushes! The children showed me a picture. It's hardly the Exxon Valdez. I find it almost obscene, with all the real problems in the world."

"I agree with you that it's a terrible waste of time and money," Charlie says. "But it's not like there's not a real problem that needs to be dealt with."

"The problem"—Helen scratches the nape of her neck; her wig itches—"is one of expensive, drawn-out busywork driven by bureaucracy and litigation, and maybe of ex-convicts wandering around while children play unsupervised. The spill itself was an unfortunate mistake. Mistakes happen. You can't control everything; sometimes you just have to move on. It's been six months."

"Four," Charlie says. "But the shoreline is still pretty devastated."

"*Devastated?*" she says. "This shoreline has seen hurricanes, torna-does, explosions, erosion. No one has ever made this much of a fuss. It's because of how litigious our culture has become. Toothbrushes on the rocks! Really, it's a travesty."

Charlie shakes his head. "There's no way to get oil off the rocks except the way they're doing it. And they're still finding birds whose wings are covered in oil. I thought you loved seabirds, Mom. If you read the paper—"

"Oh, I read the paper! Seventeen thousand people dead from an earthquake in Turkey. The gap between the rich and poor has doubled since 1997. I read the paper every day. That's why I know how to put things in proportion."

"Actually this spill was covered in the *New York Times*," Holly says.

"Months ago," says Helen.

Charlie is pacing now. "That's not the point. The west-side rocks are still black with oil, and Barney's is still closed, and the creek at Garri-sons is stopped up by a barrier. A hurricane isn't the wreckage of human stupidity. If the government had only required the barges to have double hulls. Have you really not seen any of it, Mom? Maybe you find it"—he hesitates, then meets her eye—"hard to take it in."

"Don't patronize me, Charlie."

"Then go look. If you saw the damage—"

"I'm not the gazelle I used to be. And unlike you, I'm not drawn to scenes of suffering."

"I'm not drawn to this. It's *here*," he says fiercely. "It hurts me to see it."

He sinks back down onto the hearth, looks right at her. His shirt is torn, he needs to shave, his eyes are still so blue. Her hand itches to reach out to slap him, soothe him, but she takes hold of her other wrist instead.

Holly stands. "My girls need dinner. I'd better go." She smiles wryly, waves. "Have fun!"

"Don't leave, Hol—" Helen begins, but Holly lets the screen door bang shut and then is gone.

"So," André says into the silence. "Are you putting together your tenure case, Rachel?"

"Not this weekend. She's on vacation, Dad," Charlie says.

"I'm getting close." Rachel unfolds her knees from under her. "I keep having to go back to Staples and get different binders and tabs. It's ridiculous, but the presentation is almost the hardest part."

"When do you find out if they give you tenure?" André asks.

"Not until late spring."

"I hope it works out," André says.

"Of course it will work out," Helen tells him. Rachel isn't teaching at Harvard, after all, but at Framingham State College, and her book is forthcoming with the University of Chicago Press. Helen is quite sure that, in another set of circumstances, she and Rachel could have been friends. If they'd met studying abroad or been the same age, surely they'd have hit it off, for Rachel is lively with a sense of humor, and speaks French, and is a woman unafraid of being smart. As is, Helen's encounters with her daughter-in-law, as with her son, often feel distant or fraught, and she has the disquieting sense that Rachel is judging her, watching her too hard or—worse—pitying her. "What more could they possibly want from you?" she tells Rachel. "You're brilliant, hardworking and well adjusted."

"Ha!" Rachel says.

Charlie laughs too, and Helen stiffens, unsure if they are making fun of her or of themselves. "Well, I hope you get a good raise with tenure," she says. "You'll need it. Public interest lawyers are so underpaid, and this place is a real sinkhole financially. But you must know that by now."

"We might get some money from the oil spill," Charlie says. "I've agreed to be a lead plaintiff."

She turns her head so fast it hurts. "Lead plaintiff for what?"

"The class action lawsuit, on behalf of property owners whose land was damaged by the oil."

"You're not a property owner. *I'm* the property owner, am I not? Excuse me? André? Am I not?"

"So am I," Charlie says evenly. "I own six acres at the end, with Will, Caroline and Percy. From Gaga. Remember?"

She sits up straighter and feels the pillow propped behind her slip. "You need my permission to involve our family in something like this."

"Actually, I don't, though I didn't think you'd mind. For one thing, it's money, which you tend to worry about. Potentially, quite a lot. And it's for a good cause—"

"I thought you were above caring about money."

"I wish," he says. "But the main thing is that the companies need to take responsibility for the damage. The government can't do it—the oil lobby is too strong. It's important, and not just for here. Sometimes it takes a lawsuit to force change."

"You will not litigate Ashaunt, Charlie. Leave it be. It's not a laboratory or . . . or one of your prisons where you go to save the wretched of the earth. Leave"—she cannot say why she is so terribly upset, so thrown, so *overthrown*—"it be."

"I can't do that," he says evenly.

"*Ça suffit.*" André leans in to put the pillow back behind her. "Dinner is ready. Rachel, I'm sorry for this little drama. Charlie, come help me serve the plates."

They all exit the room, then, André followed by Rachel and Charlie, the dog padding after them, leaving her alone. She turns toward the picture window, fixes her gaze outside, the light at dusk so blurry that the margins of everything—land, sky, water, porch furniture—are viscous, blurry and unclear. She did not tell Charlie that she has had dreams about the oil spill, more than once. In one dream, she was a girl skating with her brother on the black, glassy surface, cutting figure eights. In another, she was caught inside the spill, the tarry, clotted pull of it blocking her nostrils like bad blood. She did not tell him that the men in yellow plastic jumpsuits remind her of the soldiers who used to live here on the base, and everyone acted, back then, like the worst was about to happen, any second, *right here*, but then—surprise!—nothing happened here; it happened elsewhere, unspeakably, unthinkably (she has no memory of even hearing the words *Jew* or *gassed* until the war was nearly over, just as she has no memory of an officer arriving in Grace Park bearing news that her brother was dead, though apparently she answered the door). Time stands still here. Clocks break. So do telephones. Postage stamps lose their stick. At times, she has found the isolation of the place oppressive, even dangerous. Other times—when she was young, when her children were babies—she welcomed it.

Now, somehow, her life depends on it. She raises her hands to her face to make a frame, looks through, then lowers her hands and keeps her eye trained on the horizon. Such beauty. How to leave a place like this? How to leave? When she turns around, she finds Charlie standing in the doorway.

"Dinner's on the table," he says. "Salmon and corn. Let me help you get up."

She shakes her head. "I'm not hungry."

"I'm sorry." He steps closer. "I know you're not feeling well, and that . . . I'm sorry. I just—I wish you knew how much I care about this place, and that I'll—"

Take it over when you're dead and gone, she thinks.

"—fight to protect it," he finishes.

"You can only do so much." She feels tears rising.

"I know."

"Look," she whispers, and he moves closer to the window, kneels beside her, and together they look out at the sea darkening, at the light meeting it.

"When are you leaving?" she asks.

"Tomorrow."

"So are we. I have chemo. If I were you, I'd stay longer. To be here when it's gloriously emptied out."

"I'd love to, but Rachel's classes start on Tuesday, and I have to work."

"How practical you've become."

"My work means a lot to me."

She nods. "So many people waste their time on things they hate, don't they? Or things that bore them. Oh, I nearly forgot—I clipped an article for you." She pulls it from her pocket, gives it to him.

"Thanks."

"Charlie, I—I can't bear to leave," she tells him in a rush. "It's like I'm—bewitched or something. It makes me angry. Furious. Not at anyone . . . at"—she shakes her head—"myself."

"Come back next weekend," he says. "Or the weekend after. We'll come too."

She wants to say, Yes, of course she'll come, to thank him for getting her a bird feeder and keeping it filled, for coming to dinner, for *trying*, but a wave of tiredness has overcome her; her eyes keep closing, almost pleasantly.

"Come, *chérie*. You need to rest. You can have dinner later. Put your arm around my shoulder," says André, who has reappeared, and so she does, and Charlie kneels on the other side of her and she drapes her other arm around his shoulder. I love birds, she says dreamily into her son's ear, or maybe she just thinks it, she the one who taught him to name and spot the rare ones—the bar-tailed godwit, the whimbrel and Blackburnian warbler—just as her father had taught her, first from the fields and beach, then from inside, his wheelchair by the window, *Petersons* and binoculars in his lap, and she'd bike to the salt creek or climb to the top of Teal Rock and sit there waiting, then ride back and drop her bike on the grass and go inside, to where the names flew from her mouth into her father's ears, a gift for both of them.

"I love birds." She says it again, or maybe for the first time.

"I know," Charlie says.

"One two three lift, old boy," says André.

And so they lift, and so they carry her to bed.

V

MID-MOTION IS HOW he will remember it later, hoisting his bike onto the rack on the back of the car, one arm under the frame, the wheel spinning. Something has happened. The voice of Margie Childs, calm, clear. An accident.

The day is cloudy, wind ruffling the bushes. In front of him, Rachel is opening the car door to put in a grocery bag full of leftovers and a half-finished milk carton, its spout taped shut. Charlie lowers the bike and leans it against the car's rear bumper. Your mother, says Margie Childs. He watches Rachel put the bag and milk in the car, shut the door, turn around. Swimming, says Margie. Swallowed water. And then again: Accident. Choppy. Resuscitate. Breathing. Charlie registers the imprint of a bike chain greased on his calf, and below that, late summer grass, parched and rough. Rachel takes a few steps toward him, stops, then reaches for his hand. She should not have shut the groceries in the hot car, he thinks irrelevantly. The milk will sour.

"I'd have come sooner," says Margie, "but we'd thought you'd already gone home. Just about everyone has. Did you hear the sirens? Your father followed the ambulance."

"We better go," Charlie says. The colors of the day have deepened, as if a yellow scrim has slipped over the world. "Can you shut Deegan in the cabin?" he asks Margie. "He'll chase the car."

"Of course. And I'll walk him later."

Suddenly, his jaw is trembling, though his mind is flat. He had been planning to say a quick good-bye to his parents before taking off. Now, what?

Get in the car, turn on the ignition, shift into reverse. Back up. He fishes the keys from the floor of the car. Rachel puts a hand on his arm. "I can drive," she says, but Charlie tells her no, he knows the way.

~~~

AT THE HOSPITAL, THEY ARE led through the ER waiting room, past people on stretchers and a nurses' station to where André, Jane and Paul sit alone in a small, windowless room. His father, Charlie sees with a start, is crying soundlessly. Dad, Charlie says, and his father looks up, and Charlie leans to hug him and feels his father grip the fabric of his shirt. He goes to Jane next, hugs her; she too is crying. Paul reaches out to squeeze his arm. On the car ride, he'd entered into a sort of suspended state—the outcome could be almost anything; they could arrive to find his mother sitting up, chatting about her good luck, her close call, describing with a kind of wonder what it felt like to go down, come up, brush so close to one's mortality. Now, a darker place. Rachel sits down next to his father, who wipes his face with the corner of the beach towel he has folded on his lap. Charlie stands.

"Mummy drowned," his father says, and before the words can fully register, Jane says, "No, no, she didn't drown, André—she's alive!"

André nods. "I said 'near-drowned.' It's a medical term."

"Did he say that?" Jane asks.

Charlie shakes his head slightly.

"She's alive," says his father. "Breathing, with oxygen to help her. We don't know yet if she'll pull through."

"Can I—is it okay for me to see her?" Charlie asks.

"*Nurse!*" His father barks the word in the direction of the doorway, then looks abashed. A nurse appears almost immediately. "He'd like to see his mother," André says. "Our oldest son."

Charlie follows the nurse next door to a curtained room, where his mother lies on a gurney, her neck in a brace, her mouth covered with an oxygen mask, her body hidden under blankets. Her eyes are shut, her head bald (she looks, oddly, quite beautiful like this). The EMT is still there and shakes Charlie's hand. We did everything we could, he says, in a tone that implies *Don't blame me* but also makes Charlie realize that "everything" might well not be enough. *Mom*, he says, moving closer to his mother. Can she hear me, he asks the nurse, who says probably not, she's unconscious, but we encourage family to talk, it can be helpful. *It's Charlie,* Charlie says. *You're in the hospital—Dad and I are here with you.*

His mother's arms beneath the sheet appear to be tucked in a mound over her chest, but while he watches, her fingers jut over the top of the hem, then withdraw. She moved—did she understand me, he asks the nurse, who says some movements are involuntary; we'll know more later. Like when, asks Charlie. She'll probably sleep for up to twenty-four hours, the nurse says. They'll know more then. As he turns to go, he is stopped by the EMT, who hands him a white plastic bag, the top cinched shut. It's her swimsuit, the man says apologetically. We had to cut it off her; I already gave your father her ring. Charlie accepts the bag with its soaked weight and damaged, useless contents, the navy and turquoise flowers of the swimsuit showing through.

It is not until he returns to the windowless waiting area that his mouth begins to tingle and his forehead contract. It's been years since he's had a full-fledged panic attack, but he still lives with his own mind as if with a once-wild animal. *Breathe-count,* he tells himself out of long habit, and his hand reaches for Rachel's, but he must be gripping too tightly because she winces and loosens his hold. He slides his hands between his thighs, then, squeezing harder and still harder, wishing he could vise himself and make of his own finger bones an inner core. Rachel touches his arm; he shakes his head. As he counts backward from a hundred, his breathing slows, and he is back, almost back, to normal when the nurse appears and tells them cheerfully, as if delivering the first bit of good news, that a bed has opened on the ICU.

LATER, DETAILS WILL EMERGE: HOW André had packed the car, ready to go; Helen was determined to have one last swim, though the sea was rough, the day windy, and André was not in favor of her going in. I swim every day unless there's lightning, she'd said to him and, earlier, to Jane.

They had agreed to meet Jane there at noon, but as they were going out the door, she'd called to say she wasn't ready, she had too much packing to do, and in any case she didn't think Helen should swim, the wind was up and from the northeast. Of course she didn't listen, Jane will say. I should have gone with her; I should have known.

Helen swam out to the raft without a problem, but it was choppier coming back, and she swallowed water and struggled and went under. A girl, on the dock with her toddler, saw and dove, pulled her in, gave her CPR on the dock. Got her—heroically, André will say—breathing again (the "girl" being the wife of one of the Wilson boys, it will turn out, a former lifeguard who thrust her son into André's arms before she went in after Helen). And then André yelled and Margie Childs heard and came and left and called the ambulance and Jane heard sirens and they followed the ambulance in the car.

For now, just waiting. They all go up an elevator, down a maze of halls, to another waiting room, really just the dead end of a hallway, a twist and turn from the ICU. While downstairs it was hot, here it is air-conditioned and freezing. Charlie walks down the hall to find a men's room but finds, when he gets there, that he cannot pee and returns to sit shivering between Rachel and Jane. You can put this around your shoulder, his father says, offering him the striped towel, and Charlie says, No, Dad, *Jesus*, and Jane says, Easy, Charlie, and he says, You're right, I'm sorry, but his father doesn't seem to hear. A nurse passes by now and then. Food carts. Doctors in a rush. His father goes in and out of the ICU and comes back, each time, announcing that his mother is still breathing, on oxygen. Do you want me to call the other children, Jane, now dry-eyed, asks, and André says no, he will, and rises with new purpose to find a phone. Margie Childs and her husband show up at some point, leave and return with sweatshirts and fleece blankets, which they pass around. Eventually Percy shows up, having driven home to Wellesley, received a phone call, driven back. For long stretches, Jane shuts her eyes, holds Paul's hand, her lips moving. She is praying, Charlie sees, and he wishes, not for the first time, that he had even a sliver of her faith.

Every once in a while, someone speaks into the silence. The water was rough, Jane says. I had a bad feeling. I told her not to go, says André. But she insisted, and she's a good swimmer. An *excellent* swimmer, says Jane. André nods: I met her at a swimming pool in Lausanne; she challenged me to a race. You've always said you let Mummy win that race, Percy says, but *she* claims she let you think you let her win. The word *let*, Charlie silently observes, detaches from all meaning when repeated, and he says can we not talk about her as if she's dead, which shuts them all up, but then he apologizes, and Jane says the trouble is, there's nothing right to say.

At some point, Rachel offers to go find food at the cafeteria. Good idea, Jane tells her. Get something for André; he needs to eat. Jane pulls out twenty dollars, but Rachel pushes it away and shakes her head. What should I get, she asks. Maybe fruit if they have it, Jane says. Maybe, I don't know . . . bananas? I'll go with you, Charlie tells Rachel, and together they walk down the corridor and into the stairwell with its cinder block walls, then out to the lobby with its plate glass windows, and he feels a new lightness—he might walk away, go out into the sunshine, *leave*—and they do, in fact, go outside into the sunshine, gulping the fresh air, but the day looks glassy, shimmering, and the people are in wheelchairs or on crutches or holding Mylar balloons shaped like pacifiers ("It's a Girl!"), and they don't stay out long. The cafeteria isn't selling bananas, or much of anything, on Labor Day. They buy a few apples and soggy roll-up sandwiches. Bottled water. Juice.

When they return to the waiting room, his father is not there, called into the ICU. "Yes, we have no bananas," Charlie tells his aunt, who smiles thinly, takes an apple and sets it in her lap. Percy opens a water bottle and downs it in several gulps, then crushes the plastic loudly between his hands. And then their father is coming down the hallway. Stabilized, he says, tears rolling freely down his face. Still unconscious but breathing on her own. And stabilized.

"It eez possible," he says (and only then does Charlie realize that his father has fully expected her to die), "that she will be all right."

VI

TO SEE YOUR mother as a baby, that is what it's like, and therefore heartbreaking and wretched, and therefore also cleansing in some crooked way, the self wiped clean of static, pared down to its essentials, the human core that bore you, which was borne. When, the next morning, Charlie is finally let in to see his mother in the ICU, she is still unconscious. Whereas in the ER she had just one IV, now she is elaborately hooked up to drips, wires and machines. One foot sticks out from beneath the sheets in a yellow hospital sock with a nonskid sole. An arm goes up, she curls; her eyes open, sweep the room. Charlie speaks, his voice croaking: Hi, Mom. His father reaches out to pat her leg through the covers: *C'est moi, chérie. C'est André, mon lapin, c'est moi, ton mari. Salut.* For long moments, she is still; then a leg bends up, an elbow jabs and swims. Charlie takes these movements as a good sign, not knowing, yet, about abnormal flexion, the body stripped to impulse, a chicken without a head.

That she has not yet woken up can mean nothing good, but there will be no definitive answers until the doctor runs brain scans in the afternoon. Until then, largely mystery, which will leave forever open the possibility that his mother has a slow departure, a gradual fading out. As Charlie stands beside her, sometimes her eyes open, settle briefly, even, on his face. Can you hear me, Mom? It's Charlie. Mummy? Blink if you can hear. Sometimes she blinks, but then one does blink; one does hear, and there she is, so entirely herself, her long hands, the unchanged blueness of her eyes.

Midday, Charlie asks his father if he can be alone with her for a few minutes, and his father says yes, this a good idea, so after the doctors' rounds, Charlie goes in and sits with her, interrupted only by the comings and goings of the nurses, who perform their duties silently and retreat. They come, he stops talking; they leave and he begins. He shuts the curtain around the bed, pulls the chair close and sits for a good half hour, talking to a mother who may or may not be able to hear him, certainly cannot respond, but still he speaks, and extreme though the situation is, he is grateful for the chance to sit and talk to her, for his own sake, for hers—there, your firstborn, apple of your eye, bane of your existence, bending near you, telling you some of what he could not tell before.

I know I've disappointed you, he says, but I hope not entirely. He tells her that he admires her work and energy and how passionate she is, and her sense of humor and how long and close her friendships are. Were he younger and it a different time, he might also be tempted to pull out his laundry list of grievances, but they have largely lost their potency, and he tells her this and acknowledges how the strains in their relationship might sometimes lead her to think he doesn't care about her, but he does—and accepts her, and himself, more or less, and appreciates what she's given him. He tells her he is grateful for Ashaunt but sorry it has been a battleground between them. He tells her that Rachel had a miscarriage in May and will probably get pregnant again—might even be pregnant now—but if that doesn't work out, they'll adopt. I'd like to be a father, he says, and when no limbs move, no eyelids flutter open, he lays his head down on the sheet and rests there, the top of his skull lightly touching his mother's cocooned side. Perhaps he even dozes off a little, coming and going, eyes shut, breathing as she breathes.

When the scan results arrive later that day showing no brain activity whatsoever, a vegetative state, he is not surprised. The doctor explains their options, though there's really only one thing to decide: to feed or not to feed. The rest—when she, her body, will stop its breathing, is up to her, for it's still her on some level, isn't it, her pulse and heart, her life force? Charlie isn't ready, nor are the others, to stop the feeding tube, but he does not go into her room after the scans come in, not even once to say good-bye, though other people do—his sister, for one, returning and returning until the very last moment. His father. Jane. His father is making sure his mother still gets her Valium so she won't go through withdrawal, attending to her and spending time at her side in a way that almost seems, to Charlie, to disregard the test results. It feels unreal, André says several times to Charlie, who comes a few more times to sit in the waiting room with his family but never again to cross the threshold to the room. Their mother's hair, Caroline reports, is growing fast, full of perverse health, and her wig has disappeared. Friends from New Jersey call the Red House, leave messages. Suky forgets about the time difference and calls from England before dawn. For days, then a week, then over a week, the report remains the same: Helen, tube-fed, is still breathing (even mindless, she is stubborn in her will to live) on her own.

She dies ten days after Labor Day. She might have held on longer with the feeding tube, but what is life—what is sentient, wired, brainy Helen-life—without a brain? This is her idea of hell, Jane says on the ninth day, and the others agree. Only Dossy, who comes to see Helen once and then goes home to Katonah and climbs into bed and does not leave her house for several months, is not consulted. The family decides to have the feeding tube removed, and André signs the papers, and so they let her let her let her let her go.

IT IS A VIOLENCE AND a blessing, what happened that day. This is how Charlie will come to view it over time. A violence to go down so quickly; a blessing to go down so quickly. Probably, in the end, more a blessing than a violence, given what lay in store for her: ever more unremitting suffering, a wrung-dry, rasping year of it—at most a year—and at the end, death, what she liked to call, along with love, *le grand sujet. La mort, l'amour* (she'd pretend not to be able to pronounce the two words differently).

And so better off this way; they will say so eventually. Most of them will, though never Dossy, who will go temporarily and quite cheerfully out of her mind after her sister's death, chattering away to her family, to Bea and Agnes, and return to sanity largely intact but vaguer, as if always listening for someone only she can hear. Jane will host the reception after the memorial service, order food and flowers, busy herself, invite Charlie's father for dinner every Tuesday. It was the best summer of her life, she'll say of Helen. She told me more than once.

Might she have done it on purpose, Rachel's mother will ask her daughter at Thanksgiving in Poughkeepsie, while they stuff the turkey, as Charlie, just back from running, listens from the stairs. *No*, Mom, Rachel will say. But you said the water was rough and she was weak and— She loved to swim, Rachel will counter, then add, You didn't know her. It wasn't intentional, Charlie will say as he steps into the kitchen, and when Rachel's mother startles and apologizes, he'll reassure her: I can see how you'd wonder—it's just that my mother was too attached to life—she *clung* to it, more than anyone I've ever known. He will not tell her that the clipping his mother gave him the night before her accident turned out to be a *Times* obituary for a judge who had ordered dramatic reforms of living conditions in California prisons, the article left unread in his shorts pocket until an October weekend, when he retrieved the shorts from a hook in the cabin, pulled them on and found the article. He feels sure that it's the details of the man's life, not the fact of his death, that interested his mother (who, like Charlie, enjoyed a good obit): the man's life and work, and its relation to his own. Still, to come upon the obituary in his own pocket had been a quiet shock.

THE MEMORIAL SERVICE IS A huge affair at Jane's Episcopal church. Some three hundred and fifty people attend. Charlie's father has asked that he speak, and he's said yes, though as he sees the masses of people filing in, he regrets it. There are many people he knows, but also quite a few he doesn't recognize, most of whom turn out to be from his mother's life as a historian. There are old family friends, his cousins and their families on his mother's side, his father's sister—the aunt he barely knows—come from Switzerland. Streams of well-dressed white-haired women file into the church, followed by men in dark suits, looking frail and disheveled in the firm trail of their wives. Charlie sits between Rachel and Holly, his body does; his mind perches at a great distance from it all. The organ music begins, Bach swelling, overfilling the church. Around him, family members are already crying, but he, folding and unfolding his eulogy, is far from tears.

A minister friend of the family reads from Psalms. A black professor from Rutgers speaks about his mother's contributions to New Jersey African American history and her role as chair of the New Jersey State Historical Commission—how hardworking she was, how she made everyone laugh, how her passion and conversation inspired them all. She was, the professor says bluntly, a white woman from an old WASP family who made enduring contributions to black history (the following year, the annual Black History Conference at Rutgers will be dedicated to her memory). Sitting there, Charlie is surprised, even impressed; his mother always seemed restless, scattered and *unfinished*, a dilettante, but apparently she got things done, and her work crossed worlds. Jane gets up, snowy-haired and standing tall in a sky blue skirt and jacket, and talks about Helen as prankster, intellect and friend, and as a mother who was proud of each of her four children and in love with her husband till the day she died. "I've never known anyone so full of vim and verve as my sister Helen," she finishes. "I'm not sure where she is now, but wherever it is, she'll never be gone from me. In fact, I fully expect her to call me every day!"

Then it is Charlie's turn. He stands at the podium, considers abandoning his notes but turns to them. "What I'll remember most about my mother is the sparkle in her eye and how she was fascinated by everything and everybody," he reads. He talks about how she was always natural, without a trace of phoniness or pretension, and how she could be complicated, easily hurt, sometimes quick to strike back, full of contradictions, and how she believed that everyone was exceptional and thought that many of you here today were bona fide geniuses (laughter ripples through the crowd), and made everyone, with the possible exception of her children, feel like her best friend (more laughter, though perhaps uneasy now). "In the last few years"—he hears his voice grow stronger— "my mother came into her own, and although her death is tragic, I believe it happened the way she might have wanted it to: suddenly, while doing something she loved—swimming in the ocean—at the very end of a transcendently happy summer."

He returns, sapped and shaky, to the pew. Rachel and Holly both pat him on the knee. Hymns are sung, liturgy recited. The church is full of flowers—yellow roses, lilies, blue hydrangeas spilling forth—and it is on these that Charlie trains his gaze and looks for his mother, who is nowhere to be found. Not even her ashes are in the church, and no coffin, but this is less hard to comprehend than the fact that she is not herself there, a thin old bird, an egret maybe, standing on one leg, head bobbing, long neck swiveling. Contradicting, adding and subtracting. Poking fun. Peering out.

It is not until he has crossed the parking lot with Rachel that he is visited by grief, and then (he walks alone to the edge of the asphalt and stands looking into the woods) it is grief of the most arid variety, a desert creature, all hoarded water and sharp spine.

VII

HULLO, PAUL, IT'S Bea, says Bea when a male voice picks up, but the voice says it's not Paul, it's Charlie, who is this? And she says Bea—Beatrice Grubb. Oh Bea, hi—are you calling from Scotland, the voice says, and she says *Charlie*, though didn't he die a long time ago, and her own voice is echoing back in a most distracting way—Charlie, Charlie—and he says are you looking for Jane, which of course she always is so she says yes, and then Charlie—it is Helen's Charlie—tells her to hold on, just a minute, and there's nothing but background chatter for a long while, and though she has the discount phone cards, she still can't call America without a sense of time running fast, running out, and she watches the numbers on the digital clock on her hospital table flip and flip again. Her neck is sore and the bed is slanted too low, but she can't reach the lever and the girl has left; the nurses run in and out like mice. On the other end of the line, more silence, and behind the silence, noise (are they having a party? Is it American Thanksgiving?), and enough time passes that she considers hanging up, but then a voice says Bea, are you there, and she says yes, and there, it is Janie, in the flesh or not quite, but close enough to make Bea lighten and settle, both at once.

"Bea! My goodness. How are you?"

"Fine, dearie, and yourself?"

"All right. I'm . . . I've been meaning to call you—I tried a few days ago, but no one picked up."

"I'm not at home, that's why. The line is funny. My voice is echoing, do you hear that, everything coming twice?"

"No," Janie says. "But I can call you back."

"No." She will not risk it, to have Janie leave, to be obliged to find the phone number of her hospital room. "I'm not at home," she says again.

"Where are you?"

"In the rehab."

"Oh Bea. What happened? Are you all right?"

"I had a wee fall—I'm fine, just a broken hip. They said I'm too old for the surgery, which is a shame. I'd have gone for a brand-new hip."

"You broke your hip? I'm so sorry! When? And how?"

"I tripped in my very own house, in my very own kitchen! Over nothing! Can you imagine? But I got myself to the phone," she says proudly. "And they came and opened up my Message in a Bottle."

"You had a message in a bottle?"

"That I did, with all the info."

"Oh Bea. I'm glad you're all right." Janie's voice is louder now, and made even more so by the fact that the echoing of Bea's own voice has stopped. "Listen. I'm—it's not a great time to talk. I'll—can I call you back tomorrow? We have quite a lot of people here and now more have arrived, we—"

"I just need to know if I can afford to stay," Bea interrupts. "Just tell me that, dearie, quickly—or put Paul on. I won't bother you long. I need to know so I can make arrangements."

"What? Stay where?"

"Home, dearie. In my house. The lady from the Council is telling me to go to Benholm, where Callum is, but I'm quite set on the idea of going home. I'd have to hire a nurse—they say I can't manage alone until I'm back on my feet, and there's the question of the cats and the garden, but I said to the lady, I may be ninety-four but that doesn't mean I'm not capable of—"

Janie gasps. "I forgot your birthday!"

"No matter. I'd like to know if I can stay at home. Financially."

"You can stay," Janie says, almost impatiently. "You have plenty of money and the stock market is booming and if you ever ran out, which you won't, we'd help. You can live anywhere you want, Bea. Anywhere. All right?"

"I don't know." Though Bea expected to feel relieved—and in some measure, she does—the question of where she will live seems suddenly unimportant. She is asking for something else, though she can't quite say what. If she matters, maybe. If it matters to Janie where she is. Something feels off: in the conversation, in the rehab room, where her roommate, recovering from spinal surgery, is lightly moaning in her sleep. In Janie having forgotten her birthday, after having come and thrown a party for her ninetieth. In Bea having forgotten (is it the painkillers?) that Janie forgot. In the echo, especially, of her own voice, which has started up again: I don't know, I don't know.

"I'll call you back," says Janie, and then she lets out a series of extremely not-right sounds.

"You're crying!" Bea says. "What happened, love? What is it?"

"It's—oh Bea, it's Helen."

"Helen? What?"

"I . . . I can't quite bring myself to say it. I—" Her breath goes in and out. "Helen—she, well, she drowned."

Bea sits up, the motion sending a slicing pain through her hip.

"I didn't want to tell you this way," says Janie. "Bea, are you there?"

Just as suddenly as the pain arrived, it's gone. "Drowned? Helen? That's impossible! She could swim for miles! She had a cancer. You told me. Breast come back as bone."

"Yes. She was getting treatment for it," Jane says, "and she was weak, though she put on a brave face, and she . . . well, she went swimming. She didn't drown right away, we hoped . . . I tried to call you. I tried, but no one answered, and I—I should have tried harder. We just had the memorial service—the house is packed with people, that's why I was talking so loudly. I'm in the bathroom now, with the door shut. I should go back out."

A rage courses through Bea that Janie didn't invite her to the memorial service, didn't even tell her, and now Janie is saying I'll call you later and that she'll come visit to help Bea get settled back at home, within the month she'll come, will that be soon enough? And Bea says I suppose (her anger mostly gone; she can't afford it), and please put Caroline on. And then there is more noise and Caroline is on the phone saying Bea, are you all right, Jane told me you broke your hip, and then Caroline asks her to sing so she croaks out a line or two—*speed bonnie boat like a bird on the wing, onward the sailors cry*—before a nasal female voice says, "*You are running out of minutes, please complete your call.*"

And so she must hang up and does hang up and lies back down and prays for Helen's swift, winged passage, and weeps because she cannot help it, despite knowing that Helen never much liked her (and truth be told, vice versa) and only visited once for Agnes's funeral, but still was family, and Janie down to one sister and Caroline without the mother she was born from now.

And it all seems terribly unlikely that she, Bea, should be lying here in hospital, hip on the mend (she will live for four more years, at home with a caregiver), while Helen in America is dead.

VIII

JANE AND PAUL'S house is full of sunlight and beautiful things, unlike Charlie's parents' house, which feels gloomier than he'd remembered it when he returns there after his mother's memorial service, struck by how dark it is, how full of heavy furniture, worn Oriental rugs, tarnished silver, nearly all of it from Grace Park. Also, at his parents', books and books and books. His father, in an almost manic way, has already begun urging him and his siblings to take things, as if enough winnowing down might eventually convince him that his wife is really gone. The night after the memorial service, while Rachel sleeps, Charlie stays up for half the night wandering—in the attic, in his mother's study, outside, an insomniac as she was an insomniac, a searcher as she was a searcher.

Is this when he takes the cache of diaries, letters, photographs, the war scrapbook his mother kept? He will not remember, later, when each item first came into his possession; it will seem, after a time, that they were always there. Over the years, he will occasionally show Rachel or his children things that were his mother's, grandparents', or great-grandparents'—an ivory and silk fan, a clutch of hatpins, letters his mother wrote from Switzerland that will seem to his twenty-first-century daughters like ancient relics—the onionskin paper, the slanted, girlish cursive, the images on the postage stamps: a cheese-making atelier, steam engines, edelweiss. A Japanese silk kimono. A Swiss navy blue ski pullover, embroidered with white thread. The following winter, and for winters to come, Rachel will wear it skiing in Vermont.

Whether these items were given to him or taken by him will not matter much by then. His mother's money will have been divided up, most of it skipping his father (who has enough with his pension and the house) to go straight to the children and already-existing grandchildren. Charlie's inheritance, after taxes, will be enough for him and Rachel to sell the Concord bungalow and buy a rambling eighteenth-century farmhouse a mile down the road. Ownership of the Ashaunt houses will be transferred as designated in Helen's will—the Portable to Percy and Caroline (who will sell her share to Percy); the Red House and cabin to Charlie and Will, who will collect some $50,000 in damages a good eight years after the oil spill (they do not, Charlie thinks, exactly deserve the money, but he is glad to have it for house repairs and taxes and convinces his brother to give a quarter of it to the Coalition for Buzzards Bay). One corner of the cabin, straddling the property line, will technically belong to Dossy's family from inheriting the Big House, and Holly will remark on occasion that they own the porch and half a bed. Charlie will urge his siblings to place a conservation easement on the six acres of land they own together, the site of his network of paths. After some tense discussions, they will settle on an Open Space designation. It isn't a permanent restriction but will have to do.

In mid-June, Charlie will give Rachel the kimono to put in her birthing bag, both of them unprepared, despite her research on midwifery and the birthing class they took, for the actual extent of liquids—blood, mucus, iodine, orange juice, colostrum, pee, shit, vomit, spit-up, water, milk—that circulates around a baby's birth. The kimono—silk, pale peach, with a pattern of cranes and umbrellas—will remain in the bag during her hospital stay. Later, at home, she will wear it as she and their newborn daughter learn to nurse—painfully at first, eventually with ease, then with sleepy, nearly drunken pleasure that leaves Charlie envious of them both.

BUT NOW. BUT IN THE long, hard days to follow. Charlie does not talk much about his mother. Rachel teaches her classes. He goes to work, where there is little time either to grieve or to mourn grief's absence, his mind gratefully harnessed, his days packed—with a brief to write for his pay-for-stay case, heated meetings with Department of Correction officials, young lawyers at his door with pressing questions, prisons to monitor. One prisoner sends him frequent letters: *I noticed that a paper with three Words Defined went missing, Words like Milk, Creation, Opportunity*; and *The officer whom lives up to low standards Myself is feeling the stress of his meanness*; and *Myself doesn't have smooth Understanding and finds it hard to do certain Things.*

Charlie copies this last one onto a scrap of paper and tapes it to his office door. He answers the letters when he can. Sometimes he wonders: Is it true that he, as accused by his mother, courts suffering? Certainly he walks among it, chips away at it, not to do good, not exactly; he likes the prisoners, just as he likes to navigate the thorny puzzle of the legal system and figure out ways to push back against the state's heavy hand. One day he goes to the shiny high-rise offices of a big downtown law firm to give sworn testimony at a deposition for the oil-spill lawsuit. On weekends he and Rachel read or putter at the house in Concord, go for walks in the woods, have dinner by the fire. He buries his mother's bathing suit in the backyard with a few acorns he's brought back from Ashaunt, hoping for a tree, though one never sprouts. He goes for runs when his Achilles isn't acting up. Rachel drives into Cambridge to see friends and see movies. Sometimes he goes too, though not often; he relishes the time alone, and movies still unsettle him, the wall after the wall after the wall, and no way in.

When the right time arrives, he and Rachel have sex, though they try only once this cycle; they're both worn out and she's been told to skip a month of Clomid, since it gave her a cyst. They do not go back to Ashaunt for Columbus Day weekend, which comes just three weeks after his mother dies—they go camping in the Berkshires with friends instead—but they do go the following weekend to find the place almost deserted, save for Rusty and his wife, up from New York, and Margie and Gus Childs, who have winterized their summer cottage and moved there year-round after losing all ("Not *all*," says Rachel) their money in a dot-com company gone bust.

Over the course of a few weeks, another season has taken hold, asters fading, poison ivy and Virginia creeper deepening to red, the bayberries turning from blue to silver. Charlie spots a few tree swallows diving and remembers from his grandfather that the birds sometimes delay their southern migration to fill up on bayberries, nourished by the wax, eliminating the seed, sowing bushes along the migrant path. He swims both days that weekend, at high tide from Gaga's Rock, where her dock used to be—now, just one old piling attached to a boulder. On his paths, he collects bayberries, which he will later melt down, skimming off the wax to make two stubby olive green candles that burn down to the socket—a quality the early settlers believed meant good luck.

He avoids the swimming dock at the Yacht Club. He has never swum there much anyway, preferring to enter the water from the shore, but now it will be several years before he goes in there, and never again without a flicker, a flash, of his mother going down. The oil-spill workers have finished their scrubbing. You can still find coatings on the rocks, but the black spots look almost natural, a dappling, and anyway Charlie isn't in the mood to look too hard.

He catches a bluefish that they grill for dinner. He builds a fire in the woodstove. Rachel grades papers, naps, sits on the porch, plays her violin, wanders with Deegan up the empty road. She does not swim. For one thing, it's cold. For another, the water has taken on a power for her that she cannot shake. Plus she's pregnant, though only barely—the home test, then the blood test, read positive three days before—and walking carefully, as if carrying something made of spun glass (the child will turn out wiry, strong, a climber of trees, scaler of rocks). Are you excited, she asks him at night as they lie in bed, and he says it's too early to get excited. It will take a visible sign for him to believe there's truly something in the works. He leans to kiss her belly, but she contracts her stomach muscles away from him, and he feels suddenly, surprisingly left out. Are you okay being here, she asks him a few minutes later, and when he says What do you mean, she says Because of your mother, though for this question, as with her previous one, she must already know the answer, which is that Ashaunt *is* his mother, a second mother, as in a second home, except that for him it's a first home, perhaps even a first mother, both in how it holds his mother's traces and in how it nourishes him as she often could not.

"I was thinking," he tells Rachel, "of having a rock carved with her name, and maybe something she wrote. There's a boulder behind the Red House that she always liked."

"That's a nice idea."

He reaches to the floor for his backpack and pulls out a notebook with a marbled cardboard cover, and another, spiral-bound, then several more. He piles the books on the quilt in the valley made by their outstretched legs. "I thought I might find something in one of her diaries."

"You took them?" Rachel picks one up, sets it down. "Did you really? Were they just out somewhere?"

"In her study."

"But hidden?"

"Not exactly. She once told me that she'd burned a lot of her diaries and letters, around the first time she got sick."

"So you think she wanted these ones to be found?"

"Maybe. Or else she forgot about them or got distracted. I don't know."

"Have you read them?"

"As a boy I used to. Once she wrote me a note in the margin: *Dear Charlie, I know you're reading this.* I wrote *Hi Mom, Love Will* in mirror writing."

"You had fun with her."

"Sometimes."

He opens the diary with the marbled cover. In the woodstove, the fire hisses and pops. At the foot of the bed, Deegan startles in his sleep. As Charlie leans into the diary, he catches sight of the word *private* on the inside front cover, in penciled letters so faint they might have been written and erased, or perhaps they've just faded over time. If Rachel notices the word, she does not say, nor does Charlie point it out. There is Privacy and privacy, he is beginning to think, just as there is Trespassing and trespassing, the land you walk because it was there before its owners and will, with any luck, stay on after them, and because you care about it, and because it's filled with green and growing, dead and brittle, expected and unexpected things.

May 15, 1960. Back again. At last I can breathe.

ACKNOWLEDGMENTS

WHILE *THE END OF THE POINT* is a work of fiction, it draws some of its features from an actual place, whose inhabitants were unfailingly generous to me as I plumbed, borrowed, discarded, researched, collaged, refigured and freely invented. At times, I changed dates to suit my story; for example, the oil spill in the novel takes place in 1999, when in reality, the Buzzards Bay Bouchard oil spill occurred in 2003.

This novel would not exist in its current form without the many different kinds of help I received from the following people: Joan Austin, Charlotte Bacon, Joseph Bettencourt, Lydia and Louis Biglarderi, Dorothy Ann Cairns-Smith, Jacky Garraty, Beverly Glennan, Marcia Cornell Glyn, Lawrence Graver, Ruth Graver, Suzanne Graver, Bayard Henry, Sharon Jacobs, Connie Laux, Margot Livesey, Michael Lowenthal, Suzanne Matson, Marissa Matteo, Baba and Frankie Parker, Vicky Pennoyer, Brendan Rapple, George Salvador, Bridgette Sheridan, Laura Tanner and Kathy Waugh.

I am ever grateful for the support, insight and friendship of my longtime editor, Jennifer Barth, and my longtime literary agent, Richard Parks. Thanks, as well, to Jane Beirn, Shannon Ceci, Mark Ferguson, Richard Ljoenes and Danielle Plafsky at HarperCollins for all they have done for this book.

For gifts of time and space, I am grateful to the Blue Mountain Center, Boston College, the MacDowell Colony, the Massachusetts Cultural Council, the Thoreau Institute and Wellspring House.

Jimmy, Chloe and Sylvie bring gifts beyond measure.

To all, my deepest thanks.

ABOUT THE AUTHOR

Elizabeth Graver is the author of the novels *Awake*, *The Honey Thief*, and *Unravelling*. Her short story collection, *Have You Seen Me?*, won the 1991 Drue Heinz Literature Prize. Her work has been anthologized in *Best American Short Stories*; *Prize Stories: The O. Henry Awards*; *The Pushcart Prize: Best of the Small Presses*; and *Best American Essays*. She is the recipient of fellowships from the National Endowment for the Arts and the Guggenheim Foundation. The mother of two daughters, she teaches English and Creative Writing at Boston College.